VICTORIA

She dipped her pen in the gold pot, for the ink had dried on the nib while she sat thinking. Slowly she began to write, covering the pages with descriptions of the day's events: tea and the walk in the gardens, the dinner party when for once she did not record Melbourne's conversation because she had been busy talking to someone else. And at last her own feelings; the feelings she could not tell Lehzen and hardly understood herself.

'Ernst is very nice and very amiable.' In those few words her pen dismissed him from her life.

'But Albert — Albert is *beautiful*.'

**Also by the same author,
and available from Coronet:**

CURSE NOT THE KING
FAR FLY THE EAGLES
IMPERIAL HIGHNESS

Victoria

Evelyn Anthony

CORONET BOOKS
Hodder and Stoughton

First published in Great Britain in 1959

Published in 1986 by Century Hutchinson Ltd

Coronet edition 1990

Printed and bound in Great Britain for Hodder and Stoughton Children's Books, a division of Hodder and Stoughton Ltd., Mill Road, Dunton Green, Sevenoaks, Kent TN13 2YA (Editorial Office: 47 Bedford Square, London WC1B 3DP) by Cox & Wyman Ltd., Reading, Berks. Typeset by Avocet Robinson, Buckingham.

British Library C.I.P.

Anthony, Evelyn, *1928–*
Victoria
I. Title
823.914

ISBN 0 340 53022 7

Author's Foreword

So much has been written about Queen Victoria and so many of her own writings are available, that any novelist seeking to re-create her is almost handicapped by the mass of material. In particular, Lytton Strachey's biography is apt to colour one's impressions of the Queen. In most people's minds the image of Victoria is that of a stout, formidable little woman, dressed in widow's weeds, plain, unexciting and really rather dull − only one degree less dull than her illustrious Consort, Albert. Even now *his* perfections tend to turn the English stomach. But those who read this book will not find the Widow of Windsor; my story begins with her youth and marriage and ends with the death of the only human being that Victoria ever loved.

Tracing the history of her life and the first twenty years of her reign, I was struck again and again by the contradictions in her character. For a basically simple woman, her emotions were alarmingly larger than life; she was incapable of feeling or understanding anything in terms of moderation, or of appreciating anyone's view but her own. Victoria's egotism is undeniable, both in her private and in her public life; it even tinged her relationship with Albert and almost destroyed it at the beginning of their marriage. In many ways she was callous and unfeeling, thereby typifying the paradox of the Victorian Age itself. The manufacturer employing child labour at fourteen hours a day saw nothing incongruous in the text 'Suffer little Children to come unto Me', which hung in his bedroom. His insensibility was perfectly in accord with the standards of his Queen.

My portrait of Victoria is not falsified by invention. Though this is a novel, the political events described are true, so are many of the conversations and some of the written extracts. Victoria's marriage to Albert is not a romance in the accepted sense. It is ironical and tragic in one aspect in that it remained one-sided to the end: Victoria's love was never returned. While Albert gave her supreme happiness, he suffered from a lack of understanding and true companionship which made his life in England doubly hard. If some of his letters belie this, the fact remains that he died a disappointed and disillusioned man. His wife's adoration never compensated him for the enmity he found in his adopted country.

Though she was the mother of nine children, Victoria had no maternal instinct, and the future Edward the Seventh passed a miserable childhood. But in spite of her faults and in spite of the fact that she was less clever than her husband, Victoria remained the dominant personality. It has been said that he moulded her, and in so far as he disciplined her temper and taught her application, this is true. But the essential greatness of a sovereign, and the power of character that overawed some of the ablest statesmen of her day, was not Albert's gift to bestow. Where he failed, Victoria succeeded. In the midst of internal upheaval, popular hatred, war and even attempted assassination, the Queen remained immovable – vulnerable only to the husband she worshipped. Her love was her weakness, and to us it has made her human, in spite of her mistakes. Greatness is seldom lovable.

EVELYN ANTHONY
London 1958

1

A footman had opened the shutters on two of the long windows in the Green Drawing-room at Kensington Palace, and a pale dawn light spread through the room. It gave the stiff old-fashioned furniture and the big family portraits on the silk-panelled walls a grey, ghostly atmosphere. Two men, both dressed in black, stood near the empty fireplace; the taller, Lord Conyngham, Lord Chancellor of England, leant against it, and after a moment took out his watch.

'When the devil is she coming down? It's after six o'clock.'

His companion shrugged. 'They've probably broken the news as gently as possible; after all, she's little more than a child, and it may take some time.'

Conyngham smiled cynically. 'A more likely reason is that her mother is trying to come with her!'

'No, surely not,' the Archbishop of Canterbury exclaimed. 'Even the Duchess must observe protocol at this time.'

Conyngham yawned and moved away from the fireplace.

'Poor old "Sailor Bill" . . . He died with more dignity than he ever did anything else. But at least he got his wish; he lived to see Victoria come of age. There won't be a Regency now, that's one blessing.'

'I really believe that's what kept him alive,' the Archbishop said. 'Christian charity or not, Conyngham, I couldn't have borne it if the Duchess of Kent had been Regent. It'll be difficult enough to restrain her interference when she hasn't any legal right to meddle in affairs. What a pity the Princess wasn't older!'

'What a pity she wasn't a son!' Conyngham retorted.
'What a difference it would have made, my Lord, what a
difference if there'd been a man of intelligence and dignity
to follow on as king! I'm not maligning the dead, but good
God, look at the monarchy in the last three reigns; George
III, mad as a March hare for years at a time. My father told
me he used to go down to Windsor and see him walking
up and down his room, chattering like a parrot by the hour.
He said you couldn't tell the difference between him and
the damned birds he had everywhere. Then the Prince
Regent — all that mattered to him was the cut of his
waistcoat! We've had nothing but idiots and buffoons on
the throne for the past hundred years; good Lord, remember
the scandals of the Royal Dukes and their marriages? Every
strumpet on the London stage could bob up and claim she
was wife to Clarence or Sussex or Kent, and by God, as often
as not she was, with a string of children to be provided for
. . . Even King William, and he's only dead for a few hours,
he was always happier on the quarter deck than he ever was
on the throne.'

Conyngham shook his head. 'Victoria should have been
a boy; the last thing England wants after *that* procession,
is a mother-ridden miss of eighteen who's hardly been let
out of the nursery.'

'The King thought highly of her,' the Archbishop said.
'But he was apt to take likes or dislikes and stick to them
without reason. And anyway, he knew little or nothing about
her, the Duchess saw to that. No one knows what she's like;
no one's ever seen her except making tours of the country,
where she sat on the platform with her hands in her lap,
and her mother made the speeches. I don't envy Melbourne,
dealing with the Duchess.'

'Melbourne doesn't deal with anyone,' the Lord
Chancellor said. 'You know him. If the pace gets too hot
he just sighs and takes the easiest course. Once or twice I've
seen him roused, but he's carried his fashionable lethargy
to the point where it becomes a habit. He'll have the task

8

of educating the new Queen, and keeping Madam her mother in the background, and frankly, I can't see him doing it. Not only that, there are all these damned Germans living here; the Duchess is surrounded by them. The people don't like it already, and they'll like it less when this clique is round the throne itself.'

'Melbourne must be aware of the difficulties,' the Archbishop said. 'A lot will depend upon how this child acquits herself. After all, the fact that she's a woman and so young will make her popular for a time, at least. She may even be more independent than we think.'

'There's not the smallest chance of it,' Conyngham said. 'No one could expect it. She's never said a word for herself or done a thing that wasn't directed by somebody else. She's a cypher, nothing more.'

'Lower your voice,' the Archbishop interrupted quickly. I think she's coming.'

They had moved to the middle of the room and were standing together as the double doors at the far end opened. For a moment they could see very little in the dull half-light. Then they saw that a very small, very slight figure was walking towards them. She came into the circle of light let in by the opened shutters, and immediately Conyngham went to meet her. She was so tiny he was startled; small enough to be a child rather than a woman, still dressed in her night-gown, with a plain woollen shawl wrapped round her, and her fair hair hanging straight down her back.

Slowly she held out her right hand and, kneeling, he kissed it. He noticed that it was warm and perfectly steady.

'The King is dead. God save the Queen!'

'God save Your Majesty!'

'My Lord Chancellor. My Lord Archbishop. It was good of you to come. I am more grieved at your news than I can say.'

The voice was high-pitched and very young, but it was as steady as her hand. Conyngham rose from his knee and bowed.

'Your uncle the King died at two o'clock this morning, Madam. The Archbishop and I hurried here as soon as we could. We had some difficulty in rousing the porter at the gate, or we would have been earlier still.'

'I am so sorry,' the new Queen said. 'Was the King's death peaceful?'

Conyngham was watching her closely. The blue eyes were quite dry, and there wasn't a tear in them or a tremble anywhere that he could see, and for a moment he felt such composure was almost indecent.

'Perfectly peaceful,' Canterbury answered. 'I was at his bedside, and his last words were to Queen Adelaide, telling her to bear up.'

'And how is the Queen Dowager?' the cool little voice asked. 'I do hope she isn't broken with grief. If there is anything I can do to comfort her, I shall be only too pleased. My uncle and she were devoted.'

'She is very upset, Madam; as you say, they were devoted. But she will have privacy and quiet in her loss; I'm afraid that won't be extended to you.'

'I never expected it would. I know I shall be very busy. You must tell me what I have to do, Lord Conyngham, and when I shall make my first appearance as Queen. I am rather ignorant about my duties now, but I've no doubt I shall soon learn.'

The Lord Chancellor coughed.

'I have no doubt you will, Madam. Your Prime Minister, Lord Melbourne, will be here within the next hour or so, and he'll instruct you in your immediate duties. I believe the first will be a Privy Council; probably held some time later today. You can rely on his advice in all these matters.'

'I'm sure I can. My Lord Chancellor. My Lord Archbishop. Thank you for coming. You must both be tired; you have my permission to leave now.'

They had gone; the double doors were closed behind them, and Victoria, Queen of England, was alone in a room in

Kensington Palace for the first time in her life. Alone. She said the word aloud, and then slowly looked round her at the familiar furniture, the portraits of her ancestors in their dusty gilt frames. How many evenings had been spent in this room, sitting very upright on one of the straight-backed chairs, sewing and listening while her mother talked; while everyone talked except herself. She had learnt a great deal by listening, she thought; people had fallen into the habit of discussing her as if she were not there and mentioning matters which would not have been considered suitable for her ears. She was so young, her mother always said, so young and such a child. And so dependent on the Duchess . . . Too young and too small to walk down the staircase without someone holding her hand. But she had walked down alone tonight for the first time in her life, touching the banisters very lightly, trying not to let her mother, or even Baroness Lehzen her governess, see the expression on her face.

She went to the window and unlatched it, pushing it wide open. The sun was rising, filling the dull skyline with streaks of pink and gold, and outside the birds were singing in the trees.

It was over at last. There would be no more evenings spent in silence, no more lectures from her mother on how to behave with dignity, on how to be obedient and modest and keep discreetly in the background while the Duchess blustered forward. She was Queen of England. And from the time she was thirteen and Lehzen had told her she was King William's niece and heiress to the throne, she had been waiting for that day. She was sorry about her uncle; he had been a kind, if ridiculous, old man, and she quite understood how he had hated her mother thrusting herself forward, dragging Victoria behind her, constantly reminding him that he was childless and only destined for the grave.

For some time she stood by the window, holding the edges of her plain shawl together to keep out the cool morning air, and thought how impatient Mama and the other ladies must be getting while they waited for the obedient child, the dear child, to run upstairs and tell them what had happened.

'She shouldn't go down *alone*, surely? Surely I, as her mother, ought to be present to support her . . .' The words and the resentful look returned to her and she smiled. They would be waiting, and she was going to let them wait. She was the Queen.

Three other women had been Queen of England in their own right. Mary Tudor, Bloody Mary the Papist, whom the history books reviled. Papists were dreadful creatures; her rather sketchy education had made sure she understood that. And then Elizabeth. Elizabeth was praised and glorified, but privately Victoria considered her a horror, more like a pirate in skirts than a woman. Someone had said that — certainly not Lehzen, who was rather ignorant, or her tutor, Mr Davys, the Dean of Chester — but however she heard it the phrase stuck.

Not like Mary; not like Elizabeth and certainly not like Queen Anne, a much nearer ancestor. Anne was stupid and favourite-ridden. People had made fun of her as they did with her poor mad grandfather, George III, and her uncles, the Prince Regent and King William. They were her blood, and their pictures hung on the walls behind her, but they had been fools and unworthy, and she had no intention of being like them.

Conyngham had not expected much of her; she knew that when he kissed her hand. He thought she was only a girl and weak and was prepared to disregard her. But he would change his mind. She understood what the Crown meant better than anyone supposed, even if it had last been worn by a buffoon of whom no one stood in awe.

Victoria pushed the window shut, and latched it methodically; she hated leaving anything half-done.

Then she moved to the middle of the long room, and suddenly spun round in a gay little dance step which ended abruptly as she reached the door.

They were all gathered outside; the Duchess of Kent,

Baroness Lehzen, bundled in her dressing-gown like an anxious crow, with her beaked nose and darting black eyes, Lady Flora Hastings, the Duchess's favourite lady, and the Comptroller, Sir John Conroy. The Lord Chancellor and the Archbishop had left some time ago, and they had come down to see what had happened to Victoria.

When the door opened and she stood in front of them, the Duchess made a movement. Her rather florid face was redder than usual, and the quick temper which made her so many enemies was beginning to rise at the sight of her daughter, perfectly calm and well, who had dawdled downstairs when she had been distinctly told to come straight up. She opened her mouth to demand an explanation, but the words died away as she met the full force of her daughter's gaze for the first time in her life. She saw it sweep past her; the rather protuberant blue eyes, which were Victoria's only claim to prettiness, moved down the crowd of ladies and gentlemen, and then suddenly someone curtsied. The Duchess never afterwards remembered who it was, she was so confused; but the whole rank began sinking to the floor, one after another, while the new Queen stood quietly waiting in the doorway. At last mother and daughter faced each other once more. That moment seemed like a hundred years to the Duchess of Kent. Then, flushing scarlet, she too made a curtsy.

There was absolute silence while the Queen walked past them with a little nod of recognition and went calmly upstairs to dress for the day's events.

'Lord Melbourne, Your Majesty!'

They were sitting in the Duchess's sitting-room, a strained little group composed of the Duchess, stony-faced and red-eyed after an afternoon spent in tears; Baroness Lehzen, dressed in her best black silk with her chair edged as close to her former pupil as she dared, and in the stately old armchair usually reserved for her mother, Victoria, dressed in a dark brown dress edged with black braid.

It was the nearest thing to mourning that she possessed.

It was the third meeting with her Prime Minister that day. He had come first at nine o'clock in the morning, in the full uniform of a Privy Councillor, to kiss hands and present the speech the Queen was to read at her first Council.

He was a very tall, distinguished-looking man, his hair slightly greying, and much younger looking than his fifty-eight years. Victoria looked up at him and smiled.

'Madam. Your Royal Highness.' He bowed low to her first, and she caught a faint conspiratorial smile, before he turned to her mother.

'May I say, Ma'am, that Her Majesty created a furore at the Privy Council this morning. I've never heard such a chorus of praise. The Duke of Wellington himself said that the Queen not only entered the room, she filled it! This is a very happy day for England, and it must be a proud one for you.'

'I have always tried to do my duty,' the Duchess choked; she was nearly in tears again. 'And, believe me, I had no hope of personal reward. If I've brought my dear daughter up in a manner that's fitted her for her great station, then I'm fully recompensed.'

'A wonderful vocation, Ma'am, and nobly fulfilled,' Melbourne answered. He glanced quickly at the small figure in the armchair.

'Your Majesty was kind enough to suggest that I might call on you again this evening,' he prompted gently.

Victoria smiled at him.

'I did indeed. You were invaluable, my Lord. I don't know what I should have done without you.' She turned towards her mother. Melbourne thought with amusement that he had seldom seen such a cool and innocent look.

'It's been a memorable day, Mama, but a tiring one for you I'm afraid. I shall come in and say good night when Lord Melbourne leaves.'

There was nothing the Duchess could do but get up, gathering her skirts with an angry rustling — she was a woman who *always* rustled, Melbourne thought – and after the briefest good night to her daughter, she swept out of the room. The governess Lehzen still sat on, looking after the Duchess with a distinctly triumphant expression.

'Dear Lehzen – good night.'

She too found herself dismissed, though he saw Victoria squeeze her hand quite affectionately when she went, and then he was alone with her. She looked very girlish and sweet in her dark dress; one noticed the bright blue eyes and the pink mouth which couldn't quite close over her small teeth, and forgot about the arrogant jaw and the decisive, beaked nose. She blushed and suddenly held out her hand to him, melting into a smile which irradiated her whole face and made her almost pretty.

'Dear Lord Melbourne! How kind you've been to me today! Come and sit down beside me; there's so much I want to talk about I don't know where to begin.'

'Begin with the Privy Council,' he suggested. 'As I said to your mother, you were wonderful, Madam. Quite wonderful.'

'And did the Duke of Wellington really say that? That I filled the room . . . what did he mean?'

'He meant that you brought the whole dignity of the monarchy into the room with you. It was a very good phrase – I wish I'd thought of it myself. And the way you delivered your speech moved some quite hardened gentlemen to tears!'

'But it was your speech,' she pointed out, 'you wrote it for me. And I know it went well, so I'm doubly grateful.' She smiled. 'I'll admit, I was quite nervous, but I'm glad I came in and went out alone. I don't want anyone to think that I can't manage by myself.'

'No one thinks that,' Melbourne assured her, 'not after today. Shall I tell you a secret, Madam?'

She nodded eagerly, and again the contrast struck him, the sign of an impulsive temperament behind the calm facade which had caused such surprise among her ministers and peers.

15

'Before you came into the room this morning, there was a certain amount of muttering; your Royal Uncles seemed rather anxious about your ability to carry off the affair — it's no small ordeal for someone who's had no experience of public life. I knew what some were thinking, because to tell you the truth, Ma'am, I'd thought it myself before I arrived here for the first time. They thought you might falter through the speech, burst into tears — generally behave in a womanly fashion. Every excuse would have been made for you, of course, but it was a great personal triumph that you did nothing of the sort!'

'I can imagine my uncles' anxiety,' Victoria said. 'They're dear, kind men, but I feel they'd have been better satisfied if one of *them* had been making the speech this morning instead of me. Isn't it strange, Lord Melbourne, how much people long to be King . . .'

'Did you feel like that, Ma'am, when you knew it was your destiny?'

'I did,' she answered. 'From the moment I knew what my birth meant, I thought and dreamed of nothing else. Do you know how I found out?'

He shook his head.

'Lehzen told me. She didn't tell me in the ordinary sense; but one day when I opened my book to study for my history lesson, I found a genealogical tree slipped in between the pages. I saw that my father the Duke of Kent was the eldest of the King's brothers and that if he'd lived he would have succeeded. And I was his daughter. Lehzen had underlined my name. I knew then that if my Uncle William had no children, I would be Queen one day. I was thirteen.'

'And what did you do when you discovered it — ask your mother about it, I suppose?'

'I never asked Mama anything if I could help it. Later on I talked to Lehzen.'

Lehzen again. Lehzen telling the future Queen of her destiny, Lehzen watching the retreating Duchess with open dislike, and sitting on until she had to be dismissed. Lehzen seemed to have a great influence. He had better find out more about her.

'The Baroness seems very devoted to you, Ma'am,' Melbourne said. 'You must be fond of her.'

'I am,' Victoria nodded. 'Very fond. She brought me up from a child, you know, and if it hadn't been for her I doubt I'd have known what the word affection meant.' She smiled suddenly. 'Do you know, Lord Melbourne this is very odd. I've never talked to anyone like this before in my whole life! I've never discussed my feelings or talked about Lehzen or being Queen, or anything before. I hope you don't find it dull?'

'Dull, Ma'am? I only hope to God you'll always talk to me about things near to you. If I felt I had your confidence, it would be the happiest moment of my life!'

'It would be the happiest moment of mine,' she said quietly. 'Apart from the Baroness I've never confided in anyone. And though she's the dearest creature, it's not possible to be too intimate now with a subordinate. It would mean a great deal to me if I could really call on you, Lord Melbourne, for help in everything.'

He had always been a sentimentalist; it was the one characteristic which had been at war with his nature from the beginning, as well as at war with the cynical, sophisticated eighteenth-century atmosphere in which most of his life had been spent. His mother, that domineering ambitious woman, would never have forgiven her favourite son William if she had ever discovered that he possessed such a ridiculously bourgeois trait. His family and associates prized the intellect above everything, and the feelings not at all. But feeling was in him and however hard he had crushed it back in the past, it revived at moments of crisis in his life, and though he did not know it, this moment, with the eighteen-year-old Queen offering him her confidence and asking so simply for his help in return, was a turning point in his life and career.

Sentiment engulfed him; he had an impulse to kneel, as

17

he had so often knelt before to the women he thought he loved, and kiss her hand and tell her that he would spend every and moment in her service, and ask for nothing, nothing in the world, but the privilege of hearing her thoughts.

'My dear Ma'am,' he said at last. 'I am not only your Prime Minister, but Your Majesty's own devoted servant. Call on me for anything, at any time, and I shall come.'

'I will,' Victoria promised. 'I shall come to you for everything until you find it tiresome! Oh, Lord Melbourne, what a day it's been — so much, and I'm not a bit tired, are you?'

He smiled back in return, warming like a shivering man before a fire. Just when one was nearing sixty and tired and, in spite of achieving the highest office, rather disillusioned with life — when there were so many bitter and distasteful memories to look back on, that often enough one didn't care a damn about the future, because it would most likely be as futile as the past — after all that, to be offered this! He was not sure what 'this' was; he only knew that there was something strong and healthy and vital in the room radiating from the girl who might have been his daughter, the young Queen whom he would have to guide in her duties for a long time to come. She might have been another disappointment, she might have been whining and silly or coltish and undignified — how he would have hated that: whatever his wife Caroline Lamb had been, however mad and tragic and ridiculous, she had always possessed grace. Grace of movement, grace of manner . . . It was so important to him in women . . . And Victoria had grace. Teaching her to govern was going to be a pleasure instead of a dull grind, and to enjoy her friendship, to bask in the sunlight of that clear personality, so fresh, so charming and unspoiled. It was a prospect that beckoned to his vanishing youth.

'I've never been less tired, Ma'am,' he said eagerly. 'And I'm delighted to hear that you're not either. But you mustn't

18

overtax yourself. Your mother looked rather weary, I thought.'

He had been trying to introduce her into the conversation. He knew the Duchess of old, the turbulent, interfering Duchess. At all costs, she mustn't be allowed to injure Victoria, give her bad advice or bring pressure to bear. He must make sure how the Queen felt about her, before he could show her how best to deal with the situation. He had to confirm the importance of the ruthless dismissal.

'Since we're not going to have any secrets,' Victoria said, 'you may as well know she wasn't tired at all. She was angry. She's been angry all day, and, poor Mama, she hasn't been able to say a word to me about it!' And she laughed.

'What happened, Ma'am?'

'Well – ' She settled back in the chair and crossed her feet demurely on the velvet footstool. 'Well, after the Privy Council I asked her if I were really and truly Queen. She was quite cross then, because she wanted to take part in the ceremony, and there was no place for her. So I asked her, though I knew perfectly well, and when she said yes, I said then I'd like her to leave me for an hour. I made it my first request to her as *Queen*. I though it was a good way, and as kind, of making her understand that things had changed. But what really upset her was when I ordered my bed to be moved out of her room. I've always slept with her, you know, and I just couldn't wait another night to go into a room of my own. She's been dying to complain to me all day, but I've never given her the chance.'

'I thought as much,' Melbourne admitted. 'I thought something else too. I thought the Baroness disliked her.'

'She hates her,' Victoria admitted. 'Whereas I only dislike Mama, Lehzen really hates her. She's been very unkind to poor Lehzen at times. But that's all over. Mama must learn that she can't be unpleasant to the people I'm fond of any more. The real trouble is that she hoped the King would die while I was still a minor; then she could have been Regent. She's always wanted to be Regent. Don't think me disloyal, dear Lord Melbourne, Mama is a very good woman with excellent intentions, but she does everything wrong and she's dreadfully undignified. I can't allow her to take things on herself or presume to interfere in my duties. It may be unpleasant – it's bound to be, for any daughter,' she said calmly, 'but I shall have to teach her that now I'm Queen of England, our relationship is completely changed.'

'I'm thankful you see it in that light, Ma'am. Some of us were very worried about how much the Duchess would try to interfere. It wouldn't be popular with the country.'

'Have no fear, Lord Melbourne. My mother will not be allowed to interfere in anything.'

'I believe you, Ma'am, and I shall tell my colleagues in the Government.'

She rose with that astonishing, light grace of movement he had noticed, and immediately he stood. The audience was over.

'Though I'm not tired,' Victoria explained, I think I'd better go to bed. I want to be fresh for my duties tomorrow. It's been a wonderful day, Lord Melbourne. Tomorrow you must come again and help me with the despatch boxes, and tell me what I have to sign and what everything means. I have a great deal to learn, and you have promised to help me, remember.'

'I will do my utmost, Ma'am. And I make you another promise; the instruction won't be dull!'

She laughed. 'I'm sure it won't. I look forward to the teacher and the lesson. Good night.'

He kissed her hand and bowed his way out of the room. It was nearly midnight as he drove back through Kensington village, and his carriage jolted over the rough country roads towards London. Melbourne sat back with his eyes closed, more tired than he had realized, bodily tired and yet mentally stimulated. He had something to look forward to, something beyond the routine of government, much of which bored him, something beyond debates in the House, where he seldom found a subject which really exercised his wits, something quite different from dinner parties at Holland House and card parties at the clubs, where he lost or won with equal indifference.

Dealing with the late King had been the devil, he admitted; dead or alive, it was hypocrisy to pretend that William had been anything but an erratic booby, and fools were the one thing in life Melbourne had never been able to tolerate with patience. The new Queen was not a fool. She had a clear mind; decisive, too. Odd in a woman, and yet infinitely attractive because it was allied to youth and inexperience. Her appeal to him for help had been so simple, so refreshing in its honesty. He was really touched. He could never resist that particular form of child-like appeal; that had been Caroline's secret. However much she disgraced him and herself, even when he looked on the mentally defective son she had borne him, he couldn't resist her when she pleaded, wistfully like a naughty child, for yet another chance. That was why he had never divorced her, why the scandal over Byron which went round the world and made him a laughing stock, was somehow rendered paltry and excusable when she climbed on his knee and blinked back tears and promised not to make any more scenes or take another lover . . .

There was no real similarity between Caroline — unbalanced, foolish Caroline, who had always hurt herself more than she hurt him — and that self-possessed, unsullied girl who had become Queen of England. Life had yet to wound Victoria, and she faced it armoured with natural strength. No, there was no comparison between the two women, except that quality of innocence which all her follies and extravagances had never quenched in Caroline, and that gift for shining honesty, which sometimes penetrated through the dross of lies and self-deception . . . Victoria. It would be possible for a man to revere those qualities in her, without the dread of disappointment, of finding that behind the candour there lurked deceit and irresponsibility. Life, which had cheated him so often in his relationship with women, now offered a rare consolation. Friendship.

Friendship without temptation, a chance to reverence womanhood without the fear that the idol would ever step off the pedestal and show that she was made of flesh and blood.

Long before the carriage stopped at the doors of his house in St James's, he was asleep.

In the bedroom of the new Queen, lights were still burning. Lehzen had been waiting for her when she came upstairs; Lehzen had insisted on undressing her herself, and giving her long hair the one hundred brush strokes it received every night. And Lehzen had talked and talked, breaking into German in her excitement, chewing her favourite caraway seeds so vigorously that Victoria had turned away and smiled. The Baroness was sensitive about the caraway seeds because the great English ladies in the Duchess's household were always making fun of her.

How did her little Victoria feel? she enquired eagerly. Was she tired? What did she talk about to her Prime Minister? Think of it, Lehzen exulted, her little one was Queen at last! All the years of watching over her, of teaching her, of waiting for this great day . . . And now her little one was Queen and grown up! The Baroness openly blinked away sentimental tears. But she still needed her old Lehzen, didn't she, to help her dress and do her hair . . . No one could do it as well as Lehzen, after all these years. Ah, she remembered the times when the little Victoria had been no higher than her knee . . . And so naughty! So wilful already.

'It's a long time since I've been either,' Victoria reminded her. She was sitting up in bed, and the Baroness was perched on the end of it.

'And now I can be as wilful as I like!'

Immediately Lehzen was horrified. Wilful . . . Queens were not wilful — What ideas had this Lord Melbourne been putting into her head? Victoria laughed.

'Now, Lehzen, you're not to hector me. Lord Melbourne put nothing into my head; it was all there before. What did

22

you think of him? Isn't he a handsome man?'

The Baroness nodded. 'Very handsome, yes, if you like Englishmen, and English Lords at that. They have a look, these people, as if to say, No one exists except my equals . . . I don't like their pride, Victoria, and some of them — !' Her thin hands were raised in disapproval. 'Some of them lead the most terrible lives. This Lord Melbourne, he may be a great Lord and handsome and all the rest of it, but he's been a very dissolute man. The scandals there have been about him — you wouldn't believe them!'

Victoria leant forward.

'Tell me about them, Lehzen. All I ever heard was some talk about his wife.'

'Lady Caroline Lamb? Oh, that was the worst of all. But it's not fit for you, my child,' the Baroness said. 'Just take Lehzen's word, he's a bad man !'

'Lehzen dear.' There was a sudden edge to her voice. 'I am the judge of what is fit for me and what is not. I want to hear everything about Lord Melbourne. Kindly begin at the beginning.'

Lehzen coughed; the dear child, she must be tired to have spoken sharply like that.

'His mother had a bad reputation, I believe,' Lehzen said. 'Very bad. She was your uncle the Prince Regent's mistress for a time, and they say she profited by it to win a high place in society. She had many lovers besides; I've even heard that this Lord Melbourne's father was one of them . . . Lord Egremont, I think, but no one knows.'

She hesitated, a little uneasy after such a recital of immoralities, but Victoria only nodded for her to continue. In the old days, if the Duchess had heard of such talk . . . but she knew there was nothing to fear from the Duchess now, and she settled back to enjoy her own story. Every scrap of gossip, gleaned from the conversation of her superiors, had remained in that retentive memory, fixed by the fact that she had had to strain to hear it. The German title was only an honour conferred on her by King William

23

when she became governess to his niece. Lehzen was the daughter of an impoverished Prussian clergyman, and the high-born English ladies at Kensington Palace had always treated her accordingly.

'The first Lord Melbourne counted for nothing; it was his wife who meddled in politics and advanced her children by any means she could. It was she who made the marriage for her son William, your Melbourne, with this terrible Caroline. She was Lady Bessborough's daughter, and her mother, too, knew the Prince Regent better than she should!'

'Tell me about Caroline,' Victoria said. 'Was she so much worse than these other women?'

'Much worse,' Lehzen nodded. 'To start with, my child, she was quite mad. Quite mad. She used to dress up like a boy and roam the streets; she began taking lovers and making scenes so that everyone should know she was betraying her husband, and then she met that poet, Byron, and there was such a scandal over those two . . . Well, when Byron tired of her she stabbed herself with a pair of scissors in the middle of a London ballroom!'

'And did she die?' Victoria enquired after a moment.

'Die?' Lehzen snorted. 'Those women take care never to really hurt themselves. No, she just made such a scandal that people realized she was mad at last. Then she wrote some book, all about her love affair with this Byron, satirizing everyone in London including all her Melbourne relatives, and that finished her. No one in society ever received her again,' she said triumphantly. 'The mystery of it is how Lord Melbourne could have forgiven her and kept her on after such conduct . . . He can't have any sense of honour, that's all I can say. If that happened to a man of his position at home in Germany, that wife would soon be put in her place!'

'Poor man,' Victoria reflected. 'How perfectly dreadful for him. I *can't* understand why he didn't send her away. If she was mad, he should have had her shut up . . . It may have been kind, but it was very mistaken. I do pity him, though.'

'Oh, but you shouldn't!' Lehzen remonstrated. 'He's been the centre of many scandals himself, two with married women whose husbands actually sued for divorce! Lady Brandon and Mrs Norton — why, my dear child, Mrs Norton was only last year!'

'Last year . . .' Twelve months ago, while she, Victoria, still lived in the Duchess's shadow, still learnt her lessons and did needlework, and lived a life of strict routine and stricter obedience, while the world rushed on its busy course outside. And Lord Melbourne, who was so kind and so charming; and handsome . . . was in love with someone called Mrs Norton.

'What was this Mrs Norton like? Was she pretty?'

'Beautiful,' the Baroness corrected. 'I once saw her driving in the Park when we were on our way to St James's Palace. Nobody said anything at the time because you weren't to know about such things, but I saw her quite clearly, and I must say, she was a fine-looking woman. Very dark and not well-bred looking; I believe they were a family of actors or something and they came from that dreadful place Ireland. Anyway, my Lord Melbourne made a nice fool of himself with this hussy. How he's survived so many scandals the good God knows, I don't!'

'He must be very clever,' Victoria said slowly. 'I presume that no connection with this creature still exists?'

'Well, no,' Lehzen admitted unwillingly. 'I think he had sense enough, even if he hadn't the decency — to end the association.' For a moment Victoria looked at her without speaking. Lehzen was a dear; there were many kindnesses in that bleak childhood which were to the Baroness's credit. She was a dear, but she mustn't be so prejudiced against a man she didn't know; a man, after all, who was so much above her and had lived in a fashionable world of which the Baroness knew nothing but what she overheard. And most important, she thought, in those few seconds while the

Baroness watched her, unaware that anything was wrong, most important of all, Melbourne was the Queen's Prime Minister, and now that she had learned what she wanted to know, she would never allow Lehzen to speak disrespectfully of him again.

'And now, my child,' Lehzen said fondly, 'you should go to sleep. It's long past midnight.'

'I am rather tired,' Victoria admitted. 'No, you can leave the candle; I shall snuff it out myself.' There was a second's pause, then as the Baroness reached the door, 'And, Lehzen . . .'

'Yes my pet?'

'Now that I am Queen,' she said gently, 'I think you had better address me as Madam in future. Good night, dear Lehzen. Sleep well.'

At intervals the Palace clocks chimed the small hours, unheard by the Duchess, who had fallen asleep after another fit of angry weeping and a tirade to her friend, Lady Flora Hastings, on the ingratitude of children, her hope once more disappointed that Victoria would come and say good night and be subjected to her complaints in person. Lehzen slept soundly too, only waking once after a dream in which the little girl she had loved as if she were her own, suddenly looked at her and demanded to be called 'Madam', . . . and then turned over crossly, refusing to be hurt. She had been hurt so often and disappointed so often, and her one solace had been the affection of the little Princess. If she wanted to be called 'Madam', very well; she was not going to lose Victoria's confidence at the expense of her pride. She couldn't afford to be proud. She sniffed fiercely into her pillow, banished the snub out from her mind and went to sleep. But in Victoria's bedroom the candle burnt itself out, while she lay wide awake, listening to the stillness, alone at night for the first time in her life, thinking of the events of that long, crowded day. The Privy Council, entering the long room, pausing for a moment on the threshold, instinctively aware of the theatricality of her entrance . . . and silly

26

Lehzen chattering and fussing over the 'ordeal' . . . she had a feeling that the Baroness would take no more well-meaning liberties . . . all of them imagining that she was nervous or not looking forward to making her first official appearance as Queen and receiving the homage of the most powerful of her subjects. She had made every gesture, said every word, with the dedication of a great actress who had at last moved out of the wings to the centre of the stage. It was not hypocritical. It was expected; it was what a Queen should do, every moment of her public life, and what her Uncle William, and her reprobate uncle, George IV, had never done. It was not enough to be King by right and then behave with the indignity and lack of control common to ordinary people.

One simply was not ordinary. One's governess and childhood friend, however much one loved her, must not use Christian names any longer; and mothers and relatives, even if they were liked, must realize that the sovereign was above personal relationships.

Lord Melbourne seemed to understand that. But then he knew so much, while she had no experience at all. Lehzen's account of his life was rather distressing, but if his wife had really been as bad as that, it made a difference . . . He must have loved her to have put up with it. But then he was supposed to love this Mrs Norton too. It was wrong, of course, to have mistresses, but people had them just the same. And it was quite pointless, she thought firmly, to be concerned with what was past, as long as it remained past. If he were going to be her intimate, as she hoped – how amusing that would be – there could be no more scandals. No more Mrs Nortons if he hoped to enjoy his Queen's friendship . . . She had a feeling that he probably understood that too.

He was coming again tomorrow. He must explain to her about the political situation; there were Whigs and Tories and Radicals, she knew that, but she really had no idea what they stood for or what Radicals did that made everyone say they ought to be suppressed. She wanted to know everything, because now all these people who sat in Parliament and formed the Government were dependent upon her to sanction the laws they passed; without her signature they couldn't become Ministers or sign treaties or do anything – She had gathered that much at least from Melbourne's brief outline of her duties that day. How amazing . . . and how wonderful. How wonderful to be who she was. No wonder her uncles, Sussex and Cambridge, had looked disappointed when she walked into the room to hold the Privy Council. Naturally they envied her; who wouldn't?

Two incidents out of so many symbolized the change in her life. The moment when the Duke of Wellington, the great soldier and elder statesman of whom everyone stood in awe, knelt to kiss her hand, and walked backwards to his place, and the few words which closed the drawing-room door on the Duchess of Kent.

The early light was filtering through the curtain edges, and she heard the clock in the corridor chime six. Tomorrow she would have that clock removed out of earshot . . . Before she closed her eyes Victoria smiled. It was six o'clock and the date was June 21st. She had been Queen of England for twenty-four hours.

2

At her Proclamation outside St James's Palace the next day, the people had their first sight of the new Queen. They gathered in hundreds on that brilliant morning, talking, laughing, pushing, pointing at the carriages of the great Lords as they drove to the entrance, cheering the Duke of Wellington when he appeared for a moment before the Palace doorway swallowed him. But there were no cheers for Melbourne.

It was only seven years since the Agricultural Uprisings, when the miserably paid farm workers had revolted, and as a penalty for rick burning and the destruction of the farm machines which was taking the bread out of their mouths, Lord Melbourne had set up Courts where those responsible were sentenced to death, to long terms of imprisonment, or, worst of all, the condemned were reprieved and transported to Botany Bay for life. The disturbances had died down and the ships with their load of chained, degraded human misery sailed for the oblivion of the Australian Penal Settlement. The landed classes sighed with relief, congratulated themselves and the Prime Minister on their firm action, and the life of ease and absenteeism went on as before.

Times were hard and the law had been inhuman as long as anyone could remember; Melbourne might have been forgiven if he had not applied exactly the same measures to six humble labourers from Tolpuddle in Dorsetshire, only four years after the major uprising. They had been discovered planning to ask their employers for nine, instead of seven shillings a week, and this treasonable proposal was punished by life transportation. Melbourne, the indulgent, forgiving husband, with his cultured mind and gentle manner, ordered the judge that all must be found guilty and given the maximum penalty under the law. The fate of those six men had earned him more hatred than the agonies of the hundreds who had preceded them to Botany Bay in 1830.

Impervious to the silence of the hostile crowd, he hurried eagerly upstairs to the room where Victoria waited, and when the heralds appeared on the balcony and proclaimed the new Queen to her people, there were tears in his eyes.

There were tears in her eyes too. They came when the crowd suddenly cheered her, having caught sight of the tiny figure dressed in mourning, standing by the window. The noise grew louder as the moment lengthened; everywhere she looked there were faces turned up like hundreds of pale flowers, and waving hands.

Victoria, by the Grace of God, Queen of England, Ireland, Scotland and Wales . . .

The people saw a movement and the handkerchief which touched her eyes, and a wave of sentiment washed over them, blotting out dirt and hunger and grievance and the long contempt for the monarchy engendered by her predecessors. This was no fat libertine, like the Prince Regent, who hired professional pugilists to keep his wife out of the Abbey while he was being crowned. Or a buffoon like the dead King William who tripped over his own feet every time he moved. This was an angel, the crowd cried, a sweet, fair little angel . . . God bless her! God save Victoria!

And those were the cries she heard when she went driving, as she often did, just for the pleasure of seeing the people lining the road, cheering and waving and running after her carriage. She was immensely, miraculously popular, and in the first few weeks the common people's sentiment infected both Parliament and the Lords.

The Home Secretary, Lord John Russell, made a speech which Melbourne reported to Victoria, adding wryly that he hoped it wouldn't make her prefer Russell because he'd said it and her Prime Minister had not. She answered him with a gentle tap from her fan, told him to stop teasing her and tell her what Russell had said.

They had glorious female reigns before; those of Elizabeth and Anne had led them to great victories. Let them now hope they were going to have a female reign illustrious in its deeds of peace, an Elizabeth without her tyranny, an Anne without her weakness. By the total abolition of slavery, by a more enlightened method of punishing crime and the improved education of the people, the reign of Victoria might prove celebrated among the nations of the earth . . .

'What a very fine speech,' Victoria remarked. In spite of herself she had flushed with pleasure. The Court was at Windsor. Now that she had the choice of several Royal palaces, it amused the Queen to travel from one to the other. Buckingham Palace was the one she preferred while in London, and it would soon be ready.

The Court had just dined, and they were gathered in the State Drawing-room which, even if it was rather cold and bleak, was a magnificent room and the only place she considered appropriate for the sovereign to hold her evening gatherings. As usual, Melbourne was with her. He had sat on her left at dinner; that place was always reserved for him after a few months. The Queen had made it a rule that if foreign representatives were present the senior should sit on her right, but if conversation were tiresome from that quarter she could always turn to Melbourne. Or rather Lord M., as she called him and wrote of him in her diary.

'Russell has an excellent turn of phrase, Ma'am, but after all he only spoke the truth. It will be the most illustrious reign England's ever known, and without those ridiculous provisos about punishment and education and the rest of it.'

'Don't you agree with him, then?' she asked. On the surface, she couldn't see anything wrong with such ideas. They were very fine-sounding, and naturally when Lord Russell talked about revising the penal system he meant with great moderation . . .

'No, I don't!' Melbourne said. 'I think this fad for change is a perfect menace, Ma'am. The order of things should be left alone. I'm not against the principle of Reform as such, it's the practice I object to – this longing to overturn systems which have suited us for a century or more – *and* proved themselves – in favour of a lot of new notions about giving liberty and the vote to people who can't read or write, and wouldn't behave any better than wild animals if they were set down in the middle of Your Majesty's Drawing-room!'

'Well, there's some excuse for animals,' Victoria said. 'Personally I'm devoted to my dogs – but I quite see what you mean about the people.'

He turned to her earnestly.

'The lower classes are well enough, kept in their proper place, Ma'am. Believe me, I've had experience, I've seen the shadow of rabble rebellion darkening over the country while these fools of Radicals, *and* some of my own party, bleat about shorter working hours and better education! Education for what, in God's name? Does a man have to be lettered to use a spinning jenny or till a field? It's absolute nonsense, Ma'am, and dangerous nonsense too. The country's at the beginning of a new age, a prosperous age; we'll be richer than ever before, and just when we need every hour of labour and every item of goods for our markets, these rascals start trying to limit the length of employment!'

The Queen frowned. 'But surely they realize that it's good for people to work? Now if they were unemployed and starving, that would be something else! *I* work, and so do you, dear Lord M. Think of the number of papers alone I have to sign, and all the work done in the business of government! Besides whenever I drive out in London there always seems to be a crowd of people idling about waiting to see me, so they can't be too hard pressed . . . Not that I'm not fond of them,' she said quickly. She *was* fond of them. She was their Queen and they were good and loyal; they were a living manifestation of the power she was enjoying more and more as she discovered its extent. It was right that she should view her subjects with affection, but equally right that her feeling should be tempered with impartiality, that the views of men like Melbourne should be her views. Society was formed of a pyramid, with the unknown masses at the base, the middle classes forming the sides, the aristocracy the top and herself, the Queen, as the apex. It was the people's place to work obediently under the masters God had placed over them, for it was unthinkable that God, who had created the universe, was not also responsible for the social system in it.

'They don't know how fortunate they are, Ma'am, in having such a sovereign,' Melbourne assured her. 'I know you're fond of your people, and so do they. I only hope to God they appreciate it! That's the devil of it all, you see; men are venal, venal by nature, ungrateful, unseeing, untrustworthy! And yet it has always seemed to me that trying to change them − "better" them, these idiots call it − can only make things worse. You don't tame a wild beast by breaking its chains!'

Victoria laughed. She could never resist teasing Melbourne. It made such a change from the stiffness with which she treated everybody else.

'You sound far more like a Tory than a Whig, Lord M. I do say it might be the Duke of Wellington speaking to listen to you!' He smiled in return, the irritable look of an indolent man forced to bestir himself left his face; it became smooth and gay again, and his fine eyes twinkled back at her.

'Don't speak too loud, Ma'am, or you'll have me turned out of office!'

'I pity the man who tried to replace you with *me*,' she said swiftly. 'He'd find me very difficult to deal with, I assure you . . . But tell me, my Lord, why are you a Whig and not a Tory, when you feel so strongly?'

'Ah, now I've confused you,' he said. 'My dear Ma'am, let me explain myself. The Tories are dull fellows. Damned dull, if you'll permit the expression.' Victoria, who allowed no freedom of speech or laxity in her presence from anyone else, permitted it with an understanding nod.

'They oppose all progress − all reform, on the principle that Time stands motionless. What was good for our great-grandparents must be the best for us. Now there's a world of difference between those views and the Whig philosophy. If you listened to the Tories, and the Duke, for that matter, we'd all be wearing wigs and travelling by sedan chair! No, Ma'am, there's a need for a certain amount of Reform among the educated classes. It's a good thing that responsible men should take it on themselves to remedy abuses here and there, to alleviate injustice . . . that's always been our function, Ma'am. The abolition of slavery − now there was a good idea! It's perhaps not possible to enforce it *completely*, but at least it's on the Statute Book. It shows good will . . .'

'Thank Heavens you're Prime Minister,' Victoria said impulsively. 'I can't think of anyone who could combine Reform and caution as perfectly as you do. At least I know that as long as you remain at the head of my Government, no rash steps will be taken!'

'You can be quite certain of that, Ma'am. I'm an old dog at the game, and nobody will force me into anything precipitous!'

But the Queen was not listening to him. Someone in the room had so far forgotten themselves as to laugh out loud. The offender was Lady Flora Hastings, who sat playing whist in a corner with her mistress, the Duchess of Kent. The silence which descended on the room was almost tangible; the conversation of those whom the Queen was not favouring with her attention was carried out in whispers because Her Majesty objected to noise, and it too tailed off, leaving the awful quiet, while Victoria fixed Lady Flora with a cold and furious glare.

The company was mixed, because the men were no longer allowed to sit over their wine in the dining-room. The Queen was bored by female companionship, and the former custom kept Lord Melbourne away from her.

'I think it is getting late,' she said clearly. She stood, and instantly every chair scraped back and the company scrambled to their feet. The unfortunate Lady Flora was as red as a peony, and the red was rapidly turning to white under that angry, unwavering stare. Slowly Victoria turned back to Melbourne, and her expression softened.

'Dear Lord M., I've so enjoyed our evening. I shall see you tomorrow morning, shan't I, and then we can go riding in the Park in the afternoon, if it's a fine day.'

He bowed very low over her hand, and kissed it.

'I shall look forward to it, Ma'am. Good night.'

'Ladies!'

The Duchess of Sutherland, Mistress of the Robes, Lady Tavistock and Lady Lansdowne came towards her, their black skirts swaying gracefully, and Victoria politely met her mother half-way and pecked the Duchess's cheek. Nothing emphasized her unimportance more than her daughter's scrupulous observance of the niceties in public.

'Good night, dear Mama. Good night, ladies and gentlemen. You may all retire.'

The men bowed and the women curtsied as the train of ladies led by that small upright figure left the room. The last to leave was Lehzen, and as she passed him, Melbourne saluted her and smiled. The Baroness beamed in return and bustled through the doorway. In spite of her disapproval of the man, indeed of her jealousy of her beloved child's enthusiasm for him, Lehzen was fast relaxing her guard. He had been so charming to her, so really attentive and polite, and he had a way of listening to her that made her feel he appreciated how important she was to the Queen. It seemed there would be room for both of them in Victoria's favour, and with that fear allayed the Baroness basked in his flattery and was soon praising him as warmly as Victoria could wish.

Melbourne knew the possessiveness of old maids and a few compliments were a small price to pay for her friendship; he was determined that nothing should spoil his intimacy with the Queen. It was quite extraordinary how much that relationship meant to him already, after only a few months. It was reaching the point where he could find no fault with her at all. Her insistence upon etiquette amused him. She was conscious enough of her position, and by God, she saw to it that everyone else was aware of it too . . . The Court was finding life irksome and restricted; he knew very well that nothing bored the sophisticated ladies in her household more than the daily rides, the musical recitals after tea, and the stiff meals followed by an even stiffer evening . . . As for the men! He could hardly look at Mr Greville, Secretary to the Privy Council, who often found himself an unwilling guest at Windsor, without laughing in his face. He could imagine Greville's irritation at being hurried away from the port, not permitted to smoke, or lounge back in his chair – the Queen insisted on a respectful attitude – and forced to make the dullest small talk in a whisper! It was really damned funny, Melbourne decided as he went off to his own room. Damned funny and quite right . . . and, of course, only the stricture about smoking applied to him. Otherwise he could do as he liked; he could talk out loud and make jokes and laugh with her, and he always had the seat beside her and the place on her right when they went riding. He was set apart, and every time he looked into her eyes, or sometimes, when they were talking very earnestly, took her hand in his; whenever he made her laugh or extracted a compliment like the one she had paid him that evening, the old amusements receded further and further from his mind. He didn't miss the sparkling dinner parties at Melbourne House, the company of beautiful, experienced women, with their promise of a more intimate relationship. He was done with all that anyway, he told himself. Too old and too disillusioned to need women in that way. And his experience with poor Caroline Norton had shaken him badly. She had been disgraced after the divorce, and that brutish husband had been given custody of the children. The wretched woman had written him the most uncomfortable letters, imploring his help. Their association had ruined her – he felt sorry about it indeed, and a little guilty that he himself should have escaped so lightly. But it was always the way in those affairs, when the husband made a fuss. And only an oaf, like George Norton, put up to it by his political opponents, would have brought the case and exposed private matters to the vulgar gaze. Poor Caroline; the least he could do was to send her money regularly. And a little later, when he was quite sure it could be mentioned, he would ask Victoria to receive her at Court. Just once. If she did that, Mrs Norton would be automatically reinstated in society. It was the least he could do for her; especially since he never intended to see her again. It just wasn't possible, now that he was on such close terms with the Queen, to risk upsetting her by associating with a woman like Caroline Norton . . .

Downstairs in the State Drawing-room, three men remained behind. It was not yet eleven o'clock, and two of them, Charles Greville and Lord Grey, usually began the evening at such an hour. Neither felt inclined to go upstairs and find their way through the cold winding passages to their rooms, and Greville thought he would choke with irritation unless he could relieve his feelings. The third man was quite ready for bed, but he lingered on with a purpose, aware that the two Englishmen wanted to talk privately. He had been watching them during the evening and he could see they were both annoyed by the Queen's behaviour. He approached them with a smile. Baron Stockmar was a German, but he had been resident in the Duchess of Kent's household for so many years that he had become a fixture in Court circles, a man whose nominal duties of doctor had long lapsed in favour of the post of unofficial diplomat. He was a slight, pale man, with very graceful manners and an extraordinarily acute mind.

It was the measure of his abilities that having come to England in the retinue of Leopold of Coburg, husband to George IV's ill-fated daughter Charlotte, Stockmar had remained after the Princess's death in childbirth and established himself as the friend of the Duchess of Kent and the background guardian of that other heiress to the throne of England, the little Victoria.

'Ah, gentlemen,' he said, and bowed to the two Englishmen. 'Not ready to retire yet, I see. How fortunate; I was hoping to have a little conversation away from the ladies.'

'Are you sure that Her Majesty would approve?' Greville asked acidly. 'She must be the only woman in England who begrudges a man a few minutes over his port after dinner!'

Stockmar smiled. He didn't like Greville.

'The Queen is very young still,' he said gently. 'And perhaps she is a little greedy for masculine company. She's had little enough of it, you know. She never knew her father, or had the companionship of brothers.'

'Being an only child has had its advantages,' Lord Grey said. 'I doubt if the Queen would have exchanged the childish joys of romping with a brother for her present happy position.'

Greville laughed disagreeably.

'Well put, my Lord. You paint a pathetic picture, Baron, but I don't think Her Majesty needs anyone's pity.'

It was on the edge of his tongue to say that Her Majesty's subjects, especially himself, were more in need of that, but he refrained.

'I think Lord Melbourne fills the parental gap well

enough, don't you, Greville?' Lord Grey remarked. His tone, and the expression on Greville's face said quite plainly that they wished the Baron would mind his own business and go away. But the Baron did not move. Victoria was not behaving tactfully. She was becoming more headstrong and autocratic every day, and the Baron, who had a profound mistrust for the English and a deep desire to see her succeed in spite of the character of her subjects, felt it his duty to excuse her.

'She relies completely upon Lord Melbourne,' he agreed. 'And what could be more fortunate? After all, gentlemen, think how aggrieved we might have been had she chosen a foreigner as her confidant instead!'

It was a shrewd point, but Greville parried it.

'It's certainly lucky that the voice whispering into Her Majesty's ear has an English accent, but it's rumoured that this governess Lehzen does more than her share of whispering too. The thing is, my dear Baron, it's always been thought best for the sovereign of England to have *no* confidant; to repose her trust equally among her Ministers and Household. Not that anyone objects to Lord Melbourne, you understand — or indeed to yourself, for that matter, if her choice should fall on you at any time . . .'

The Baron shook his head.

'Her Majesty regards me as a kind of distant uncle; believe me, if I had any sway with her at all, we should be dallying over the port every evening, Mr Greville.'

Lord Grey laughed, and the atmosphere relaxed.

'In that case, for God's sake try and oust Melbourne! I can't think why he hasn't pointed out to the Queen that a little laxity would be much appreciated.'

'Perhaps because he doesn't suffer the strictures,' Stockmar suggested. 'Royal favour is a potent draught, my Lord, and it's gone to stronger heads than his. No, gentlemen, let us be frank. I've known the Queen from a child, and I'm truly devoted to her. I beg of you, be a little patient. She's so young, and all this insistence on etiquette, these tiresome rules of conduct, if you like, are only a young girl's way of asserting herself. She'll relax when she's more at her ease — more sure of her dignity.'

'I think she's sure of it already,' Greville interposed. 'And since we're speaking frankly, and I know I can count on you as a man of honour, Baron, not to repeat my remarks —' he bowed, 'I think the Queen finds it perfectly fascinating to alter our lives and regulate our movements, and watch us having to obey her whether we like it or not. Did you notice the reception Lady Flora got this evening after that unfortunate guffaw? I'm not saying it was a pretty noise, but by God, when the Queen stared her out like that I nearly shrivelled in my seat myself! A child she may have been, and a girl she may be, but don't let that bird voice and that lack of inches deceive you. The Queen has the makings of a formidable woman already. You think age will improve her, Baron. I think her character is only just developing.'

'If what you say is true, Mr Greville,' Stockmar said quietly ' — and I shan't argue with you — then there's only one solution which will keep Her Majesty's popularity and check any wild impulses she may have.'

'And what is that?' Lord Grey enquired.

'The Queen must marry the right man,' the Baron answered. 'I say to you now, that I believe that everything — her reign, her happiness, indeed the happiness of England — will depend upon that!'

Greville laughed unkindly.

'If she marries anyone, it'll probably be Melbourne at this rate. Come, gentlemen, let's go upstairs. We've said enough indiscretions for one evening!'

Alone in his room, Stockmar began a long letter to Leopold, King of the Belgians. He was extremely tired, and he felt symptoms of dyspepsia returning; his digestive system always suffered if he over-taxed himself, and the conversation with Greville and Grey had certainly upset his juices again. He swallowed a draught, mixed from the well-stocked medicine cabinet that went everywhere with him, and sacrificed his sleep to the composition of his letter. He was devoted to Leopold. The friendship between them had grown during the short time the Prince's marriage to Charlotte had lasted, and it was cemented for life on the night she died, when the distracted husband had flung himself into Stockmar's arms and begged him never to leave his side. Stockmar had kept that promise. He had remained in England to comfort the Royal widower, and firmly ignored the fact that the frustration of his hopes of being Consort to the Queen of England, formed the major part of Leopold's grief for his wife. The young man's talents and ambition were wasted in this country, and his position was rendered all the more intolerable by the dislike of his father-in-law, George IV. But the tragic death of Princess Charlotte and her infant son had aroused widespread sympathy, and earned the bereaved husband a degree of popularity which made it easy for Stockmar to enlist supporters for him.

The Baron's gift for making friends in the right places proved invaluable to the young man; Stockmar's efforts to secure a consolation prize for Leopold were strengthened by the fact that he himself had nothing to gain. He was recognized as that phenomenon, a loyal and disinterested friend to a stranger in a foreign land, and thanks to his tireless efforts and connections, the vacant throne of Belgium was offered to his protégé.

It was Leopold's suggestion that he should remain in the household of his sister, the Duchess of Kent. After all, his little niece Victoria would one day occupy the place which should have been his dead wife's . . . it was a duty to be on hand through a loyal proxy and guide her judicially when the time came. The time had come; the little niece was Queen indeed, and her affectionate uncle wrote copious letters full of advice to which she replied with equal fondness and effusion, and the Baron maintained a tactful watching brief.

King Leopold had two nephews, two excellent young men, both of whom had been reared with the object of fitting them for marriage, since their home state of Saxe-Coburg offered little scope for political ambitions. And Victoria was the most eligible girl in Europe. When the time came for her to marry, it was essential, as Stockmar had just pointed out, that she should choose the right man. And the right man was obviously either Ernst or Albert of Saxe-Coburg, cousins by blood, nephews of her dearest uncle, protégés again of Baron Stockmar, who had spent some years as their tutor. As soon as the Queen was crowned, as soon as the Court was out of mourning and a decent interval had elapsed, the subject of that marriage must be raised more seriously.

The candle burnt low on the Baron's desk, as his neat writing covered page after page with news of Leopold's dearest niece, her country and her Court. The conversation with Greville and Lord Grey was faithfully reported, and the Baron regretfully admitted that some of their complaints had been justified, though in common with the English aristocratic class they were expressed with a most distressing lack of respect for the sovereign. Undoubtedly it was her consciousness of this attitude which made the Queen adopt her somewhat autocratic habits. The pen hesitated for a moment, and then wrote on, impelled to tell the truth however disagreeable. It described with some pain Her Majesty's increasing hauteur – not quite becoming in one so young – her disinclination to discuss serious matters other than with Lord Melbourne, who was obviously devoted to her, but hardly the right person to imbue her with a true concept of her moral duties . . . Her insistence on following her own pleasures, though these were certainly innocent enough, regardless of the comfort or wishes of others, and her unfilial exclusion of her mother from her confidence. She favoured her former governess Lehzen far more than the woman's position or intelligence deserved, and the Baron was forced to conclude that the

Baroness's complete subservience to the Queen's smallest whim was the secret of her elevation . . . The Queen also enjoyed flattery more than was wise, and reacted with unbecoming hostility to the least criticism, as he feared even Leopold himself had noticed, judging by their last exchange of letters. He hastened to add that in spite of these failings which he was sure were due to extreme youth, the Queen's innate honesty, courage and innocence remained unaltered, and the more he saw the more convinced he became that the best means of ensuring a happy life for Victoria was marriage with one of Leopold's nephews. It was unnatural for a woman to bear the great burden of sovereignty alone, without a husband's guidance and authority to strengthen her, and only a husband would protect her from the dangers of intimacy with men like Melbourne, and from the ultimate loss of dignity which must ensue from such an association.

In the meantime he took care to remain on good terms with the Prime Minister, with Lehzen, indeed with everyone, confident that all would accord with Leopold's desires if they were patient.

He purposely omitted Greville's jibe that Victoria might marry Melbourne because he considered it too offensive and waspish to repeat, and he feared that his beloved Leopold, whose anxiety sometimes overcame his tact, might mention it to the Queen if he were told.

The rumours of that marriage which were soon to sweep the country did not originate with Stockmar.

'Lady Tavistock! *Lady Tavistock!*'

The Marchioness of Tavistock hurried into the Queen's private sitting-room at Buckingham Palace as fast as she could without actually running. She had come to recognize the angry note in that voice; by the early part of 1838 it was well known to those who attended on Her Majesty. Victoria stood in the middle of the room, holding a copy of *The Times* newspaper in both hands. Her lady-in-waiting

43

saw with alarm that the Queen was trembling with rage, and her cheeks were scarlet.

'Yes, Madam,' she said breathlessly, 'I came at once, I was only talking to Lady Durham in the next room . . .'

'Never mind what you were doing! Have you seen this . . . this disgusting article? Have you read it'

'No . . . er . . . no, Madam, I'm afraid I haven't.'

'Then listen to this description of Lord Melbourne! . . . "a mere dangler after the frivolous courtesies of the ballroom and the boudoir . . ." Did you ever hear of such impertinence?'

'No indeed,' Lady Tavistock agreed quickly. For one awful moment she had imagined that the Queen's annoyance was connected with her. 'Most disgraceful!'

'Oh, but wait,' Victoria snapped. 'That is nothing! Nothing to the insult that has been offered me! They have the kindness to point out, these creatures, that my friendship with Lord Melbourne is bringing me into disrepute! "There are rumours," it says here, "that our beloved and innocent young sovereign is contemplating a matrimonial step which her most loyal subjects would find utterly abhorrent. Those same loyal subjects are already suffering on their Queen's behalf hearing her described as Mrs Melbourne . . ." *Mrs Melbourne!*'

The principal Tory newspaper was flung towards Lady Tavistock, who hesitated, not knowing whether it would further enrage her mistress if she picked it up.

'Have that scandal sheet taken away,' Victoria said. 'Oh, where's Lehzen, where's anyone who can advise me how to counter this?'

'Lord Melbourne will be here within an hour,' her lady-in-waiting soothed. 'Don't distress yourself, Madam, he'll know how to deal with it.'

'I know how I'd like to deal with it!' The Queen swung round on her and the bloody temper of her ancestors, of "Butcher Cumberland" and her own father, spoke out incongruously in the nineteenth-century room.

'I'd have the author of it flogged!'

It was an impossible threat and she knew it; the days were past when the late Duke of Kent had been able to order nine hundred lashes for a delinquent soldier, but at that moment his daughter could think of nothing more fitting for the man who had dared to call her Mrs Melbourne.

'If they think they'll make me give up my friendship with Lord Melbourne by doing this,' she promised, 'they'll discover their mistake. They shall be excluded! No Tory shall set foot at my receptions and I shan't even speak to one of them if I can help it!'

'But, Madam, it's impossible to alienate such a large number of your subjects,' Elizabeth Tavistock protested. Even she was shocked by the vehemence of the threat, and the possible consequences. It was all very well for the Queen, who tyrannized with impunity, but how awkward it was going to be for the Whig Lords and their wives, if she adopted such an attitude . . . Some of the Tavistocks' friends were Tories — and in any case, the time would certainly come when the Whigs would be voted out of office . . .

'I'm not aware that your duties include giving me political advice,' the Queen said. 'Loyalty to Lord Melbourne, Madam, is only second to loyalty to me. Kindly remember that in future.'

'I beg Your Majesty's pardon,' she murmured. 'I was only trying to make light of what was written for your own sake.'

'Thank you,' Victoria retorted. 'Now will you please fetch Lehzen for me? And order me a glass of water; I feel quite faint.'

It was some time before the Baroness could be found, and Victoria waited alone, walking up and down the new carpet in her new Palace, quivering with temper and very near to tears. Finally she shed a few, but they were tears of outraged pride and anger. It was such a rude shock to discover that in the outside world people actually thought and spoke of her disrespectfully, that her dignity should be smirched by those beyond her power to punish.

The Tories. Ever since her accession those detestable people had been writing and saying things which were a veiled criticism of her. They hated Melbourne . . . pure jealousy, of course, because he was so clever and she found him so amusing, and had made no intimates of any one of them. When they voted in the House over her Civil List they had the impertinence to quibble over her allowance of £380,000 a year, and their miserable newspapers attacked Melbourne and the Whigs in every article they printed. That had been bad enough, but now they were daring to mention her by name, to imply that she was in the wrong . . . She wiped her eyes furiously and pushed the handkerchief into her sleeve.

The next moment Lehzen had come up to her, and seeing the signs of tears, gathered her into her arms exactly as if she were a child again and they were back at Kensington Palace.

'Oh, Madam, Madam, my little love . . . Don't upset yourself so.' It was only temper, as the Baroness knew, but she treated it like distress.

Lady Tavistock had whispered something about an article in *The Times* when she routed the Baroness out of her room, where she had been dozing on her bed after lunch. The Queen was beside herself with anger, and the Baroness had better hurry up to her at once . . .

An incongruous friendship had sprung up between the great lady and the once-insignificant governess. Lady Tavistock gossiped with her and rushed to her for advice in dealing with the Queen, and gradually Lehzen thawed. All Victoria's ladies treated her with respect, conscious of the fact that the wind of Royal favour blew strongly in the Baroness's direction. Only the Duchess of Kent and her entourage maintained their old indifference to her, and Lehzen still smarted from privately administered snubs. The most arrogant of all was that insufferable Lady Flora Hastings . . .

She listened patiently while the story of the infamy committed by *The Times* in particular and the Tories in general was poured out by Victoria, and clucked sympathetically. Poor Lord Melbourne, to be attacked like that . . . as for calling her precious mistress Mrs Melbourne — words failed Lehzen at the impertinence.

'I shall discuss this with him as soon as he arrives,' Victoria said. 'Just think of it, Lehzen, saying there is talk of my marrying him! How embarrassed he must be!'

'I'm afraid your mother will say that he's responsible,' Lehzen said spitefully. 'You know, Madam, she's never liked Lord Melbourne, and I really think she's jealous of the friendship . . .'

It was an unnecessary piece of trouble-making, for the Duchess had long since given up advising her daughter or attempting any interference. But she was still making the mistake of being cool to Lehzen.

'Mama won't dare say anything like that to me!'

At that moment a footman put his head round the door, and then moved cautiously into the room. News travelled fast in the Palace, and everyone from the Duchess of Sutherland, Mistress of the Robes, to the meanest kitchen maid, knew that Her Majesty was in a temper.

'Lord Melbourne to see Her Majesty,' the footman murmured.

'Show him up at once,' Lehzen ordered. The Queen never directly addressed a servant or was spoken to by them, if she could help it. The Baroness had gone before Melbourne came; he found the Queen sitting alone in a chair by the window, her posture very stiff and her eyes still red. His pulse always quickened when he saw her; he had begun to think her quite beautiful lately, and to dream of a light, graceful figure which sometimes danced towards him, holding out both hands.

He saw at once that she was upset, and his heart gave a ridiculous jump. It used to do exactly that when Caroline, his wife, rushed weeping into his arms, after the discovery of a fresh peccadillo. He had never been able to bear a woman's tears. And he had seen *The Times* that morning.

She got up and came to him, and impulsively he took her hand in both his own and kissed it, holding it a fraction longer than was necessary.

'You don't have to tell me something is wrong, Ma'am; I can see it, and I know exactly what it is. It's that damnable newspaper again!'

'Come and sit down with me,' she begged. 'I'm so angry, so furious, that I shall burst into tears in another minute. How could they print such things? How dare they!'

He drew his chair close to hers.

'They can and do. I'm used to being slandered, Ma'am. Nothing my enemies say can hurt me; but I can't bear that this sort of thing should touch you. Try to ignore it, I beg you; treat it with the contempt it deserves!'

'Ignore it?' Victoria stared at him in amazement. 'But, my dear Lord M., how can I possibly ignore these – these references to my marriage . . .. and mentioning you in that connection! It's too monstrous! Why, it's a deliberate attempt to make us both ridiculous!'

She did not see him flinch, or notice the very faint colour that came into his face. She was right, of course, he insisted to himself. To talk of their marrying *was* ridiculous . . . there had never been any question of it, certainly not in his mind. And if he hadn't foreseen how much she would object to it, it was entirely his own fault, and he had no right to be hurt.

'Besides,' Victoria continued, 'what right have they to discuss such a personal thing? This isn't the first reference to my marrying, you know, though at least the others were respectful. It's most unseemly that my private life should be open to comment from Members of Parliament and newspapers.'

'I'm afraid it's the penalty of your position, Ma'am,' he explained. How well he understood her indignation, her resentment of intrusion into the secret places of her life.

Poor child, he thought tenderly, exposed to the pitiless curiosity of the crowd. But it was the price she had to pay and would go on paying all her life, for being who she was. The least he could do was try and explain and help her bear it.

'You see yourself as a private person,' he said earnestly, 'and, of course, you are. That's the curse as well as the glory of kingship, my dear Ma'am, that sovereigns are human beings, with feelings and hopes and affections the same as everybody else. But because they're set apart from, above, the commonality, the commonality demands that these private things should be exposed to view. Everything you do and say will be important to your people; stories will be spread about you and many of them will be lying and cruel. But you must try not to mind. It's human nature to be jealous of the great and try to lower them . . . What you eat and what you wear and who you favour with your friendship is of absorbing interest to thousands who have never even seen you and probably never will. And that most private of all matters, who you honour with your love and choose to marry − that above all, must be shared with your people. The husband of the Queen of England must be approved by England, because he will stand nearest to England's most important personage. And he will be the father of a future King. See it in that light Ma'am, and you wont be quite so angry with *The Times*.'

'I appreciate what you say,' she admitted, 'but I still think it's a liberty that has grown up unnecessarily. As for *The Times* − you may forgive that vicious article, but I never shall. If I am Queen, Lord M.' − she faced him, and tapped his sleeve emphatically − 'if I am set apart and above, then I shouldn't be disrespected. All people have a right to privacy. I don't demand to know everything about even those who come in daily contact with me, and I shall insist on being shown the same consideration. They can question and speculate as much as they please − I shall make it a rule to let them know *nothing*!'

He knew that it was useless to pursue the subject; and it was hardly likely that she meant to irritate public opinion in such a way. Naturally her judgment was biased by that attack upon her; she was still angry and, damn it all, who could expect her to be otherwise . . .

'And since we're on the subject,' Victoria's voice broke in on him. He looked up and found that she had left her chair and was walking towards the window. Without turning round she sensed him move to stand also, and said quickly, 'Dear Lord M., please don't get up. You know I like you to be quite at home when we're alone. Just stay in your chair and let me walk about. It helps me think. As I was saying, about my marrying, I've had another letter from my Uncle Leopold.'

'Yes?' Melbourne said cautiously. Personally he detested Leopold, whom he regarded as a humbug and a foreigner, still trading on the memory of his dead English wife. And an insufferable meddler, he thought angrily, always writing his damned letters to the Queen full of advice she didn't want . . . 'What had he to say, Ma'am?'

'It was a very nice letter,' she answered. 'Full of kind enquiries – too full, really, for I'm afraid my uncle's apt to ask about State business in the most awkward way, and naturally it puts me to the trouble of answering in such a fashion that I tell him nothing . . . But that's another matter. The point is he's anxious for my cousins Ernst and Albert to come to England.'

She turned and faced him, very small and very upright, with the pale sunlight streaming through the window at her back, and he could tell by her voice that she was irritated.

'You know my uncle's always wanted me to marry one or other of them. It's been taken for granted for as long as I can remember. Victoria will marry Ernst or Albert. When I a child and we used to spend a lot of time at the house at Claremont – when my uncle lived there before he went to Belgium – Mama and he were always discussing it. I suppose I accepted it then without thinking. But now, Lord M., I'm not so sure!'

He was ashamed of the way his heart bounded with relief; he didn't know whether his feelings showed and whether she saw them on his face. Probably not. Like all the very young, Victoria was not over perceptive to the reactions of others.

'That's quite natural,' he agreed. 'After all, Ma'am, you've only just acceded; life is opening out before you – isn't it a little premature to think of curbing your freedom with a husband and children?'

'How perfectly you understand!'

She hurried back to him and subsided into the seat beside him, and again he found himself holding her hand in his. Comforting her, he thought happily, and ventured a little squeeze which was returned with warmth.

'I don't want to get married yet,' Victoria insisted. 'I don't *feel* like marriage! It's all very well to take something for granted as a child, before you've any knowledge of what the step means. Personally, if I wasn't so fond of my Uncle Leopold, I would say it was unfair of him to try and hold me to a promise which was never made by me, but only by Mama, and harry me with letters before I've even been Queen for twelve months.'

'Fair or not, my dear Ma'am, all he *can* do is harry,' Melbourne smiled. 'The decision rests with you, and I'm hanged if I see why you should be pushed into marrying until you're ready. Enjoy life a little first! Think of the Balls and parties you can give, and how much gayer it will be without a worthy husband in the background claiming every dance. You may even allow me the occasional honour . . .'

She laughed, and he thought again how infectious a laugh it was, though some people said it was too loud and the Queen showed too much teeth and gum. Personally he found it irresistible.

'Occasional honour? If you're not careful, my Lord, I

shall make you lead out at the first Ball I have, and then think what *The Times* will have to say! But seriously — what fun it will be! I had so few parties when I was a child. Mama was always quarrelling with King William and rushing away to Claremont to sulk in the country, or staying shut up in Kensington. Now I have this lovely Palace, all newly decorated, and a *lot* of money . . .' She laughed again, and withdrew her hands to clasp them with excitement. 'I think we've been in mourning long enough, and anyway there's the coronation in June, and a thousand preparations to be made — I think I ought to give a Ball!'

'I think so too,' he said heartily. 'And if I may suggest it, Ma'am, it won't do the brothers Ernst and Albert any harm to cool their heels and wait a while for the hand of the Queen of England. That is if she decides on one of them in the end.'

'Exactly!' Victoria nodded. 'Thank goodness that's settled. Dear Lord M. Whatever should I do without you? Now I insist that you stay to tea, and I'll go through the papers you want me to sign afterwards. By then it'll be nearly time to change for dinner, and I expect you at my table as usual.'

The new year of the new reign advanced through the dismal winter months and into the brisk English spring. From behind the tall windows of the new Buckingham Palace, lights and music filtered out into the night, and at dawn a long procession of carriages could be seen driving ladies and gentlemen in elaborate Court dress back to their homes. And sometimes the Queen of England, sheltering in a fur cloak, went on to the Palace roof with her ladies to watch the sun rise over London before she went to bed. The black dresses were put away; silks and satins of every colour filled the Royal dressing closets, scarlet robes trimmed with ermine for State occasions, the ribbons and stars of the various orders — Victoria's favourite was the Garter, she thought the blue sash pretty — cases of jewellery, tiaras and necklaces and stomachers, most of them too massive for her to wear, heirlooms from centuries of monarchy, including the fabulous rope of pearls which had once belonged to poor Mary Queen of Scots, and which the rebel lords had sold to her acquisitive rival, Elizabeth . . . Victoria had given orders for much of the jewellery to be reset, the lightest and most elegant to be kept for informal use, and the rest to be locked away. There were cupboards full of bonnets, impractical and pretty, trimmed in profusion with ribbons and flowers and the graceful ostrich plumes which the Queen loved. She had really ordered far too many bonnets − but every time she tried one on it seemed that her reflection was not quite so plain, and for once the offending *Times* had gratified her by praising a new portrait in which, the writer said, the artist had painted the Royal bosom in admirable rotundity. Her features weren't good; Victoria knew that, and contented herself with a clear complexion and bright blue eyes, but even if she were too small, as she had once complained to Melbourne, her shoulders and bosom were very well formed, though naturally one did not mention that. And in spite of the jeers of the Tory newspapers, who had suddenly decided to harp on the Queen's physical delicacy and insist that she marry and give England an heir − the inference was that she would probably die performing that duty − Victoria's health bloomed. She worked hard; the red despatch boxes had to be opened, the contents examined, and signed when necessary, the newspapers had to be read through, deputations received, petitions and correspondence answered; Ministers came and went and the general business of being Queen went on relentlessly day after day. Melbourne was always at hand, of course; he went through the boxes with her and explained the reports from the Foreign Minister. He told her which to read carefully and which she need only glance through; he looked through the audience list and advised who should be received and what she should say and pointed out items in the papers which were likely to interest or amuse her. She sometimes thought it would have been easier with a secretary, but Lord M. didn't think she needed one, and it was much nicer to deal with the day's business direct with him. And if spiteful people said he spent more time at the Palace than he did at the House . . . well she couldn't spare him, and that was the end of it. In between there were luncheon parties, and then a drive in the afternoon, or a ride in Windsor Great Park if she were staying at the Castle, embroidery and gossip with her ladies, and private talks with Lehzen, who *never* contradicted her now, and was the dearest of companions. There was always time to put on a big apron and bath her spaniel; she found it so relaxing to splash about with soap and water like an ordinary woman, before going to her rooms to change into one of her magnificent new dresses for the evening dinner party. And often there was a Ball in the white-and-gold Ballroom, where she could catch glimpses of herself in the long mirrors, dancing with some of the handsomest and most eligible men in England.

And in the first months of that new year, all she wanted to do was dance with them, talk a little, albeit self-consciously because they lacked the easy conversational gift of dear Lord M., and whereas he was elderly and safe they were single and young and, often as not, vaguely embarrassed. It was an embarrassment that Victoria enjoyed and it made up to her for the lack of beauty which she was too honest not to admit. She might not be pretty and able to draw sighs and blushes like some of the young women who attended her Court, but she was Queen and everyone was only too anxious to please her. It was enchanting to be able to choose the music and the dances, and dictate the conversation, so that whatever happened she was sure she would never be bored, and if she wanted to get rid of someone, she had only to nod and smile and they had to go away, discomfited or not . . . And no matter who was tired, the gaieties continued until the Queen decided it was time to go to bed. As she needed very little sleep and always woke full of energy, it was usually dawn before the carriages, occupied by many less youthful and vigorous than their Royal hostess, rolled away from the Palace.

And as the spring passed and the month of June, set aside for the coronation, approached, the Tory newspapers and the lesser scandal sheets began making unkind references to the Banquets and entertainments given by the Queen, while so many of her subjects were starving that Parliament was struggling to get the Poor Law amended so as to give some relief to the unfortunates. Naturally, her critics said, part of the blame for such extravagance and lack of feeling must be laid on that elder statesman who lived with his feet under the Royal dining-table and could well have pointed out to Her Majesty that wasting so much money in light pleasures was causing pain to her people . . .

The elder statesman, who found himself forced to sit up until five in the morning after a gruelling day alternating between the Queen and his Cabinet duties, cursed the papers for this attempt to spoil Victoria's innocent enjoyments. Why the devil shouldn't she spend, he grumbled: what else was money for, except to buy the few pleasures available in life. And God bless her, she was young and carefree, and the few paltry thousands her critics wanted her to save wouldn't have made any real difference to the poor. Melbourne was becoming very tired of the poor, and very tired of the people, that nebulous, irritating body in whose name change was constantly invoked. The people . . . what did the Reformers mean by that lumping together of humanity? Everyone fell into that category, the same as they all subdivided into classes, and quite rightly. God, if there was one — and his beloved Queen was always trying to convince him of His existence — God had made the world and the system by which it operated. And if God made the poor, as well as the rich, presumably He knew

55

what He was doing. No one would ever convince Melbourne that the lower classes were not better and happier left undisturbed, safe from the perils of an education they could never appreciate, lucky enough to be employed, and adequately paid, damn it, when there was employment.

And if they suffered, then he felt sure that, like animals, their capacity for feeling was much less than the sensibilities of their betters. If Victoria had any doubts on these points, he was quick to reassure her. Also the coronation would dispel the few clouds of unpopularity which had gathered since her accession, blown up by his political enemies and by the professional kill-joys, who couldn't bear to see their superiors enjoying themselves.

On the 25th of June the sound of cannon woke Victoria at half past five. It was the morning of her coronation, and outside she could hear the murmur of an immense crowd which had gathered outside Buckingham Palace, prepared to wait for many hours to see her set out for the Abbey. It was a fine day, sunny and warm and the temper of the people was cheerful and expectant. Popular sentiment was touched by the age of the small, fragile girl who was to take her solemn vows of sovereignty that day, and be burdened with the weight, both physical and symbolic, of the mighty English crown. When she appeared at last shortly before noon, dressed in a crimson velvet mantle and a white gown glittering with embroidery, riding in the enormous State Coach like some winsome fairy, the sentimental crowds went mad with enthusiasm. They cheered her even more loudly than their former enemy, Marshal Soult, veteran of the Napoleonic wars, who had come as representative of the French King, Louis Philippe. The old man's eyes had filled with tears at the warmth of his reception; if he wondered at the mentality of a people who shouted louder for him than for the Duke of Wellington he kept his opinions to himself. Victoria too found herself near to tears, as she made the journey to Westminster Abbey, jolted uncomfortably in the historic but unsprung State Coach. She waved to the crowds and smiled, and thought that if she once began to cry from emotion, she would never stop. All through the ceremony she could hear the swell and murmur of the multitude outside the Abbey, and her heart was strangely touched. For that day Lord M.'s cynical doctrines were forgotten, the loyalty and approval of the unknown masses seemed for once just as important as the formal homage made by her peers after she was crowned. It was a muddled service, made more confused by the ignorance and nervousness of the Archbishop of Canterbury, who actually whispered to her in desperation, asking what he should do next. The music was very beautiful, and the colours of the massed peers and peeresses in their crimson robes and jewels gave the grey Abbey interior a magnificent glow. The altar was covered with gold plate, and the anthems in praise of God and the new Queen, Victoria of England, seemed to hang like mist in the roof, long after the human voices had died away.

The Crown of St Edward was so heavy that she had a headache within ten minutes of putting it on, and no one had warned her of the weight of the orb. The coronation ring was forced on to the wrong finger by the Archbishop in his confusion, and there were several moments when she felt like fainting with the pain as her attendants tried to ease it off when she retired for a rest to the privacy of St Edward's Chapel. She was displeased to see that the altar itself had been covered with a cloth and stacked with bottles of wine and sandwiches. It was sacrilegious to use the tiny chapel as if it were a buffet, but it was nearly four o'clock and she was desperately hungry.

Then came the long procession down the aisle, holding her head up under the crushing weight of solid gold and jewels and ermine, balancing the orb and sceptre, taking slow, tiny steps until it seemed as if the West Door of the Abbey would never be reached. And outside the crowd's roar met her, and broke over her like a tidal wave. In spite of her tiredness and the feeling of anti-climax engendered by the inefficiency of the ceremonial, the colour rushed into her face at the sound of that tremendous greeting. The dull booming of the cannon firing a Royal salute from the Tower echoed down the river through the harsh volume of cheers. For a moment Victoria stood there, forgetting the heat and discomfort of her heavy train, the ache in her head and wrists from carrying the impediments of Royalty, unaware of anything but that wonderful heart-warming cry which seemed to come from a hundred thousand throats in unison, and which grew almost frightening as the people saw her outlined in the dark archway of the Abbey door.

Then she began to move again, bending her head automatically as she entered the State Coach, laying aside the orb and sceptre for a moment as her pages and ladies folded the long velvet train and arranged it on the floor by her feet. Then the coach door closed and the sickening swaying movement began as it rolled out into the streets. She had taken orb and sceptre up again, and hardly seemed to notice, and her heart was beating very quickly. Tears were burning behind her eyes as she looked out of the windows, turning from right to left and smiling, and she knew that to weep would be only an expression of unbearable happiness.

This should have come to her when she was crowned, but it hadn't; she had felt just the same, and looked up to the seat where Lehzen, crimson with pride and emotion, was watching her, and exchanged a friendly smile. She had felt nothing, no uprush of emotion, no sense of dedication to her tremendous duty, and no love, no love at all for the countless millions she had sworn to serve and protect in the name of God. And now it had come to her, separated from her own kind, alone in the Coach with the sound of her people's acclamation roaring in her ears. And suddenly the words spoken in the Abbey had real meaning. The crown she wore was blessed, the symbol of the highest human authority, the rod in her right hand was Majesty and justice, and the orb was a tiny universe; and she, who was only a woman after all, was Queen of all England. For this she had been born, and this was all that mattered; the petty feuds and little tyrannies of her protected life, and the small powers she exercised within her narrow circle – all these were meaningless beside the tremendous destiny which she saw for the first time on that drive home to Buckingham Palace. She had sworn to protect her subjects, the same people as those crowds who cried and waved to her at that moment, and now they were personal and painfully near to her. Their glory and their welfare were hers, united by the mystic bond of kingship. She was Queen of England, and for ever after, in spite of her own feelings, in spite of ties of blood which were alien, England would come first.

3

Christmas passed; it was celebrated at Windsor with the mixture of extravagance and naïveté which formed the pattern of Court life. There was a Ball, a brilliant affair, but stiff, because the etiquette was growing stricter in accordance with the Queen's wishes; and there were long evenings of interminable dullness for the guests when Victoria made conversation and then played games at a round table, or retired with her beloved Melbourne to turn over the pages of a book of drawings.

The serenity of this existence was disturbed by an ugly incident involving one of the Duchess of Kent's ladies. The unfortunate Lady Flora Hastings, the object of Lehzen's relentless hatred and the Queen's dislike, showed a sudden change of figure. The rumour that she was pregnant reached Victoria's ears, and a harsh message was sent to Lady Flora that she must submit to a medical examination and prove her innocence before appearing at Court. After a humiliating interview with the Royal physician, Sir James Clark, Lady Flora's virginity was established beyond question, but though the Queen reinstated her personally, expecting the affair to be forgotten, the Hastings family made their kinswoman's treatment public. A general outcry ensued, letters were published in the newspapers and the scandal reverberated abroad. Victoria was accused of harshness on the one hand, and of protecting an adulteress on the other. The pleas of the Hastings for a public apology and the dismissal of the offending doctor were ignored; so was the tardy advice of Melbourne, who had at first counselled the Queen to do nothing about the rumours and then suggested marrying Lady Flora to some ambitious Whig politician. Dismiss Sir James Clark, he begged her, give public opinion a victim, and she would escape the bitter censure which was being poured upon her, not only in England but in Europe, where the story of her treatment of an innocent woman had lost nothing in the telling. For the first time Melbourne experienced the force of the willpower which he had indulged so freely, directed against himself. Nothing, Victoria said coldly, would make her punish Sir James for carrying out her instructions. Nothing would induce her to admit that she had not acted rightly in protecting her reputation and ensuring that an immoral person was not attending her Court. And nothing would make her forgive the Marquis of Hastings and Lady Flora for daring to publish correspondence in the newspapers and cause the scandal. She had apologized in private, permitted the woman to remain at Court in her mother's entourage, and that was more than enough. As for saying that Lehzen, who was her dear friend and trusted companion, had engendered the intrigue because she bore Lady Flora Hastings a grudge, there was not a word of truth in it. The Queen supposed, she said acidly, that public opinion would want her to dismiss the Baroness as well as Sir James.

All Melbourne's persuasive words were wasted; his pleas and reasoned arguments only intensified that look of stony obstinacy, and had he loved her less and been less prejudiced, her indifference to the suffering and disgrace of an innocent woman would have shocked him. It shocked many, both inside and outside the Court, and rent the sentimental veil covering the little Queen from top to bottom. From end to end of the country, in the poorest homes and the great houses, Victoria was denounced as a heartless minx, who had sacrificed a blameless English lady to the malice of her German confidante. Throughout the storm, Lehzen sheltered behind her mistress's skirts, defiant and chewing more caraway seeds than ever, assuring

Victoria that she was in the right and not to yield to anyone – unless, she wept, she would rather her poor old Lehzen left her side as her enemies demanded. Sir James Clark, ignorant, opinionated and notoriously bad-mannered, also remained in the Royal household, while the cause of the trouble moved more and more feebly through her duties as lady-in-waiting to the Duchess, and the ominous swelling and changed appearance which had caused the pregnancy rumours, became daily more pronounced. Within a few months it was established that Lady Flora, far from paying the natural consequences of an illicit love affair, was dying of a malignant kidney disease. The storm of abuse and unpopularity which now broke over the Queen's head appalled Melbourne and terrified her advisers. Some were even more disturbed by the iron indifference with which the nineteen-year-old Queen met that storm, by the tight little jaw and hard eyes, bright with temper and defiance. Popular condemnation reached its height when Victoria was greeted with hisses as she drove down the racecourse at Ascot. But whatever anyone said, no public statement was issued and the doctor whose role in the affair had been magnified out of all proportion, stayed in the Queen's service. And when Flora Hastings died, the Queen's only concession was to cancel a Ball at Buckingham Palace that evening.

The clouds of unpopularity which had threatened before the coronation, were massed round the throne like a thunderstorm, and the projected visit of her two Saxe-Coburg cousins did nothing to lighten it or to improve Victoria's temper. She should have been excited; instead she was exasperated, and surprised too, because a polite but pointed letter from her younger cousin, Albert, had informed her that unless she allowed him to come to England and also made up her mind, he must clarify his own position in the eyes of the world. In other words, he was tired of being put off and humiliated, and unless she decided one way or the other, he would withdraw his suit.

That threat had more effect than all Uncle Leopold's entreaties and reproaches. It was unthinkable that the young man should reject *her* . . . better that he and Ernst should come to England for a short visit and then the refusal could be hers!

Crossly, and with little grace, she fixed a date for October; but long before that, the visit and its implications were forgotten in a political crisis which struck straight at Victoria's heart.

In May 1839, Melbourne's Government fell.

Their hold on power had always been precarious; the Whig Administration was symptomatic of the warring elements in English politics, composed as it was of a collection of Whig Lords, all highly individualistic and none really in agreement even with each other. In an age when extreme Tories, led by the Duke of Wellington, fought every measure for Reform, and their opposites, the Radicals, demanded almost Republican measures, the Whig Party tried to steer a middle course. But Melbourne's Government was constantly harried by both opposing groups and, worse still, was divided in itself. Men like Lord John Russell, who was a moderate, warred with near Radicals like Lord Durham; the sound sense of an individualist like Lord Althorp clashed with the reckless impudent temperament of the Foreign Secretary, Palmerston. At their head, Melbourne himself presented as much of a paradox as the rest put together. The duties of Prime Minister bored and discouraged him; half the projects for Reform he was forced to sanction in the name of his Party seemed dangerous and futile to him; he found the pushing mentality of Palmerston and Durham and their friends inimical to his own leisurely philosophy, compounded of disinterest and despair which solved every problem by leaving it undisturbed.

Many times Melbourne would have gladly resigned and retired to his magnificent estate at Brocket and his books, content with trips to London and dinners at Holland House and an occasional attendance at the Lords when he felt there was something interesting to hear or a sense of lazy mischief moved him to intervene in a debate.

But Victoria's accession had changed all that, as it had changed his mode of life. Loss of office would mean exile from her. The irritations of John Russell, whose odd manners and profound convictions made him more enemies than friends, the insufferable bravado of Durham, always roaring in support of the extremes, the bounding confidence and drive of Palmerston, who refused to let *anything* alone and was always causing trouble, and the maddening inefficiency of Glenelg, who could blunder to his heart's content because Melbourne didn't consider the Colonial Office important – all these pinpricks meant nothing compared to the pleasure and stimulation of the hours spent with the Queen. The less lovable she lately appeared, the more Melbourne adored her, unequivocally and ruthlessly, as he had once loved Caroline, his wife, and he shielded her when she had placed herself beyond excusing. He imagined he was *protecting* the Queen, though somewhere he admitted that the wild, foolish quality of Caroline was lacking, that his idol's feet were made of iron and not of clay. But she filled his life and his heart and if it meant bearing the tiresome burden of office indefinitely, he was happy and willing to do so, rather than be parted from her. Disaster had nearly overtaken him earlier that year, when he sent the rumbustious Durham out to quell a rebellion in Canada and found the Government under violent attack from the Tories for granting too much and from the Radicals for granting too little. And Durham, loosing his head completely, had not helped by pressing for self-government for the Colony. Most ministries would have resigned in the face of that particular storm, but the Whigs hung on, clinging to their small majority in the House. The mishandling of the Flora Hastings affair provided Melbourne's enemies with a strong stick and they used it unmercifully. Radicals and Tories alike abused the

Prime Minister for not exercising his influence over an inexperienced girl and preventing the episode from reaching such unfortunate proportions that the Queen and her Court were vilified abroad. It would be unfair, the papers said slyly, to suggest that Victoria was responsible for the harsh treatment meted out to a woman whose reputation had only been properly cleared by a terrible death . . . Melbourne and her Court advisers were to blame.

No sooner had the crisis over Canada subsided than a new one arose. Much against his will, Melbourne had agreed to the freeing of slaves in the Crown Colony of Jamaica. He regarded the measure as premature and certain to cause rioting and trouble, but pressure from the Radicals in Parliament and the Reformers in his own Party forced him to agree. His forebodings proved justified, for within a few weeks the island was in turmoil. Glenelg, fatuous and inefficient as usual, blundered right and left, John Russell repeated his threat to resign because his colleagues couldn't agree with his views, Althorp infuriated Melbourne by insisting that in spite of the trouble, emancipation was right in principle and must be so in practise, and as a result the Whig Government's handling of the situation satisfied nobody. The Radicals regarded it as inept and illiberal, so they abstained from voting on the motion in the House and Melbourne's Government avoided defeat by only five votes. It was the lowest majority the Government had ever had, and there was nothing they could do but resign after such proof that they had lost the country's confidence.

The news paralysed Victoria. Melbourne wrote a formal letter to the Queen, informing her of the resignation of his Government, and a few hours later he came in person to explain and say good-bye.

She received him in her sitting-room, and rushed towards him with both hands outstretched, white and shaking from agitation.

'I can't believe it! I won't believe it!'

He had a most improper longing to take her in his arms,

forgetting that she was the sovereign and he no longer even head of her Government. If he had ever had a daughter, he told himself hastily, he would have felt like this on being parted from her.

'I've been crying from the moment I read your letter,' she declared, 'and I only hope you've come to tell me that you've changed your mind, and you're not going to do this dreadful thing after all.'

'I have no choice,' he said gently. It was he who led her to the little sofa where they usually sat, and rubbed her cold hands to warm them while he explained as calmly as he could why he had to leave her.

'Abandon me, you mean,' Victoria interjected passionately. 'How am I going to manage without you? This means I shall have to have another Government – a new Prime Minister! Lord M., I won't have it. I won't allow anyone else to take your place.'

'It won't be as difficult as you imagine,' he soothed. 'We've been very lucky to have lasted as long as this, the way things are. And we can't stay in – not now. Dearest Ma'am, five votes . . . you must understand what that means. We haven't the confidence of the House; no Ministry can cling to office under such circumstances and hope to govern properly.'

'I don't care what the House thinks!' Victoria blazed, the tears overflowing on to her cheeks. 'It simply means they don't appreciate you. They're idiots, and that's no reason why *I* should have to suffer!'

'But I promise you, you won't,' he insisted. 'All that will happen is this. You must send for the Duke of Wellington and invite him to form a Government.'

'A *Tory* Government! I shall do nothing of the kind!'

'You will, Ma'am, and you must,' Melbourne said gently. 'I doubt if the Duke will agree to lead the new Ministry himself; he's old and disinclined for office – I can't say I blame him,' he added. 'He'll recommend Sir Robert Peel to you, and you will see him and complete the formalities.'

66

She turned sharply towards him, her small, projecting teeth biting into her lower lip, and that ominous look he knew so well, gleaming in her eyes.

'I *detest* Sir Robert Peel,' she said.

'You won't when you know him better,' Melbourne assured her. 'He's a very shy man; I grant you his manner's unfortunate, but behind it he's full of good sense, and absolutely trustworthy. He'll serve you as devotedly as anyone in England.'

'His service will mean nothing to me,' Victoria went on. 'As for trustworthiness – I shall never trust a Tory. Oh, I shall never trust anyone or depend on anyone as I do with you!' And she burst into tears.

It was too much for Melbourne; within the cynic a sentimentalist had long been struggling to get out, and the next moment he was wiping his own eyes, and for a few timeless minutes the Queen of England's head rested on his shoulder, and the Royal tears were wiped away into his handkerchief. He afterwards treasured that handkerchief as if it had been St Veronica's veil.

'Don't make it more difficult for me,' he begged her. 'I tell you, Ma'am, my heart is breaking at the thought of losing you – of being separated, I mean.'

'But we needn't be parted completely,' she insisted. 'Even if this wretched situation does come about, and it won't if *I* can prevent it – you'll still dine with me and come to Windsor for week-ends!'

'No, Ma'am, I won't. I can't, when I'm no longer Prime Minister. My successor mustn't have a rival for your confidence. I can only see you occasionally, if at all.'

'Do you mean our *friendship* can't continue as before?' she asked in horror.

Melbourne shook his head. 'Only in our hearts,' he said.

Something about her expression worried him then; she sat very upright, the soft little hands he loved were no longer twisting with grief, they clenched into two determined fists in her lap.

'Am I supposed to make an intimate of Sir Robert Peel?' she asked quietly. 'Will he expect to sit at my dinner table and come as my guest? Lord M., I said something to you once, not long after my succession. I said I pitied the man who tried to replace you with me. If he were the most charming and amiable person alive he would still find it impossible. And I don't think Sir Robert is exactly noted for his grace. If my life is to be made miserable in this way, then I shall see to it that I'm not the only one to suffer!'

He was really alarmed by then. His own feelings went to the winds in his anxiety to prevent her from doing something which would place her in a false position on his account. It was all very well to be Queen, but she was only a child still and no match for the experienced statesman with whom she must soon deal.

'I assure you, you'll grow to like and trust Peel as much as ever you do me,' he said quickly. 'Please, Ma'am, listen to me and believe me. I wouldn't recommend him to you if I thought he was a rogue — I'd tell you to take care. But I have a great respect for him and admiration for his abilities. Don't judge him on the few occasions he's been presented to you; everyone knows he's as stiff as a stick on first meeting, but he'll soon melt with you. How could he help it? And, however you feel, he'll be your new Prime Minister and responsible for the Government of your country. I beg you to keep an open mind, and consider your duties as sovereign. Send for the Duke first and then see what comes of it.'

Victoria stood up and walked to the window. She pulled back the curtain and appeared to be looking out on to the Palace grounds for a moment before she turned round to him.

'Very well, Lord M., I shall do as you say. I'll summon the Duke in the morning. And now I must say good-bye to you for the present.'

He kissed her hand and bowed very low over it.

'Good-bye, Ma'am. This past year has been the happiest of my whole life . . .'

'Please,' she checked him. 'Don't say any more or I shall begin to cry again. Go now – quickly . . .'

He left her, feeling a little hurt in spite of everything because there had been so much he wanted to say and she had not allowed it; after the tears and storms that last farewell had been an anti-climax. He noticed that she had not pressed him to stay and dine that night or asked when he could come again. As he drove wearily back to his rooms in the Commons to clear out his desk for his successor, he supposed that she had accepted the inevitable.

The next morning the Duke of Wellington presented himself at the Palace. The victor of Waterloo was an old man, bent and hesitant in his movements, but the commanding personality had not diminished with the years. He received the impression that the Queen was not daunted by it, and her nod of agreement when he refused the office of Prime Minister was distinctly curt. For a moment the keen blue eyes of the greatest soldier and toughest statesman of his day held the look in those other eyes, also blue, and oddly disconcerting in the steady way they stared. He advised her to send for Sir Robert Peel and appoint him head of the new Tory Government. Again she nodded; she had a curious quality of rigidity even when sitting down that made the great man feel uncomfortable.

She expressed her regret at his decision and promised to see Sir Robert that afternoon. Then she held out her hand for him to kiss and the audience was over.

Victoria lunched on broth that day, to the dismay of her ladies and Lehzen, who were all hungry and condemned to the same menu, and then she hurried to her room to dress. She was receiving the new Prime Minister, she said shortly, and simplicity would not do. No one mentioned Melbourne. Expressions of sympathy only made her cry; indeed she had broken down and wept for nearly two hours after he left, surrounded by Lehzen and Lady Tavistock and the Duchess of Sutherland, whose commiserations only made her worse. Now the subject was forbidden. She had to see Sir Robert Peel, and that was the end of it.

She chose a dress of pale gold velvet, with a deep edging of fine Brussels lace around the shoulders, and wore the rich blue Garter ribbon, its jewelled star pinned to her breast. Two bracelets containing miniatures of the late Kings, George III and William IV, set in diamonds, and a diamond hair ornament completed her toilet.

It was a very regal figure that met Sir Robert Peel in the White Drawing-room at Buckingham Palace that afternoon.

The White Drawing-room was enormously long and rather narrow. The Queen proved to be waiting at the farthest end of it, when Peel was announced, and he had a long, silent walk before he reached her. He was a small, pale man, with a terse manner accentuated by nerves, and the procession down the long room, between the portraits of frowning Royal ancestors in different attitudes of Majesty, did little to put him at his ease. When he reached the small golden figure of the Queen, he bowed.

The same sharp little nod which had greeted the Duke of Wellington that morning was her only sign that she was aware of his arrival, and he found himself clearing his throat, avoiding the unfriendly stare, and studying the carpet. It seemed a long time to Peel before the Queen put him out of his misery and spoke.

'As Lord Melbourne's Government have resigned,' she said, 'and His Grace the Duke declines to form a Ministry, I have sent for you, Sir Robert, to ask if you will head the new Government. This is something of an ordeal for me on two accounts. Firstly, because I have no previous experience of the procedure, and secondly because of my profound regret at losing the services of such an excellent and trusted servant as my dear Lord Melbourne.'

Peel reddened. Any vestige of self-assurance he had left was dissipated by that last remark.

'I am honoured, Madam. And naturally I appreciate Your Majesty's feelings. I only hope I shall be able to replace Lord Melbourne in your estimation.'

'That would be expecting far too much of you. Would you be good enough to explain what Ministries you intend to give to whom, and anything else you think I should know about the new Government.'

In one of his frequent bouts of indiscretion, Melbourne had amused the Queen by telling her that his brilliant Tory rival was known as the Dancing Master, because, he said, Peel shifted and postured as if he were about to break into a quadrille, as if his feet had a life of their own . . . She had laughed very much at the description, and it returned to her, as she watched Sir Robert turning red while fixing her eyes unkindly on his pointing toes. Dancing Master. Prim, detestable, cold little man, after dear Lord M. Daring to say he hoped he might replace Melbourne in her estimation. She listened politely, generating hostility without saying a word or moving an inch, while he put forward a list of names for the new Ministry. She could find no fault with his suggestions; they were all Tories anyway and equally detestable. She only interrupted once to suggest that the Duke of Wellington should be included in the Cabinet. It was unthinkable that this miserable little man should omit the great statesman. Whatever the Duke's politics, she had a genuine respect and trust for him, and there had to be *someone* in this odious Ministry with whom she could deal . . .

'And now, Madam –' Peel had begun to relax slightly, thinking the worst was over. Also the interview would soon be ending. Thank God, he said to himself. 'Now, Madam, about the ladies of your household.'

'My ladies? What about them?' The Queen's thin brows were raised in surprise.

'Well, naturally, I must ask you to make some changes,' Peel said awkwardly.

'Changes? What changes, if you please?' A faint angry

colour was creeping into her face and the blue eyes snapped at him.

'All the ladies in attendance upon you are Whigs,' Peel said stiffly; he was so ill at ease that he sounded quite abrupt. 'Some, like Lady Sutherland, are the wives of former Cabinet Ministers. It is the custom for the Queen to change members of her household and choose others belonging to the party of the Ministry in power.'

Victoria glared at him.

'You are referring to a Queen *Consort*, not a Queen Regnant. That is quite different, Sir Robert. I have never heard of such a proposal. What precedent has been set for it?'

Peel was caught and he knew it. There was no precedent simply because the last Queen in her own right had been Anne, and if there was one thing well known about her, it was the immovability of some of her female intimates . . .

'Madam,' he pleaded, 'Madam, please let me explain my position. As your Prime Minister I must feel that I have your confidence. How can I achieve that when my political enemies are with you day and night??'

'Sir Robert! Are you suggesting that I am governed by my ladies?'

'No, Madam, God forbid you should be *governed* by anyone, that's not what I meant at all . . .'

'Then what did you mean?'

Beads of sweat were standing out on his forehead. He had quite forgotten that his opponent in this contest of wills was only a girl of nineteen. Desperately, he tried another argument.

'Supposing Lord Melbourne had been in my position. Would you have expected him to carry out the business of Government knowing that Your Majesty's entire household was composed of Tory sympathizers and that it would be impossible for you to have a full understanding of the aims of the Whig policy? Madam, I do put it to you, it would have been unthinkable for him.'

'Lord Melbourne,' Victoria answered triumphantly 'would never have asked me to do anything so inhuman; whatever inconvenience he suffered himself, Lord Melbourne always put my comfort and happiness first. That, Sir Robert, was the secret of the confidence he enjoyed. It is unthinkable for *me* that I should part with my friends and submit to the company of strangers who I'm sure would be most disagreeable to me. There is no precedent for such a request, and therefore I must refuse it. I cannot part with any of my ladies.'

Peel drew a deep breath.

'Does Your Majesty mean to keep all your ladies?'

'All.'

'The Mistress of the Robes and the Ladies of the Bedchamber?'

'*All!*' the Queen said.

'Then I do not see how I can form a Government. I shall have to consult the Duke of Wellington, with your permission, Madam.' He bowed and she nodded. She watched him walk out of the long room and as soon as the door had closed on him Victoria lifted her skirts and almost ran to her own sitting-room. There she wrote a letter to dear Lord M., describing with much angry underlining the infamy which Peel had suggested and her reaction to it. If she was trembling with anger as she wrote, it was fast turning into excitement. 'Then I cannot form a Government.' Those were the Dancing Master's words, and oh, how wonderful if they were true! If she persisted, resisting the pressure she knew would be put on her from many quarters, even from Melbourne himself, because he was so noble and just to his opponents − if she forced that pious little man into that position, then she could have Melbourne back! For a second her pen hesitated, searching for the right words. Then it wrote on in the fluent, strong hand which betrayed so much of her character.

'I was calm, but very decided and I think you would have been pleased to see my composure and great firmness;

the Queen of England will not submit to such trickery. Keep yourself in readiness for you may soon be wanted.'

Within a few days, neither the pleas of Melbourne, nor the arguments of Peel and Wellington having had the slightest effect upon her, the Bedchamber Crisis brought the Whigs back into office. The Duchess of Sutherland, Lady Tavistock, Lady Normanby and all the rest were safely established under the Queen's roof, with Lehzen flitting from her room to Victoria's for midnight confidences; Lord Melbourne was back in his old place at the dinner table and the country was under Whig Government. To celebrate her happiness, the Queen arranged a Ball and a concert for the middle of the month of May, and invited only those Tories like the Duke of Wellington whom it was impossible to leave out.

In spite of her victory or, as some unkindly said, because of it, the Queen's temper deteriorated; her tongue sharpened and her eye grew colder when it encountered the mildest offender. She was as affectionate and possessive about Lord M. as she had ever been, but there was a sharp note in her voice when he disagreed with her that seemed to remind him that it was thanks to her strength of mind that he was there at all — The tiny figure appeared to gain inches in height because the Queen's carriage was so erect and her manner so sweeping. Even her dear friend the Duchess of Sutherland felt the sting of Her Majesty's displeasure when she gave a Ball at Stafford House in the Queen's honour and came to meet her at the door in a magnificent dress, blazing with diamonds. The Queen arrived in a simple muslin ball gown, and after viewing the brilliant setting, the ballroom glowing with uniforms and lovely dresses, turned to her hostess.

'I come,' the cold little voice said, 'from my house to your palace.'

By the summer of 1839 dislike of Her Majesty was spreading to some of the Whigs, and Baron Stockmar wrote anxiously to Leopold that Victoria was pitifully in need of a husband's restraining influence. Melbourne, the elderly roué, had entirely succumbed to the Queen's personality and seemed incapable of crossing her, even for her own benefit. He prayed God, he declared, that when her cousins Ernst and Albert came in October they would find her in a more feminine mood. Especially Albert, who was so sensitive and placed such value on womanly gentleness. Stockmar's forebodings seemed borne out by the tone of a letter from Victoria to her dear uncle, in which she made it plain in far from affectionate terms that the coming visit of her cousins committed her to nothing. She had given no promise and did not consider herself bound in any way. On that understanding she was looking forward to their arrival. Strangely, only one person read the signs correctly. Melbourne, with all his worldly experience, was baffled by the quick changes of mood, the bursts of temper, the tendency to cry for no reason, and the rather angry gaiety with which Victoria attacked her life. Stockmar, always watching and noting in his painstaking Teutonic way, dismissed her behaviour as wilfulness and lack of discipline.

It was Lehzen, the old maid, who understood. She knew by instinct what others far more clever could not reason out; she knew it out of her own dim experiences of long ago – the unsatisfied yearnings for fulfilment which had found sublimation in her care of the child Victoria. The Queen was marriageable in the true sense. She was restless and bad-tempered and mercurial, because the fond attentions of a man old enough to be her father were beginning to frustrate rather than please her vanity. Life, which had seemed so gay and promising, was spoilt by a nameless feeling of irritation, and the girl who had danced till dawn and watched the sunrise from the Palace roof only a few months ago, now came from the Ballroom and sat on Lehzen's bed and confessed that parties left her tired and disappointed.

Lehzen said nothing; she was jealous again, because it

was so obvious that her love for Victoria was not enough
and never would be and that the harmless devotion of
Melbourne would some day give place to the sway of a
younger, stronger rival. She was jealous and at the same
time sympathetic, because she knew that the Queen's love
of independence and her repugnance to marital subjection
were warring bitterly with all her feminine needs. The
coming of her cousins had brought the conflict to a head,
and only two nights before their arrival, Victoria sat up
in her night-gown and wrapper talking to the Baroness.
Lehzen was tired and had been looking forward to bed.
Bed was a warm and comforting place and as the years
advanced Lehzen looked forward to it more and more; but
lately her beloved Victoria had developed the habit of
sending for her in the middle of the night when she came
upstairs after a Ball or an official Banquet. Lord Melbourne
had been to dinner as usual that evening; the Court was
at Windsor, and the Duchess of Kent, whose relations with
her daughter were severely strained after Lady Flora
Hasting's death, had been invited to meet her nephews and
give an appearance of family unity. It had been a quiet
gathering; the Queen had carried Melbourne off to a corner
of the room and sat in silence while he turned the pages
of a book of pictures. His attempts to cheer her had failed
so obviously that in the end he gave them up, and when
the Queen rose to retire the company dispersed with a sigh
of relief.

'It was tedious tonight,' Victoria said suddenly. 'I've
never felt bored before. Even Lord M. was a little dull.
Didn't you think so, Lehzen?'

The Baroness shrugged.

'I thought it was very pleasant, very restful, Madam my
love. You're over-tired, that's what I think. You'll have
all the bother of entertaining your cousins from Saxe-
Coburg the day after tomorrow, and you ought to be
sleeping now instead of sitting up.'

Victoria looked at her.

'I'm not tired, Lehzen; I only wish I were. As for sleeping, I wouldn't close my eyes all night if I went to bed now. Lehzen, I wish they weren't coming!'

The Baroness straightened her shawl and pursed her lips.

'They've got to come,' she said. 'Once and for all and get it over. You'll have no peace from your uncle, King Leopold, till you've made a choice one way or the other; and if you don't like them, then that's the end of it. Besides, you might find one of them to be suitable,' she added with an effort.

'But I don't *want* to get married!' Victoria turned on her so vehemently that she jumped. 'I don't want to lose my freedom and surrender my rights to a husband. For the first eighteen years of my life I said nothing but "yes" to Mama and now I'm expected to give up my independence and marry and start saying "yes" to a husband! I don't want to, Lehzen; I want to stay as I am!'

'You can stay as you are,' the Baroness said quickly, 'whether you marry or not. You're the Queen; you're not an ordinary woman however high born. The Queen. That's different. Queens aren't subject to anyone, husband or no husband. Anyone you marry, dearest Madam, will be subject to *you* and don't let people tell you otherwise! You'll have to choose one day,' she went on, 'whether it's Prince Ernst or Prince Albert or someone else, but don't fear to lose your freedom. If anything it's the bridegroom who will lose his. Therefore choose carefully. Choose a man who will understand that and be agreeable.'

'You're very wise, Lehzen,' Victoria said slowly. 'It won't do if either of my cousins are of a managing nature. I couldn't bear it. I would rather stay unmarried.'

The Baroness shook her head and smiled.

'Oh, no, Madam, you wouldn't, not in the end. Listen to me, for I've never married and I know what it's like. I've been fortunate because I had you to care for and love, but compensations like that are only given to humble women, not to Queens. When you nurse a child, it can only be your own.'

'Dear Lehzen . . . Poor Lehzen!'

She suddenly held out her arms, and the Baroness, blushing and nearly in tears with emotion, came over and was warmly embraced.

'You've been so good to me,' the Queen said in a whisper. 'Don't think I've ever forgotten. You *were* my mother, in everything but name. And I love you very dearly. But you're not to cry, or I shall begin too!'

'No, Madam,' Lehzen mumbled, wiping her eyes. 'And don't you fret over a husband; you do what you feel like and any time you're troubled, just promise that you'll come to me!'

'I will,' Victoria said. 'And I shan't be nervous about the visit. I shall be very polite and nice to everyone and probably send them both away. As long as I have you and Lord M. I don't need anyone else.'

'And when you do marry,' the Baroness implored, 'you'll still have need of Lehzen, won't you? You won't let a new husband turn me out?'

'No one shall turn you out,' Victoria promised. 'You ought to know that by now, Lehzen, it's very bad of you to mention such a thing. Have you forgotten all the trouble over Lady Flora and the questions asked about you in Parliament? If that didn't move me, why should I listen to a husband? Don't be silly, and don't mention it again.'

'I won't,' Lehzen smiled. 'And you mustn't lie sleepless thinking about your cousins tonight or you'll only be cross and snap when you meet them!'

Victoria laughed. 'Quite likely! Anyway, I've met them once, though it was some years ago, and I think they were pleasant enough. I don't suppose they've changed very much. Of course, dear Stockmar likes Albert best; he's always praising him to me. Which probably means,' she said firmly, 'that I shall dislike him on sight! Anyway, we shall see . . . You'd better go to bed now, Lehzen. It's late and I'm more tired than I thought.' She sighed; her spirits were low again, in spite of the relief of talking to the Baroness. When the candles were put out she would probably cry, she thought irritably. There was only one more day left before they came and the whole wretched issue had to be faced.

'We should be there in ten minutes.' Prince Ernst of Saxe-Coburg-Gotha replaced his watch in his pocket and turned to his brother. Albert had been staring out of the carriage window, appraising the rather flat green country. It was difficult to judge whether he was more handsome full face than in profile. The features were faultless, a high forehead, shadowed by thick brown hair, fine eyes, very blue and expressive, a noble nose and mouth with soft moustaches and, even cramped on the carriage seat, a beautifully proportioned figure . . . Only the English taste, with its suspicion of anything masculine which was too regular, would have pronounced him less than perfect in looks. Ernst was a poor contrast to his brother; he had a rather humorous face, in which the chiselled beauty of Albert was entirely lacking; his expression was lively rather than sensitive and he talked far more.

'What an ugly country!' Albert nodded towards the window. 'So flat and uninspiring.'

'Don't be too unenthusiastic,' Ernst warned. 'One of us may have to live here and it will probably be you.'

'Why me?' Albert said quickly. 'Why not you, Ernst? Our cousin will probably prefer you to me — you're much better company, you know, and I hear she loves gaiety and amusing herself.'

Ernst smiled back at him. 'My dear brother, in a way I hope she fancies me, because I've a feeling you're miserable enough before you've even seen her. Come, Albert, don't be low-spirited. I ought to be gnawing my nails with jealousy at having such a handsome brother as a rival in the marriage market. Think how eligible she is.

And flat and uninspiring or not, this is England! Isn't it worth a few Coburg mountains to be King?'

Albert laughed. 'Consort,' he corrected. 'And if I miss Coburg after being here for only a day or two, how much worse I'd feel if I had to stay here for ever— How much longer now?'

'No longer,' Ernst told him. 'Look to your right. Those grey towers must be Windsor Castle.'

4

Victoria had come to meet them at the Castle steps. The concession was due to Stockmar's tactful suggestion that the two young cousins would be shy and tired after their long journey, and an informal welcome would help to make them feel at home. It was not quite cousinly to receive them in audience like strangers . . . Reluctantly she had agreed, because Stockmar had managed to make her proposal sound more like cowardice than dignity, and cowardice she knew it was. So Albert's first sight of his Royal cousin was against the grey background of Windsor stone, surrounded by ladies in colourful dresses and the gentlemen of her suite, and his first impression was astonishment because she was so tiny and yet she overshadowed everyone in her simple blue gown and feathered bonnet. The rest of the meeting was confused; he remembered afterwards kissing the Duchess of Kent, who squeezed his hand so hard that he winced and then turned away quickly. He felt somehow that she was uncomfortable and upset. He knew that Ernst acquitted himself well; he heard him say something to Victoria and was surprised to hear her laugh out loud. In Germany great ladies murmured when they were amused; surely a Queen should merely smile . . .

After he and Ernst had changed and explored their rooms, they drank tea in the Blue Drawing-room with the Queen, the Duchess and some ladies and gentlemen. The Blue Drawing-room had long windows which opened out on to a fine view, the first agreeable sight he had seen since he landed. The Castle stood on a hill, and below there was a panorama of fields and woods, with the town of Windsor itself growing like a mushroom under the shadow of the Castle walls. It was on a very small scale, but it reminded him of home. Staring out, Albert forgot for a moment that he had been seated next to his cousin until her rather high voice interrupted his thoughts. She sounded like a bird; the round face with the sharp little aquiline nose and the heavy-lidded, prominent eyes reminded him of a small eagle. When he last had seen her three years before, he had thought her more pleasing than he did now, and she had never been pretty.

'How do you find the view, Cousin?'

'I find it charming. We have a similar view in my home at Coburg, but our mountains are higher.'

'We have very few mountains in England. I prefer hills, like this. I hope you prefer them too?'

He had no idea what to say in reply without being curt, so he smiled instead, and was startled to see his cousin blush, as if she had been paid a compliment.

After a moment she began again, her head tilted back to look up at him.

'Personally I find gardens very boring. I told Lord Melbourne so and he said he quite agreed. He thought a garden was a dull thing. But he likes flowers and knows a great deal about them. You shall meet him at dinner this evening, Cousin. I know you will like him; he's so knowledgeable and so witty. I am *devoted* to him.'

'I much look forward to it,' he said solemnly; in fact his anticipation of meeting the scandalous old man who held such a dubious place in his young cousin's life was distinctly unpleasant. He was sure they would have nothing in common and that, as usual when he was shy or awkward, he would find himself standing in front of the English statesman unable to think of a word to say. And Victoria was devoted to him. What a frightening emphasis she put on that word. He felt suddenly that devotion from Victoria could be an enveloping experience, and began hastily drinking the tea he disliked. He was only twenty and on approval with this small, self-possessed creature who kept on staring at him with her bright eyes, her cheeks growing pinker every minute. He wished she would turn away and talk to Ernst.

Victoria was unaware of his embarrassment, for he showed no sign of it. His extraordinarily handsome face was pale and composed; if he didn't answer her directly, he smiled, and however irritable and on her dignity she had felt at first, she couldn't deny that his smile was quite charming. When he stared out of the window instead of paying her attention, she felt like pulling his sleeve.

The tea party lasted an hour. Both young men paid their respects to the Duchess of Kent, asked after mutual relations and made conversation for a few moments before resuming their places on either side of the Queen. Ernst talked a good deal; he was lively and quickly made friends with several of the ladies-in-waiting, but after a few pleasantries Victoria's shoulder turned a few inches away from him and he accepted the hint. Most of her remarks, concerning the weather, the countryside and the details of their journey, were directed at his brother Albert.

'Well, brother, there's no doubt which one of us she favours.' Ernst yawned and let the yawn turn into a smile. 'No doubt at all. I've never seen such an expressive shoulder; in fact I know it better than her face, for it was turned to me most of the evening!'

'I wish you wouldn't joke, Ernst, I'm sure she didn't mean it.' Albert sat down heavily and stared at the toes of his polished Court pumps. After tea there had been a walk in the gardens, and then a short respite while the Queen and her ladies retired and the gentlemen went to their rooms. Dinner had been interminable; Albert had lost count of the courses which were served, noticing only that his cousin Victoria ate a helping of all of them and that, as reported, her table manners were highly individual. After dinner they gathered in the Yellow Drawing-room, an immense salon furnished in a mixture of Regency and Louis XVI. He had thought it terribly stiff and antiquated and wondered how any woman could feel at ease surrounded by so much grandeur. It had no apparent effect upon Victoria; she had been very gay during the meal, plying him with questions, telling him about the visit of their Uncle Leopold, who had come to England in August, and doing everything she could to entertain him. He appreciated it and liked her better than he had that afternoon. And it was not her fault if he felt lonely and restrained.

After dinner he had talked to Lord Melbourne. He had felt Victoria watching them together and sensed that she was anxious Melbourne should approve of him; the knowledge only made him shyer. It was impossible to dislike the Englishman or to suspect that his friendliness was insincere. It was merely difficult because he himself was incapable of bantering small-talk which seemed the rule in this odd Court, and Melbourne lightly parried any attempt to discuss anything serious. He had moved away from the Prime Minister with the uncomfortable impression that Melbourne thought him harmless, but a dull dog. He could almost hear him saying it.

'If she paid me more attention than you, then I can't understand it,' he said to his brother. 'I think she was probably trying to be kind because she felt I wasn't quite at ease.'

'Nonsense.' Ernst came and stood beside him. He was extremely fond of his handsome brother; no one knew better than he how hard Leopold and Stockmar had worked to bring about a marriage with their cousin of England, or how dutifully Albert had prepared himself in case he should be chosen, but he also knew that everything sensitive, proud and unsure in his brother shrank from the prospect.

'You underestimate yourself, Albert,' he said firmly. 'And perhaps you overestimate the good nature of our little cousin. She was obviously enchanted by you, just as obviously as she was unmoved by me − listen to me for a moment . . . My dear brother, we've never had secrets from each other, have we?'

Albert shook his head and smiled.

'Never; you've been my best friend, Ernst, and you always will be.'

'Then let's discuss this frankly. Since we were children we've been educated and brought up on the assumption that one of us would marry the Queen of England. We've taken it for granted, but I personally have also recognized that the general opinion favoured you rather than me. You knew it too, for you wrote to her and told her you'd withdraw as a suitor unless she made up her mind, remember?'

'I know I did,' Albert sighed. 'I know everything you say is true, Ernst. When I sent that letter, I meant it. I would have withdrawn. In my heart perhaps I hoped to be able to. And I hadn't met her again then.'

'And now that you have, what do you feel . . . supposing I'm right and she decides to marry you?'

Ernst sat on the arm of the chair and placed an arm round his young brother's shoulders. Albert shook his head slowly.

'I don't know. I can't conceive it happening.'

Ernst looked down at him, and when Albert raised his head and faced him he said quietly: 'You don't like her, do you?'

It was a moment before he answered.

'No. Not very much.'

After that neither said any more. They embraced and Ernst went down the corridor to his own room. Albert's valet came and undressed him and blew out the candles. It was a long time, however, before he fell asleep.

For the first time Victoria was reticent when Lehzen came to say good night. She did not really understand why she avoided the personal references about her cousins which she normally made so freely about everyone else. Perhaps it was because the Baroness showed too much interest, questioned her too eagerly; perhaps because she was a little confused by her own feelings. It had been a long and crowded day, but not difficult or tiresome as she had expected. Yes, she had enjoyed it, she told Lehzen, it was quite gay and both Prince Ernst and Prince Albert had been very nice. Everyone was nice in fact; the conversation flowed easily through dinner and wasn't it pleasant in the drawing-room afterwards? Lehzen had been there; didn't she agree? Lehzen agreed. She had been very interested to see how the two young Princes made friends with Lord Melbourne. Prince Ernst seemed more at ease than his brother, she said casually, and had her suspicions confirmed by Victoria's quick rebuttal. Ernst was very nice, but he could never compete with Albert for charm, she said firmly. In her opinion, Lord Melbourne had preferred Albert, though he was too tactful to show it. And now, as another busy day awaited her tomorrow she would say good night to her dearest Lehzen . . .

When she was alone, Victoria went to her writing table and opened her Journal. She devoted at least an hour out of every day to recording her activities, her thoughts and her feelings in intimate detail; the Journal received confidences forbidden even to the Baroness. How curious Lehzen had been . . . Normally she would have been irritated, but that evening she felt too happy to be cross with anyone. And not only happy, but excited, as if something wonderful were about to happen. Victoria laid down her pen and pressed one hand against her cheek. It was quite pink again.

It had been a *lovely* day. How odd to think she had dreaded it and tried to put it off. It seemed incredible that only two nights before she had grumbled bitterly to Lehzen and cried herself to sleep because her cousins were expected. They were so nice. She was trying hard to think of Ernst, of how nice Ernst was, but Albert's face kept blotting him out. Ernst was like lots of other young men, talkative and pleasant and ordinary, but when Albert spoke one listened,

86

knowing that what he said would matter. He was so different. Different from the young Englishmen who came to Court, different from the Russian Grand Duke who had paid her a visit earlier that year and caused a romantic fluttering, leavened by amusement because he was really a barbarian and no match was thinkable . . .

It was so difficult to explain Albert, or to understand why the sight of that noble profile, or the melting charm of his infrequent smile should cause a nagging pain in her heart – and set her trying to think of excuses to prolong the visit when he had only just arrived.

She dipped her pen in the gold pot, for the ink had dried on the nib while she sat thinking. Slowly she began to write, covering the pages with descriptions of the day's events: tea and the walk in the gardens, the dinner party when for once she did not record Melbourne's conversation because she had been busy talking to someone else. And at last her own feelings; the feelings she could not tell Lehzen and hardly understood herself.

'Ernst is very nice and very amiable.' In those few words her pen dismissed him from her life.

'But Albert – Albert is *beautiful*.'

Within the next three days it was obvious that a change had overtaken the Queen. There was no need for Lehzen's anxious prying or the sidelong looks of her ladies. No point in the Duchess of Kent complaining that in this most personal matter of her only child's future, she was the last to be informed; the announcement when it came could only be an anti-climax. The Queen was openly and unashamedly in love with Albert. The Royal party went for long rides in Windsor Park, and by unspoken agreement Victoria and the prince were allowed to gallop far ahead. They disappeared for quiet walks in the Palace gardens, in spite of the lowering October weather; she went in to dinner on his arm every night, and the seat beside her on the sofa which had once been Melbourne's was now occupied by Albert. She seemed to be always laughing, always flushed, gazing up into his face like a delighted little bird; she worked at her despatch boxes, reading, annotating and signing with furious energy, impatient to hurry out in search of her cousin.

And if anyone noticed that the Prince was paler since his arrival, or that his manner was hardly in keeping with the role of an ardent suitor, it was soon forgotten. If he was quiet and downcast, no one cared; his feelings did not matter. He tried hard; he smiled at Victoria's jokes and paid her shy little compliments, and told himself over and over again that this was his destiny, and he had no right to shrink from it. She was affectionate, kind, thoughtful . . . she had many virtues, he argued wretchedly; it was not her fault if she left him unmoved in mind and body. And she loved him. Even to himself he refused to admit that it was her love which disquieted him most. Ernst and he had discussed it frankly, and Ernst had pointed out the immense advantages of a marriage where there was genuine affection, at least on one side. Most Royal unions were cold-blooded affairs; it was refreshing to see Victoria's devotion. And it would make his position as Consort so much easier if he had a loving wife. She would do everything to make him happy; Ernst was sure of that. Already she took infinite pains to please him, hung on his words and asked his opinions. And if she was a little high-handed with others, she was gentleness itself with Albert. He agreed with all his brother said, because it was the truth, and yet it made the prospect harder. If she were only less intense, he said unhappily, less blind in her own infatuation . . . A loveless marriage was what he had expected, contracted with calm and dignity, a match where he would have been chosen on his merits as a Prince, a future 'helpmeet'. He had never wished or supposed that he would be the object of a romantic passion. Passion was the word he stumbled on, and for the first time Ernst understood his underlying dread. Wretchedly, Albert admitted that he felt nothing for Victoria. Nothing at all, except gratitude because she had tried so hard to please him and make him welcome. His emotions were untouched, and what he had said the first night after they arrived at Windsor was still true. There were things about her that he actually disliked. She was headstrong. She was proud. She loved great state and revelled in her position. His ideal in a woman was the opposite of all these traits. Meekness, femininity, modesty, humility. The country bored her; going to bed early was ridiculous, simplicity of living was for commoners and not for Royalty. Her tastes were the antitheses of his own. Tranquillity and intellectual exercise, the study of science and philosophy – there was not a trace of such things in Victoria or the people who surrounded her. The conversation was either flippant or composed of platitudes. She was terribly ignorant, he suspected; whenever he tried to interest her in a serious subject, she turned the talk to something else. She had dismissed the whole of Scottish history by saying there were too many Jameses and too many murders and, laughing, told him that was her dear Lord Melbourne's opinion and wasn't it both true and witty?

There was nothing Ernst could say to comfort him in the end. He would receive some indication at the proper time, and then propose. And when that moment came, and he was certain that he had been chosen, he would do his best not to disappoint his family.

On the 13th of October, Victoria sent for Melbourne. He came to her in her little boudoir overlooking the same height which Albert had admired, and found her sitting, waiting for him, smiling. She looked painfully young, he thought tenderly. Not yet twenty, and about to take this tremendous step in her life; he knew exactly why she had sent for him.

Without a word she held out her hand and drew him down beside her.

'My dear Lord M., I am so very happy, and I want you to be the first to know. I have decided to marry my cousin Albert.'

'May I say I'm not surprised, Ma'am? And may I also

89

say I think he's the most fortunate young man in the whole world.'

He kissed her hand and when he looked up she saw that his eyes were full of tears.

'You do like him, don't you?' she asked. 'It's so important to me you should both be friends.'

'I like him very much,' he said solemnly. 'And I think you've decided very wisely. It's unthinkable that you should go on bearing your burdens alone at your age, Ma'am. He'll make you an excellent husband, and he'll be at your side always. Not like a Prime Minister. They're temporary creatures, as we both know.'

Her eyes opened wide. 'Oh, I don't think of Albert in *that* way,' she said. 'He wouldn't know anything about politics. But it'll be so lovely to spend my leisure with him. He's the most perfect companion, and really, Lord M., I never tire of looking at him! Do you think me very silly?' she asked shyly.

'Indeed I don't,' he smiled. 'He's a most handsome young man, and no Narcissus either, thank God! That would never have done. Everyone will approve of your choice. As for myself, all I ask is that he should make you happy. And I feel sure he will.'

'So do I,' Victoria said happily. 'Life is very wonderful, isn't it? The very thing I dreaded most is now my heart's desire. Just to think I said I'd never marry!' she laughed up at him. 'Perhaps I'm unmaidenly, but I can't wait to have him with me all the time. I'm so in love with him, Lord M., and I'm so happy!'

'If you are,' he told her gently, 'then so am I. God bless you, Ma'am.'

He walked more slowly away from her room than he had come to it. She was happy, and because he loved her so deeply, he couldn't help being glad for her sake. But he was sad for his own. Naturally she would marry and transfer her affections to a man of her own age; the harmless idyll which had filled his empty life had to end some time, he had always known that. She was vigorous and passionate and in the unique position of being able to choose. But in his heart he had not expected her to make up her mind so soon. And mixed with his own feelings there was one unselfish regret. He wished he could feel that the love she expressed so generously was returned. It was not; he had seen that, and resented it. But he smothered his anger. Albert was no adventurer; he was over-sensitive, if anything, and like all these Germans he had been brought up as if it were a sin to laugh. He was shy and lost and driven by duty. And perhaps he was bewildered by the vigorous character of his little cousin, Melbourne thought wryly. When they were married, he would appreciate her; love for her would grow. And for her sake, to ensure her happiness, he would help Albert in every way he could.

The next morning it was Albert who went to the little boudoir and sat down on the sofa beside Victoria. Her face was very flushed but otherwise she was calm. They sat together, Victoria very upright, with her hands clasped in her lap; her air of resolution belied the demure attitude. Then, very simply, Victoria proposed.

'Dear Cousin,' she began, 'I have something to say to you and also something to ask you. I hope you'll be patient with me, for it isn't easy.' She hesitated for a moment and her colour deepened. 'In these days since you've been here, you have gained my heart completely. It would make me intensely happy if you would consent to share my life.'

He could never have refused; he could never have hurt her and seen the expectant, almost shy expression on her face turn to pain and disappointment. It was impossible to do anything but lift her hand and kiss it.

'Nothing would give me greater happiness,' he said.

'It will be a sacrifice for you,' Victoria went on, holding his hand tightly in her own. 'It will mean living here and leaving your family and your home, and I know how much you love them both. The only thing I fear is that I won't be worthy of you.'

This was as it should be; nobility and high sentiment always moved him, and on an impulse compounded of emotion and pity, he leant towards her and for the first time kissed her cheek.

'It is I who must try to be worthy of you,' he said. 'Dear Cousin — I shall always do my best.'

He found that she had slipped her arms round his neck and that her head was resting on his shoulder. Kindly, he kissed her forehead.

'I am so happy, Albert, so terribly, terribly happy.'

Again there was only one thing he could say. 'Dear Victoria, so am I.'

A lot of other people were happy too. King Leopold wept tears of sentimental joy; Stockmar, holidaying in Germany, thanked God that all had come about as he had hoped, and re-read the letter from Albert in which he described the Queen's proposal and said how much it had touched him and how generous and amiable she was. In Germany and in the Queen's immediate circle, everyone rejoiced. Victoria read the declaration of her intentions before Parliament, and wrote long, loving letters to Albert, who had returned to Coburg for a last visit before the wedding. She wished he had been there, she said passionately, she wished he could have heard the people cheering her and felt the atmosphere of goodwill. Above all, she needed him beside her and was counting the days till he returned, *never*, her pen underlined the word, to leave her again.

To her aunt, the formidable old Duchess of Gloucester, she said she had never expected to be so happy, and had quite recovered from any nervousness about facing Parliament. After all, what could have been more trying than having to propose to Albert? And she had to do it because, naturally, he would never have presumed to take the liberty of asking the Queen of England . . .

When she heard that, the old Duchess smiled grimly. The Coburg faction might have triumphed, but she had a feeling they would gain very little from her niece.

In a burst of sentiment the London crowds had cheered Victoria and there were loyal and friendly messages when the news was first released. But like shafts of sunlight before a cloudburst, they were soon closed out. The Tory Party and Press and a large section of the populace were only waiting for an opportunity to show their ill-will towards the Queen and everything connected with her.

The men who had been deprived of office by her subterfuge over the Ladies of the Bedchamber, excluded from her entertainments and stung by repeated snubs, gathered to revenge themselves.

Melbourne, blinded by his own infatuation, had no idea how his idol was hated. He presented the Bill asking for an allowance of £50,000 a year for the Queen's future husband, confidently expecting that it would be passed as a matter of course.

It was met by the bitterest opposition; the Queen's fiancé was jeered at as a pauper and a nobody. Albert's religion was not clearly stated, someone pointed out, and there were howls of suspicion that Victoria's Consort was a secret Papist. His Uncle Leopold had married a Papist when he became King of the Belgians — how could the country be sure that this was not another Roman plot to introduce Popery into England?

Albert's Protestantism must be affirmed to the people's satisfaction, and as for the sum Her Majesty's Government proposed to allow him, surely Her Majesty realized how incongruous the figure was. On what would it be spent? The gentleman in question might be the Queen's husband, but he had yet to prove himself of consequence to the country in any other capacity . . .

Even some of the Bishops, incensed by the rumours of hidden Popery, spoke out with unchristian vigour in the Lords. The allowance was written about and criticized in every newspaper, cartoons of the future Consort, dressed in patched breeches with his hand out, were circulated in the streets, and when the question of his precedence arose, the Royal Uncles, whose hopes of succession were properly doomed by the coming marriage, rose in a body to protest. It was so obvious, even to Melbourne, that Parliament would support them against the Queen's wishes, that he withdrew the Bill. Albert's position must be settled by an Order in Council. At least the details of the proceedings could be kept quiet.

Mr Greville, who spent a lot of time at Buckingham Palace and Windsor in his capacity of Secretary, noted the Queen's fury and humiliation with unkind amusement. He also noticed that Melbourne appeared to be feeling the strain. He was greyer and thinner; his movements had begun to slow down as if he were intolerably tired. It was well known that Victoria's temper and her tongue spared no one. The Duchess of Kent had been violently rebuked for coming to her daughter's apartments uninvited. There were tears and angry scenes when the newspapers arrived, and it was rumoured that the favoured Minister himself had been berated several times. Meeting Melbourne in the corridor at Buckingham Palace one morning, Greville stopped him. Victoria had been persuaded to accept a reduced allowance of £30,000 for Albert and to waive any claim to precedence over her uncles. It was a triumph for her enemies, but also for Melbourne. Greville had never liked him, but he could imagine the tact and patience and pleading which must have been employed to turn Her Majesty away from insisting on her wishes and causing further trouble.

'God morning, my Lord. I find you here early.'

Melbourne pushed back his hair from his forehead with a weary gesture.

'I have just left the Queen,' he said. 'Dammit, Greville, I'd no idea there were so many tag ends to be tied up when Royalty married!'

'The major problems appear to have been solved,' Greville answered. 'And I hope you get the credit you deserve.

You've performed miracles in keeping the Queen straight.

'By God,' Melbourne retorted, 'I'm at it morning, noon and night!'

Greville looked after him and smiled. She must have given him the very devil. And if Melbourne with his experience and charm found it exasperating, he wondered how that stiff young German princeling would fare when her Majesty recovered from the first raptures of married life . . .

For the second time that year Albert drove up to Windsor Castle. But Ernst was not with him, and he knew there would be no return to Coburg. When Victoria received him she did so alone and, instead of a cousinly greeting, came forward blushing and offered him her lips. He found that he was expected to kiss them more than once during their first evening together; he found her hand always seeking his, her eyes always fixed on him with that look of innocent eagerness which was so disconcerting. He was desperately tired and his spirits were sinking; every memory of those happy months spent at his home at Coburg, the affection of his family, the quiet pursuits of country life, above all the solitude he loved, tormented him with homesickness and dread of the future. Who was this ardent little creature who edged close to him and talked and talked, with her assumption of the master role . . . Was it possible that in a few months she would really be his wife, that the solace of retreating to his own rooms would be denied him then, that she would follow him there too . . .

He didn't even know her. And yet the rest of his life must be spent with her. He would have to make love to her, not with propriety and one eye on the door, but in a way that he had always felt indecent in the absence of love. Almost in the absence of liking.

'I've missed you so badly, dearest,' she told him. 'And I was so excited to think you were coming today that I couldn't sleep at all last night! Oh, Albert, aren't you glad we're together again?'

'Of course I'm glad. Dear Cousin,' he said quickly, 'if you didn't sleep, you must be tired. Don't let me keep you up, it's late already.'

'Oh, but I'm not tired *now*!' Her eyes were bright with energy. 'Not with you here. And you mustn't call me cousin any longer. You must say "Victoria" or anything else you like . . . we shall be husband and wife before long,' she added.

'Very well, Victoria.'

'I have so much to tell you I don't know where to begin! First, your allowance has been settled. You're to receive £30,000 from the Civil List. Parliament have passed the Bill.'

'I know,' he said, 'but Stockmar told me it was usual for the Sovereign's Consort to be voted more.' He turned to her, frowning. Knowing every point of precedent, Stockmar had innocently told him what he could expect before the controversy became known in Germany. The money was not important, but the idea that the English Parliament had awarded him less mattered very much.

'Times have changed,' Victoria said quickly. 'And as Lord Melbourne said, it's foolish not to get what you can. Besides, you won't be poor on that sum.'

'I have never been rich,' he pointed out. 'That doesn't concern me. I'd rather have nothing than feel your people made me a grant against their will.'

'Your people.' He had not meant to say that, and he saw her stiffen.

'They will be your people too, Albert. Not in the same way as they're mine, because I am the Queen, but once you marry me you will become an Englishman.'

'I quite appreciate that.' He had become stiff in his turn. 'Until that time, I have my personal pride.'

'And so have I,' Victoria answered so sharply that she surprised herself. Really, after her loyal attempts to get everything possible for him, after the wranglings and insults which she had had to bear alone, and of which he knew nothing, it was too irritating to have *him* complain.

'Since you will be my husband, my pride is just as much affected. Believe me, I would have preferred my Parliament to vote the usual sum, just as much as you. I did everything in my power. And since we're discussing the subject, Albert dear, I may as well warn you that those responsible for cutting it down were the Tories. I don't wish you to meddle in politics, it would be most unfair to you, but the Tories are quite insupportable. I have nothing to do with them, and I know you will take the same attitude.'

'I have not had time to consider what attitude I shall take.' His voice was unsteady with anger. No woman had ever spoken to him like that in his life. '*I don't wish you to meddle in politics.*' He might have been a child. *Meddle in politics.* Most of his training under Stockmar had been concerned with English political usage; it had always been assumed that if he married Victoria he would take an active part in her government of the country.

'Now, Albert, you mustn't misunderstand me.'

He looked so strained and angry that suddenly her own annoyance was cooled by dismay. This was their first evening alone after weeks of waiting and all those long, affectionate letters. It was almost as if they were quarrelling.

'Naturally you don't know anything about the Tories,' she said patiently. 'When I've explained things to you, I know you'll agree with me. You must rely on me to know best about such matters. Now don't let's talk about it any more. You must be very tired after that long journey, and I've been so thoughtless . . .'

'I am tired,' he admitted. As usual anger was turning into despair; he longed to leave, to shut himself up alone. He had a most unmanly desire to burst into tears, he was suddenly so unbearably unhappy. It should have been Ernst, he thought desperately; Ernst wouldn't have cared so much or been so sensitive to his position. He would have taken the allowance and ignored the insult; he would have laughed and told his future wife that it was better to be interested in politics, however mildly, than in pretty ladies, like a lot of Consorts with nothing better to do. Ernst would have managed the situation without choking with anger and resentment and wanting to order his bags and take the first coach down to the coast and re-embark for Germany before it was too late . . .

'Then I'll say good night, dearest Albert.'

They were standing and she lifted her face and put her arms round his neck. She had to stand on tiptoe to reach up. He saw the eager mouth, a little open, showing her teeth, and lacked the courage to ignore it and kiss her cheek.

They kissed, and he felt the small body press quickly against him.

'Oh, Albert!'

It was over and she was standing against him with her head on his breast, blushing and breathless.

'Albert, I do love you . . .'

He said nothing; his mind was a blank, his body cold and stiff with lack of feeling.

'Albert?' She was looking up at him, imploringly, with tears in her eyes.

'Albert, why don't you answer? Are you still angry . . . Albert, how can you be, after that most wonderful kiss . . . Please, don't be angry. Everything will come right; I only want you to be happy. Oh, my darling Albert, I've never felt anything so beautiful in my whole life.'

He thought for a moment that she was going to kiss him again and he stepped back quickly, catching both her hands.

'It was beautiful for me too,' he said. 'And I'm not angry, Victoria, not in the least. Why should I be?'

She laughed with relief.

'Of course you're not − forgive me for being silly, my love. Why should you be cross, as you say? Oh, dear Albert, I suppose I must let you leave me now and go to bed . . .'

'I'm tired,' he said gently. 'Quite tired really. I hate to say good night, but, dear Victoria, I think I'd better. Tomorrow we can spend all day together.'

'So we can,' she said delightedly. 'I've planned so many

nice things for us to do, but I won't tell you about them; they shall be a surprise tomorrow. Good night, beloved. Sleep well.'

He kissed her hands and quickly touched her cheek, and forced himself to smile at her so that she wouldn't see how anxious he was to get away.

He fell asleep reading his Bible, having prayed hard for strength. He was going to marry a woman he didn't love, and never could, and live in a country he found as alien as a desert island. God, who had directed his life, must help him to live it as best he could.

'I can't help feeling,' Baroness Lehzen insisted, 'that the Prince doesn't like me.'

'Nonsense!' Victoria laid down her cup of chocolate without tasting it. 'Nonsense, Lehzen, of course he likes you. He knows how fond of you I am!'

'That doesn't make any difference.' Lehzen shook her head. 'I can't help noticing things, and I've felt it more and more in the last few weeks. I've not mentioned it before because I hoped to get round him, and then you needn't have known, Madam, my pet, but I really feel so unhappy about it I think I'd better keep out of his way!'

'Lehzen . . .' Victoria leant back against her pillows. It was still early morning and the Baroness was sitting with her while she drank her chocolate and breakfasted on hot rolls and butter.

'Lehzen, you don't mean to say Prince Albert's been *rude* to you! I don't believe it!'

She felt like bursting into tears. Of course Lehzen was right; she knew Albert disliked the Baroness and had been trying to ignore it because she loved Lehzen and it upset her to think that Albert was hostile to her.

'Oh, no, Madam, not rude. The Prince is much too gentle to be that,' Lehzen said. 'It's just that I've tried so hard to be nice to him, because I *want* him to like me. But he's like stone.'

She screwed up her eyes and squeezed out some tears. *Prig. Self-important young puppy, with his fine airs.* How she hated him. *Just a nobody who'd got above himself because her Madam had a fancy for him . . . Thinking he could get between them, no doubt. All men were the same. They couldn't bear a true friendship between women.* She'd brought Victoria up like her own daughter and no upstart Adonis was going to come along and lure her away with a few nasty kisses. *And God knew what other tricks,* she thought balefully; she'd never seen a girl in such a nervous state since he came back from Coburg, restless and cross and emotional. The poor child, she was so affectionate; Lehzen's gorge rose thinking of her in his arms, being upset like this before her wedding day. Oh, he had his weapons, and he was using them. While she only had her years of service and her love to offer. But he wasn't going to get his way. Oh, dear no. Victoria might be a Guelph and they were all hot-blooded, but they all cooled in time . . .

'Perhaps it would be better if I didn't come into the drawing-room in the evenings,' she suggested mournfully. 'I don't want to feel that I'm intruding on the Prince.'

'How can you intrude any more than all my other ladies and my mother and heaven knows who else!' Victoria said sharply. 'Besides, you've always joined me in the evenings, and I won't hear of such nonsense. Once and for all, Lehzen, I'm sure the Prince likes you. In any case I shall tell him that he must; I can't have a strain between you, it makes me unhappy!'

'Oh, if he knows you mind, I'm sure he'll be nicer to me,' the Baroness said. *He wouldn't be; he would be thoroughly irritated and he'd show it.*

'One thing I'm sure of; he wouldn't want to do anything to upset you, Madam. But don't say anything to him on my account! After all, I don't matter — I'm only poor old Lehzen and as long as I have your confidence and your love, I can bear it if the Prince is against me.'

'Will you stop,' Victoria cried out, 'saying that he's

against you! And if you don't mind and it doesn't matter, why did you tell me in the first place? Lehzen, if you say another word I shall be really angry with you. I'm going to speak to the Prince and that's the end of it.'

'Oh, don't cry!' Lehzen rushed forward, genuinely upset and gratified at the same time. 'Don't cry . . . We'll be friends one day, you'll see . . .'

She spoke to Albert that morning, during the long ride back through Windsor Park. They had had a fast gallop, in which he shouted to her to rein in, frightened that the horse would bolt or throw her at that pace. He had noticed her red eyes and tense manner, and knew that the furious gallop was some kind of release, but all the same he felt it was not quite womanly to ride like that.

'Oh, I feel better now!' She was quite out of breath and very red in the face.

'Your hat is not quite straight,' he said.

The horses had slowed to a walk, and Victoria reached up and pulled at the brim of her tall silk hat. It was the same as men wore to the opera, and Albert thought it a peculiar English affectation to allow their women to take the field wearing an article of male dress, even a hat. He was a superb horseman, but taking the exercise for its own sake had always seemed pointless; however Victoria loved riding, and they rode every day when they were at Windsor.

'You shouldn't ride so hard,' Albert said. 'If the horse were to throw you, Victoria, you could be seriously injured. I beg you, don't do it again.'

She smiled at him; it was so nice to think he was anxious about her. Even if she didn't always take his advice, it still made her very happy to know that he minded. He was so thoughtful; and so loving. He was much less shy than he had been at first, though sometimes when he drew back and tried to explain that too many kisses were unwise before marriage, she felt irritable and upset for days. It showed the fineness of his nature — no one could say there was

101

anything gross or worldly about Albert – his mind was really as pure and beautiful as his face – and if she didn't sleep too well and felt at times that he would be shocked if he knew how affectionate she was feeling, it would soon be over. Christmas was very near, and they were to be married in the following February.

'If I promise to ride more sedately, will you do something for me?' she asked suddenly.

'Of course, if I can. What is it?'

'Be nice to Lehzen,' Victoria burst out. 'Poor thing, she thinks you don't like her, and she's quite upset.'

'Oh.' Albert's voice was cold. What an odd request. He disliked that beady-eyed, interfering old woman intensely, and he felt instinctively that she hated him. He had been polite, but distant and he didn't see what more he could do.

'I'm sorry she feels that,' he said. 'Certainly I'll speak to her a little more; after all, she is an old and trusted servant of yours.'

It was not the answer Victoria wanted; it annoyed her to hear Lehzen described as a servant; Lehzen had brought her up, jiggled her on her knee, kissed her good night and heard her prayers. And she had told Lehzen more secrets than anyone alive. Lehzen was *not* a servant . . . But he had not meant to sound derogatory, she thought quickly. And he had promised to be nicer to her. She consoled herself with that, and they rode back to the Castle at a gentle canter.

That evening, when the ladies and gentlemen were gathered after dinner, Victoria watched her beloved and her closest friend very carefully. Certainly, Albert spoke to the Baroness; but the warmth and ease with which Melbourne greeted her was missing. He was stiff and cold and very formal, and she suddenly felt extremely angry with him. Why didn't he like Lehzen? Why didn't he try, when he knew how important she was to Victoria . . .? She turned away quickly and suggested shortly to the Duchess of Sutherland that they should sit round the big polished salon table and play a letter game.

In the weeks that followed one bitter quarrel already shadowed her happiness, but she never doubted that she was in the right, and she insisted on having her way. The new Consort had to have a household, and the Queen promptly began choosing every member of it without consulting him. There was no necessity, none at all, to ask Albert's opinion when he hardly knew anyone in English circles, whereas she was the proper person to judge who would be suitable and who would not. When he questioned her right she was astonished. She was patient at first, unaware that she was explaining as lightly and patronizingly as if she were talking to a child. Albert had grown colder and stiffer, a sign of anger that she had already recognized; when he came on the name of George Anson, selected to be his Private Secretary, he turned quite red. The post of Private Secretary was the most important of all. The man who filled it should have his complete confidence and *must* be congenial to him; they would spend hours working together and the appointment of a comparative stranger to a place of such intimacy was most repugnant to him. He did not wish to have Anson, he said. For a moment their eyes had met with real hostility. Victoria's lips tightened and a sharp note entered her voice. George Anson was the only man suitable; besides he had once been secretary to Lord Melbourne, what better recommendation could he have than that!

That, Albert answered, was yet another reason why he disapproved. The Crown should be neutral if it was to be properly effective. The Consort should not have a Whig as his Private Secretary. Again there was a moment when they stared at each other in silence, and Victoria felt the conflict of a will strong enough to challenge her own. In that moment she forgot her love for him, or the unhappiness which always followed if she felt a strain between them; she forgot how handsome he looked, even when he was angry, and the delight of his enchanting kisses; she forgot everything except the fact that he had dared to infringe on her authority by suggesting what the monarchy should or should not do.

She had to remind him, she said, that she was Queen, and therefore qualified to decide on such matters. She also had to point out that he had neither knowledge nor experience of English politics, and that his judgment was of no practical value. It would please her, she snapped, if he would be guided by her. The list would stand. She had left the room very quickly and taken her spaniel Dash out for a long walk. It was the best way to escape Lehzen's sharp eyes, because if Lehzen sympathized with her or asked her what was wrong, or anyone mentioned *anything* she would really lose her temper . . .

When Victoria returned she was tired, but calm; anger had given way to kindly determination, partly influenced by the fact that she had to dine with Albert and spend the evening with him, and she did not want it to be spoilt by a cold atmosphere. She had sent him a little note while he was dressing, a most affectionate and conciliatory note, saying how miserable their quarrel – she hastily changed the word disagreement – had made her. She was only concerned for his happiness and his welfare, and anxious that in this strange country he should have the best possible guidance. Therefore she hoped he would not pre-judge her choice, especially Anson, who was so charming and whom she knew he would like . . . She looked forward to seeing him at dinner.

It was very near Christmas, and Albert, who had been equally miserable for different reasons, accepted the note and the dictum that in this instance Victoria knew best.

Christmas passed; outwardly it was the gayest since Victoria's accession. It was spent at Windsor, where a host of German cousins came to stay, and some favoured friends, including, of course, the Prime Minister. There was a gigantic tree, covered in decorations and coloured lamps, it was a German custom and becoming very popular; there were presents for everyone, the more personal packed and addressed in the Queen's own hand. A Christmas Service was held in St. George's Chapel, which moved Victoria to tears of emotion. While Albert praised the music he gently deplored some of the ritual, saying he thought the plainer the form of worship the better — fancy his being called a secret Papist — why, he absolutely loathed them! By contrast, she suspected, with mixed annoyance and amusement, that during most of the Service, Lord Melbourne had been asleep . . . But in spite of the parcels, the elaborate dinner, where her astonished fiancé thought it impossible that any woman, least of all a small one, could eat as much as she did, in spite of the kisses and pleasantries and the fact that some of the cousins from Germany behaved quite boisterously, forgetting that their relation was the Queen of England — in spite of everything the atmosphere was strained.

On the surface her quarrel with Albert was made up, but it grumbled beneath the thin crust of Christmas harmony like a threatening volcano. The Queen's laugh was a little too loud, her eyes too bright, and her manner too nervous to deceive the two people who knew her best. She was not really happy, and both Melbourne and Lehzen knew it. Lehzen made the most of her opportunity when the Prince failed to thank her for her Christmas present. She allowed Victoria to find her crying bitterly, and burst into a torrent of complaint and self-pity. He didn't like her, and nothing she could do would change him. Oh, she could see that as soon as they were married, he'd turn her beloved Madam against her . . . Victoria, who believed her, forbade her to say another word; and as soon as the Queen had gone, Lehzen dried her eyes and settled back for a contented nap in her chair. The seeds of suspicion and resentment were not being idly scattered, whatever Victoria said. *Toys had no right to like or dislike and that was just what the young puppy was. A handsome toy for her darling to play with, and the sooner he realized it and behaved accordingly, the better*. Lehzen knew he had upset the Queen by signs of independence, and her jealous heart rejoiced. Victoria would never allow that. She was making much of him and imagining herself to be in love — romantic nonsense, culled out of novels — and she was going to marry him, because, of course, she had to have an heir. But if the young man imagined that she was going to assume the role of an obedient wife like any ordinary woman, he was going to be rudely disillusioned. And Lehzen would be there to make sure that her mistress guarded her rights and kept His Royal Highness of Saxe-Coburg-Gotha in his proper place.

Melbourne, as usual, did nothing. He watched Victoria, saddened because he felt her to be strained and ill at ease; and the fatal ability to judge even those he loved impartially, forced him to admit that the more he saw of Albert, the less fault he could truthfully find with him, while his beloved Queen made numerous mistakes. She was inexperienced, of course, he said to himself, but so was the Prince. She was wildly in love, and so sweetly generous and impulsive, forgetting that to a man of Albert's nature, there was nothing stimulating or attractive about a tempest. And she was dictatorial too, quite innocently, since the habit of command came so easily to her. There were few men, and fewer Kings, who possessed the gift of authority as strongly as she did already . . . She seemed unaware of her fiancé's pride, or of the delicacy of his position. She was excruciatingly tactless with him at times, and at others so gentle and winning that Melbourne could imagine how bewildered Albert was. And if Albert was worthy and serious-minded, and frankly boring, he was also impeccably honest with himself and others, quite without guile or malice and painfully anxious to do what he believed to be right. He would never be cruel to Victoria or take advantage of her; Melbourne had watched him keenly and he was sure of that. He didn't love her, and Melbourne forgave him for that too. Remembering old attachments with ladies whose enthusiasm hadn't cooled as quickly as his own, he supposed the situation could be rather trying, especially when there was no possibility of escape . . .

The ingredients for happiness were there. Good intentions, duty, self-discipline, and a simple belief in the ultimate triumph of virtue which he found rather touching. Qualities like that in a marriage would have driven him out of the house in a week, but then their opposites hadn't made him happy either, so it was hardly fair to judge. They should be happy. They should adjust themselves after marriage, when Victoria's feelings were tempered by common sense, and the Prince's pride by deeper understanding of his wife and how to manage her. It would all come right if it were left alone.

5

'Wilt thou, Alexandrina Victoria, take this man to be your lawful wedded husband?'

'I will.'

It was a whisper, inaudible to everyone except the Archbishop of Canterbury, who stood on the altar steps in front of her, magnificent in his gold-embroidered cope and the tall mitre; it was so faint and her voice shook, so that Albert only just heard the words.

She kept thinking how beautiful the altar looked, and wondering quite irrelevantly whether Albert thought so too, because there were rather a lot of candles and all the gold plate, and she knew he didn't like theatricality in church. Her eye kept noticing small things, trivialities, and conveying the message to her mind. The Archbishop had a cold, his voice was quite hoarse, and he had a habit of pausing in the middle of a sentence to clear his throat. The sun had come out and was diffused in majestic colour through the reds and blues of the stained-glass window over the altar. St. James's Palace. How glad she was they were being married in the small church there instead of in the vast Abbey. And how odd that she should be so frightened and so near to tears at this simple ceremony, when she had been so calm at her own coronation.

Albert looked wonderful. Indescribable. She was so proud of him and so glad he had worn the full uniform of an English Field Marshal, with knee breeches and gold lace and the Star and order of the Garter. Some of the flowers in her bouquet were caught on the edge of her

wedding veil. She tried to disentangle them while the
Archbishop's voice mumbled on; what he was saying did
not matter now. They were married. She was Albert's wife.
For better for worse, for richer or poorer, in sickness and
in health. For ever and ever until death. She just could
not realize it properly; even while she made those awful
vows, it seemed a little unreal, as if the finality could not
be as binding as it sounded. And yet she was so happy.
Tears filled her eyes, and the delicate bouquet trembled.
So very happy, in spite of being frightened. She had sent
him a note before the ceremony, a silly stilted little note
mentioning the weather, because she was suddenly shy and
unable to put on paper the things which were in her heart
that morning. They remained unexpressed, the regrets for
past misunderstandings, the passionate hope that he loved
her as much as she did him, and the promise that she would
do everything possible to make his life happy in the future.
Perhaps she could tell him these things when they were
alone at Windsor on their honeymoon, later in the day.
It was a pity their time had to be so short, but she had
explained to him, when he remonstrated, that two or three
days of solitude was all a Queen could spare away from
her duties. But by that time they would surely be united
perfectly as husband and wife . . .

Brides were said to look pretty on their wedding day,
as if the magic of the greatest occasion in their lives
smoothed away all their faults and gave them beauty. She
had looked very nice when she stood in front of the tall
looking-glass that morning, nicer than ever before —
definitely pretty. And she had been able to believe her
mother and her relatives and her bridesmaids when they
told her so. Her white satin dress was gathered over half
a dozen stiff petticoats which gave her height; the flounce
of Honiton lace was as fragile as cobwebs, two white ostrich
plumes swept down from the diamond coronet which held
her veil, and softened the contour of her face.

How ridiculous to think of one's appearance at such a

moment . . . or to wish that she could, without being seen, push back the plume which was tickling her left cheek . . . Albert was so dignified. He had made his responses in such a firm, clear voice, as if he understood and appreciated the solemnity of everything they said and did. She was sure that he was not dazed and silly like herself.

Oh, when would the Archbishop finish the address? She hadn't heard a word of it, and she wanted so desperately to be able to turn and see Albert's face before they went down the aisle together. He *would* look happy – he must . . .

The anthem began, triumphant and pealing from the choir, and the organ, reverberating through the dark and ancient church, and the two figures at the altar moved as one. Victoria gave her hand to her husband, and for a moment they hesitated. Those standing near saw the Queen give him a quick, adoring smile, and the more romantic insisted that it was returned with equal fervour. Then the procession moved slowly down the church and out into the February sunshine.

They said nothing to each other in the carriage during the short drive back to Buckingham Palace. As the roar of cheering crowds met them, Victoria caught his hand and squeezed it. The feeling of unreality vanished immediately; the world was familiar again, she was back in her right place, smiling and waving out of the window, the Queen being greeted by her people on her wedding day. And because the sun was out, and the figure in the coach looked like a tiny glittering fairy in her white and diamonds, the crowd forgot the scandal sheets, the caricatures of the new Consort, and the fascinating rumours of discord which had cheered the long hours of waiting, and yelled and waved and pushed, in a paroxysm of transient loyalty.

There was now a long, stiff Banquet at the Palace, where the right things had to be said and there would be little chance for more than a few whispered words between husband and wife. The Duke of Saxe-Coburg bowed very

110

low over the hand of his new daughter-in-law, and Ernst paid her a charming compliment before congratulating his brother. They were very fond, those two; it was so nice to be united as a family, Victoria thought, watching them, prepared to resist any over-familiarity on her own mother's part as the Duchess approached her. There was no need. The guests took their places and the Banquet began. There were too many courses; for once Victoria had no appetite, and she noticed that Albert left most of his food untouched. He must be tired, she thought tenderly, and managed to turn and ask him how he felt. Very happy, he murmured, but anxious to start for Windsor as soon as the meal finished.

He had no dread of being alone with her now, no distaste for the performance of his marital duty, nothing but a terrible ache of resignation and a passionate desire to get away from the Court, away even from his own father and brother, and face his future without anyone watching him except the woman he had just promised to love and cherish for the rest of his life. The service had given him a peculiar sense of unity with Victoria; it was probably an emotional figment, but it helped him, it provided a companion in the lonely, uncertain existence to which he had committed himself. He would live in a strange country among strangers, his home would always be a palace belonging to someone else, furnished in alien taste; his life and his habits would be regulated by the customs of a foreign nation. Everything would be English, his clothes, his hobbies, his entourage, his food. And he had grown to dislike these people among whom he had to live; he had tried hard to understand them, to appreciate their love of sport — their passion for it, rather — their distrust of all things foreign, their contempt for intellectual interests, for the arts and sciences, their lax morals and strong heads. He had tried most sincerely and failed, and at the root of his failure lay the knowledge that they had tried to understand him and been equally disappointed. He would be alone, except for the woman he had married. Any hope of happiness or tranquillity lay with her, and he knew it. He was indeed anxious to get down to Windsor.

When the meal was finished and the dessert cleared away, Victoria gave the signal, and the whole company rose to its feet as her footman pulled back her chair. Taking Albert's arm, she left the banqueting-room, smiling from right to left, and behind them the guests began to file out in strict order of precedence.

'I shan't be too long, my dearest,' she whispered to Albert. 'As soon as I'm changed and ready we shall start.'

He kissed her hand and smiled; she realized again how tired he looked, and the new tenderness in her feeling for him returned. It made her feel that in spite of the crowd of ladies and gentlemen surrounding them, they were already alone.

'I am quite ready, except for these,' he said, and touched his uniform. 'I shall be waiting for you, my dear Victoria, and not very patiently, I'm afraid.'

She almost ran up the wide staircase. Oh, to be gone! To get away from the Palace, from her large retinue, even from Lehzen — how upset she had been when she learnt that though she was being taken on the honeymoon, she was to keep to her own quarters for the three days — but Victoria had had to be firm. Albert had pointed out so tactfully that if the Baroness came with them they might not have as much privacy as they wished. Victoria had agreed. She was such an old friend and might not realize, but, of course, she could not be left behind. Oh, how she longed to be off to Windsor to enjoy the three days she had set aside from her duties . . . And how happy she was that that was what Albert wanted, too.

In her own apartments, Lehzen supervised the changing of her clothes, wiping her eyes and fussing, and saying over and over again that Madam was certainly the most beautiful bride in the world. The diamond coronet was lifted off, and for the first time Victoria realized how heavy it was;

there was a faint red line at the edge of her hair which had to be sponged with rose water. Her necklace and earrings were locked away and she stepped out of the virgin satin-and-lace wedding dress, changed her little jewelled slippers for plain pumps, and put on her travelling dress. That too was white, with a short pelisse edged with ermine for warmth, and a white bonnet with a delicate trimming of orange blossom under the brim. Her mother came when she was almost ready, with her aunts, the Royal Duchesses, and some of her cousins.

'I didn't wish to intrude, Ma'am,' her mother said awkwardly, 'but I know you would wish me to follow custom and come and say good-bye to you privately.'

Victoria turned towards her with a smile. She had forgotten all about her in the excitement and the chattering.

'Dear Mama, how nice of you. I hope you enjoyed the ceremony? I thought it went very well.'

For a moment the Duchess of Kent's lower lip pouted, exactly as if she were a child, and her eyes suddenly suffused with tears. She had wept into a handkerchief all through the wedding, aggrieved and hurt, and quivering with sentiment at the sight of her only child taking a husband. Now the child stood in front of her, a bride who was soon to be a wife, about to leave alone with the man she had chosen, and to draw still further away from her . . .

'My child,' she burst out, 'my little Victoria!' She opened her arms wide, and the small figure glided into them, left a cool kiss on the Duchess's red cheek, and slipped out of reach, almost in one movement.

'Dearest Mama,' the Queen said lightly, 'I must be going now. Won't you come down?'

There was a crowd of people round the side entrance; the doors were open, and she could see the carriage drawn up outside, but the faces of her Court were blurred, their figures indistinct. At last she saw Albert, waiting a little apart from the rest, dressed in a plain travelling suit, his silk hat held in the crook of his arm, and her eyes never left him as she descended the staircase.

It was only a moment of intimacy, because immediately she was engulfed by the faceless, formless people who had lined up to see her off and some of whom expected to say a few words. She suddenly saw Lord Melbourne, looking quite magnificent in a plum-coloured coat with gold lace, very straight and elegant and somehow delightfully old-fashioned in his Court dress, like some fine old painting.

She remembered the coat; they had joked about it, and he had teased her by saying that he expected his coat would be the thing most people would be looking at on that particular occasion. She made a move towards him, and he came to her at once and kissed her hand, the ready tears shining in his eyes, and she felt such affection for him, exactly as if he were the father she had never known, and was sorry that she could not kiss his cheek instead of some of her relations whom she didn't like at all.

'Dear Lord M.'

'My dear Ma'am. What can I say to you, except – all happiness go with you, and God speed?'

And what can I say to you?' she answered. How could the two years of their intimacy be compressed into a few words— Their talks together; their laughter, the ironic and rather shocking things he used to say, which always amused her in spite of her protests; the rides through the forests at Windsor when the leaves were turning brown and gold and they galloped as hard as they liked. He was a splendid horseman, and never tried to slow the pace as Albert did. And the hours spent over the red despatch boxes, when she followed his advice and discarded the dull bits; his anecdotes and her confidences. Even their sharp little quarrels. It was all there between them and yet it was already in the past, delightful and nostalgic and rapidly losing substance. He looked like a portrait of one of his own ancestors; he really did . . .

'What can I say to you, Lord M., except to thank you,'

114

she said. 'Not only for your good wishes, but for all your kindnesses to me, from the day you first came to me at Kensington Palace. I can never forget it. This is the happiest day in my whole life, and it is completed by seeing you. Good-bye, Lord M., and don't forget — you dine with us at Windsor on Sunday. Just as usual!'

And she laughed, and gave her hand to her new husband, and stepped out into the bright February sunshine to drive away with him. Melbourne might go to Windsor and sit down at the Queen's table, exactly as he had done so often in the last two years. But it would never be the same again, and he knew it.

The carriage passed out of the Palace courtyard, and once more the cheers of the waiting crowds rose on either side of them. There were people everywhere they looked, a bank of heads and hands and handkerchiefs and hats, all bobbing and waving, with a child held up here and there to get a view of the Queen and Prince Albert. With her right hand Victoria waved back till her wrist ached, but her left was clasped in Albert's fingers, and it remained there until at last they drove under the grey stone gateway to Windsor Castle.

'Dearest love — isn't it funny to be quite alone? I keep thinking someone is going to come in at any moment!'

'That's the one thing which makes me regret my birth, Victoria — the awful lack of privacy. Thank God, we really are safe from intruders, just for a few days!'

'Regret your birth? Oh, Albert, you know you're not serious. I think it's wonderful to be who one is — I wouldn't change it for anything in the world, and nor would you, you naughty creature! Life is so exciting, there's so much to do, and here I am, at the centre of affairs, hearing everything and knowing everything, and being Queen of England. Put your arm round me, my love; there, that's more comfortable. Did you think the dinner was good? I was so hungry. I couldn't eat anything at the Banquet.'

'Dinner was excellent. I must admit that I was hungry, too. I thought the Banquet was never going to end! Did it have to be so elaborate? I sometimes think one's Comptroller subjects everyone to more ceremony than is necessary. Have you ever looked into things like that, my dear?'

'Never. Besides, I like the way things are done, and anyway, they've always been so. But I do agree with you, Albert, it was tedious; but it's over now, and here we are quite by ourselves for three whole days, with the best cook in the world − I must send word down saying we approved the meal tonight − the Park to ride in, the gardens, books, the piano − everything! Oh, I'm so happy! I do hope you're happy too?'

'Very happy. Very happy indeed.'

'I thought you looked sad a minute ago. Are you missing Ernst and your father? You'll see them quite soon, you know, because all the Court comes here in three days, and we shall have everyone with us as usual.'

'I miss Ernst a little − but hardly now, when I know he's going to be in England for a while. And I wasn't sad, Victoria. My dear wife, believe me, I'm extremely happy.'

'Tell me, Albert, what did you feel when we were being married?'

'Feel? Why − how do you mean?'

'Well, what did you think about? Or didn't you think of anything at all? *I* couldn't concentrate. It was most irreligious, but all I could think of was how irritating the Archbishop sounded, clearing his throat like that, and whether my train was straight, and what people were doing behind . . . It was so odd, Albert, it seemed like a dream. Was it like that for you, too?'

'A little. Except for the marriage service. I felt that was very real.'

'Dearest. How sweet of you. It's absolutely real for me, too. The most real and happy thing that's ever happened to me. And this time I shan't ask if it's so for you, too, because I *know* it is!'

Albert squeezed her hand.

'I thought your mother looked a little disconsolate. She said a great many very kind things to me, and I do believe she's very devoted to you.'

'Mothers usually cry on these occasions – it's expected. I'm glad she was pleasant to you, Albert; I'm sure she likes you, but she can be quite tactless at times. I had such a lot of trouble when I became Queen at first, making her understand that she really couldn't overbear and thrust herself forward. She used to come to my rooms without permission! She did it again, after we were engaged, and I had to be quite sharp with her.'

He couldn't help pitying the Duchess. She looked so hurt and ill-at-ease in her daughter's presence. And she *was* her mother, after all.

'I'm sure she understands now, Victoria. Perhaps when she comes down you might be a little less formal with her: I'm sure she'd appreciate it.'

'Dear Albert – what a kind heart you have. I do so love you for it. Don't let's talk about Mama. Listen! It's striking eleven o'clock. How quickly the time goes.'

'Eleven is late; it's been an exhausting day. Do you wish to sit on here or are you tired? If you're very tired, Victoria, dearest, and want a long rest, I shall quite understand. If you feel in any way that you would like to be alone . . .'

'Oh, no! But I think I might go upstairs first . . . I think that would be very nice and very kind of you, Albert, if you wouldn't mind. Dear Albert. I feel so hot suddenly – it might be the middle of summer. Darling Albert. I'll go now. And I shall be awake when you come.'

She woke before dawn; the bedroom was quite dark and everything was very still, and she lay without moving, feeling Albert's arm close to her side. She was married. Really and properly married. Married to the gentlest and

117

most perfect of men. No woman – she didn't care whether it sounded ridiculous or not – no woman had ever known, or ever would know, such happiness. People had no *idea* how wonderful marriage was. Now the Archbishop's mutterings made sense. It was sacred. It was a gift from God. One could be married and have this happiness for the rest of one's life, apart from all the other joys of existence. It was possible to be Queen and therefore set apart, and still to find a husband like Albert, and wake in a warm dark room, and feel suffused with love and this beautiful tranquillity, knowing that such awakenings could go on over the years. As the grey morning light filtered through the curtain edges, if she turned her head she could see his face and hear his quiet breathing. God had indeed been good to her . . .

'And are you happy, Madam, my love?'

The three days had passed all too quickly; the Court joined the Queen at Windsor and Lehzen, who had spent the time consumed with jealousy, rushed to re-establish her old intimacy.

'Very, very happy, Lehzen.'

'Thank God,' the Baroness said piously. 'I've been praying for you every moment, and thinking of you. Your well-being is the most important thing in the world to me. I think you look a little pale, though. Do you really feel quite well?'

Victoria laughed. Her eyes shone and her complexion bloomed with health; she was as near to prettiness as she would ever be in her life.

'Perfectly well! – Dear Lehzen, you mustn't be silly, fussing over me as if I were in the nursery. I'm in such high spirits I could dance round the room. And I'm so pleased to see you again.'

Really, she *was* pleased to see everybody. No one as happy as she was could fail to feel benevolent to all humanity, even to people she didn't like normally, and she was very fond of dear old Lehzen, and very touched that she should have worried over her and prayed for her. She was so good and so genuine. And Albert was sure to recognize her worth. Darling Albert. She wished he hadn't been so depressed at the prospect of resuming a normal life. They couldn't be alone for longer, and after all, how gay it was to see everyone and parade her happiness; even her duties were a joy, because she knew now that at the end of them, she could run back to Albert. And the big dinner parties had always amused her, especially since she could discuss the guests and the conversations with him afterwards. It was still rather strange to sit up in bed and talk to a husband instead of Lehzen—

'And how is the Prince?' the Baroness enquired.

'The Prince is an angel! Oh, Lehzen, if only you knew how perfect he is! I'm the most fortunate woman in the world.'

'How generous you are, Madam,' Lehzen murmured. 'He's fortunate, at any rate, to have such a wife. He's a good young man, and I hope he'll be worthy of you — indeed I *know* he will. I hope he's well, too; he seemed somewhat downcast, I thought. But perhaps I imagined it,' she added. Sullen was really the word. Sullen and cold and stiff. Wanting the Queen to himself, so that he could influence her against her friends. She hadn't trusted him before, and she trusted him less than ever after seeing the Queen so besotted. It nauseated her to think of the nasty creature, worming his way into her darling child's affections.

'After all, it's only natural he should resent everyone coming round you so soon,' she said.

'Resent it?' Victoria's smile faded for a moment. 'Of course he doesn't resent it, Lehzen — why should he? He knows perfectly well that I'm Queen and not free to please myself.'

He didn't resent it, he couldn't be so unfair; he must understand that she wasn't an ordinary woman. Then why

119

had he looked so depressed, when she was so happy? Lehzen had noticed it, too, so she wasn't imagining things. She couldn't bear it if there was going to be a strained atmosphere, after those three wonderful days. After all, if she could put up with the interruption and welcome her Court, why couldn't he? She felt her temper rising, and was bewildered by the speed with which her feelings changed. One moment she was unbelievably happy, basking in the sunshine of her new married life, prepared to do *anything* for Albert, and then she had only to suspect that he was not in harmony with her wishes to feel absolutely furious . . .

'Lehzen, I'm going for a drive!'

'Yes, Madam.'

She turned and saw the Baroness watching her hopefully, and on an impulse of inexplicable spite towards her husband, said shortly:

'And I want you to come, too.'

By the time she returned from her drive with Lehzen, her mood had changed. The Baroness had surpassed herself as a companion. She was tactful, amusing, affectionate, and she never mentioned the Prince's name again. As Victoria relaxed, her enjoyment of the fresh air and the gossip was tempered by regret that she should have felt so cross with Albert, and for so little, too; dear Albert — never mind, as soon as they reached the Castle she would find him and have an hour alone with him.

She worked herself up into such a fever of self-reproach that the Prince, who had been reading quietly in the Library, was astonished by the outburst of affection with which she greeted him. He put his book aside and Victoria slipped on to his knee, one arm round his neck; she sighed with relief and quickly kissed him, exactly as if they were mending the quarrel which had taken place in her own thoughts. It was so miserable to feel at odds with him, even in secret. Now that they were together, sitting so peacefully in the old Library, it seemed impossible, almost sacrilegious,

120

that she should have been angry and resentful when she thought how close they now were, and would be again; things changed when one was married, and the frictions and disunity which sometimes marred an engagement *always* melted away in the new relationship. Darling Albert. As if to prove this to herself she began deliberately to talk about Lehzen. When she left to go to her own apartments and change for dinner, her step was as quick and her eyes as bright as when she found him in the Library. She was still perfectly happy, she insisted; she was not tense and holding herself in check. And he had not stiffened and lapsed into silence when she mentioned the Baroness. She was not going to allow herself to think that when she loved him so much and had done everything possible to show that love, he should nurture a groundless dislike for someone he knew quite well meant a great deal to her. No, she had merely imagined it.

Conversation at the Queen's table was lively that night. Lord Melbourne was there, seated on her left, and she was suddenly so pleased to see him that she could have burst into tears. He was more gay than usual; he never allowed a silence to develop, almost as if she were not deceiving him, and he knew that she was upset.

Her head had begun to ache by the time the ladies and gentlemen gathered in the White Drawing-room, and she was surprised when Melbourne suddenly asked permission to leave her.

'If you won't think me unfaithful, Ma'am, I should like to speak to His Royal Highness. May I desert you?'

'Of course, Lord M.! I've been so selfish and kept you to myself during dinner.'

She began talking to Mr Greville. She disliked the secretary, and the conversation was confined to questions and answers about her morning ride. Then she saw Melbourne and Albert moving towards her, both smiling and talking, and she released Mr Greville from his ordeal with a curt nod.

121

'The Prince and I have been enjoying a fascinating conversation, Ma'am,' Melbourne said. 'I've been proving to him that I'm not such a worldly old ignoramus as he thought!'

'Really? You must tell me the topic.'

'Lord Melbourne has been discussing theology,' Albert explained. He was smiling and she thought it was the first time she had seen him look at his ease since their honeymoon ended.

'I fear *I* am the ignoramus! You must have made a very deep study of it, my Lord.'

'Only as a hobby,' Melbourne admitted. 'As Her Majesty will tell you, I'm not a religious man. She's made several attempts to convert me, but I regret to say my soul's as black as it ever was!'

He was gratified to see them move closer together, quite unconsciously, physically united by their moral agreement. Both were religious, especially the Prince; both were a little shocked by his remark and consequently pleased with themselves. Melbourne didn't mind; he was only thankful to see the strained expression fading out of the Queen's eyes. Albert took her hand. 'I'm sure you exaggerate,' he said kindly. 'Doesn't he, my dear?'

'Of course he does,' Victoria returned. 'Lord M. has the kindest heart in the world!'

For a moment she wondered rather guiltily whether Albert knew about Caroline Norton, and what he would think of her meeting such a woman. He would be horribly shocked; she was already shocked with herself. But she had promised Melbourne she would receive her as soon as she had married Albert.

'I envy you both your nobility of mind,' the Prime Minister said gently, 'and especially you, Sir. A pure spirit is a rare thing in a young man. I only wish I had ever possessed it.'

He stepped back without being noticed, because Victoria had turned towards her husband and quickly squeezed his hand. How right Melbourne was when he paid Albert that beautiful compliment. He *was* noble – and pure; for the second time that day she melted, and the suspicions so cleverly sown by Lehzen receded. But not even Melbourne could divine either their nature or who had put them into her mind. And already they had established a firm hold.

Beneath the glittering surface of Court and aristocratic life there were volcanic grumbles of unrest in the country. The sounds were less violent than in the previous years; death and transportation had weakened the Chartist movement and the watery measures for Educational Reform and the introduction of the Penny Post had left both the extreme Tories and the Radicals without the excuse to attack the Government on a positive issue. But within the Government the factions bickered as usual; nerves became frayed under the strain of confronting Parliament and the Lords with such a slight majority, and the personality of Lord Palmerston, the Foreign Secretary, was not conducive to harmony. He had immediately antagonized Prince Albert, to whom he intimated that he considered him archaic in outlook, inexperienced, a foreigner and a bore. To Albert, still bewildered by the contradictions in the lives and behaviour of English statesmen and constantly offended by their arrogance, Palmerston seemed the personification of the worst aspects of advanced Whiggery. He was told little or nothing of political events by Victoria; the weeks had gone by since their marriage and he had found himself firmly relegated to the position of companion in her leisure hours and husband after dark. He had waited patiently for some sign of responsibility, for the promise of some useful purpose in his new life, absorbing facts from Stockmar and from his secretary, George Anson, whom he had soon admitted to be an admirable choice, and generally fitting himself to serve Victoria when she came to him for advice. But she neither asked his opinions nor proffered any of her own. They quarrelled over trifles and were reconciled;

she was as loving and ecstatic as ever, but when the red despatch boxes arrived and her Ministers called for consultation, she became the Queen, and withdrew into her own sphere. The Court was back in London, which he hated; there were endless Balls and supper parties and late hours, evenings when he actually nodded in his chair with boredom, or else played tedious games of chess with Anson. There was no serious conversation or any male companion, except the secretary and Baron Stockmar, with whom he felt at ease. His world was filled with men like Melbourne, for whose respect and friendliness he was grateful, but with whom he had nothing in common; with the awesome presence of the Duke of Wellington, who managed to enter every room, as some wit once remarked, as if he were surveying the field of Waterloo; with leaders of society, like Lord and Lady Holland, whose house was a forcing ground for scandal and political intrigue — and, of course, with Lord Palmerston. He had only to meet Palmerston to stiffen with a feeling of helpless inferiority; he was not Victoria, who was Queen, and could quell anyone with a look or a few words. He was only the Consort, unimportant and alien, with no voice in anything, and that impudent Englishman, with his casual manners, managed to humiliate him without even knowing it.

One late spring day the Queen was shut up with Lord Melbourne as usual, going through State papers, and Albert suddenly gave up all attempts to find amusement or occupation in the rambling Palace and burst into Stockmar's rooms. He found the Baron writing to King Leopold, but immediately the pen and paper were pushed aside and the old man drew up a chair for him.

'I'm interrupting you,' the Prince said gloomily. 'Forgive me, I'll come another time . . .'

'My dear boy,' the Baron said gently, 'nothing is more important than seeing you. I was only writing to your Uncle Leopold, and I have plenty of time to finish the letter later on. Come and sit down. Where's the Queen?'

Stockmar knew there had been quarrels, but wisely he had kept in the background, trusting that the two young people would adjust themselves of their own accord. He only hoped that another quarrel was not the reason for Albert's visit, or for his depressed expression.

'The Queen is with Lord Melbourne. Conducting the country's affairs. At least that's what I suppose. She doesn't deign to discuss such things with me.'

'Ah' – so that was it. Stockmar sighed and pulled his chair away from the writing table. The time had come to interfere at last, and he knew it. He had never heard such bitterness in Albert's voice or seen him look so wretched.

'Have you mentioned political matters yourself?' he asked.

'Several times. And always with the same result. My wife smiles vaguely – you know that determined vagueness of hers, when her mind is made up and she is going to change the subject without offence – she squeezes my hand and says she doesn't want to talk about *that*, she's been wearied with it all day long. And I find myself discussing the dogs, or some anecdote or other. Good heavens, Stockmar, am I considered such an idiot that she denies me the confidence she gives her Ministers?'

'She doesn't underestimate your intelligence,' Stockmar answered. 'No one could, it's far superior to hers; we both know that. That, my dear boy, is probably what she fears. Without knowing it, of course. She's very jealous of her power, I should have warned you about that, but I myself had no idea how jealous . . . And I can't help feeling that some suspicion, or bad advice, has been put into her mind to make her shut you out of her life in this one way, when you obviously fill it in every other!'

'Fill it in every other!' Albert turned to him bitterly. 'I fill nothing, I mean nothing! I am a cypher, an arm to hang on to, a partner to dance with – I sit at the other end of the table and people bow to me when they curtsy to her. I come and complain to you that she doesn't allow

125

me to take any part in politics, not even an interest — why don't I tell you the truth and say she allows me no part in anything! Do you know something, Stockmar? When I rang the bell the other day and ordered the fire to be lit in her boudoir, the footman refused to do it without the Queen's permission! That's what my position is. The Queen can give an order, or that insufferable Lehzen, and the servants obey, but I, her husband, must sit in the cold.'

After a moment spent studying his hands, the Baron looked up and answered:

'I had no idea it was as bad as that; why didn't you come to me sooner?'

'At first I hoped things would improve. She said so often she loved me — she has never stopped saying it. We've had many disagreements, Stockmar, especially concerning that wretched Lehzen, but when I face the truth it is always I who have given way! I make a point of speaking to the Baroness when I dislike her and think she's a thoroughly inferior person with too much influence. I stay up dancing and making small talk at these endless functions when all I long for is peace and my own room. And I stand there like a waxwork, while her Ministers condescend towards me and pass on. They've done their duty, they've said a few words to the Queen's Consort — that dull fellow who hates hunting and doesn't know how to look and behave like an Englishman — but he has to be humoured to please Her Majesty! They must think me very insensitive,' he said violently. 'That is, if they think of me at all!'

'You had better calm yourself,' Stockmar advised quickly. He had never seen Albert so agitated; he was white, and his hands were trembling. This was not what he and Leopold had planned; this was a travesty of their high dream of a perfect alliance directing a noble policy. Albert was not meant to be a domestic puppet, the companion of the Queen's leisure and the father of an English heir. All the Baron's affection for him welled up as if it were his own son who sat there, despised and lonely in the

126

position chosen for him by others. Thank God he had found out in time the trend their relationship was taking. It had gone wrong, but if Albert acted now, with his tact and worldly wisdom to guide him, it was not too late. Victoria loved him; Stockmar knew that. He knew it by her own words to him, by her effusive letters during their engagement, and from Leopold to whom she described her husband, in characteristic capital letters, as an Angel. It was all the more inconsistent that she should exclude him from her confidence and leave him with less authority than a mere member of her household.

The footman refused to light the fire, without the Queen's permission. Or an order from Baroness Lehzen. Lehzen. A vague suspicion stirred. They had quarrelled over Lehzen and Albert spoke of her with particular bitterness. She was now superintendent of the Royal household and the privy Purse, and didn't she also manage Victoria's private correspondence? These were great responsibilities for an ignorant governess. He remembered that before marriage her room had adjoined the Queen's and that the unfortunate Flora Hastings affair had momentarily highlighted the shadowy figure behind the throne. Questions had been asked about her in Parliament at the time, and there were some very pointed demands for her dismissal. He had thought little of them then, regarding them as no more than a facet of the Queen's unpopularity and a desire on her subjects' part to punish her by banishing a personal servant. He had been wrong, he thought suddenly. Very wrong. While the English papers and Members of Parliament had been unaccountably right. Someone had been putting suspicions into Victoria's mind, someone had been subtly turning her against her husband, spurred on by the fact that the husband openly disliked her. It was Lehzen, of course. Clever Lehzen, so subservient to her imperious young mistress, motivated by an old maid's cunning jealousy of the man who threatened to end her influence.

'The source of your unhappiness doesn't lie in the Queen, thank God,' he said, facing the Prince and laying one hand on his knee. 'Of that I'm quite certain. I said some bad influence had been at work and I believe I know whose it is. Like all very strong characters, Victoria is helpless when her weaknesses have been discovered. She is proud and frightened of being dominated – she always was – that was her objection to marriage before she saw you again last year. She fell in love with you, but those fears remained. A mother might have exploited them and produced exactly these results, but her mother had no place in her affections and no influence. It is the substitute for that mother who is to blame. The person who brought her up, who is part of her childhood – and therefore has a stronger hold on the Queen than anyone imagined. Your evil genius is Baroness Lehzen, my boy.'

'Are you really suggesting that old woman could sway Victoria to that extent?' Albert shook his head. 'You can't know her as well as I thought.'

'Better,' Stockmar retorted. 'Husbands, especially those with a grievance, are never good judges of their wives. She's hurt you very deeply, Albert, but I'd swear she's done it in ignorance. I know she loves you. I also know, God forgive me, that you don't love her and never did. I only pray this hasn't made you hate her.'

Albert stood up, and half turned away from the Baron, his hands clasped behind his back. It was some time before he answered.

'No, I don't hate her,' he said. 'If I did, life would be really unbearable. It's not possible to hate someone who thinks she is making you happy – who tries, in her own way, and has no idea how miserably she is failing. She makes me presents, Stockmar, and the more valuable they are the more humiliated I feel, because the things I would give her, things which would mean something to me, could only seem worthless and sentimental. And by God,' he said passionately, 'that's how I shall appear before all the world as well as in front of myself — worthless and sentimental! The Consort — the Queen's lap dog . . . I know how I've been written and spoken about from the beginning! I know exactly what the English think of me, and I'm not even sure that Victoria doesn't think like it, too, without realizing!'

'Keep your sense of proportion,' the Baron said evenly. 'If we have a difficulty, let us face it firmly and then think how to deal with it. I have an idea, and I'm going to tell you what I would do in your place, and in your circumstances. I warn you beforehand that you won't like it. It's not pleasant advice to give, but I think it may have to be taken.'

'Whatever it is,' Albert said wearily, 'I know it will be wise. What do you think I should do?'

'First,' Stockmar began, 'consider your assets, my boy. Consider one asset, if you like, because it's the only one that matters. The Queen is in love with you. Deeply in love. She is capricious and much too self-willed, and she undoubtedly takes your happiness for granted. She takes your love for granted, too. All is well with Victoria's world, but only because she thinks all is well between you and her. If she lost confidence in your love — if she felt that you were withdrawing from her, the shock would bring her to reason. If you keep her at arm's length, and do it consistently, she'll capitulate on her knees to get you back!'

As Albert did not answer, the Baron nodded, half smiling.

'I said you'd find it unpleasant advice. Now I'll go further. Treat her with coldness, and I give you my word that all the Lehzens in the world won't be able to make up to Victoria for what she is losing. It's a struggle between you, my dear boy, a struggle in which you'll either emerge with honour and authority or else utterly lose your self-respect, waste your gifts and probably be unable to stay in England.'

'My mother's marriage failed,' Albert said, almost under

his breath. 'I have always sworn, all my life, that I wouldn't follow her example.'

'Then do what I suggest,' Stockmar retorted. 'Harden your heart. You can make amends later — you can be the most devoted and affectionate husband in the world, once you *are* a husband — and not a lap dog, if I may borrow the phrase. You mentioned your mother just now; well, weakness was her ruin: moral weakness.' He saw Albert flinch, but the hard voice went on. 'You show no sign of being her son; all your life your Uncle Leopold and I have watched and guarded you in case you had inherited some flaw. You can never afford to be lax, my dear boy. Only the highest standards will do for you, and only in a life of service and self-sacrifice can you fulfil yourself, as that unhappy woman never did. You cannot afford to be weak with the Queen now. You must assert yourself, whether it's unpleasant or not. You owe it to your uncle and to me, not to disappoint our hopes for you.'

'I pity my mother,' Albert muttered. 'She used to write to Ernst and me — God, what tragic letters they were — I used to cry over them for hours as a boy. And whatever she did, she suffered for it.'

'I never approved of the correspondence,' Stockmar said. 'And if your mother suffered, you must remember that she also sinned. Sinned through weakness.'

'I know, I know . . .' Albert stood up suddenly. He knew that if the Baron went on, even though what he said was true, hammering home the fallibility of that shadowy figure who had died in isolation and disgrace, he would break down and burst into tears in front of him. And how Stockmar would despise him. Weakness again, he would point out calmly. Princes did not cry. Princes never lost control of themselves or shirked a duty, however hard.

'If you really advise that course,' he said at last, 'then I'll do it. But I must first tell you this, Baron. The Queen believes she is expecting a child. No one knows yet, but I'm confiding her secret to you in view of this counsel

130

you've given me.'

'All the better,' the Baron said coolly. 'She won't come to any harm, I promise you, and in that condition she'll be even more dependent on you.'

'Very well. I'll report to you how things go on between us.'

Stockmar stood up and patted Albert affectionately on the back.

'You're being very wise, and very firm, my boy. Your uncle and I will be proud of you yet!'

The change was not noticed by anyone but Lehzen at first, and by Stockmar, who was watching for it. The first sign was Victoria's temper. It was sharper and more uncontrolled. She rounded on her ladies for the slightest mistake, and there were rumours that Melbourne's daily conferences were sometimes very stormy. She was nervy and irritable; at times too gay and vivacious to be quite natural, and at others haughty and stilted, even with her intimates. The rumours took a more definite form. The Queen was pregnant, and all women in that condition became difficult. Lehzen, who often found her red-eyed from weeping, and who knew she was having a child, made the fatal mistake of attributing Victoria's tempers and depressions to this cause. She soothed and chattered as usual, and talked so much about the future heir of England that the Queen felt like crying out to her to stop.

It would be a son, Lehzen rejoiced, a dear little boy. And then her darling Madam would have done her duty to the country. She would be Queen, with a little Prince of Wales. The inference was that the odious marriage could recede a good deal out of Victoria's life, once the baby was born. And in her rhapsodies over the coming child, the old Baroness managed to ignore the fact that Albert was in any way responsible. If Victoria brought his name into the conversation she avoided it and changed to something else, or sat silently with her eyes fixed on a point

131

above Victoria's shoulder, with a cheerful expression that seemed to say the nasty subject would soon be dropped. She no longer complained about the Prince or sowed suspicions in Victoria's mind. That part of her campaign had been successful; the second phase was to exclude him entirely from her relationships with her mistress.

She knew that he was told nothing and consulted on nothing; she knew and enjoyed the full extent of his humiliations, and increased her own powers of management in the Royal household at every opportunity. And because she no longer invited Victoria's confidence about her husband, she remained ignorant of the new situation which had arisen.

For some time Victoria refused to admit to herself that anything was wrong. She saw Albert smiling and polite in public, correct in word and deed towards her, and tried desperately to close her mind to the fact that when they were alone he was depressed and silent, always making excuses to go off for walks by himself, to ride alone, because the exercise wasn't allowed her, easing his hand away when she took it in hers. He was polite and gentle and terrifyingly distant.

She began to quarrel with him over trifles, striking out in the attempt to bring him near, even in anger. But he either ignored the challenge or else left the room. And one thing she couldn't ignore. He was obviously unhappy. It was unbelievable, she thought, working herself into a rage to disguise her fear. How could he be miserable when they were married and expecting a child, and when she had done everything to please him? Lehzen was right — he had wanted to interfere, to take on her authority! The happy life they led together, where he could do what he liked while she was occupied — that wasn't enough for him. He didn't love her, she said to herself — and then denied it, in floods of tears. He did love her . . . he *must*. They might have misunderstandings and little struggles of will — all married couples needed time — but if she thought he didn't love her, life would have no meaning at all. The more Lehzen babbled on about the baby, the more irritated she felt, as if the unborn child was all-important and could compensate her for the relationship which had suddenly taken a wrong turning. She didn't care about the child; only one never admitted a thing like that. It was very nice and she didn't feel ill and it was the result of the beautiful affection which existed between her and Albert, but that was all. If she had to live without Albert's love, and continue seeing him melancholy and withdrawn, then she really didn't care if she died at the end like her cousin Charlotte . . . She probably would die, she thought wretchedly. And then he would regret having been so ungrateful.

Resentment made her more high-handed in her treatment of her husband; she politely avoided discussing anything about Melbourne's visits, and swept in to her despatch boxes and her conferences with her sharp little chin thrust out and an increasing heartache, because defying Albert didn't relieve her feelings in the least. And she began to resent Lehzen's attitude even more. If only her confidante would give her the chance to talk about him, to express the anxiety which had no outlet − what a relief it would have been. What a relief to quarrel with Lehzen about him, and give vent to her feelings. But the Baroness defeated her efforts; she swam serenely past every bait, leaving Victoria alone with her pride and her uncertainty.

Albert hated every move in the campaign; he often wept because he loathed being deliberately unkind, and her condition made it harder still. But Stockmar was there at his elbow, strengthening his resolve, encouraging him to persist. His life must follow the right pattern. Service to the community, self-sacrifice in the cause of peace and better morality in the world. No man had such an opportunity for doing good as he had, of living a useful, dedicated life, once Victoria admitted him to a share of her power. And she would, Stockmar maintained. As long as he didn't weaken.

* * *

'I'm so glad you decided to come to Windsor this weekend, Madam,' Stockmar said. 'The air does agree with the Prince and I thought he was looking a little pale lately.'

He was alone with Victoria in the music room; together they had been choosing the music to be sung at a concert that evening. Some of the ladies-in-waiting, especially Lady Lyttelton, had fine voices, and they were often called on to entertain the Queen and the Prince after dinner. Sometimes the Queen sang, while Albert accompanied her, but that habit had lapsed in the last few weeks, because he did everything she suggested with such an air of resignation that there was no longer any pleasure in it.

Albert did look tired; but not as tired as Victoria, the Baron thought as she looked up at him. She was thickening slightly, but no mention could be made of her condition. Albert thought interest in such a private matter was indelicate, and in that she seemed to agree with him. She was agreeing on several minor points, almost as if the major issue could be avoided by giving way on trifles which didn't really matter to her. But every concession gained at the expense of that iron will was a victory. Albert couldn't see that; he only despaired and gave way to depression as the strain between them increased and she showed no sign of yielding.

'Albert is very fond of Windsor,' Victoria said. 'He's often told me how much he dislikes London.' It was such a pity he didn't enjoy life in the capital, that the parties and receptions bored him, because now she no longer enjoyed them, either. She sighed, and bent over the music album.

'I think he finds the time dragging,' the Baron remarked gently. 'He has so little to do in London, while you are very occupied, Ma'am.'

She looked up at him sharply.

'Little to do? But good heavens, Baron, there's the Library . . . and his correspondence . . . *I* can't find time enough to deal with mine!'

134

'Yours is perhaps more interesting,' Stockmar said. 'There's a limit to the number of letters one can write to one's family. Even a limit to the number of books one can read. If he had something to occupy him . . .'

He saw the expression in her eyes and decided that this was not the time to make an issue of Albert's position. No wonder he found her hard to deal with; even he, who had known her since she was a child, felt uncomfortable before the intensity of her opposition.

'In Coburg he had certain interests,' he went on carefully. 'He's a serious-minded young man, and science used to occupy him. And theology. If he could perhaps meet some of the men who work in these fields . . .'

'That has been suggested already.' Victoria closed the album with a snap. She was only waiting for Stockmar to add politics to the list of Albert's hobbies, and then she could really lose her temper. 'Unfortunately my education in these matters was neglected. I would feel most unhappy in such company. Quite ill at ease, my dear Baron. I can't believe Albert longs for conversations in which he knows I cannot join.'

'Of course not,' Stockmar retreated hastily.

'You are not suggesting that the Prince finds the Court boring?' There was an angry patch of pink in both cheeks. 'I shall soon begin to feel that he finds me dull . . .'

The Baron laughed as if she had made a joke. 'My dear Ma'am, you know he only lives for you. All I meant to say was, that he's been approached by the Society for the Abolition of Slavery and the Civilization of Africa. They would like him to be their President. It's really a mark of esteem,' he explained. 'A gesture towards the Prince from your people. He could study the subject and make a speech. I know how strongly he feels about slavery, and in addition of course, it would make him feel that he was being really useful to you.'

The Abolition of Slavery. It was a very laudable project. If that was the sort of work he wanted, perhaps she needn't

135

have been so jealous of her privileges. Slavery had nothing to do with her government or her policies. The Society was a gathering of worthy people who wanted an equally worthy Royal Personage to support them. If Albert would be content with good works of this kind . . . Above all, if he would only look happier and behave more warmly towards her.'

'Do you think he would accept?'

'I'm sure of it, Ma'am. It would make him very happy.'

'In that case,' Victoria opened the music album again,' I shall press him to do so — Now, Baron, we really must make a selection of these songs.'

His address to the Society was Albert's first public duty. He made a speech in which Anson and Stockmar had collaborated, and which he had learnt by heart. It was entirely non-political, and his audience was composed of members of all parties and religions. He was extremely nervous, and for once his stiffness was appropriate to the occasion. The audience was staid and righteous; the subject was uplifting; the new President comported himself exactly as they thought he should, and when his speech was finished they cheered him warmly. *The Times* reported the incident in terms which implied that the Queen's Consort was at last doing something to earn his keep, but otherwise managed to praise rather than criticize. Hearing the accounts of his success — above all seeing him animated and happy for the first time in weeks, Victoria felt such a surge of relief and pride in him that Lehzen quickly reminded her that the King of Portugal, who had interests in Africa, might take the speech to mean that England had designs there. How lucky that she had overheard Mr Greville saying that; she knew nothing about Portugal and less about Africa, but it enabled her to damp her mistress's enthusiasm. Unctuous puppy, the Baroness muttered to herself. Not yet twenty-one, and presuming to make speeches and set himself up. Oh, her darling had better be careful. Victoria snapped at her not to talk about things she didn't understand, and a few minutes later went to tell Albert that he must write to the King of Portugal *immediately* and explain that the speech had no political significance at all.

In June they went to the Derby. It was a democratic gesture, for no sovereign had mixed with the crowd at Epsom before, and the people gave them both a reception that brought tears to the Queen's eyes. *Her* people. They were rough and dirty and rather frightening at close quarters, but hardly as dangerous as Melbourne made them out. How they cheered her. Even the little children waved. The sight of them made her feel quite sentimental towards the child she herself carried. It was wonderful to be Queen and to be popular. It was wonderful to feel that the crowd loved her, and in return she could love them. It almost made up for the fact that still all was not well with Albert. In spite of her gesture over the Abolitionists, he wasn't happy. She refused to admit that lecturing him over Portugal might have spoilt anything. She had to point it out; he was inexperienced and she couldn't let him make mistakes in her name. As she had said at the time, everything he did was scrutinized, just because he was the husband of the Queen of England.

She sat very upright in the carriage as they drove to the racecourse and said firmly to herself that being Queen was all that mattered, and that it was enough to know her people loved her.

But a few days later her confidence in the affection of the masses suffered a blow from which it never quite recovered.

As she was driving out from Buckingham Palace with Albert to pay a duty visit to her mother, an attempt was made on her life.

She was looking the other way, and it was Albert who saw the figure first, leaning against the railings of Green Park, pointing something that glinted in the early evening sunlight. The next moment a shot cracked past them. The terrified horses whinnied and stopped; the small carriage with its guard of two postilions pulled up, and Victoria, turning, saw the assassin with the pistol smoking in his hand.

The next moment Albert's arms were round her, trying to draw her down out of sight, and she heard his voice, trembling with anxiety, asking if she were hurt. In that moment of nightmare she looked up at him and laughed. It was so brave it was incongruous. She was pregnant and a woman, and a man had tried to kill her. She should have fainted. He had no time to reflect on the character of the woman he had married, whom Stockmar said was less intelligent than he was, because in those few seconds he only saw one thing. The assassin had two pistols.

'Victoria — in God's name, get down!' It was too late to do anything but try and shield her with his own body, and as he did so he felt her stiffen, refusing to be frightened into sheltering on the floor. The second and last shot smashed into the wall just above her head. There had been quite a crowd of people hanging about in groups to watch the Queen drive out, or strolling through Green Park. Up to that moment, they had hesitated, petrified by the scene; as the sound of that final shot cracked through the still air, the spell or horror was broken. They came running towards the man, who stood quite motionless, slowly lowering his pistols and staring at the face of the Queen he had tried to murder. He was still in the same position, his eyes fixed in the lunatic's glare, when the cry was raised.

'Kill him! Kill him!'

Victoria turned to look; people were running towards the man, with fists and sticks raised. Only then did she quail.

'Oh, Albert,' she whispered, and hid her face against his shoulder. He could see, though she could not, that her attacker was surrounded. The next moment they would witness a mob lynching.

138

'Drive on!' he shouted to the coachman. 'Use your whip, but get the Queen out of this!' The carriage jerked forward and began to race down the road. As they turned out of Constitution Hill, Victoria gently freed herself and sat upright.

'Oh, Victoria, are you all right?'

Dear Albert. How worried he looked. And hc had put his own body between her and the assassin. It was worth having nearly been murdered to see him look at her like that.

'Perfectly all right, just trembling a little. Darling Albert, don't be anxious: I'm not hurt in the least. I was more frightened of seeing that wretch torn to pieces than anything else. And let me sit up now. People mustn't think that I'm injured.'

And she drew herself very upright and ordered the coachman to drive at their usual pace. But she held on tightly to Albert's hand under cover of the carriage rug, and he comforted himself with the thought that she had been afraid and womanly after all, in spite of that extraordinary, defiant laugh at a moment which might well have been her last. It was as if all her roistering, arrogant ancestors had spoken through her lips. Poor child, he thought tenderly, resolutely forgetting that he had been the more alarmed of the two, poor little Victoria, so small and frail, poor unborn infant . . . He had to bite his lips to avoid shedding tears of emotion. There was a good deal of guilt mixed with the sentiment, because of the way he had treated her. For the rest of the evening and for the whole of the next week, Baron Stockmar's advice was put aside, and Victoria's happiness blossomed.

They went to the opera, where the audience rose and gave them a tremendous ovation. There was a special cheer for the Prince, whose attempt to shield the Queen had been widely repeated, and when they saw Victoria, very regal and yet tiny, bowing from the Royal Box, they cheered and clapped and sang the National Anthem. The Queen's

139

unpopularity was momentarily forgotten in the general fury at the attack upon her. The heartless little autocrat of the Flora Hastings affair, the partisan monarch who had retained the Whigs because she liked their leader at her dinner parties, became a national heroine, and for a brief moment Albert shared in the reflection of her glory. For a foreigner, he had come out of the affair quite well. Even the aristocracy admitted that, though a few sour voices declared that, had they been in his place, they'd have knocked the scoundrel flying before he took a second shot. For a little while the sun shone on them again, both in private as well as before the world. Victoria was happy, even-tempered, kindly; everyone round her breathed more easily. Albert loved her; he was being just as affectionate and companionable as before. Nothing had been wrong with him at all; she had simply imagined it. She went back to her daily conferences with Melbourne and her Ministers, dealt with her vast correspondence and shut her husband out of her public life as firmly as before.

As Stockmar pointed out, she thought she had won. Not consciously, of course. God forbid that Albert should think she was calculating. But his foolish relaxation had led her to believe that he was content with a sop like the Presidency of the Abolitionists and a round of applause at the opera because he had tried to prevent his wife being murdered in front of him. Slowly Albert retreated into himself, so gradually that Victoria couldn't be sure at first that the tension between them was not in her imagination. In an effort to please him she went down to Windsor more often and stayed longer, but he spent so much time away from her, walking and hunting that, in a burst of jealousy, she insisted on his returning for lunch, which effectively spoiled those relaxations. The idyll was over, and she could not but realize it. Her social activities were curtailed by her advancing pregnancy and a morbid fancy that she was going to die like her cousin Charlotte became so strong that she ordered Claremont, the house where the mother and child had died, to be prepared for her own confinement. By the end of June her nerves were taut to breaking point; she cried very easily, lost her temper twenty times a day and horrified Melbourne by the vigour of her interference in affairs of government. Day by day he watched her, and because he loved her as he had never loved any human being in his life, he knew that underneath the arrogance and tantrums she was desperately unhappy and afraid. And this same love divined the reason. He was not taken in by the domestic play between husband and wife; he saw through the polite attentions and courtesies exchanged in public. He was not deceived. He had suffered the misery of a wrecked marriage too acutely himself not to sense the same deadly atmosphere in others. He also admitted that in this instance inaction was not the right policy; all his life he had avoided taking sides or forcing a decision, but lethargy was his besetting sin, and when his marriage lay in ruins, lethargy had helped him bear it. Base metals bend under the weight of circumstances, but the fine-tempered steel of the Queen's nature would eventually break. He could not stand by and let that happen to her, as he had let things happen to himself. One late June afternoon at Windsor he asked to see her privately.

6

'Am I to understand that *you* are going to lecture me about Albert, too?'

'I am not attempting to lecture you, Ma'am. God forbid someone like myself should have that much presumption. But I am asking you about him because, whether that is presumptuous or not, the happiness and welfare of both of you matters more to me than anything in the world.'

They were facing each other in the Queen's sitting-room, with the June sunshine making patterns on the magnificent Persian carpet, and the rigid, angry figure of the Queen stood in a patch of yellow light. Her head was up and the determined chin was matched by the anger in her eyes. Why was it, Melbourne thought irrelevantly, that one was inclined to think she had no chin until one saw her really angry. She was very angry; not giving way to the short tempests which sent everyone flying out of reach, but quivering with deep, controlled rage. He had seen her like this with her mother, and also seen humiliations and rebuffs heaped on the Duchess which had broken her heart as well as her spirit. There was something truly formidable about Victoria in those moments. If he were mistaken and her heart could not be touched, it would go hard with Albert. And with him. If there was no true love for the Prince, there was nothing anyone could do. For a moment he glimpsed a side of Albert's life formerly unsuspected, and he pitied him.

'If anyone had been lecturing you, and I can't think who would dare,' he said quietly, 'be sure that I shan't. Be sure that nothing but absolute devotion to you prompts me to bring the matter up.'

'Then if you're devoted to me, how can you tell me you think he looks unhappy, and upset me at such a time as this?'

Melbourne hesitated, and then looked away.

'Because I think *you* look unhappy, Ma'am, and I can't bear to see it. Especially, as you say – at a time like this.

No one had mentioned her feelings before. All Stockmar and Uncle Leopold had hinted at was Albert's melancholy; even her mother had tried to join in on his behalf, just because he liked her and paid her little respects . . . No one had given *her* unhappiness a thought . . . Quite suddenly, she was no longer on the defensive.

'I'm not unhappy,' she said. 'Why should I be, Lord M.?'

'Because any wife who loves her husband and is trying to please him becomes miserable if she isn't succeeding. Unless, Ma'am, I'm mistaken, and you are no longer fond of the Prince.'

He had his answer then because her eyes flooded with tears, and immediately he crossed to her and took her arm and gently guided her to a chair by the long window. He had a ridiculous impulse to go down on his knees and kiss both her hands and ruin himself completely by telling her that he loved her so much that he would weep with her unless she stopped.

'Oh, dear. Oh, Lord M., how can you say that . . . of course I'm fond of him.' She raised her wet face to him and he saw the lower lip trembling as if she were a child. 'He's the only person in the world that matters to me. I should *die* without him.'

'That's what I thought,' he answered. 'My most – most dear Ma'am, please don't cry. Think of your own health and be calm. If you'll only confide in me, come to me,' he said passionately. 'You know I'd do anything in the world for you. I've watched you growing pale and losing your gaiety. I've come to you with cares of State and burdened you, and known that you carried some load of your own

143

. . . And it's not right that you should. You should be content now, and happy. You have everything to look forward to.'

'I *was* content.' There was no pretence between them now.

'I was perfectly happy, and I thought Albert was, too. We had our difficulties, but they were only trifles − I loved him and did everything I could to please him. You know how long his brother Ernst stayed with us . . . When he left\I found Albert white and weeping, and I was so sorry for him. But I thought that *I* would be enough. I thought we led such an interesting and amusing life he'd stop being homesick for Coburg. But whatever I do, whether I leave London and come to Windsor, whether I go to bed when I'm not at all tired, and refuse engagements because I know he doesn't like them, nothing pleases him. That's the truth of it. Nothing will satisfy Albert but to have a finger in my authority, and that I won't allow. Not to him or anyone.'

'I see,' Melbourne said. 'I see now what is the matter.'

'Then you must see that he's being unreasonable,' Victoria insisted. 'He knew I was Queen when I married him; I made the position perfectly clear and he accepted it. You yourself said that he mustn't have the title of King, or assume any status like that, when we were engaged.'

'I did, and I would say the same thing now. There is only one sovereign of England, Ma'am, and that's yourself. But I also said something else to you, if I may remind you. When you told me of your engagement I said I was glad that you'd have someone to share your burdens with you. And I meant that, too. I have been married, Ma'am, and you know that sorry story; by rights I'm in no position to give anyone advice . . . But I do know this. You must have trust between husband and wife. You are the Queen − the power is yours, nothing can alter that. You share your opinions with me and your Ministers; you trust us, yet we are only strangers, men who can be turned out of office and never have the right to approach you again. Wouldn't you be a little jealous and forlorn if you were the Prince, and the woman you loved shut you out where she let others in?'

'But he can't come in! He's inexperienced, Lord M. He might make terrible mistakes . . . He isn't English.'

'I don't think he'd make mistakes,' Melbourne said. 'Truly I don't. I think he's one of the most intelligent men I've ever met. Good God, Ma'am, compare him with some of the buffoons who sit in my own Cabinet! I think he could be trusted absolutely, and I think that he deserves to be. May I speak really frankly?'

'You always have,' she answered. 'And whatever you say I promise I won't be angry.'

'Or upset? Because I won't continue if you are.'

'Or upset,' she promised. 'Please go on.'

'I think he's been in the most difficult circumstances possible for any man, and he's acquitted himself wonderfully well. Men are odd creatures, you know. Nature didn't intend them to be subservient to women; it doesn't come easily to a man to walk behind his wife however much he loves her. And the Prince had an unfortunate reception when your marriage was announced; there was squabbling over his allowance, squabbling over his precedence . . .'

'And didn't I take his part?' Victoria demanded. 'Didn't I insist on every respect being shown him?'

'Of course you did,' Melbourne smiled patiently. 'And of course he appreciated what you did. But it didn't alter the fact that it was your wish which prevailed – not his merits. The Prince is very proud, Ma'am. And sensitive. If he was some stupid young brute, like so many I can think of, he'd have shrugged his shoulders and set out to enjoy himself. He certainly would not have loved you as Albert does. And I wouldn't be advising you to lean on him a little in the important things as well as the trivial. Far from it! He feels useless; he has a good brain and nothing to exercise it on – sound judgment and no one wants an opinion from him! He wants to help you, shoulder some of the more tiresome of your burdens, feel that you respect him as a man as well as love him as a husband. He wants most of all to respect himself. And he can't in his present situation.'

She looked down at the damp handkerchief which she had been knotting and twisting in her lap as she listened.

'Lehzen thinks he will try to rule me,' she said slowly. 'I couldn't bear that. If he were allowed to know things and interfere, he might try to supersede my authority, so that people looked to him as the Crown instead of me.'

'Does Lehzen say that?' – The old snake! – As Victoria didn't answer he slid past the governess and returned to his arguments. Now the picture was painted in at last. The doubts in that proud, suspicious mind, the understandable ignorance of the feelings of a man in Albert's delicate position – and insensitivity to anything but the fact that she was happy and according to her lights her young husband had no right to be otherwise. Insensitivity was an ugly word to apply to the poor child, he thought quickly. Innocence of the world was a better description of her mistakes. In all his career he had never talked more persuasively or skilfully than he did then, trying to inject subtlety into that supremely literal mind.

'Good Lord, Ma'am!' He laughed out loud. 'Rule you? I've never heard anything more ridiculous! You're the last person in the world to surrender for any reason except because you want to; and the Prince is the last person in the world who would try to make you. You've sadly misjudged yourself as well as him when you say that. The danger to your happiness doesn't lie in that direction.'

'Danger?' She stared at him, frowning. 'That's a terrible word to use about Albert and me. We're not in danger . . . We may have difficulties . . .'

No, he thought, she won't face that. That's where the steel would break. But she will have to face it now, in theory, before it presents itself in fact. And I, God help me, will have to make her.

'You are in danger, Ma'am.' He wasn't laughing then. 'You gave me permission to speak out, and at the risk of

146

hurting you I'm going to do it. The danger lies with Albert. People have told you he's unhappy. Well, they're right. He is. I told you just now, he can't respect himself. He's the Queen's husband in name and he's a nobody in fact. And that is your responsibility, Ma'am. He knows it. He knows that you can make a useless life possible to him, and that you alone have the power to turn his gifts and his energies to a good purpose. If you deny him that right, the right of every man to justify himself rather than live in the shadow of his wife, then I believe he'll come to you one day and ask to go home to Coburg.'

'Coburg?' She had lost every tinge of colour; he thought for one awful moment that she was going to fall off the chair and faint at his feet. He half rose and quickly caught her hand.

'Ma'am . . .'

'Are you trying to say,' the strained voice said, 'that Albert would *leave* me?'

'If his self-respect was at stake — yes, I think he might,' Melbourne said quietly. 'Other men would take a mistress, but he would leave.'

She withdrew her hand, and turning away from him stood up. After some moments she spoke:

'Thank you for your advice, Lord M. You may go now. We shall see you at dinner.'

He bowed very low and went to the door. She was standing with her back towards him, looking stonily out of the window at the rolling view that Albert loved. As he closed the door behind him, he wondered suddenly whether she would ever forgive him, for what he had said, even if his advice prevailed.

'In my opinion, the Turkish Empire is an essential bulwark against the ambitions of France and Russia in the Eastern Mediterranean.'

The speaker was standing with his back to the fireplace in the Green Drawing-room at Buckingham Palace. He was a tall man, with a ruddy complexion, bright blue eyes, side-whiskers dyed an outrageous red, and a manner that suggested he would have had both his hands in his pockets if the Queen hadn't been within a few feet of him. There was quite a gathering of people; Albert, standing beside Victoria's chair, Mr Greville, Lord Grey, towering over the tiny figure of Lord John Russell, several gentlemen-in-waiting, and most of the great Whig ladies who attended the Queen.

Palmerston beamed round at all of them. He had had quite enough of the Royal small talk, and Her Majesty's coolness had made him mischievous. He turned towards the little figure, sitting in the big gilt-chair as upright as a pin-cushion, and as prickly – and bowed.

'With your knowledge of foreign affairs, Ma'am, would you consider that opinion correct?'

'If I did, I should hardly express my views here, on such a secret political matter, Lord Palmerston. Besides, I think Lord Melbourne has explained my attitude already.'

She was furious with that bumptious man for daring to mention politics in her drawing-room. Her expression as she looked at him would have daunted anyone else. But Palmerston's smile only widened as if he were making the happiest impression on her.

'Lord Melbourne seems inclined to the view that the Sultan of Turkey is not worth befriending – that the Ottoman Empire is a rotten structure, liable to topple at the first sign of insurrection. I agree with him, Ma'am, but I deplore it, for the reasons I've just mentioned.'

'You are referring to the rumours that the Pasha of Egypt is about to rebel, I believe.'

Palmerston's smile was positively cherubic with surprised contempt as he turned to Albert.

'Why, Sir, how well informed you are! Perhaps you can persuade Her Majesty to give me her opinion at first hand. You might even persuade her to be of mine in the end.'

Albert felt his hands clenching and moved them behind

his back. He knew to his annoyance that he was blushing.

'I don't speak for Lord Melbourne, but as a reigning Sovereign the Queen could *hardly* approve of a revolt against the authority of another reigning sovereign, even an Infidel, and even if it appeared to suit our interests. There are moral principles involved . . .'

'Albert – !'

Victoria made the word sound like a whip-crack, and the rest of the sentence went unspoken. Palmerston had already changed his position and was gazing at his polished boots as if his attention was miles away.

'Albert dear, I'm quite tired. And I must remind you, Lord Palmerston, that I dislike politics as a topic of conversation at social gatherings. If you want my opinions, be good enough to ask for them at the appropriate time.'

'A thousand apologies, Ma'am. Most inconsiderate of me, burdening you in your leisure hours. Far too much is expected of you – far too much. I've told Melbourne over and over again . . .'

Nothing stopped the creature, she thought; nothing. Snubs, commands, protocol, all the restraints which worked so well with everybody else were brushed aside like cobwebs. If one did rebuke him publicly as she had done, he only said something more irritating. And she was already furious with Albert for committing her about the Sultan of Turkey, when she had never discussed it with him and the affair was mostly rumours. Naturally England would support him against the Pasha, but how dare Albert say she couldn't approve, and stand there voicing his own principles as if they were hers. . . How dare Palmerston draw him out like that. He only did it to make him look ridiculous. She would tell Albert once and for all that he had to be careful and not make a fool of himself with such people . . .

She had meant to be tactful; her temper had cooled a little by the time they reached their rooms. Quite calmly she asked him to come into her boudoir, and sent all her ladies away – even Lehzen, who tried to linger; and then she began pointing out that he really mustn't talk about things he didn't understand. Neither of them knew how the quarrel developed; before she could stop herself Victoria's voice had risen and her tone had sharpened. She felt her nerves quivering as if the intolerable strain she had been under during the last few weeks had suddenly become more than she could bear. It had begun calmly; that much she remembered afterwards, but it ended with her shouting at Albert that she wouldn't brook his interference and that he had better remember who she was . . .

One moment he was standing, white-faced with anger, looking at her with an expression of hurt and amazement exactly as if she had struck him. The next he had walked out of the room and slammed the door with a crash that shook the ornaments. He had gone to his own apartments. She stood there, trembling. He had dared to turn his back on her. He had actually dared to go before she had finished and leave her to go to bed with their quarrel still in progress. Without thinking further she ran out of the room and crossed the corridor to his suite. She saw a footman standing at the far end, his figure blurred through her tears, and then forgot about him and anyone else who might be watching. She stopped in front of Albert's door and turned the handle. It was locked. She rapped on the panels.

'Open this door at once!' There was a pause, and then his voice answered:

'Who is it?'

'The Queen!'

'The seconds while she waited seemed like hours. There was no movement from inside. She caught the handle and rattled it furiously. Her own voice was hoarse and shaking.

'Open this door! I command you!'

A moment later she heard his voice again:

'Who is it?'

Her fist banged against the wood.

'The Queen! The Queen of England!'

She thought she shouted it; she felt as if she were trying

to bring her own terror under control by the words. She was the Queen. No husband would dare to lock her out. No husband would dare to stop loving her and want to leave her as Melbourne said . . .

But he was not going to let her in and suddenly she knew it. She covered her face with both hands and knew that if that door remained between them she would lose Albert for ever. She would be Queen, but her happiness with him, her joy in their life together, would be lost forever. For one more moment her pride and her self-will struggled against her love.

Inside his room Albert waited. This was the test, the test Stockmar had foreseen. If he bowed to her autocracy and let her in his life would be intolerable. And if she went back to her room it would be a marriage in name only. He heard the sound of a timid knock. He cleared his throat and asked again:

'Who is it?'

'Your wife, Albert. Please let me in.'

The next moment he had unlocked the door and Victoria ran, weeping, into his arms.

One night at the end of August, when the little town of Windsor was sleeping, and the only sound was the changing of the sentries outside the Castle, an old woman lay awake in her room. The room adjoined the Queen's, but Victoria's candles had been put out hours ago. She no longer stayed up till midnight, talking to Lehzen. She had adopted Albert's habit and went to bed soon after ten; and everyone in her household had to do the same. And now the door which communicated with the Baroness's little room was shut.

Lehzen's candles burnt on, the flame guttering in the melting wax, flickering and weak. It would soon die, drowned by the substance which had first given it life; and as she watched it, the Baroness felt as if her own future was symbolized by the tongue of light.

She had lost Victoria. She did not know how it had happened, but her hold over the Queen was broken. She turned her head away and allowed the tears which had been gathering to spill out over her face and soak the pillow; her ugly mouth opened and turned down in a soundless cry of pain and despair and bitter rage.

Once before she had lain like this, unable to sleep, faced with the prospect of losing her child, the child she had taught and brought up who had suddenly told her to call her Madam like everyone else. The night Victoria became Queen, there might have been no place for her old governess in the new life she was going to lead. But Lehzen had made a place. She had gone to sleep that night with hope to comfort her, and the determination to be needed whatever the cost. She had made a place for herself at Victoria's side, and fought to keep it with the cunning and tenacity of a wiry old tigress. Now there was no hope, and no courage to continue; she had been suddenly squeezed out of Victoria's affections, and she knew at last that she could never get back.

The Queen was not unkind. She was never rude or irritable as she had been in the old happy days, when Lehzen's words or actions were important to her. She was gentle and considerate, almost as if she were aware that she had withdrawn the intimacy which meant more than anything in the world to the Baroness.

When Lehzen fawned and fussed, she smiled and thanked her nicely, and when the Baroness tried to strike out at Albert in her terror, Victoria's indifference confirmed her fears. She could no longer upset the Queen, and now she was afraid to go too far in case she made her really angry. She could no longer afford that luxury, because she knew that Victoria could do without her. Three months before her child's birth, the Queen was calmer and happier than she had ever been, with a curious serenity which was equally proof against caresses and attack. A few weeks ago she had come to Lehzen with her confidences; now the little handbell never rang to bring her back when the Ladies of the Bedchamber had retired. And twice when the Court went down to Windsor, she had left the Baroness behind. Lehzen knew who had supplanted her. In the moment when he seemed defeated, Albert had won his wife away from her. Now she went to Albert for advice, clung to him, even sat by the window and watched for him when he went out for a walk, which he did less and less as she was unable to take much exercise. When he first joined the Queen at her daily interview with Melbourne, Lehzen's heart nearly burst with jealousy.

He was victorious, and the Baroness lay there weeping because she knew that the time would surely come when he would suggest her dismissal. And when he did, Victoria would agree. On that same day in August, Parliament had passed a Bill making him Regent for the unborn child in the event of the Queen's death. Lehzen's candle flared suddenly; then, with a splutter, it went out.

The weeks passed slowly. Victoria amused herself sewing for the baby, embroidering little caps with silk thread which she showed Albert, blushing when he praised the work. He praised everything she did, from making clothes for the baby to writing letters to Melbourne on the crisis which had arisen over Turkey. How strange to think they had quarrelled about that — how absolutely extraordinary that she should have feared his interference when now she felt dissatisfied with everything unless she had his approval. Palmerston had been right that evening when he talked about a possible revolt against the Sultan.

The Pasha of Egypt had attacked him, and Palmerston's plan for an alliance to protect Turkey had brought about a most dangerous situation. France had sided with Egypt and refused to join the pact. As the Pasha's armies advanced, there were threats of French intervention, and counter threats that England would give Turkey aid.

Nobody agreed with the vigour of Palmerston's policy. Albert was horrified by it, and Lord M., who should have known better and controlled the creature, faced a split within

153

his own party. Think of it, she said to Albert, think if she had to face a change of government now, and the misery of accepting Peel, just because that odious Palmerston had dared to bring England to the verge of war and the Cabinet to the point of a mass resignation!

She was surprised when Albert said that a Tory administration might not be as bad as she supposed; he thought Peel a rather fine man, with very serious ideas. Naturally an upheaval must be avoided, he said kindly – how she loved him to be solicitous and think of her health – but what really worried him was the danger of war with France. They were in no position to face a major conflict, and the insolent assurances of Palmerston that the French were even less so, did nothing to relieve his mind. Together they went through pages of correspondence and kept Melbourne hurrying backwards and forwards for endless consultations on every point. In September, primed by Albert, Victoria interfered officially.

France must be accommodated before the country found itself at war. The Queen could not face such anxiety without becoming seriously ill. Albert read the letter and said that he entirely approved of it. Melbourne, who only dreaded injuring Victoria's health more than he dreaded her active intervention, managed to prevent Lord John Russell from resigning and Palmerston from provoking the French to a declaration of war, by appealing to their sense of chivalry. But by the end of October the Egyptian Pasha had been defeated, the King of France had hurriedly dismissed his anti-English Minister Thiers, and Palmerston settled into his chair in the Foreign Office more firmly than ever. He had bluffed and he had won, and whether the Queen and the Prince resented his stratagems or not, the English people loved them. Melbourne, relieved of the appalling strain, suddenly realized how very tired and ill he felt. Thank God she had Albert. Thank God she had taken his advice and saved her own happiness. That was all that mattered to him. It was a pity the Prince was so methodical and was teaching her to be the same. Papers came back to him covered in marginal notes and queries which he had to answer with the same exactitude. But if it wearied him, it was worth while. She would learn more of the machinery of government in that way than she ever had under his easy tuition, and in spite of her condition she was able to perform her duties with the same energy she had once devoted to dancing and enjoyment. The secret, she confided to him, was early hours and an orderly routine. And besides, she had an easy mind. If she were to die and leave a child as sovereign of England, that child would have the most perfect of men as guide and father. Albert.

She gazed past Melbourne and sighed with admiration as she spoke his name. She did not see the shadow of a smile as he listened. All women were extremists; and no woman more so than the Queen who had once been so suspicious of her husband that she wouldn't let him see a letter. She had made her decision and typically committed herself heart and soul. She was supremely happy in her surrender, so happy that it seemed she couldn't shed her independence fast enough in order to attain still further ecstasy, and that was enough for him.

No mention was ever made of their conversation that July day at Windsor. The sunshine of fulfilment was flooding Victoria's life; she had no more need of fitful flames like him and Lehzen.

7

On November 21st 1840 Victoria gave birth to her first child. It was not the son she had hoped for, or rather that Albert had hoped for because he felt more strongly about children, but a healthy little girl with blonde hair and large blue eyes. She was christened Victoria Adelaide Mary Louisa, and Uncle Leopold, who was now permitted to offer his advice, because Albert valued it, was godfather, and gave the baby a very handsome cross, set with turquoises and large diamonds.

The Duke of Wellington was also sponsor to the new Princess; it was a gracious gesture to the revered old statesman, and the Duke quite realized that he could thank the young Prince for it, rather than the Queen. Since the arguments over Albert's allowance, when he had voted for less, Victoria's eye had rested on Wellington with definite coldness. Conciliation was not natural to her, but he understood that the truce between them had become peace, and Albert suddenly found that the most powerful member of the Tory aristocracy had become his friend.

The christening was a happy family event, with Victoria smiling and very gay, and looking healthier than ever. Her mother was standing in a corner, talking to Albert, smiling hopefully up into his face. She felt very trembly and weak, not at all like the vigorous bustling woman of two and a half years ago, and public functions where she had to appear with her daughter made her quite tearful with nerves. Without Albert to single her out and be courteous, she would never have faced many of them. She longed to sweep over to the little Princess and pick her up and advise and admire as any grandmother was entitled to do, but she just didn't dare. But there was a historic moment when Victoria crossed to her husband's side, and squeezing his arm as if she were doing something specially pleasing to him, talked amiably to the old Duchess for nearly ten minutes.

Stockmar was present, looking very pleased. After the Regency Bill he had considered it permissible to leave Albert to entrench himself further without supervision, and spent a holiday in Coburg with his wife and family. Now he had redoubled his activities; there were no secrets, either personal or political, kept from Albert, and therefore none from the Baron either. For a young man of twenty-one, the prince did work hard, he admitted. It was a pity he tired so easily and became suddenly depressed. He had no reason to despair now, and the Baron chided him severely. He had an adoring wife — truly adoring, who went out of her way to submit to his wishes, and a nice little daughter. Stockmar and Uncle Leopold were very pleased with him; he was gaining in esteem every day. He had no excuse for looking downcast; and because he felt Albert's despondency to be a sign of weakness, Stockmar lectured him mercilessly. He did not love Victoria, that was the truth, and it made the Baron feel almost guilty when he caught the empty look of sadness in Albert's eyes. He did not love her and Stockmar had helped to push him into the marriage. In spite of all the care in his training and education, something of his reprobate mother's romantic nature had survived in him. And though he was grateful and affectionate to his wife, Victoria's uncomplicated love would never satisfy that need. Resolutely, Stockmar refused to feel regret; Albert was his and Leopold's life's work; all their unrealized ambitions could be fulfilled through him. And if there was an emotional vacuum in Albert's marriage, a son would succeed where Victoria failed.

The Royal couple spent more time than ever at Windsor,

where Albert enjoyed himself planting and re-organizing the gardens. And gardens were no longer dull things to Victoria as they had once seemed when she and Melbourne talked about them, because if Albert was interested in botany then she wanted to know about it, too. She listened while he explained the different species, memorizing the fascinating names, and astonishing her ladies by regaling them with the information. Suddenly all her intimates began studying flowers, and one more subject was added to the curriculum which had to be learnt by those who attended her drawing-rooms and dinner parties.

Men like Lord Grey and Lord John Russell and the acid Mr Greville found Court life more boring than ever. Domesticity seemed to have settled on the Royal circle like a blight. An atmosphere of gentility began to pervade the air, and the sophisticated English aristocracy found it almost difficult to breathe. Motherhood and married bliss had never been a noticeable part of life in the Royal family before, Greville said, after one interminable evening spent turning over books of drawings and watching the Queen watching Albert playing chess with Anson. God forgive him, he said sourly, but he was tempted to long for the rough explosions of Sailor Bill and the undignified excesses of her Uncle Prinny.

Under the restraint of virtue, the debts and debauches of Victoria's Hanoverian ancestors assumed a rosy hue; better be judged by the consumption of port or the cut of your coat, Lord Grey exploded, than by your ability to identify some damned tree in the garden! Those who had grumbled so bitterly in the days when Melbourne was supreme were only beginning to feel the effects of the Prince's influence. They had always been bored when they attended on the Queen, because, with unbecoming selfishness, the Queen insisted on doing only what pleased her; it now seemed as if they must spend their time doing what also pleased Albert. The great ladies, accustomed to gaiety and splendour, found their Royal mistress affecting simple dresses with a minimum of jewels, and, to their chagrin, had to follow her example. The slanderous tongues of Lady Tavistock and Lady Portman were no longer free to repeat gossip to the Queen; Albert, and therefore Victoria, frowned on scandal. Her own life was so happy, and luckily so spotless, that the sins of lesser mortals appeared indefensible. She had discovered perfect bliss in her union with Albert – the friction and near crisis of a few months earlier were quite forgotten – and if she, with all her responsibilities, could reach such a standard of moral and emotional perfection, she had no patience and no pity for anyone else who failed. The Queen was happily married and submitted joyfully to her husband; her husband was the model of marital fidelity, thoughtfulness and nobility. Woe betide the wife who showed signs of independence now that Victoria had surrendered hers, or the husband whose private life failed to reflect the virtues of her Consort. As the Whig courtiers said: where life had once been tedious it was fast becoming intolerable.

By the spring of 1841, they were relieved of the burden. Melbourne's feeble administration split like a piece of rotten silk over the problem of the Repeal of the Corn Laws; for a few weeks the Government stayed in office, as if Melbourne's apathy had reached the point where he was too lazy to resign. The great issues of Reform had really dislodged him, but it was the minor question of a tax on Colonial sugar that brought his defeat in the House of Commons. On August 28th he rose in the House and announced that the Government had resigned. And then, for the second time, he went to say good-bye to Victoria.

The dining-room at Windsor looked more beautiful than usual on that last evening; he thought that everything seemed especially brilliant, the candlelight reflected in the magnificent silver plate – perhaps there was more silver and more flowers on the table than normally; the Queen might have ordered it just for him – and surely the crystal glass was different, only used on special occasions –

everything seemed to glitter and sparkle at him as if he were taking his place on her left hand, and bowing to her before he sat down, and at the same time watching the scene and himself through very clear water. He blinked and with an effort forced his mind back to reality.

The silver was no more valuable than that in common use at the Royal table; he had seen the crystal service used a dozen times, and the Queen took a keen interest in the floral decorations only because Albert liked them. He turned to her with a smile and set out to be amusing. He could never remember what they talked about during the meal, and the lapse was a trial to him during the long, empty evenings that stretched ahead of him, when all he could do was try to picture her and escape the present in the past.

He knew that she laughed and seemed very animated; several times she repeated his remarks to Albert, who bent forward and smiled at him in his awkward way. He was a waxwork, Melbourne thought, suddenly irritated and bitterly intolerant; a stiff, pompous young ass, so ill at ease that his mentors ought to be kicked for not teaching him how to comport himself like a gentleman. Why, good God, if he or his brothers had sat at a table in that pose, straight-backed and solemn, like some poor devil of a curate whose benefactor had said 'Damn', they'd have been kicked till they couldn't sit at all. How besotted she was with him; he only had to speak and she turned towards him, beaming with pride and admiration as if he were the Oracle of Delphi.

The ridiculous thing was that Albert was being gracious; he was actually trying to express sympathy with Melbourne because of his resignation, and Melbourne summoned every conversational art and every trick of the polished world which was already becoming out-of-date, to show the Prince and the company seated at the table that he was as flippant and casual as ever and had no regrets. And even if he couldn't remember afterwards how he did it, he knew that he had succeeded. None of them would know his heart was breaking, that the most ravening grief he had ever experienced reached its climax during that dinner party. If they had known they would have misunderstood, he thought contemptuously. They would have thought he minded losing office — as if that pipe-dream Power had ever seemed reality to him. They would never believe that he was tired of office, tired to death, and had been for some time. The motive which made him steer his fractious colleagues through internal crisis and keep his political opponents from exploiting the Government's weakness had nothing to do with love of Ministerial position. He had only wanted to be Prime Minister because it kept him near the Queen. And now that the time had come to part from her, he felt it as if it were a minor form of death. The last of his youth was dying that night, even while he talked, and with it his interest in a life that had been so empty and disappointing until Victoria came into it. And this time there would be no reprieve; this time she would not duel with Peel and keep the Tories out of office just to keep Lord M. beside her. Those high, romantic days were past. She had another stand-by now, whose place did not depend upon the whim of the electorate.

'Lord M.'

For a moment her fingers rested on his arm. They were standing in the Green Drawing-room, and they had been talking lightly about something, when she suddenly spoke in a serious tone.

'Lord M., I know you want to speak to me, and I want to speak to you. We have no privacy here. Let us go out on to the terrace.'

The long windows were open; it was a warm and lovely evening, and the sky was full of stars. For a little while they stood in silence, Victoria still holding his arm, his head a little bent because he was so much taller, while the lights of Windsor twinkled in the distance and the sound of subdued voices followed them out on to the terrace from the room.

'You will be leaving me, Lord M.,' she said. 'And I wanted to tell you that I find it very hard to bear.'

'God bless you, Ma'am. God bless you for minding. But be comforted; it won't be all that bad.'

She turned towards him and the light from the windows shone on her face.

'It means Sir Robert Peel again, and I do dislike him,' she explained. He noticed that she was frowning. 'I do wish it was someone more congenial to me. As I have to lose you, dear Lord M., it might have helped had he been a man like you in manner — someone you trusted.'

'Oh, but I do!' he said quickly. He was going; nothing had emphasized the fact more than the way she spoke of it. And accepted it. But she mustn't begin with distrust of Peel, or it might cause her a lot of difficulty. And he wouldn't be there to smooth them out for her and dissuade her from taking some course of violent action. She must learn to work with Peel if she was not to be continually upset.

'I trust Peel absolutely,' Melbourne said. 'I don't always agree with him, but I have the highest opinion of his honesty, and you must remember how he said he'd rather die before he caused you distress over the Ladies of the Bedchamber. After all, Ma'am, some men would have persisted and tried to take office on that occasion. He behaved very creditably towards you.'

'That's what Albert said.' She opened her fan and looked up at him. 'But I think Peel was more wise than chivalrous. I think he knew he couldn't move me, and if I was prepared for a Constitutional crisis, he was not! And I would be again, if he did anything I thought was wrong.'

Melbourne swallowed and began again. Patience, patience. He had quite forgotten his own impending exit in his acute anxiety that, Albert or no Albert, that autocratic nature was as rash as ever.

'Peel will do nothing to bring such a situation about. Peel is a moderate,' he explained. 'Ma'am, I implore you not to form your judgment on him by the past.'

'On what else can I form it? You must admit, Lord M., my only experience of him was hardly favourable. His first action was to try and trespass on my rights.'

'He won't make that mistake again,' Melbourne insisted.

'Also I detested his manners; he was so stiff it was positively rude.'

'Dear Ma'am, he's a shy fellow — damned shy; I've seen him turning pink like a schoolboy on occasions, and I know that if you put him at his ease you'll find he's got more pleasant qualities than I have. He needs a little help, that's all. And whatever he's like in private, he's a great politician.'

'How generous you are,' she said. 'I shall always find him tiresome, or anyone else for that matter, by comparison with you. Oh dear, Lord M. Just when I'm so happy with the Prince, and the baby is so good, and everything is so peaceful, this wretched upheaval has to take place and I have to lose you!'

'You won't notice it after a time,' he said, and as she shook her head he smiled. She was happy with her husband and her child, and quite innocently she had put him in perspective. He could remember that other time when he had taken leave of her, and she had cried and declared passionately that she could not bear it. Now he was just part of an upheaval, as she said, an inconvenience which was going to disturb her routine and bring her in contact with someone she disliked. He knew as she stood and he looked down at her that within a few months he would be forgotten, and he turned away for a moment and fixed his eyes on the lights of Windsor winking up at them. This was the irony of life; he should have accepted it and laughed, as he had laughed at all the misfortunes of his life, great and small, but he bowed his head and knew that cynicism was a cold comfort to the old. And he had never been a genuine cynic where his emotions were concerned; this girl of twenty-one had touched some sentimental chord in him which had never vibrated to any other woman. And to the end he thought of her before himself.

'Promise me that you'll give Peel a chance, Ma'am. There's so much at stake in the country, and he must have your approval if he's to hold his Government together. I know what a difference it made to me, and frankly I don't envy Peel taking on at this moment.'

'I know things are difficult,' Victoria admitted. 'Albert and I often discuss all these new movements; he's so wise, Lord M. I'm always being surprised by the amount he knows. He spent the whole morning yesterday explaining why the Corn Laws will have to be repealed. One might think he had been born and bred to English politics!'

Melbourne forced back the retort that only someone who had not been born and bred as she described would have advocated such a course.

'Opinion is very divided on that question, Ma'am. The electorate wants them repealed, and as I showed no sign of doing so, they've put the Tories into power because they think they may. God knows I can't see the Duke of Wellington humouring the masses!'

'Albert says the Duke knows when to bow to public opinion,' Victoria remarked. 'He says that's what makes him a great man.'

'Personally I think Waterloo had something to do with the Duke's greatness,' Melbourne said, more sharply than he meant to; damn the fellow, pontificating about everything and everyone. 'Also, Peel and not Wellington is the real leader of the Tory Party. And Peel will consider the interests of the gentry and the landowners before he opens the English market to a flood of foreign corn at prices which will ruin our own land-owners. I know the cry – cheap food for the people – give them bread! Abolish the tax on corn from abroad and let all men eat their fill, while the corn from our own English fields rots in the barns and the best men in England become beggars!

Peel will never do it, Ma'am. Peel couldn't do it. He's a gentleman.'

'Albert thinks he should,' she said slowly. 'Albert thinks that if food were cheaper it would remove much of the industrial unrest. He's so humane and kind, Lord M. He says the trouble lies in the attitude of our aristocracy; he said yesterday they were rather like the old French ruling classes — without a sense of responsibility to their dependents. *He* thinks one is morally bound to set a right example to one's inferiors, and to practise those virtues we wish them to have. He says if the landlord shows no concern for the people under his care, and puts his own interest before theirs, then they are bound to behave badly. After all, the lower classes *do* look to us for an example.'

'If His Royal Highness had seen the work of the Chartist mobs burning and destroying property and smashing machinery and murdering their betters, he might not think them so easily controlled. I once said the people were animals, and I haven't changed my opinion. As far as the French ruling classes are concerned, I think I prefer them to the civilities of the Reign of Terror!' Only when he had finished did he know how near he had come to losing his temper.

'Now, Lord M., you are not to speak like that.' She rebuked him gently but with steely firmness. She knew quite well what Albert meant, while he did not. She thought the people were animals, too, but she also thought that it was far nicer to speak of them soberly and talk about responsibility as Albert did, than to make everything sound cynical and worldly like Lord M. It would have been quite useless to point out that, however unworthy one's inferiors, a Christian had to do his duty, because dear Lord M. was simply not a Christian . . .

'Albert certainly did not mean that the French Revolution was justified — he simply meant that the aristocracy brought it on themselves. And I agree with him.'

Melbourne did not answer for a moment. He had lost

165

the thread of the conversation; what had happened to the wise and cautious things he had been about to say to her over the new Government?

They had got lost, pushed aside to make room for the moralizing of the young man who owed his pre-eminence as a Prince and a husband to that worldly wisdom of Melbourne's which he was teaching Victoria to despise. *That* was irony, and some of his old spirit returned and enabled him to make her a mocking little bow and say gently: 'Why, Ma'am, you sound almost angry with me. Would you send me away with a flea in my ear over the French Revolution?'

Immediately she softened. Dear old Lord M. It was true, she had been quite cross with him just then for speaking so sharply against Albert's opinions. And he *had* come to say good-bye. For a moment sentiment overflowed in her; for the same moment she found room in her own contented heart for gratitude and regret on behalf of the man who stood in front of her. They had been so close and such good friends, and if it weren't for her new reliance upon Albert she would be frantic at losing him and having to put up with Peel instead. As it was, his resignation was very sad; she would miss not only his guidance but his company.

'My dear friend.' There were tears in her eyes, but they were compassionate ones, and did not quite spill on to her cheeks.

'I shall miss you so much. We both will. But I shall write to you just the same, and ask your help. And for your sake I shall try and bear with Peel. Thank Heavens, Albert seems to like him.'

She gave him her hand and he kissed it very humbly, and without lingering as he once did in the days before her sentences began and ended with what Albert thought and did and liked.

'If I have been of any service to you, Ma'am, then that's all I ask from life. If I can go on serving you, I have a reason for living. May God bless you. I should like to take my last leave of you here. I don't think,' he said suddenly, 'that I can bear an audience tonight.'

'This is our good-bye. And only for a little while, Lord M., because I shall soon want you as my guest again. I shall go in now, and you can find your way out along this terrace. Good-bye. And thank you.'

He stood back to let her pass, and waited for a moment, hidden in the shadows, watching the little figure in the spreading pink dress glide into the room and go at once to Albert, who was standing by the fireplace talking to Anson. Melbourne saw her hand go out and touch his arm, and without seeing her face he knew that she was smiling. He walked down the dark terrace, turning his collar up against a sudden breeze, and slipped back into the Castle, where a footman showed him to his room. He slept deeply without dreaming, but when he left for London early the next morning, he felt very old and very tired.

'If I hadn't got you to encourage me, I don't know how I could have got through it! Really, Albert, I felt so irritable when I saw him come into the room and when he stood in front of me and pointed his feet again I could have screamed!'

Victoria swept the skirts of her dress aside and made room for Albert to sit beside her in the window seat. She had just come back from her interview with Sir Robert Peel, but this time she had received him in one of the less formidable State rooms; at the Prince's suggestion he had been spared that long nerve-racking walk down the White Drawing-room, with its unpleasant memories of that other meeting two years earlier.

Melbourne's Government had resigned and the Tories were in power. Albert was only too thankful for the assistance of Stockmar and Anson in persuading the Queen to welcome Peel and his associates as gracefully as possible. He had never appreciated how difficult she could be, or

how hard-pressed Melbourne must have felt at times. Her
refuge from anything she disliked was her own impregnable
position as Queen; whatever the electorate decided, she was
able and only too ready to show that she did not approve
of its choice, and to make the sweets of office very
indigestible to the men who were unable to govern without
her. That was her privilege, and it took hours of patient
argument and tactful pleading to dissuade her from
exploiting it to the utmost. Peel was a worthy and honest
man, only too anxious to earn her trust and forgiveness
for past mistakes — any hint that she had been in the wrong
or that she had no real alternative but to be nice to him
would have been disastrous — and the combined efforts
of the Prince and her advisers had soothed her resentment
into polite hostility. Albert sat beside her and patted her
hand.

'I know what an effort it was for you, dearest; but I
do hope it went off well.'

'Yes, I think it did,' she admitted. 'I didn't say anything
disagreeable, and I avoided staring at his feet.' She smiled
at the memory. 'I think you would have been proud of
me, I was so controlled. Perhaps I may be able to tolerate
him after a time. But he'll never be as pleasant as Lord M.'

'Pleasantness isn't the most important quality in a Prime
Minister,' Albert said. Melbourne must be banished out
of her mind as well as her sight. Stockmar had been so
emphatic on that point that he couldn't allow the
comparison to pass unchallenged. Melbourne was already
writing long letters to her, which he had no right to do
as a member of the Opposition, and that would have to
be stopped.

'No, but it is a help,' Victoria sighed. 'Especially since
I am in this condition again.'

She was not at all pleased to be pregnant again so soon,
and her attitude had shocked Albert. He felt it was not
quite womanly and proper to enjoy the privileges of married
life so heartily and so obviously for their own sake. A

woman's noblest function was to bear children: it raised her above the coarse appetites of men. He looked into the small face turned up towards him and decided that it was unfair to criticize her mentally. Or to envy her, he thought with a flash of insight, because she was so uncomplicated and so sure of herself.

'What did Sir Robert say?'

'Oh, the usual things – how he hoped to serve me as well as his predecessor – he said that the last time and I gave him such a snub! But I just said I hoped so, too; and he said the new Government had every intention of widening our trade with other countries because he believed it was the only way to bring true prosperity, and he gave me the impression that he would probably repeal the Corn Laws, too, after an interval. Much as I dislike him, I do believe he's quite able. I noticed that as soon as he stopped trying to make courtly speeches and shifting from one leg to the other in case he said something tactless, he had a very shrewd grasp of affairs. And he never mentioned my ladies. Thanks to you, my love.'

She reached up and kissed him impulsively on the cheek. The question of the Whig ladies remaining in her service had been neatly resolved, and the Prince had earned general approval by his conduct of the negotiations with Sir Robert. The question must not be raised because the Queen would not concede any of her rights; so it was tacitly agreed that the principal members of her household would resign and make way for the wives and daughters of the Tory peers.

'It was nothing,' he said. 'Peel was very reasonable.' He liked Peel. It was odd, because the man was as cold and awkward socially as he was himself, but he felt more in sympathy with him than he had ever done with Melbourne. Polished manners never made Albert feel at ease; they only pricked him with the suspicion that he was being treated with familiarity, or, worst of all, that he was being laughed at secretly. He had no such fear with Peel. Conversation with Melbourne and Grey and Lord John Russell was always liable to degenerate into a discussion of the trivialities, or an exchange of banter which they treated as humour but which seemed to him as if they were insulting each other. Palmerston's remarks would have made any self-respecting German call him out. He would never, never understand them or like them, and unfortunately their kind predominated at his wife's Court. And the common people were appalling: dirty and drunken and undisciplined. Nothing was further from the clean, orderly little Coburg villages than the sprawling, smelly City of London, and the hideous industrial towns which were springing up like patches of black eczema over the English countryside.

Only the middle classes seemed to have those virtues he respected and longed to find in his intimates. They were sober and serious and led very methodical lives; but like the burghers and shopkeepers in his native Germany, they were separated from their betters by an unbridgeable social gap. Yet Peel's ancestors came from that level of society; they had traded in calico and made a fortune.

And only in a country as mad as this one could their descendant rise to the leadership of the party dedicated to the interests of the aristocracy, while blue bloods like John Russell and the abominable Palmerston expended their energies and passions on behalf of the inferior masses.

'Darling Albert, the credit for the whole affair is *entirely* yours.' Victoria's voice recalled him to the present, and again she kissed him. She was very demonstrative, and the habit of kissing him and squeezing his hand seemed to grow as time passed.

'And there's no question of that little man being *reasonable* – he knew very well that he had to be! But you did it all so well, my darling, and you saved me all the trouble of settling it myself. What a boon it was! I shall see that everyone knows what a service you did to those wretched Tories, and I hope they feel ashamed for having cut down your allowance.'

Really, she never forgave, he thought, half listening while

she began a fresh eulogy of his tact and cleverness. She had an infinite capacity for feeling, both affectionate and hostile, that left him quite exhausted. She hated or she loved. Lord Melbourne, the roué, was her *dearest* friend; Peel, whom most men respected, was that wretched little man . . . God knew if anything would persuade her to change her opinions about either. And the venerable Bishop of Exeter was a fiend, if he remembered her description rightly, and likely to wear horns and tail in Victoria's sight for the rest of his life.

In spite of everything, he felt suddenly depressed. Their life was led in perfect harmony, because she studied his wishes and deferred to him on every point. He was in a unique position, as Stockmar, exulting, pointed out almost every day. He was no longer powerless and excluded. As far as his wife was concerned, he could play as large a part in her government of England as he wished, and whether her subjects liked him or not, he was safe from their contempt. Everything had turned out admirably, and yet that knowledge only made it harder to admit that he was still unhappy. Sometimes, as at that moment, he felt as if the tiny, loving, eager little woman at his side was suffocating him, and that the mountain peaks of duty and achievement he had set himself to scale would be as bleak at the top as they were at the slope.

'Now don't let's talk about Peel and tiresome things any more. Come, Albert darling, we have a whole half an hour to ourselves before we have to change for dinner. Let's go to the music room. I feel so gay, now the interview's over! Perhaps I shall manage with the Tories in the end. Come, Albert. Come, darling.'

'I do hope you'll forgive this intrusion, my Lord.'

George Anson coughed; he had never felt so uncomfortable in his life. This was not the first visit he had paid to Brocket, the Melbournes' magnificent country house. In the days when he was Melbourne's secretary the two men had passed many pleasant hours together, shooting or hunting, and then conducting their business almost as an afterthought, with a decanter of port on the table.

Melbourne leant back in his chair and smiled. 'You could never intrude, my dear fellow. I'm always delighted to see you; come and sit down.'

He watched Anson, and noticed the despatch case under his arm, and the careful way he placed it by his chair, looking very solemn and rather ill at ease. He thought with amusement that secretaries and dogs soon began to look like their masters; when Anson had worked for him he had had quite a fashionable air.

The Library was a large, beautiful room. The sunshine of late autumn poured through the long windows, and there was a faint smell of old leather from the hundreds of books. Melbourne spent most of his time there when he came to Brocket.

He poured Anson a glass of wine; it was a rather good Burgundy he had been sipping while he read in preparation for his contemporary on the life of St Chrysostom. As his old friend Anson knew, he had often complained that politics left him no time for serious pursuits. Anson agreed with him, and said quickly that he must be glad of the rest in the country after the busy social life he had been leading in the past few months.

Melbourne smiled again.

'I have been visiting all my friends, and having a very amusing time, my dear Anson. I had quite forgotten how to enjoy the pleasures of society. Her Majesty left me very little leisure.'

He had gone to a great many Balls that season, and left them feeling more tired and uninterested than ever. He had stayed with the Leicesters and the Duke of Bedford, and with Palmerston, who had at last married Melbourne's sister Emily; how typical of Palmerston to regulate a love affair of many years and present himself with impish enjoyment as a respectable husband! He had dined with

Lady Holland and listened to all the scandal and intrigue; he had deceived everyone into thinking that he enjoyed himself and did not miss the Queen. He had even begun seeing Caroline Norton again, because he was too listless to resist her overtures, and now that his connection with Victoria was severed, he had no need to guard his reputation. But it was all empty and futile; he lived in a vacuum, eating, sleeping badly, making conversation out of habit, and living only for the letter which came regularly from the Palace. He often took them out and re-read them when he was alone.

'How is the Queen?' he asked at last.

'In very good health.' Anson answered.

'And Prince Albert?' I hope he's well?'

'I think so. He works very hard.'

'Yes,' Melbourne said, 'I'm sure he does. I'm sure he's invaluable to her. I wouldn't have rested easy for a moment if I'd thought she was going to be left alone. How is she with Peel? I feared fireworks there, you know, Anson, but I hear from her from time to time, and she seems to have accepted him.'

'As a matter of fact,' Anson hesitated. It was going to hurt Melbourne, but it had better be said. 'As a matter of fact the Queen has completely changed towards him. She speaks very well of him now.'

'Does she?'

He hid the pang of jealousy so well that Anson went on, relieved.

'The Prince likes him very much. It's strange, isn't it; you wouldn't think they'd have anything in common. The Prince is still very shy, and I thought it would be the devil working with Peel, he's so awkward mannered. But they understand each other perfectly, and the Prince has won the Queen over to his opinion of him.'

'I'm very glad to hear it. But she does me the honour of asking my advice occasionally, even so.'

'I know.'

Anson picked up the despatch case and opened it on his knees. He took out a thick envelope and held it out to Melbourne.

'I'm afraid that's why I've come, sir. Baron Stockmar asked me to give you this. It's about your correspondence with the Queen.'

It was a long letter, and the Baron had pointed out in the most painstaking detail why Lord Melbourne should not give the Queen political advice. He was out of office, his party was in opposition, and it must seriously damage her good name if it was known that she consulted him behind her Prime Minister's back. He felt sure that Lord Melbourne realized how wrong his conduct was, and that it was his duty to ignore the Queen's requests. In any case, she only made them out of habit. At last he put the letter down; Anson saw that his hands were trembling.

'This is a very decided opinion. Quite an apple-pie opinion!'

Anson steeled himself against the note of bitter sarcasm and against those shaking hands.

'The Baron thinks it is even worse considering the attack you made on the Government in the Lords a few days ago.'

'God Eternal damn it!'

Melbourne sprang up and Stockmar's letter scattered on the floor. He was quite white with anger; in all the years they had been associated, Anson had never seen him lose his self-control as he did then.

'Flesh and blood can't stand this! Am I to give up my position in the country? Am I to submit my speeches to the Baron for approval, and ignore my sovereign when she writes to me because he thinks I should? Good God, sir, how dare you come down with an errand like this?'

'The Baron isn't thinking of you, nor is the Prince,' Anson said quietly. 'I'm very sorry, very sorry indeed, but you've no idea how worried they are in case some of Sir Robert's party get to hear of this. Think what it would mean to the Queen if it was brought up in Parliament!

174

She'd be open to public rebuke for dishonest political dealing, and you'd be entirely responsible for it. Make what speeches you like, but all the Baron and the Prince want is that you should not involve the Queen.'

'Involve the Queen? Damnation, Anson, you know I'd die rather than bring any harm to her!'

'Then stop writing to her on politics, sir. I've told you she's gaining confidence in Peel every day. Leave her alone and let her trust his judgment, or the Prince's, instead of yours.'

'Oh God above!'

Melbourne sat down suddenly. He covered his face with his hands and the impetus of rage went out of him. He was cornered and he knew it. The correspondence had been wrong, but it was all he had to live for. He had only seen her once since his resignation, and then in his excitement he knew he had talked too much and rather embarrassed her. She was so cool and happy in her new life, and he had known that his display of feeling had seemed incongruous. In spite of the letter he wrote apologizing, she had not asked him to visit her again. But she had written; out of habit, as they said – how that had hurt him – asking him about appointments and discussing the moves Peel intended making, and he had spent hours thinking out the best advice to give her. Now that was to be stopped. The Prince and Baron considered it dangerous, and they had cocked their pistols at his heart by saying he would get her into trouble.

After a long pause he raised his head and looked wearily at Anson.

'How you've changed,' he said. 'How you've changed since the days we used to work together. But then, everything is changing. All my old friends are dying, too. I feel less and less at home among all of you. You can tell His Royal Highness and Baron Stockmar that they need not worry any longer. I shall stop my correspondence with the Queen.'

'They'll be very glad to know it,' Anson said hastily. 'Thank you for seeing me, sir.'

'It was a pleasure.' Melbourne had leant back and was staring at the ceiling. 'Now be a good fellow, and leave me alone.'

November came, that grey month when the winds stripped the last burnished leaf from the trees, and the new phenomenon of fog covered London and the industrial towns up and down the country. It was a bleak and bitter month for most of the subjects of the Queen; a month when the damp and rickety houses of the poor let in the cold and the squalls of driving rain, and the foul drains flooded up into the streets. It was a time when hunger gnawed more cruelly, and the wretches who worked in the factories and attic workshops for fourteen hours a day hardly ever saw the daylight.

In the summer, at least, the children under twelve had often fallen asleep on the roadside, worn out from hours of grinding mechanical work, too tired to drag themselves to the pile of rags which served most of them for a bed, and too tired to eat the miserable diet of crusts and bone stew on which their families lived. But in November it was far too cold to sleep out; those who did quickly caught chills and died a little earlier.

November was the month when all the countless sufferers from tuberculosis, that ravening disease which the romantics called consumption and attributed to disappointed love in novels, coughed and coughed in a racking chorus up and down the country. The grinders, the weavers, the pottery workers, seamstresses and lace makers, the miners whose lungs were caked with dust – November was a dreadful month for them, and they knew December would be even worse. But the epidemics had died down; in summer cholera and typhus had stalked the stinking slums, bred in the refuse and excrement emptied into the open streets, and thousands had died as they died every year. That was the only comfort which the winter brought the poor of Her Majesty's kingdom.

The wealthy settled into their comfortable houses and prepared to amuse themselves for the winter, or to travel abroad to kinder climates. The routine of life continued as it had done for generations. There were house-parties and Balls in the great houses, laughter and scandal and love affairs, but the general tone was muted to an echo of the riotous exciting past, when the example of high-living came from the Court itself. For now Royal debts and mistresses and indiscretions were as out-dated as the high-busted, transparent fashions of the Regency. The ghost of Prinny and his disreputable ancestors was laid once and for all by the sedate figure of the Queen in her simple gowns, playing and singing sentimental German lieder at the piano, while her husband stood by and turned the pages. At Windsor and Buckingham Palace life was calm and ordered; the days were filled with duties and improving relaxations like music or reading aloud, and visits to the nursery, where the little Princess Royal enchanted her parents by her good behaviour. She did none of the disagreeable things associated with babies; as if she knew how offended her mother and father would be if she cried or was sick, the child was always smiling and sweet smelling, and Albert thought her perfect. So did Victoria, who called her Pussy and wrote about her in her Journal, and thought comfortably that when Albert had a son – the new baby was certain to be a boy this time – he would not make quite such a fuss of his little daughter. It would be such a pity if Pussy were to receive too much attention from her father and get *spoiled* . . .

On November 9th, Her Majesty announced in tones of resignation to her Mistress of the Robes that she felt unwell and had better go to bed. A few hours later, Albert Edward, heir to the throne of England, was laid for a moment in Victoria's arms. The dear child. Her dear little son; what a pity new-born babies looked so red and ugly and made

177

such a noise. What a big nose he had . . . Darling Albert seemed so pleased, so proud of her. Really it was worth the awful nuisance of it all just to see his face and have him bend down so gently and kiss her forehead. And now that the baby had been taken away she could lie back and sleep.

In that bleak month of November the light of domestic joy shone out from the Palace like a beacon. The slave-driven poor blinked wearily without understanding; the aristocracy were amused and faintly contemptuous, but the rising middle-classes basked in its radiance. The homely little Queen with her two children and her serious young husband symbolized the households of the new rich, where the wives of the drapers and corn merchants and tool manufacturers found themselves installed in large houses with staffs of servants who were only a degree lower than themselves. Sophistication, the prerogative of the well-born, was unknown in the class which still bore the stigma of 'trade'. There was no place for them in the world of fashionable society, and their new wealth had dug an enormous chasm between them and the labouring community. The middle-classes were becoming rich as England's trade expanded; fortunes were being made by people who had the traditions of prudence and sobriety bred into them, and now had no niche in the sphere where money had always pertained by right. In that year of 1841, with the birth of the Queen's second child, the bourgeoisie beheld a Royal family whose life and habits appeared the mirror of their own. The Queen went to bed early, dressed plainly, frowned upon any form of immodesty, either in speech or reputation, went to church every Sunday, and, in spite of her exalted position, was properly subject to her husband. Life at Windsor and Buckingham Palace was very like life at the newly-built Lodge; the prolific middle-class mama could point to the Queen as her example with two children in two years, and ignore the pretensions of great ladies who preferred hunting to pregnancy.

In spite of the discontent among the industrial and agricultural classes, and the agitations of the Chartists, still pressing for Parliamentary Reform, trade was swelling in volume, new veins of riches were being discovered every day waiting for exploitation, and from the nation's heart there beat a steady pulse of energy, thrusting more strongly towards power and profits. There were bright gleams of humanitarianism, stirrings of conscience and ideas, bitter conflicts between those who wished to stop the rush of progress for fear that they and their way of life would be submerged, and those who could not let it flood out fast enough. Though an army straddled Ireland, and troops were busy suppressing rebellion in the Colonies, in the West Indies and the Cape, England had been moving forward through industrial expansion to that point where in the person of a little, homely woman, she would dominate the world.

8

It was summer, and the Rosenau country home of the Dukes of Coburg might have been an enchanted palace set against the background of the deep pine forests and the vivid blue sky. There was colour everywhere, colour in the grass where the chicory flowers grew, in the petunias glowing in pots against the grey Castle walls, in the dress of the harvesters and peasants who paused to wave to the carriages which rolled up the hill. It was summer 1845, and Victoria had come to Albert's birthplace for the first time. They had left England in August, with a long happy journey ahead of them, with visits planned to Uncle Leopold in Belgium and to the King of Prussia. At last, after so many years of exile, Albert could show her Germany, and the tour through the land of her ancestors became an experience of successive delight. It was just as beautiful as he had said; it was clean and fresh and miniature, like a toy country; everywhere they went they heard the German language which they used to each other at home in England, and everywhere politeness and enthusiasm met them. It was all unbelievably pretty; the children were so sweet in their neat national dress of green and white and their tidy hair and scrubbed faces, and when the Burgomaster of Albert's native town made his address to them and stammered with emotion, Victoria's eyes grew wet with happiness. This was Thuringia, this was Coburg which Albert loved and had described to her so often. He was so happy and excited that there were moments when she felt as if England and their life there was only a dream and this was the reality. They had talked of this visit for several years; whenever he grew depressed she would remind him of it quickly, and see his face light up. This was the honeymoon she had refused him when they married, the blessed escape from formality and duty which they had both earned in the last four years.

They had taken a very small party with them, carefully chosen, because a bevy of haughty English aristocrats would have spoiled her darling Albert's pleasure. Lord Aberdeen, Lord Liverpool and two ladies, Lady Canning and Lady Gainsborough, accompanied them; they had been tested by a visit to Scotland, where the Royal couple enjoyed a holiday as private persons in a simple little house. There was no need for elaborate entertainment, Albert assured his brother Ernst; their companions would make no pretensions. The old Duke of Coburg had died three years earlier and Ernst and his wife now lived and reigned in the little Duchy. An ugly scandal had touched Albert's brother some years before; he had horrified them all by showing signs of the inherited maternal trait so dreaded by Stockmar, and contracting debts and an alliance with undesirables which precluded him visiting the chaste Court of Windsor until he had expiated his sins by penance and a suitable marriage. He was Duke of Coburg now and re-united with his family; the terrible disease which was the result of his indiscretion had been cured, but the second son of Victoria and Albert, born the year before, would one day take his place at Rosenau, for Ernst would never have children.

This was Albert's home, and it was also the future home of the little Prince Alfred. As she stepped out of her carriage, Victoria caught Albert's hand and pressed it lovingly.

'My darling,' she said in German, 'I think it is the most beautiful place in the world.'

Ernst and his wife Alexandra led them into the Castle, and a figure who had once lived in the shadows also moved forward to greet them. The Queen threw her arms round her mother. Her mistrust of the Duchess of Kent was over. Two years had passed since a carriage loaded with trunks

181

and bags had passed under the arch at Windsor Castle, taking Lehzen on the road to Germany for the holiday which she and Victoria and Albert knew would never end. And the Duchess had been gently led forward by her son-in-law to a full reconciliation with her daughter, while her old enemy passed the remaining years of her life at Hamburg in a house where the walls of every room were covered with pictures of the Queen. The old Baroness still wrote to her, rambling, humble letters enquiring hungrily about her darling Madam and the precious children, two of whom had been born since she left, and Victoria replied. But she wrote less and less, and the letters from Lehzen were too long to read through to the end so that she rather wished she wouldn't write so often; and the weeks dragged by for the lonely woman in her place of exile, forever waiting for the post.

'Dearest Mama! I'm so happy to see you!'

The Duchess could never quite believe it when Victoria embraced her and kissed her warmly on both cheeks; she still glanced nervously at Albert for confirmation, and he always smiled at her and nodded. He had taught Victoria to appreciate her; it was wrong to disrespect a parent or to withhold affection from them, and obediently, convinced that he was right, she had forgiven her mother and admitted her to a corner in her life.

The interior of Albert's home enchanted her. It was so small, she exclaimed in wonder, thinking of the vast rooms at Windsor and Buckingham Palace, and look, the walls were painted with frescoes of Swiss waterfalls, and the ceilings were bright blue with little silver stars. It was like living in a garden!

There was a happy family dinner party with the rich homely German food she loved, and there was so much news to be exchanged that it was past eleven before she realized Albert was nodding in his chair. How cross she used to feel when they first married when he fell asleep at her receptions and she thought that he was bored — and how unkind she felt when she remembered it. She rose immediately and they went up alone together, arm in arm.

She woke before he did and lay looking at the ceiling, thinking suddenly of the morning after they were married, when she had first glimpsed the happiness that lay ahead. How strange to remember their quarrels and difficulties, and to know that they had all been caused by her own blindness and mistrust of him. Lehzen had done a lot of harm, she realized that, and she had been rather pleased to punish her by sending her away. Lehzen had delayed their happiness and when Victoria read her letters and knew that she was lonely it was no more than she deserved. It had been so easy to part with her; easy, too, to say good-bye to Melbourne. She really had been ridiculous in her opinion of him, but then she was very young. She had re-read some passages in her Journal in which she wrote of her dear Lord M. and declared passionately that no Minister could ever enjoy her confidence as he did. The memory of her old feelings made her so angry that she had disclaimed them in the margin, and with them all the ideas of her youth when pride and frivolity still guided her heart. Melbourne had passed out of her life like Lehzen; he might have been dead since he had suffered that stroke three years ago. She was quite embarrassed when she saw him afterwards, he seemed so aged and uncertain.

She turned and looked at Albert sleeping beside her, and covered his arm with the bedclothes. It was quite true to say she loved him better every day, for she was always discovering new things to love about him. He was such a fine musician — an organ had been installed at Windsor and he played most beautifully. She often heard him improvising when he was alone, and was only disturbed because the memories were always sad; he had such a keen artistic sense, a wonderful eye for colour and line which never hesitated to improve things, when she would have been lazy and left them alone. They had a lovely home of their own at Osborne now, a house built on the Isle of Wight, where Southampton

Water separated them from the intrusions of Ministers, with the most perfect gardens which Albert had laid out. He hated Buckingham Palace and now she disliked it too, and Windsor was too big and also too near London to give them the privacy they wanted.

The children were all very sweet and she didn't mind having them every year any longer. It was part of the joy of family life and if it was unpleasant for a few hours, she always recovered very quickly. The last two babies were particularly nice: the little Princess Alice and then Alfred . . . what a pity he was not the eldest and then Bertie needn't be the heir. Bertie was not quite as nice as the others, and she certainly didn't like him as much. He was a noisy child and even at his early age showed signs of temper and self-will that thoroughly alarmed her. He wasn't at all docile or pretty and she new instinctively that Albert was disappointed in him. And as she wrote to Uncle Leopold a few days after he was born, her most fervent wish for him was that he should grow up to resemble his perfect father in every possible way. It was annoying because Albert simply doted on their eldest daughter Pussy, and she would much rather he had loved his son, as fathers ought to do.

Yes, Bertie *was* naughty. And even if he was only four years old, he would have to be disciplined. She made up her mind to talk to Albert about it, and then decided not to, because it was her darling's birthday and she didn't want to spoil it by worrying him about the child. Bertie would be good like all the others in the end; he only needed training.

They had breakfast on the terrace, and the town choir came up the hill to serenade them. The Prince looked extremely well, she thought, suddenly realizing that in England he often seemed tired and had little colour. They sat for some time listening to the cheerful German songs and applauding heartily. Victoria laughed out loud at the continuous bows the choir director made towards them, and noticed that Albert smiled too. He didn't laugh loudly very often, but it was pure spite on the part of those who said he had no sense of humour.

'Victoria?'

'Yes, my dearest?'

He held out his hand towards her and stood up. 'Come with me; I want to show you the room where I was born.'

He opened the door for her and for a moment she stood on the threshold; it was a small room with a large bed in the centre and furniture in the Empire style, not very good furniture, because the German families had not been able to fill their houses with anything better than copies of the elegance which was so essentially French. It was full of sunlight, and yet the atmosphere was still as if the room were never used.

'Come to the window, there's a wonderful view.'

She stood side by side with him and he unfastened the catch; the sounds of the choir singing below floated up to them. There was the pine forest, dark and velvety in the distance, with a waterfall shining and splashing, competing with the artificial fountain in the garden, and the distant fields were brilliant patches of meadow saffron and red clover.

She leant her head against his shoulder and he slipped his arm round her. He was not nearly as shy as he used to be, when every gesture of affection seemed to come from her.

'It's the most perfect view I've ever seen,' she said. 'And this is the most perfect room, just because you were born here.'

'I've often wondered how my mother felt when she had to leave it. I've often wondered how she could have lived here in all this peace and beauty and still have done what she did.'

He had never mentioned his mother before; in all his reminiscences of his childhood, the stories of his father and his grandmother and Ernst, the Duchess Luise's name had been omitted as if she had never existed. He reached out and closed the window.

'Darling Albert,' she said tenderly, 'why talk about something sad today?'

'Because I've been thinking of her since we came here, and I've never told you about her. I would like to tell you, Victoria.'

'You don't have to,' she said quickly; all the happiness had gone out of his face, he looked so sad she longed to drag him out of the bright, stuffy room and down into the real sunlight.

'You don't have to tell me unless you really want to, because I know it was all most unhappy . . .'

'She was unfaithful to my father,' he said. He was staring out of the window, and the arm holding her had tightened. 'She fell in love with an officer; his name was Von Hanstein. She was denounced to my father and he divorced her. Do you know that she was much loved by the people, Victoria? There was a riot when they heard she was being sent away . . . I was only four years old, and I remember it because I had whooping cough. She came and said good-bye to Ernst and me, and she was crying. I believe she was very pretty; I know she was small, like you. I can see her now, standing there, holding a handkerchief to her face, and Ernst and I both crying because she had said good-bye.'

'Oh darling, darling Albert . . . how dreadful for you! And how *wicked* of her to do such a thing and have to leave you!'

He looked at her and saw that she was in tears, tears of anger and indignation because the picture of the child weeping for its mother had painted a picture of the man she loved in pain. She was overflowing with pity for him; she loved him and she was inherently good and strong and it was too much to expect that she should have perhaps pitied the pathetic, sinful little ghost . . .

'Don't think about it, Albert. Nothing like that can happen in our lives.'

'It happened to Ernst,' he reminded her quietly. 'You were so kind and understanding about that, and it gave me the strength to help him. But her nature came out in him, just the same. Stockmar used to warn me about it when I was a boy. 'Your blood is tainted, you must always be on your guard.'

'But, dearest love,' Victoria exclaimed, 'you have nothing to fear — no man ever lived who was purer and nobler than you!'

'I've tried to be,' he said. 'I only pray to God that you will be able to say those words at the end of my life as you do now.'

'I will always be able to say them! Always!'

'I've known what immorality means,' he went on. 'That's why I said to you long ago that your Court must be an example and that nobody should approach you with a stain on their character. I remember Melbourne saying you couldn't lay down a rule like that because of the people you'd offend.'

'Lord M. had no moral sense himself,' Victoria said. 'But I understood what you meant and I entirely agreed then as I do now. Darling Albert, what's troubling you now? You've been so happy since we came here, and today is your birthday and it's the one day I want you to be happy all the time. Come out of this room, and let us listen to the choir outside.'

'If I lived to see one of the children growing up like my mother or like Ernst, it would kill me, Victoria. I could not bear it.'

'Our children will be like *you*, so how could they do anything wrong? We can keep a close watch on them and have them brought up in the best possible way. I don't think such a thing could happen for a minute! Now, darling, please come downstairs. And promise me you will forget this little room and all these unhappy things and enjoy your birthday? Please, Albert?'

He bent and kissed her forehead.

'I will, my dearest. We'll go down now.'

They were very gay for the rest of the day and in the

evening he took her to the forest where he had wandered as a child, and they walked hand in hand until it was time to return for dinner. He said nothing more about the Duchess Luise and his fear that her moral lapse might be repeated, but Victoria felt sure ever afterwards that when he talked of their children, he was thinking of their wayward little eldest son.

The England they had left was comparatively calm; Peel, now the trusted friend of his sovereign, had assured them that the disturbances in Ireland had died down and there had been few manifestations of industrial discontent. The Queen and her husband could enjoy their holiday with an easy mind. While Albert and Victoria picked flowers in the woods round the Rosenau, and sang German songs together around Duke Ernst's piano in the evenings, the skies above the British Isles were dark with rain clouds. It was the wettest year in living memory; the rain poured in a continuous grey sheet, and still the clouds rolled forward over the Atlantic like an invading army, and emptied themselves over the fields of England and Ireland. The corn lay flattened and soaking in seas of mud; the landowners cursed and declared themselves ruined and everyone said that the price of bread would rise.

In Ireland there was little corn; the people's principal food was potatoes, dug up from their own sparse patches of ground. Price bore no relation to their problem; the potato crop was ruined, rotting under the soaking earth, and the semi-starvation of Ireland's eight million inhabitants plummeted to stark famine.

That was the word which Peel used to Victoria when he came to tell her of the situation. They were at Buckingham Palace, because it was impossible for Ministers to make the journey down to the coast and cross Southampton Water to the seclusion of Osborne House in the middle of the crisis; the Queen had to be in London, or Windsor, and Albert, who loved Osborne even more than she did, soothed her irritation at this restriction.

Peel looked very drawn; he was a bad colour which accentuated the rings under his eyes. He looked as if he had hardly slept at all. He was no longer shy of the Queen and no longer abrupt and clumsy because he dreaded being compared to his polished predecessor and found wanting. She trusted him, and in her own inimitable way, Victoria had let him know that she neither expected nor wished for another Melbourne.

'Famine, Sir Robert? What a terrible word to use!'

'I'm afraid no other will do, Ma'am,' he answered. 'The people are falling by the roads from starvation and dying where they fall. And I tell you frankly that I lie awake thinking how close our own people are to the plight of the Irish.'

'We don't depend upon potatoes, thank God,' the Queen said quickly. 'We should have a sufficient stock of corn to meet our own needs.'

'I wouldn't gamble on it,' Peel said. 'I couldn't, in all conscience. Holland and Belgium and Norway have suffered just as we have; their potato crop is ruined and they're opening their ports to foreign corn. Ma'am — that's what we must do, now, before it's too late!'

Victoria looked at him.

'If we open the ports now, Sir Robert, they can never be closed again. This must inevitably lead to repealing the Corn Laws.'

He was always amazed by her grasp of a point; her mind cut through side issues with masculine directness, and however much she owed to the advice of Albert, that gift was entirely her own.

'I don't see any other way, Ma'am,' he said. 'After this disaster, we must consider the good of the majority of your subjects; the landowners must give up their monopoly and allow cheap food to come into the country.'

'Do you really think the Tory Party will support you, Sir Robert? The Whigs fell on this issue, and nobody has felt strong enough to carry it through the House.'

189

'We weren't on the edge of starvation then,' he exclaimed. 'I was as cautious as anybody until this happened. They can't see the plight of the Irish and risk similar conditions here!'

'I know Albert would agree that the Laws should be repealed,' Victoria said, 'and I shall certainly support you in whatever you do. After all, Ireland is mainly agricultural and their standards are far lower than ours – the people are better able to sustain a famine than we would be.'

'However low their standards are, Ma'am,' Peel said grimly, 'you can't imagine their misery; we shall have to help the distress in every way we can.'

She clasped her hands in her lap and said firmly, 'You can't expect me to feel too much sympathy for the Irish, Sir Robert. They're a source of endless trouble to us, and while I agree that the people's sufferings must be relieved, I insist that nothing is done to jeopardize our own position for a moment! Ireland really deserves no help at all, considering her disloyalty and ingratitude to this country!'

He met the cold blue eyes, pitiless with prejudice against the most rebellious of her subjects, and glanced away. He knew that the Queen disliked the Irish, that the rare visits she had made there had only intensified her antipathy to a country that was Papist, poverty stricken, and determined to resist the benefit of English rule. There was no place in her orderly, Teutonic scheme of things for that wild, romantic, inconsistent race.

'A Relief Fund is being set up,' he said at last. 'We hope to collect a large sum of money from private contributions as well as official aid.'

'I very much doubt whether anyone who has either been to Ireland or knows anything about it, will give very much,' Victoria remarked.

Peel coughed. Though he admired her, and had come to value her friendship almost as much as Melbourne had done, there were times when he recoiled from the callousness he was seeing then.

Albert the foreigner, with his ideals and high-minded approach to life, possessed more human sympathy that this small woman who discussed so much suffering with an indifference worthy of Melbourne at his worst.

'That is quite true,' he said. 'And that's why if you were to set the example, Ma'am . . . I know it would establish the Fund.'

'Are you suggesting that I should give money, Sir Robert?'

'For the women and children, Ma'am,' he said desperately. She had four children of her own; surely to God, her heart could soften a little . . .

'Mothers are being found dead with their babies at the breast — they're eating dirt!'

He forbore to add that in some districts there were reports of cannibalism . . . 'Whatever your feelings about Ireland politically, Ma'am, I do beg you to make a donation.'

'I find it difficult to see why I should,' she answered. 'After all, Sir Robert, I am the Crown, and it might appear that we were seeking their favour if I make a public gesture, and that would never do!'

'Believe me,' he urged, 'believe me, no one in that unhappy country is concerned with politics at this moment!'

'Then it will be for the first time for six hundred years,' she retorted. 'No, Sir Robert, I shan't promise anything till I've thought about it.'

'Speak to the Prince,' Peel suggested, 'and let me know your decision. But the gift must be made public if it's to have any value. I assure you, the Irish will respond whole-heartedly to any act of kindness from you; or indeed from England. If we help Ireland now and prove the value of English sovereignty, the whole Irish question may be resolved for good!'

'Nothing would please me more,' Victoria said. 'I assure *you*, Sir Robert, I am sick to death of the troubles we have with that miserable country. And I do advise you not to let sentiment for them influence you too much. I can foresee a lot of difficulty for you over the Corn Laws here, without stretching your supporters' patience further on behalf of Ireland.'

Christmas passed with all the Germanic festivities of trees and carol-singing which the Queen's example had made popular, and in the early months of the new year the mass of the people came a little closer to starvation; there were riots in the industrial towns and talk of revolution; in Ireland the dead were tumbled into hastily dug pits and covered over, and the hard core of the Tory Party began to consolidate under the nominal leadership of Lord George Bentinck to oppose Peel's abolition of the Corn Laws. They had rejected his proposal to open the ports to cheap foreign corn, and, as the split widened in his party, Peel gave his resignation to the Queen. However, the Whigs were unable to form a Government, bedeviled as usual by strife among themselves, and Sir Robert remained in office.

There was no alternative but to face the issue of the Corn Laws in the House; not to do so would be to risk plunging England into the horror of famine which was creeping over Ireland. There was no doubt in Peel's mind; the sentiments about humanity and duty which rolled so glibly of most politicians' tongues were deeply rooted in his heart. Beneath his cold and stiff exterior there existed a genuine love and a genuine pity for the suffering inarticulate masses, and a sense of responsibility towards them which was sadly lacking in his nobler born compatriots. Food must be brought into the country, and food must be sent to the Irish, whether the wealthy landowners' profits suffered from the competition or not.

He knew a faction was gathering against him, under Bentinck's leadership; he also knew that the men whose interests would suffer by the repeal of the Laws were among his oldest friends and most loyal supporters of his party and that they had taken it for granted that his primary duty was to them.

It was a hard choice and it carried the danger his shrewd

sovereign had mentioned – political disaster to himself. But in the summer of that year the Act to remove the Corn Laws was introduced into the House of Commons.

The Whigs approved and were prepared to vote for it; the Radicals backed the motion and it was assumed that those opposing him within the Tory Party would either change their minds or prove a very small minority. But behind the unimpressive figure of George Bentinck there darted a new personality, a quick-moving, satin-tongued Jewish politician named Benjamin Disraeli whose sympathies were wholly Protectionist and Imperialist. He was also known as a master of verbal castigation and a brilliant intellectual; his undoubted abilities had erased much of the prejudice against his race and his early flamboyance of dress and manner were now subdued. Nine years before, the young Disraeli's maiden speech in the House had been drowned in a chorus of catcalls and laughter, but now when he rose to speak there was an expectant silence. He was known to be a dangerous man and Peel had never liked or understood him; in the summer months of 1846 it was he who rallied the Protectionists under Bentinck's leadership and plotted the downfall of Sir Robert Peel.

Peel had betrayed his trust; nothing could stop the Corn Laws being abolished and the country abandoning its ancient policy of agricultural insularity in favour of industrialism and the perils of Free Trade. But the man who had revoked his Tory principles would pay for it with the ruin of his political career. That was Disraeli's intention and he found a host of supporters; it was also his intention to dispose of the most serious rival to his own ambition, which was eventually to assume the Party leadership himself. That night in August the House was packed for the debate; the atmosphere was stifling with heat and tension as speaker after speaker rose from the Government Benches to oppose the Prime Minister. When Disraeli stood and, in the bitterest phrases of mockery and reproach, attacked the Bill, Peel sat quite motionless, staring ahead of him with his arms folded. There was a move to save him, made by the powerful Duke of Buckingham and Chandos, and there were cheers from the Treasury Bench. But when the vote was taken there was a moment's hesitation; for the first time Peel looked up, and as he watched, the first members of his party moved forward to the hostile Lobby. Eighty Protectionists filed in to vote with Whigs and Independents, men, as Disraeli afterwards noted, who were not only Peel's colleagues but his friends. When the House rose, the Corn Laws were repealed by a small majority, but the political career of Peel was finished.

He travelled to Osborne, and there Victoria and Albert received him, and the Queen accepted his resignation. She was distressed and indignant to learn of the harsh words used against him in that fateful debate; she was heart-broken at losing him, she said, and the tears were in her eyes as he bent to kiss her hand for the last time. It was so awful, she said passionately to Albert, when the door had closed on him, to have the Whigs in power again when she had got so used to Sir Robert and worked with him so well.

As Peel stepped into the shadows another figure, long living in the twilight, stirred expectantly. The old man idling his days away at Brocket, living on memories of his last visit to the Queen at Windsor, watched the windows for the messenger from London calling him back into office with the new Whig Government, perhaps even to lead it . . . But Melbourne waited in vain; Lord John Russell formed his Cabinet and presented it to the Queen for her approval, and the name of her old favourite was not mentioned by either of them. He had had a stroke, his memory was impaired, he had a disconcerting trick of talking to himself in public; the last time Victoria had seen him she had been forced to rebuke the old man firmly for criticizing Peel. She approved Lord John's Cabinet list, and no message disturbed the peace of Brocket.

Slowly Melbourne's resurgence of hope died, and with

it the last of his attachment to life; his books were unopened, his treatise unwritten, and his mind, if not his body, moved faster in the direction of the grave.

'Ah, my dear Russell! What a splendid morning! But then all mornings are splendid when one's in office, eh?' Palmerston grinned down at the new Prime Minister. He was standing by the window looking out on to Downing Street with both thumbs hooked into his waistcoat; he had an almost proprietary air, as if he had just vacated the Premier's seat to let his old friend rest in it for a moment. Russell did not smile in return. He frowned and tapped his paper-knife on the edge of his desk.

'I've a great deal to discuss with you,' he said, 'and the weather isn't included. Nobody doubts your enjoyment of office, my dear Henry, but considering the state everything's in, our term is likely to be short, so we'd better make the most of it!'

'Short?' Palmerston raised his eyebrows, and the bright blue eyes twinkled. 'Nonsense! The Tories are split down the middle like a rotten apple, and thanks to our friend Mr Disraeli, Peel won't be able to put it together again. Thank God for the Jews — I've always maintained they're a splendid race — and nobody could possibly take that ass Bentinck seriously, so I really don't see who's to turn us out? Come, come, don't be such a pessimist, man; and stop tapping that paper-knife like an old schoolmaster!'

Russell's lips tightened. He really sympathized with the Queen in her dislike of Palmerston; he would have been only too pleased to dispense with him if there had been anyone else in the Whig administration with his experience and flair for Foreign Affairs. He had spent a most uncomfortable morning explaining to Her Majesty that though Lord Palmerston was objectionable to her, he must beg her indulgence because he simply couldn't be done without in the new Government.

'If you underestimate the Tories, I do not. I'd be obliged,

my dear Henry, if you can tear yourself away from the window and settle to some business.'

'By all means. Let me salute the faithful onlookers below on your behalf — you really ought to show yourself, it's you they've come to see, not me, you know.'

He waved cheerfully to the straggling sightseers below, and was rewarded with a cheer.

'If never hurts to be popular,' he observed gaily. 'We're only the servants of the people, after all.'

'I've never found it necessary to be approved by my inferiors,' Russell snapped.

'That's where we differ,' Palmerston pointed out. 'It's the opinion of my equals which is unimportant to me. Now then, to business, to business,' and he clapped Russell affectionately on the shoulder.

'Henry,' Russell looked at him, 'Henry, this is not the time to make jokes: I want you to be serious and listen and, if you can't be serious, then for God's sake be quiet!'

'Two very hard things to ask of an Irishman,' Palmerston retorted, 'but I'll try.'

'The situation in Ireland is getting worse; the second potato crop has failed, and the landlords have begun evicting because the peasants can't pay rents or work the land. The refugees are crossing to Liverpool in hundreds, and they're bringing typhus and cholera with them. In Ireland there's no food, no agricultural implements, and no one who knows how to use them if there were any. There's no work we can put them to, no system of wages, and the workhouses haven't the room or the food to cope with the thousands besieging them. The famine is growing, not lessening, and God knows how we're going to begin to get it under control.'

'We can import cheap food and supply them,' Palmerston said.

'There's a limit to what the Exchequer can afford,' Russell answered. 'We need most of it to keep our own people from down-right hunger. The best we can do is not enough, now that the second crop has failed. Have you any idea how difficult it is to organize a people like that? Teach them to grow wheat − sow against the winter harvest . . . Do you realize, Henry, that the only implement the wretches have ever seen is a spade, the only thing they know about the earth is how to plant potatoes and dig them up again? We send food there − very well, but how is it distributed? What do you do in a country where there are no shops, where the villages are just a few hovels built out of turf and slate, where bread and sugar and coal and candles are unknown! How do you stop disease when the people are leaving their homes in droves and carrying pestilence from one end of Ireland to the other? I said all this to the Queen today, I told her it would need a miracle if the whole population were not to be wiped out.'

'And what did Her Majesty say? ' Palmerston asked. 'I imagine some pearl of wisdom fell from our Prince's lips, at least.'

'His attitude was more humane than hers,' Russell said gloomily. 'I suppose it's too much to expect a woman to visualize such things; I'm beginning to believe Marie Antoinette really suggested the French people should eat cake!'

'Her Majesty's excellent Uncle Cambridge recommended grass,' Palmerston remarked. 'I hear that the idea was not appreciated in Irish circles. I don't think you need expect much understanding from the Queen, my dear Russell. Women are not only unimaginative, they're extremely unfeeling. However, I've no doubt the Prince will suggest building a Library or a Museum so that at least the Irish can perish in an atmosphere of culture.'

'The Prince is a foreigner,' Russell said. 'What's the use of pillorying him, when you know the Queen looks on his word as law?'

'I don't have to share her view,' Palmerston said promptly. 'I find his artistic airs as irritating as you find my levity, except that I don't try to form our Foreign Policy on my jokes. The Queen, God bless her, is the Queen, and one must overlook her little foibles. I'm damned sure they'd be less tiresome if they didn't emanate from him!'

'If you are going to antagonize the Queen,' Russell said coldly, 'our Administration will fall in a few months. That's one thing I must make clear to you from the first. She dislikes you, Henry, and I can't say I'm surprised.'

'I don't see why she should,' Palmerston grinned. 'I'm a kind, fatherly old man, and Melbourne set a marvellous precedent for middle age!'

'She's devoted to the Prince, and making fun of him behind his back and provoking him to his face isn't the way to endear yourself to her. And I shall have to bear the brunt of her displeasure. Once and for all, Henry, tread carefully with the Court.'

'My dear Russell, I shall be the soul of tact,' he promised. 'I'll even offer to give His Royal Highness English lessons to get rid of that damned Coburg accent, if you think it will help. Besides, my province is Foreign Affairs, and I can't see why there should be any conflict between the Queen and myself so long as I'm not interfered with; the Queen requires lip service — she shall have it! I'll reign in the Foreign Office, subject to yourself, of course, and Her Majesty and her noble Consort can meddle with every other Government office with my blessing! Now you've delivered your lecture; what else is there?'

'Grey is at the Colonial Office,' Russell said. 'I'd be obliged if you'd refrain from quarrelling with him.'

Palmerston laughed. 'Good God, what a list! Don't antagonize the Queen or the noble Prince — same thing, according to you — and don't quarrel with Grey! My dear Russell, I've always quarrelled with Grey, it's part of the fun of life. You're drawing up a terribly dull programme for me, aren't you?'

'The bickering between you nearly brought Melbourne down several times,' Russell said acidly. 'I don't intend to lose office because you two can't control your dislike. I repeat, don't provoke Grey; he has a powerful following and if he resigns, we go out of office.'

'That's a point,' Palmerston said cheerfully. 'The devil of it is, Grey's always threatening to resign, and I always feel it'd be such a boon if only he would! However, I'll bear with him. Palmerston the Peacemaker! You can count on me, my dear fellow. By the way, I hope you and Lady John will dine with us next week. Emily has persuaded Melbourne to leave Brocket for a few days and stay with us – she's a very devoted sister, you know, and it would cheer the poor fellow to see a few friends and feel in the swim of things.'

'We shall be delighted; it really distresses me to see how feeble he's become. I must say, Henry, you're very good to him.'

'Emily worries about him,' Palmerston explained. 'And naturally I'd do anything for Emily. Besides, I remember the days when every man with political ambitions in London used to besiege him, myself among them. He was the best conversationalist I ever met in my life. But if you'll make a show of asking his opinion and talk about the Queen, he'll live off it for weeks. He badgers everyone he sees for news of her; she's all he really wants to talk about.'

'She could invite him more often, now,' Russell said. 'It was difficult while the Tories were in power, but perhaps now . . .'

Palmerston smiled cynically.

'He's partly paralysed and deaf, and his mind wanders. We're his old colleagues, Russell; we'll find time for him somehow, but I doubt if Her Majesty would be amused any longer. She has all the virtues, but a soft heart isn't among them. I saw a crowd of hopefuls waiting in the rooms outside, so I'll be off. The sweets of office, my dear Russell – you're every man's friend while it lasts!'

The months went by and the new Government established itself as firmly as a small majority would allow. The problem of Ireland overshadowed everything throughout that year.

Work began on a system of roads, to give employment

to the starving, homeless people, but it was insufficient for the numbers in need, and the wages were too low. Murder and robbery followed in the wake of famine and disease; the countryside was ravaged by bands of thieves. The landlords applied their own remedies to the stricken people, while the Government considered one measure after another for relieving the distress, and the different factions in Parliament bickered over which methods should be used.

Ireland was over-populated and under-developed; the land was divided and sub-divided between families until as many as eight or ten people were living off the produce of a quarter acre, and the only crop was the potato.

The landowners' solution was wholesale eviction. Bailiffs began turning tenants out of their shacks; in the case of those who refused to go or were too weak to gather their belongings and take to the road, the houses were pulled down over their heads, and the livestock driven off. The landowners cleared their estates ruthlessly of the sick and faltering population, who could neither cultivate nor pay the rents, and a mass of homeless starving men and women began their trek to the ports and the emigrant ships. There was no food in Ireland, no work and no shelter; for a few pounds, often donated by relatives living in America, families could sail for the New World and begin a fresh life. The Laws of Correction instituted by the English Government were putting down the lawlessness and terror, but they were forcing able-bodied men into the workhouse and separating the fanatically close Irish families: what had begun as a measure of mercy and assistance became an oppression.

Thousands of emigrants set sail that year and in the year that followed, crossing the Atlantic in ships so unseaworthy that many floundered in the first storm, and in conditions of such squalor and brutality that men who had sailed in the old slave ships pronounced the emigrant voyages far worse. Shippers and agents made fortunes out of the exodus; the traffic was so shameless that emigrants' fares were accepted, and the passengers thrown overboard to ease the overcrowding when the vessels had left harbour. Battened beneath the holds, plague and scurvy and starvation raged among the living cargo, and a high proportion were found to have died on arrival. Protests were made in the House of Commons. There were attempts from some of the more eccentric English peers to stop the evictions and supervise the emigrant traffic, and in the comfortable isolation of Osborne House, Victoria read the newspapers and asked Albert angrily if people had nothing better to do than criticise the sensible course which the Government was taking. It was too irritating to be worried about Ireland and at the trouble that wretched people had brought upon themselves, when her darling Albert had been made Chancellor of Cambridge University.

She was no longer so jealous of intellectual interests which were beyond her; she had long accepted, indeed embraced, the idea that Albert was infinitely more clever and artistic, and his success in the election for Chancellor delighted Victoria more than any honour they could have shown her personally. He was so interested in theology and physics and architecture and the classics; they were all quite beyond her appreciation, and because she was so stupid, she found them rather dull, but he understood everything, and the Chancellorship proved that at last her ungrateful people were beginning to see how brilliantly clever he was. She was overjoyed, and her generous enthusiasm glossed over the sneers and hostility of some of the Press and most of the university dons.

The post was honourary; nobody had expected the Prince to take it seriously or to interfere with the ancient scholarship of the university. When he explained in surprise to Victoria that such subjects as modern and oriental languages, metaphysics, geography and political economy were excluded, she said promptly that he must insist on them being taught at once. But experience, and the strong hand of Stockmar, had made Albert cautious. The changes were introduced with such tact that it was hardly noticed that the Prince was responsible, and when Victoria complained that he received no credit he calmed her by pointing out that he had achieved his object and was satisfied. That should have been true; he should have been proof against the human weakness which longed to be acknowledged, and not suffered any hurt. But he was hurt. He was hurt continuously by the knowledge that, though a few men like Peel and Anson and the ageing Duke of Wellington thought well of him, the majority of all classes did not. He had never won the liking of the aristocracy. The more he indulged his taste for music, drew up plans for public buildings, encouraged foreign artists to visit the Court, the more hostile they became. He played the piano well and the organ superbly; these accomplishments did not endear him to the class who adhered to the view of Lord Chesterfield that, while it was permissible to hire a fiddler if one loved music, it was unthinkable that a gentleman should play himself.

His political advice was listened to and sometimes followed but only because it became the Queen's and her views could hardly be defied. Working with Sir Robert Peel had been deeply satisfying; for the first time he had begun to feel useful on his own account. But he found Lord John Russell very different. He was reserved, morose, and inclined to be sharp; he gave the impression that Albert's tactfully worded suggestions were trying his patience but that he was determined to humour him if possible. He was extraordinarily narrow in outlook; his prejudices were almost as strong as Victoria's, and his tastes far removed from the water colours and porcelain views and Landseer paintings which brought such warm feelings to the heart of the Queen and her husband when they admired them together. He was a cold man, in whom there was no soft-hued sentiment, only a hard core of honour and duty and loyalty to the Crown, and a fiercely intellectual belief in the principles of liberal reform. But if the business of governing with Russell was disappointing and uninspiring to Victoria and Albert, dealing with Lord Palmerston in the Foreign Office was a nightmare.

The rumblings of revolution, never wholly subdued since the uprising of the French people in 1792, burst out with a roar in Italy, where the Austrian Empire had to maintain its sovereignty with a force of 75,000 men; and the pamphlets written by Robespierre and Marat were again circulating among the Parisian artisans. Discontent was rising all over Europe, in countries held in bondage by stronger alien powers, and among the mass of the people whose cry for justice and reform had not been satisfied. The decaying Bourbon dynasty had crumbled, leaving Louis Philippe, son of the Duc d'Orléans who had voted for Louis XVI's execution and died on the guillotine himself, to sit uneasily on the throne of his ancestors, with the title of King of the French. The middle-class monarch carried the stain of his father's treachery; he was suspect by Victoria, who detested false humility in a sovereign, and disliked by Albert who was sure he would yield to temptation and try to re-establish France as a great power.

But though he was a feeble figure, he represented the only bulwark against the mighty faction in France who were agitating for a Republic, and no one supported the rights of other monarchs more jealously than Victoria. However unworthy, tyrannical or imbecile a King might be, the security of all Royal dynasties depended on the safety of each individual throne. To the fury and amazement of the Queen and Albert, Lord Palmerston made it plain that he did not share this view. While his allegiance to the English Crown was unquestioned, he only expressed contempt for the ridiculous monarch of France, hatred of the Russian despot, and complete unconcern over the fate of the rulers of Portugal and Spain. To the delight of the English people and the embarrassment of his Prime Minister, he loudly sympathized with the demand of Europe's people for freedom of speech and republican government if they wanted it. The tone of despatches abroad was full of encouragement for Liberal movements and condemnation of reaction; in an attempt to control him, the Queen supervised every paper and telegram before it was sent, only to discover that her Foreign Minister had blandly altered them to suit himself, or even neglected to submit them at all. The atmosphere between the Court and the Cabinet became so frosty that Russell dreaded every interview, but hints and outright orders to Palmerston were cheerfully ignored. His policy reflected popular opinion, he retorted, and while he respected the concern of Her Majesty for her fellow sovereigns, some of whom were relatives, it was England's duty to point out to them the error of their ways. England had survived the clamour for reform by granting it, as these idiots abroad refused to do; England had added Australia and Ceylon to her possessions, and kept Canada, while Austria and Russia were forced to use their armies to hold down what they had. Feudalism and the Divine Right were precepts of the past; it was inviting disaster to try and impose them, and besides, it was immoral. While the Irish died of starvation in their thousands, the House of Commons cheered these sentiments, and indulged in the national pastime of patronizing and admonishing the foreigner. The champion of this attitude was strongly emerging in the person of that Irishman who was more English than the native race themselves, Lord Palmerston. And pitted against him, and all that he represented, was the ambition of Stockmar, the policies of Albert, and the pride of Victoria. A long and bitter struggle between the Crown and the Constitution had begun.

9

The bedroom at Brocket was very quiet, with the strange stillness that follows after convulsions of human sickness and despair. The November wind had stripped the last leaves off the trees outside the window. It was nearly dark, and two candles had been lit close to the canopied bed; they shed a kind light on the pale sunken features of the man lying propped up on the pillows. His hair was completely white, and the skin had drawn back, showing the prominence of a fine forehead and the high-bridged nose, but the lips were blue and the breath came faintly between them.

Only the gleam under his half-closed eyelids showed that life and intelligence remained. For two days Melbourne had lain there, tortured by convulsive fits, his mind and body racked with pain, and now at last a blessed calm had come to him. The ghosts had left him; the bloody phantoms of the Chartists rioters, the gaunt and manacled creatures who had gone to life deportation in Australia at his order, had faded out of sight, and with them went the shadows of his enemy, the people, bent under an intolerable burden of labour and starvation which he had done nothing to relieve.

His mistresses had flitted through the twilight of self-judgment, and a small, graceful figure had detached itself and run towards him, mocking, laughing, mad, and he had writhed and croaked her name. Caroline. Caroline. The idiot son she had borne him joined her, and turned into Caroline Norton, weeping because she was disgraced and separated from her children. His friends and enemies came to him too,

205

and he heard the applause of the House and the cries of dissent, and wrestled for a speech that would not come . . .

He saw his proud, ambitious mother, forever urging him to action and beside her a nightmare figure of himself, reclining in inertia because he knew he lacked the courage to fight for himself and the heart to fight for others. And then another came out of the hobgoblin creation of his mind, gliding as gracefully as a swan, dressed in riding habit of Windsor green, and asked in a high voice whether he were coming for a canter in the Castle Great Park. Victoria. He tried to speak her name but the power of speech was gone; but with her the darkness and the pain receded. She waltzed with him, resplendent in diamonds, and he heard her laugh at something he had said. She wept because he was leaving her, and the tears seeped under his eyelids and ran down his sunken cheeks. The room was full of light and music and he was standing by her, and the wealth and splendour of Windsor and Buckingham Palace were all intermingled in the background. She turned to him and smiled, wearing the heavy Crown of St Edward, and the mighty anthem pealed out in triumph as he followed down the nave of the Abbey. And then inexorably she began to fade, and he shivered, feeling the cold evening breeze that swept the Terrace at Windsor, as he walked down it into retirement from office and out of her life.

The lights and the visions dimmed and blurred, and he lay still at last. When he opened his eyes he recognized the bedroom at Brocket, and saw that the woman standing by his bed, holding his hand and crying, was his sister, Emily Palmerston. They had been very good to him − all his family; his younger brother and sister-in-law, and dear Emily. They had looked after his household and rescued him from debt when it appeared that he had overspent in the distracted, empty years after his stroke. Such a vacuum those years had been, living long after he should have been dead, while other men governed and did what he had never done. He had been useless and unwanted for so long; what a relief to slide into oblivion, beyond the pain of regret and disillusion. And to be able to admit that she had forgotten him and hardly mind. He had served her well; that was to his credit. He had saved her marriage and helped her to happiness, and if she had neglected and forgotten him in his decline, what did it matter now? Nothing mattered, except rest. He tried to squeeze Emily's hand to show her he was grateful and that she was not to cry, but the effort was too much for him. He lapsed into a coma, and thirty-six hours afterwards, he died.

'I have been talking to Stockmar, my dear, and I feel I must tell you that he's very worried.'

Victoria looked up from her embroidery. They were sitting in their private room at Osborne, their own sanctuary from the cold, grandiose palaces, and she had been sewing happily by the fire after dinner. Life was as informal as possible when there were no Ministers or guests to entertain, and nothing relaxed her more after a day spent studying State papers and writing her endless correspondence, than to come to the pretty room with its comfortable furniture and the lovely Landseer picture of the stag, and rest alone with Albert. Albert had designed the house and chosen the furniture; she loved the rich mahogany and the table covered with miniatures of the family and porcelain views. As he said, it was their own, real home.

'Worried? Oh, Albert, dearest, what about?'

The Prince sat forward and sighed. She noticed tenderly that the hair on top of his head was thinning. It was rather early, but then he worked so hard, the darling, and he was so tired, even at Osborne.

'He's worried about Bertie. And so am I.'

Victoria's expression changed at the mention of her seven-year-old eldest son.

'Tell me,' she said.

'Stockmar's been watching his progress,' Albert said. 'He's so conscientious, so devoted to us, I don't know what we'd do without him – and he thinks the boy's undisciplined. He thinks his character isn't developing well.'

Victoria put her sewing on one side.

'He's certainly less intelligent than the others. And I must say I don't like his nature *quite* as much. But what did the Baron say about him?'

'He said he's frivolous. He said he's much too spoilt and self-willed and that all he seems to want to do is play. He's been looking into his studies and he says his progress is disgracefully slow. He has no application at all!'

Victoria frowned. What was the Royal governess, Lady Lyttelton, doing, that she had said nothing about this? There were three governesses in the nursery, French, German and English, chosen by Stockmar, of course, who knew everything about children since he had practically brought up Albert. And now it was discovered that Bertie wasn't working properly.

'I must say I'm surprised,' she said. 'You know, dearest, I take the closest interest in all our children do, and especially Bertie because he's my heir, but I never received a report from Lady Lyttelton or I should have done something about it!'

'I mentioned that to Stockmar,' Albert answered, 'and he said she indulges the boy too much. He says she's over-affectionate to him, and that's not good for him at all. I think he's right; women are too sentimental with children. What Bertie needs is a tutor.'

'And a proper rule of conduct for every day,' Victoria interposed. 'If he's frivolous, then the best way to cure him is to remove the opportunity. I think a tutor is an excellent idea. I shall certainly let Lady Lyttelton know that Bertie isn't to be pampered in the meantime!'

Really, he was a tiresome child. It infuriated her to see dear Albert looking anxious and disappointed on account of the wretched boy. Why couldn't he have been studious and clever like Pussy – he didn't even look like his father, which was annoying, and whenever he was with them she always felt a sense of strain and irritation. He laughed too loudly, and when he was reproved he had a trick of bursting into tears and hanging his head so that she could have shaken him. He wasn't neat and orderly like the other children, even the smallest; he seemed to do everything in a hurry, to run out to play, to fall over and dirty himself, to eat too many sweet things and be sick. He was really unattractive, and now it seemed he was stupid as well. Everyone said he was a handsome little boy, but she had looked in vain for any trace of Albert's beauty; all she saw was the blue eyes and strong little features of her own Hanoverian ancestors, and the fear was growing in her that he resembled them in character as well as looks.

That was what Stockmar suspected, and her darling was sitting there worrying because he was mistaking it for the weakness in his own family. She could never forget his anguish in that room at Rosenau, and his admission that he couldn't bear it if one of their children should turn out like his mother or Ernst. Ernst was still behaving badly; his wife lived in separate rooms and bore with his conduct as best she could, poor thing, and Albert was so distressed about that too. How miserable for him not to feel pleased with his eldest son . . . it was bad enough that so many people in England showed him hostility, the newspapers were always ready to criticize him, and she knew that he was unpopular with the Court. He had done *everything* he could to ingratiate himself, worked long hours helping her with State papers, studied every despatch and memorandum, and come forward with a sound solution for all England's problems from agriculture to Foreign Policy, and she knew, with intense disappointment, that his efforts were not appreciated but actually resented.

In that moment, her anger with her Ministers and her people concentrated into a furious dislike of her eldest son. The others were out of reach; she could not make them love Albert, or alter them to please him, but no child of seven was going to grow up into a man displeasing to his father.

209

She came over and knelt beside his chair, and held his hand in both her own.

'Dearest love,' she said, 'if Bertie is going to be King, then I want him to be and do what you think he should. That was my greatest hope when he was born — that England would one day have a ruler just like you. That is what we must make him, and I promise you, I'll support you in everything. You and Stockmar must take Bertie in hand before he grows any older. We shall engage a tutor for him immediately, and you must lay down the rules for his education and upbringing. Then I *know* he will be a credit to us.'

'He must be,' Albert said. 'I've felt all along he wasn't like the other children. Stockmar's right; he's lazy and light-minded. And, dearest, I used to be the same. Oh, yes, I had no real ambition, I was afraid of responsibility and my will was deplorably weak. But Stockmar trained me. He taught me to discipline my mind and body, he made me what I am. And what he did for me I can do for Bertie. I've discussed a tutor with him, and he suggested someone called Henry Birch. He's the rector of Prestwich, he took high honours at Cambridge, and he was a master at Eton for four years. I think he'd be the right man, if you agree.'

'Of course I agree,' Victoria said. 'From this moment, Bertie is in your hands, my darling.'

At seven years old, childhood was at an end for Prince Albert Edward.

Stockmar viewed the new tutor with approval, and therefore Albert liked him. Nothing more was needed to ensure that Victoria sanctioned his appointment. He was a quiet, scholarly man, immensely learned, with a firm yet deferential manner that the Queen and the Prince found most agreeable. He listened to the parental opinion of his charge. When Albert described the boy as obstinate, lazy and undisciplined, he only nodded. When he read the curriculum drawn up by the Baron and the Prince, he glanced quickly at Victoria, and then decided that any protest would be useless. He said he hoped to bring up His Royal Highness to their entire satisfaction, and then went to the nursery to meet his pupil.

Stockmar had taken great pains with the schedule. He had sat up late, pondering the problem of a child who preferred play to study and the company of other boys to sober walks with his parents or talks with the Baron. He was unaware that jealousy of the little Prince was mixed with his concern. He also had nothing in common with Albert's exuberant son; noise and high spirits repelled him; so did the attempts to show affection when the child tried to climb on his knee. His one love was Albert, Albert moulded, almost created by him; his one pride was Albert, who now worked harder than any Minister of the Crown, who was diligent, painstaking and guided by Stockmar's deity, logic. He had transformed the gentle sentimental youth into a man of vision, the power behind the English throne. He had guided him in his struggle with Victoria and had shown him how to win; he had advised him how to advance himself and yet keep in the background, how to separate her from influences like Melbourne and incline her away from the Whigs, with their dangerous Liberal policies. He had fulfilled every dream cherished by Leopold for bringing England under Coburg domination through the medium of Albert, until he knew that in many ways Albert was virtually King. But his power depended upon the life of Victoria; without Victoria he was nothing, merely a Regent for his son. And the son would never be worthy of his father's place; the son had no right to inherit, compared to the natural right of Albert . . . No, Stockmar would never make friends with the boy, or tolerate signs of individuality. If the young Prince disliked his lessons, then he must study more and more until he learnt to like them. All minds succumbed to discipline in the end. If he was to grow up as high principled as his father, he must avoid the contamination of other children and draw companionship from his tutor or other adults. He must not be encouraged into the English passion

211

for sport. It was a waste of time and energy; an afternoon walk or an occasional ride were sufficient exercise for health. If he deserved amusement, he could recite, or play in suitable amateur theatricals. And every day a memorandum of his progress should be submitted to his parents.

That, Stockmar decided, should correct the errors of character the Prince was showing. That should bring him completely under his father's rule and subject him to the continuous pressure of his father's ideas. The new tutor would quickly learn that severity and justice were quite compatible in the treatment of small boys, and that Albert, Victoria and himself would be watching events very closely.

In 1848 the sun had shone and the crops flourished; the famine and disease which ravaged Ireland disappeared, but of a population of eight million, only three were left. Hunger, plague and emigration had wiped out the rest; the landlords were in undisputed possession of their estates, and the quarrels over English assistance to the Catholic Church were no more virulent than usual. Ireland was in a state of political ferment, but as Russell said, when had it ever been otherwise – when had that unhappy country ever submitted gratefully to English domination and given proper allegiance to the sovereign. It was almost a mercy that the famine had depleted Ireland's strength and that such a large proportion of trouble-makers had either died or crossed the Atlantic to America. The chance of a permanent peace which Peel had foreseen through the disaster slipped away, forfeited by Russell's antipathy to all things Catholic, and by the rule of force and terror employed by the landlords. In their agony the people clung more fiercely to their ancient faith; Catholicism was more than ever the symbol of Irish freedom, but to the staunchly Protestant Prime Minister and his Government it was unthinkable to divert funds from the Established Church for the benefit of an alien religion, however much it might have reconciled the population. So

212

the sores of neglect and oppression festered, and what sympathy there had been in England for the distress of those three terrible years gave way to irritation at Irish intransigence.

Victoria and Albert made a State visit to Ireland in the following year. The Queen began her journey with the fixed belief that it would be unpleasant, and though the people gathered in their curiosity and cheered with unexpected warmth when they saw the homely little Queen of England with her husband and her brood of children, Victoria's heart remained cold, and her mind hostile. She had never liked or understood them; there was an atmosphere of stress which she found most unpleasing, and they seemed much more affected by the pink and white Princes and Princesses than by the essential majesty of their rightful sovereign. She returned to England with a sigh of relief and promptly forgot about Ireland. They had bought a new home in the Highlands of Scotland, on a magnificent site called Balmoral where they would retire every summer, crowding their household into the small country mansion and playing happily at being private people. Albert loved Scotland; he loved the mountains and the wild, glorious scenery; the keen air and the views reminded him of Germany, and Victoria noticed happily how much healthier he looked.

Osborne was delightful, but it was still too near to London; Southampton Water was not sufficient barrier between them and the demands of the outside world. But in Balmoral they were really free. It was while staying in the great bleak fortresses of the Scottish Lords that Albert had conceived the plan of building a fastness of their own. The idea of Balmoral Castle enchanted the Queen, who still enjoyed a show of the regal grandeur Albert found so stifling. But if Albert were to design the Castle he would surely love it, and it could be planned and furnished from top to bottom exactly as they wished, without regard to the taste and traditions of former kings. It would provide full scope for her darling's artistry and passion for detail; they could indulge every sentimental whim, and live there in a medieval dream.

Besides, she was now so rich that they could easily afford it, thanks to Albert's brilliant management of her affairs. He had already re-organized the running of the Royal palaces, dismissing hordes of useless servants, tightening the rules of household management and abolishing the system of perquisite and abuse which had grown up over centuries of mismanagement. His actions had not made him popular, of course. people were so blind, and so ungrateful; they resented him saving the Crown money and called it meanness. They protested when practices like removing the candles, used or otherwise, from every room each day were stopped, and they made cheap jibes about Albert saving candle ends. Whatever he did was criticized, and she sprang to his defence with redoubled obstinacy and anger. They owed Osborne to his careful husbandry, and it would give them Balmoral too, without extracting a penny from her ungrateful Parliament. Though the Queen's public and private letters were full of praise for his efforts, her subjects stubbornly refused to acknowledge their debt to Albert. And Albert had another plan, a tremendous concept so dazzling in its vision that she was breathless when he explained it.

He proposed a great exhibition of the products of the world. As he pointed out, Europe was engaged in a bitter class war, blinded by political and national passions to the truth that commerce and not revolution was the means of man's emancipation. Trade was soaring in England; the manufacturers were drawing rivers of gold into the country's coffers. They had discovered a new world of wealth comparable to the gift Columbus had laid at the feet of the King and Queen of Spain, and the living proof of the progress and ingenuity of trade would confront the world in an exhibition to be held in the greatest trading country in Europe.

There was a good deal of enthusiasm for the plan from manufacturers, members of that blessed middle-class whose

214

common sense drew them towards a man of Albert's genius, and the idea had gained much support abroad. Every country could exhibit and compete; orders would flow and prosperity for everyone would follow. So Albert reasoned, and Victoria agreed. But experience had not yet taught her that what Albert proposed, the majority of her subjects vetoed on principle. There was an outcry in Parliament, where the expense was discussed. A furore of disapproval erupted in the newspapers, which dismissed the whole scheme as a monument of arrogance and said that the proposal to house the exhibition in a glass building was the concept of a madman. The medical profession issued warnings that plague would break out if large crowds assembled. An influx of foreigners could only result in riots; the first downpour would destroy the glass structure and cost countless lives. The Church declared vehemently that such an idea would bring the wrath of God down on the heads of all responsible. Every excuse, valid or ludicrous, was put forward to frustrate Albert's plan, and there were many nights when Victoria came quietly to his study and found him with his head buried in his hands, staring at the blue prints and papers in soundless despair. All the power of her love for him broke out on those occasions, until she sometimes felt as if her heart must break at her inability to give him the one happiness she knew he wanted, appreciation from her people. She often held his head against her breast, with a maternal passion she had never felt for any of her children, and promised him with tears, that *nothing* and *no one* should spoil his wonderful plan, and that when they saw the shining palace filled with treasures from all over the world, they would admit their indebtedness on their knees.

And backed by support from some public men, from the manufacturing classes and by enthusiasm from the Continent, the project went ahead, propelled by Victoria's enthusiasm.

There was also the constant irritant of Palmerston who was fast becoming the personification of that side of

England which frustrated Albert, resisted Albert, and did not appreciate him. Palmerston was impossible; she had always thought so, even in Melbourne's day – how long ago that seemed, he might have been dead a hundred years her memories of him were so faded – and now, faced with that imperturbable, devious defiance of her authority and Albert's wishes, Victoria really hated him. And her hatred, as Palmerston was soon to learn, could end his political career. There was a time in 1850, when it seemed that his hold on the public imagination had weakened, and the policy of encouraging insurrection abroad and making wild claims for English rights had lost their magic for the Commons. Don Pacifico, a Portuguese Jew, but a native of Gibraltar and therefore a British subject, had demanded compensation from the Greek Government after his house was pillaged by a mob in Athens. The Greeks refused, and an order from the Foreign Office despatched the British Fleet to Grecian waters to persuade them to change their minds on the matter. France, who had been mediating in the affair, was so incensed by the attitude of Her Majesty's Foreign Minister, that England came to the verge of war. Immediately the storm of disapproval broke over Palmerston's head. Victoria and Albert faced Russell triumphantly and said they had no doubt that when the motion of censure was introduced in the Commons against him, it would be rightly carried. In his sanctum at the Foreign Office, Palmerston waited, quietly for once, twisting his dyed side whiskers and whistling under his breath. He knew that his enemies regarded him as fallen. He knew that poor old Russell, who never got any limelight, was jealous and would be pleased to accept his resignation. Besides, the Queen had been giving him the devil of a time, and Russell took beratings to heart. As for the excellent Prince Albert – Palmerston grinned; he'd rub his hands and find some damned unctuous phrase appropriate to the occasion, and rejoice in the prospect of meddling in English affairs to his heart's content. They all counted him beaten, but he loved his dear Emily far too much to let a parcel of faint-hearts and spoil-sports deprive her of the joys of being the foremost political hostess in England and himself of the fun of treading on alien corns. He gathered his papers and set off for the House of Commons. The Lords had already voted against him, but he didn't care a fiddler's curse for anything except the Commons.

He sat nonchalantly during the speeches against him, his lips pursed in a soundless whistle, and then when they had all finished he rose to answer his critics. He spoke for four hours, defending himself and his actions in one of the greatest speeches ever delivered in the House. He proved himself a master of persuasion and invective, of reasoned argument and brilliant rhetoric; he tore the charges against him to shreds, he reduced his audience to shouts of laughter and roars of patriotism, watched by the admiring eyes of the young Mr Disraeli, who was no novice at the parliamentary game himself. At the end Palmerston sat down to watch the motion of censure being soundly defeated.

When the news of his triumph reached Victoria at Windsor, she burst into tears of disappointment. The wretch had won again. Furiously she concocted a memorandum, with which Stockmar and Albert assisted, and laid down the only conditions under which she would work with Lord Palmerston. He was to show her every despatch, and to alter nothing after she had approved it; he was to send nothing without her approval, and he was to make his intentions perfectly clear on every point beforehand. If he failed to comply with her wishes, she would be forced to dismiss him, as was the sovereign's Constitutional right.

'I hope you see now, the position you've placed yourself in,' Russell spoke quietly. He had been watching Palmerston read the copy of Victoria's memorandum.

'You went too far too often, Henry, and I warned you not to irritate her. She's said she'll dismiss you and she will. And I would naturally have to resign if she did.'

Palmerston made a grimace and handed the paper back.

'A very clear piece of work that,' he remarked. 'All set out with Teutonic thoroughness; I'm damned sure our Prince and that old pill peddler Stockmar wrote this out for her.'

'Whoever wrote it out,' Russell said dryly, 'you can be quite sure it expresses the Queen's views. Can I seriously hope that you understand the position now and you'll take it to heart? If you flout her authority once more, Henry, she'll turn you out of the Foreign Office!'

'I've no doubt she would,' Palmerston said. 'It might cause some adverse comment, mind you, but I don't under-estimate our sovereign's will-power − don't let's call it obstinacy − that would be ungallant. It appears, my dear fellow, that you've been right and I've been wrong. Ah well, I can repent!'

'What are you going to do?' Russell asked. He wished he could trust Palmerston, and ignore that mischievous gleam in his eye. He would *say* anything, Russell knew that, but it gave no indication of what he was going to do. The Queen had threatened him, and in spite of that bluff manner, Russell knew he was a bad enemy.

'Do? Why, I shall go down to Osborne and make my apologies in person. I shall prostrate myself if necessary, clear up this misunderstanding, and come back to London to get on with some serious work.'

'I don't envy you your interview with the Queen, Henry. She'll make it damnably difficult for you.'

Palmerston smiled. 'I don't intend to let her. Being a woman, and a formidable one at that, she'll *never* forgive me. I trust I shall melt our noble Prince's heart, however. He, in turn, will soften her.'

There was no doubt about it, Palmerston thought, Osborne was the most hideous place he'd ever seen. Ignoring the gardens, which were pretty enough, though too orderly and artificial in his opinion, the house itself was in such awful taste it took his breath away. The lines were ugly, fussy with detail – good God Almighty – who had thought of building a colonnade with alcoves painted blue and surmounted by gilded scallop shells, and filling them with the busts of the Queen's German uncles? It was so inelegant that Palmerston wanted to laugh out loud. While he waited in the ante-room for his interview with Albert, he noted the chairs made of antlers, shot by the Consort while in Scotland, the mixture of mock baronial and middle-class German which made his surroundings a travesty, and wondered what had happened to the lovely furniture and pictures accumulated by the Crown over so many centuries. No doubt they mouldered in some store-house. The Gainsboroughs, the Adam and Chippendale furniture, the exquisite products of eighteenth-century France, with all the blended grace and charm of master workmanship – the taste of Prince Albert and his wife had replaced them with pictures of deer, hand-painted porcelain views of Windsor Castle, and the stucco busts of the porcine German uncles in the colonnade. He allowed himself one sniff of contempt, and then the door leading to Albert's room opened, and his name was announced.

The Prince received him standing. He had thought very carefully how to set the scene for the interview with this man whom he disliked so much and so heartily distrusted. And he had decided that as Palmerston obviously came to make his peace, he should be received with severity. He must be made to understand how deeply the Queen was offended and that his political survival depended on a genuine reformation. Albert was not sure how the Minister would behave, whether the jaunty arrogance which always annoyed him would be muted, whether indeed he would even appear embarrassed by the stinging rebuke he had received. Anything was possible; Victoria had already said she believed the old man incapable of behaving properly. A man of feeling would have resigned, after such a memorandum. Perhaps, they both wondered, that was what he had come to do. That hope was immediately disappointed by Palmerston's first words.

'It's so very good of your Royal Highness to receive me. I've been so distressed since I discovered I'd inconvenienced Her Majesty that I couldn't attend to affairs until I'd made a full apology.'

'Inconvenienced is not quite the description,' Albert said stiffly. 'The Queen has been terribly anxious these last few months; she has been grievously disturbed by your conduct, Lord Palmerston, and little though I wish to interfere, I must say I agree with her.'

He felt himself reddening as he spoke. Although Palmerston stood there as a supplicant Albert felt just as unsure and uncomfortable as ever in his presence.

'I'm more upset than ever,' Palmerston burst out. He spoke with such vehemence that Albert was surprised, too surprised to halt the flow of words which followed.

'How could I ever have been so blind? Good God, I'd rather die than cause the Queen a moment's unhappiness. Sir, I assure you, with all my heart, that if I've offended the Queen and you, it was only through ignorance — zeal for Her Majesty's welfare! I want nothing for myself — I'm sixty, I'm not ambitious now for my own glory. Everything I've done, I've done for the Queen and for England. I've made mistakes, and I acknowledge them — humbly.' There was a pause and to Albert's astonishment, Palmerston took out his handkerchief and wiped his eyes. There was no doubt about it, they were full of tears. He felt suddenly extremely uncomfortable to discover that the thick-skin could be pierced. Whatever his faults, it was embarrassing to see him crying, humiliated. It was not quite dignified either, Albert thought, to be so eager to abase himself and beg. Yet it was noble. His self-doubt supplied an answer quickly: pride was wrong; the inability to admit error — that was wrong; and he suffered from both faults, so did Victoria. How could he inveigh against his eldest son because he didn't show enough contrition, and then ignore the generous apology of Palmerston, just because he didn't like him?

'I feel quite sure you didn't mean to annoy the Queen,' he said. 'Quite sure. No one ever questioned your motives, Lord Palmerston, only your methods.'

'Thank God!' Palmerston's handkerchief went back into his pocket. 'Thank God for that. As for the methods – they shall be changed, Sir, just as Her Majesty commanded.'

'I must warn you,' Albert said solemnly, 'that the Queen is adamant; you cannot afford to lose her confidence a second time.'

That threat again, Palmerston thought; flout her, and of course *you*, you popinjay, and I shall be dismissed . . . Very well then, we shall see what happens if the people's favourite is displaced. Not now but later. We shall see.

'I understand,' he said at once. 'I understand perfectly and I give you my word. I'll earn the Queen's confidence if it's the last thing I do. I should much like to feel that I have yours too, Sir.'

'My opinion doesn't count,' Albert answered. 'I am only her Consort, and I would never presume to interfere. I only try to help, Lord Palmerston. It is the Queen who must be satisfied, not me.'

'I know I have no right to ask you,' Palmerston said gently, 'but I'd be eternally grateful if you'd speak to the Queen for me. Nothing would help me more than a word from you. Reassure Her Majesty that she has nothing to fear from me; I shall fulfil her wishes to the letter. Will you tell her that, Sir?'

'Of course.' Albert said. 'Certainly. But it might help if we were to take a few examples of the things which have caused this misunderstanding. Sit down, Lord Palmerston.'

Palmerston thanked him and relaxed. He had won and he knew it. He would sit down and listen to the Prince's second-hand opinions and agree with every one of them; he'd promise and flatter to gain the truce he needed, rather than lose the Foreign Office. He had no trouble digesting humble pie. They talked for an hour, while he avoided giving a definite answer to a question concerning Schleswig, which the Prince was trying to make a test case. Damn these paltry Germans and their problems . . . and damn his impertinence in expecting a statesman to have cut-and-dried plans for all eventualities. But how could he understand, or the Queen who was rigid like all women, that policies evolved from situations, and situations could change in a few hours. How useless to try and point out to him that one could not work out the destinies of nations with pencil and paper, that the only thing to do with a preconceived plan was to tear it up? He would never understand; he saw everything in terms of detail, painstaking, time wasting detail. To Albert, everything could be reduced to the level of a schoolmaster's thesis; the erratic course of genius, the breadth of true vision were incomprehensible to him. He had the soul of a counting-house clerk.

At the end of the hour, Palmerston left. He had given no answer to the Prince's question; he had made a lot of promises which he intended to break; and he had committed Albert to healing his relationship with the Queen. He returned to London as gay and self-confident as ever.

The closing months of the year 1850 were full of sadness and anxiety for the Queen and the Prince. There was trouble in Germany, where the spirit of revolt kept breaking out, and no one in England agreed with Albert that union under Prussian sovereignty was the best solution for his unhappy homeland. No one appreciated the virtues of the Prussian mentality, or would admit that strength and orderliness was the best safeguard against insurrection. The English expressed a rooted dislike for these essentially German qualities, chiefly, he suspected, because he admired and advocated them. The love for his own country, long disguised by his activities in English affairs, burst out openly in his attempts to use the power of England in Germany's interests. There were icy disagreements with Lord John Russell, who showed inflexible opposition to Victoria and Albert on the subject, and in spite of his promises,

Palmerston had begun his old practices within a few weeks. The Queen was furious; furious with her Prime Minister, volcanic over Palmerston, and wretched because the attacks on Albert and the Exhibition were growing more and more violent in the Press and the Commons. Public disappointment was joined by private grief, for death had taken his one friend in politics, Sir Robert Peel; and then Anson, who had become closer to him than anyone except Stockmar, also died. Victoria noticed his pallor and loss of appetite, and wrote agonized letters to the Baron, who was visiting Germany, to return as soon as possible, for her darling's health was suffering after so many blows. He slept so badly since Anson's death; he was silent and depressed and even talked of abandoning the Exhibition. The death of old King Louis Philippe at Claremont, where the Royal family had allowed him to live since his dethronement, upset them out of all proportion. His misdemeanours were forgotten; Victoria recalled his flight from Paris and humble acceptance of English protection, and burst into tears. Death was so terrible, so final. She clung to Albert, terrified by the thought that one day she must be separated from him by an authority higher than her own, and plunged everyone into mourning. Death was not to be taken lightly; she was shocked when she realized how casually she had thought of it in the past, and sitting hand-in-hand with Albert in the dusk at Osborne, they talked of it in whispers. Black should be worn, entertainments should be avoided, widow's weeds and memorial rings and pictures of the departed were the due of death; and from the Court's example, Victoria's pre-occupation with mourning began to gain ground with her people. It was part of Albert's philosophy, part of the Teutonic passion for doom and sentimentality which found so little outlet in the lusty English atmosphere. Together they grieved for Peel and Anson and the old King of the French, and everyone round them was plunged into compulsory gloom. One of the most discordant notes was the evident gaiety of the little Prince of Wales who seemed inordinately

223

fond of his tutor. However closely the Royal parents studied Mr Birch's daily reports, they could find no fault with them. Bertie was studying hard, Bertie was making excellent progress, he was obedient, intelligent and affectionate. When Stockmar returned, Victoria and Albert conferred anxiously with him. Surely Birch took too lenient a view? It was impossible that the boy's character should have changed so completely that there was nothing adverse to report? The Baron pursed his thin lips and said he would look into the matter. He asked to see the little Prince's papers, often sitting by during lessons, and after a time he delivered his opinion. Admirable as Birch was, he lacked the firmness necessary in dealing with the Prince. He had become too attached to the child and was indulging him. The strict routine laid down by Prince Albert was modified to suit Mr Birch's ideas. Lessons were shorter than they were supposed to be and enlivened by unbecoming anecdotes; there were too many walks and too many games. The Prince was often seen romping with his tutor or swinging on his hand, and there were rumours of story books at bed-time instead of the proper lecture about the faults committee through the days. Birch's reports were too favourable, they could not be true, and the Baron suggested that a change would have to be made again.

But in the spring of the new year their dissatisfaction with their son was forgotten in the fruition of the tremendous scheme which Albert had planned and worked for so zealously. On a site in Hyde Park a glittering glass building one thousand feet long marked the Prince's triumph over the malice and opposition of his enemies. The Press, the Commons and the Church had indulged in an orgy of hysterical abuse at the end, one Member of Parliament having publicly called on the elements to destroy the abomination before it was opened. There were cries that the foreigners swarming into London would cause a revolution, that the Queen would be murdered — she had suffered two further attempts on her life in the last few years, and had been struck across the face with a heavy cane by a demented ex-officer named Pate — there would be plague, riots, and the vengeance of God. But in spite of everything the Crystal Palace was completed, the visitors began pouring into the capital, and the mass of exhibits from all over the world were laid out. On the first of May, in brilliant sunshine, Victoria, Albert, and their two eldest children, Bertie and the Princess Royal, drove out to open the Exhibition.

Side by side, with their children by the hand, Victoria and Albert walked through the iron gates, past the palm trees towering overhead, through lines of trumpeters who gave a magnificent fanfare of welcome, watched by a dense crowd of people of every race and degree. The Queen walked very slowly, with that peculiar grace which always lent her height and state, wearing a new dress of pink and silver tissue which glittered in the light.. She glanced from side to side, bewildered and breathless with emotion, pride and wonder at the embodiment of her beloved one's achievements. It was indescribable. The sun filled the immense glass building with a diffusion of gold and was reflected back a thousand times; a crystal fountain played in the centre hall, shooting great jets of silver water into the air, and everywhere there was colour, beauty and novelty to enchant the eye. She looked quickly at Albert and smiled, a trembling little smile of passionate love and admiration, a smile which said that now the accolade, so long withheld by England, must be his. This was his work; this wonderful gathering of the treasures of the world, laid out in a dazzling display for the instruction and enjoyment of countless thousands. There were treasures from the East, gorgeous silks and embroideries, an ivory throne from India, jewelled swords, lacquer work, brasses and bronzes, statues with coloured waters bubbling at their feet, terra cotta and majolica, English country pottery, lace, gold and silver plate, bedsteads and chairs in zebra wood, cabinets from Switzerland elaborately carved. In a daze of happiness Victoria heard the Archbishop make his address and pronounce a prayer; then a chorus of six hundred filled the huge building with the majestic *Hallelujah* from Handel's *Messiah*, and the tears shone on the Queen's cheeks.

She saw the glistening machinery, so complicated and able to do such marvels, and then passed on to admire the beautiful wax flower models which were quite the prettiest decorations she had ever seen, and listened to the twittering of mechanical birds so cleverly made that they might have been real. There was such a mixture of large and small exhibits, and eleven miles of tables, that it was impossible to do more than make a cursory inspection of a part of the Exhibition and receive the homage of the people, and tell Albert again and again in a loud voice that it was the most wonderful thing she had ever seen and that every bit of it was due to him.

They returned to Buckingham Palace that day, exhausted emotionally and physically, after passing through masses of people who cheered and waved from the door of the Exhibition to the Palace gates.

'Darling Albert! Oh, my darling, aren't you happy today?' She caught both his hands and gazed up at him. They were alone in her boudoir. Victoria was so anxious to tell him how wonderful she thought it was that she had taken off her own bonnet and pelisse and flung them on a chair.

'I am happy, yes.' For once he looked it; he was rather flushed and smiling. He put his arm round her tenderly. She was a dear wife, a good wife. He really depended upon her a great deal. 'It was a great success, I think,' he said. 'I really believe everyone is pleased now.'

'Pleased? My dearest, they're overwhelmed! It was a miracle. I never imagined anything could be so big, so beautiful! Oh, Albert, you are the most wonderful man in the world. I've always known it, now everybody else will too.'

However blind and mean they had been to him in the past, they couldn't help seeing his true worth after this. They

226

couldn't fail to love him and appreciate him as they should have done years before. That was why she had wept at the Exhibition, why the tears were near again. His unpopularity had pained her so deeply for so long, that the prospect of the country accepting him, loving him, seeing him as she did, was almost more than she could bear without breaking down with joy and relief. Her darling. How she loved him! How good and conscientious and noble he was! To think that scene of splendour was his doing, that glory which attached to her Crown and her capital was his brain-child, planned by him down to the last detail!

She put her arms around him and leaned against his chest.

'I know, my love, how hard it's been for you here in England. I know how you've been hurt, though you've never really complained or tried to defend yourself. I know it all, and my heart has almost broken at times. But from this day I know things will be different. I know my people realize what they owe you at last. I know it. I know it so truly that I can't wait to see tomorrow's papers and all the enthusiastic things they're going to print about you.'

'Meine kleine Frau,' he said gently, lapsing into the German they used in moments of intimacy, 'my little wife, if you're pleased that's all that matters to me. This is your country, but you know I've worked for it since we were married as if it were my own. Everything I've done has been for the good of England and for you. If the people take me to their hearts at last I shall be very happy. But chiefly because I know it will make *you* happy. Let us pray that they do.'

They woke very early as usual the next morning, for Albert believed in rising promptly and getting down to work; and when they saw the newspapers Victoria jumped up and kissed him. There was nothing but praise for the Exhibition, and at last, without one discordant note, praise for the Prince. They went to their desks as usual to deal with the mass of papers which accumulated every day, and Victoria wrote a long, passionately enthusiastic letter to her Uncle

Leopold describing the scene at the Crystal Palace and assuring him that the Exhibition was a personal triumph for her dearest Albert. Her pen flowed on, writing and underlining, saying again and again how wonderful he was and how at last his efforts were appreciated. It had been the happiest and proudest day of her whole life.

'You understand our anxiety for the Prince, Mr Gibbs. As Baron Stockmar has explained, your predecessor failed to maintain the standard of discipline necessary to my son's education. I trust you will not make the same mistake.'

Frederick Gibbs, tutor to His Royal Highness the Prince of Wales, bowed low to the Queen. He was a tall thin man, with a pale face and dour, set features.

'I shall pay the closest attention to Your Majesty's wishes,' he said. 'I share the Baron's views on the right method for developing character in boys. Discipline shall not be neglected, I promise you.'

The Queen and the Prince and the Baron had each described the failings of his charge, exactly as they had done to Birch two years before. Unlike Birch, who was surprised by their prejudice, Gibbs listened with sympathy. He had no time for sentiment in dealing with children and he was relieved to find that the Royal parents demanded such high standards from their son. He had no patience with levity and time-wasting himself and was gratified that they had none either; the more they explained their wishes the easier he felt it would be to satisfy them.

'He must be made to work,' Albert said firmly. 'We want his memory trained so that whatever subject comes up in later life he can produce some facts about it; it's essential that a king should know something of everything. Above all, Mr Gibbs, he must be made to take an interest in serious subjects. To give you an example, he enjoys history and lags behind in mathematics and physics.'

'He also has a highly coloured imagination,' Stockmar added. 'His accounts of the simplest things are much exaggerated.' In other words, the young Prince was inclined to tell lies. Mr Gibbs nodded grimly.

'I shall do my best to discourage that,' he said.

'And we shall require a detailed report of his progress every day,' Victoria said. 'We are very anxious about him as I said, and please omit nothing, however trivial, that he says or does.'

Again the tutor bowed.

'And now, Baron, will you take Mr Gibbs and present him to Bertie.'

The Royal nursery presented a charming picture when the Baron entered with Gibbs. There were five little Princes and Princesses, all very near in age, from the baby Louise who lay playing in her elaborately frilled cradle, to the blonde Princess Royal, who was reading aloud to Lady Lyttelton from a geography book. Except the baby, three of the children were usefully employed; the girls were drawing or spelling out words, the younger Prince was in a corner with his governess taking French lessons. But sitting in the window seat, staring out into the gardens, Gibbs saw a small boy dressed in a sailor suit, and knew instinctively that this was his charge, the unsatisfactory Bertie. Stockmar crossed the room with a nod to the governesses to continue their lessons undisturbed. He was frowning and his tight lips were compressed. It was typical of what he and the boy's parents had been saying that, of all the children, Bertie should be the only one sitting in idleness, wasting his time looking out of the window, with his hands in his lap.

'Your Royal Highness!' The boy turned with a start at the sound of that sharp voice, a voice he always connected with some rebuke, and slid quickly down to the floor.

'This is your new tutor, Mr Gibbs.'

For a moment the Prince and Gibbs looked at each other. He was not an ugly child, Gibbs decided, though his mother had conveyed the impression that his moral defects were matched by his appearance. He was very fair, with Victoria's bright, protuberant blue eyes and a fresh complexion, but he had a hang-dog air as he stood there, which Gibbs immediately disliked. He must be taught to stand up straight and look people directly in the eye, and answer promptly when he was spoken to.

'How do you do, Your Royal Highness.'

Bertie hesitated for a second. He did not like Gibbs's voice. He did not like that unsmiling expression and the close-set eyes watching him. In that instant before he put out his hand, he sensed that, like the Baron, this was not a friend.

'How do you do,' he said.

'Mr Gibbs,' Stockmar prompted.

'Mr Gibbs,' he added. They shook hands.

'I have come to take Mr Birch's place,' Gibbs said. 'I hope you will work well with me, Your Royal Highness, and please your parents.'

Bertie said nothing. For three weeks before Birch left he had cried himself to sleep, and sometimes sneaked out of bed to hide a note or a childish present under his tutor's pillow. He had loved Birch, and Birch had loved him. Birch had somehow stood between him and that awful feeling that his mother and his father didn't like him very much. He could forget about them when he had Birch to talk to and play with, and knew Birch would say good things about him. He was never going to love this man. He bit his lip and for one awkward moment Stockmar thought the wretched boy was going to disgrace himself and burst into tears.

He turned to Lady Lyttelton. He knew that she was watching, showing as much disapproval as she dared, and he said peremptorily, 'His Royal Highness may go out for a walk with Mr Gibbs. They can begin lessons after tea.'

'Certainly,' Lady Lyttelton's voice was very cold. How he detested the arrogance of these English women! She would never have dared speak like that if the Queen had been there. He glared at her and determined to put in a word against her at the first opportunity. She had started all this trouble by shielding the boy from criticism and fussing over him instead of reporting his bad habits at once. He nodded to Gibbs and walked out of the room. Lady Lyttelton smiled at the new tutor. Privately she hoped his nature was not as forbidding as his face. Poor little Bertie. He looked so shifty and miserable waiting there, trying not to cry, with this dour ramrod standing over him.

'Go and get your cap,' she said kindly. The boy looked up at her and fled into the next room. Then she turned to Gibbs. This might be her best chance to say something nice about the child. She could imagine how the Queen and Prince Albert had prejudiced him, as they had tried to prejudice Birch. As for Stockmar . . . It was just possible that this man was not as unbending as he looked.

'I am so glad you are going to tutor the Prince,' she said, 'you'll find him a most lovable little boy. Mr Birch was devoted to him.'

'So I believe.' Gibbs looked at her, and Lady Lyttelton's smile began to fade. 'But I understand Her Majesty was not satisfied with him. Nor was Prince Albert. I intend to give satisfaction. I believe it is a boy's duty to love his parents, not his tutor. I shall concern myself with his mind, not his emotions, Madam.'

Five minutes later she watched them from the window, walking slowly down the pathway to the lake, Gibbs very stiff, measuring his steps to the pace of the small boy, who trudged beside him, his hands hanging by his sides.

'Do you think Bertie will be good now?' That was the Princess Royal; she had put down her geography book and watched the little scene with interest. Lady Lyttelton turned round. She was always good; she had never said or done anything to annoy the Queen or Albert since she was a tiny child.

'Kindly continue with your lesson,' Lady Lyttelton snapped suddenly. There were times when she really disliked that child just because she was her parents' favourite.

The summer passed and the Court went to Balmoral. It was the happiest time of the year for Victoria, for she and Albert went for long drives through the Highlands and picnicked in the heather, attended only by one lady-in-waiting and Albert's ghillie. Brown. Brown was an excellent man, and devoted to the Prince; she loved to hear his soft Scots accent, and to have him wait on them while they sat on the grass and lunched off cold chicken and game pie, and afterwards went off alone to gather flowers or wander by some highland stream. How they loved Scotland! And how wonderful it would be when the Castle Albert was designing for Balmoral would be built and finished and they could really live there. They were both very occupied with the plans, and the drawing of Gothic towers and turrets excited her imagination; also her darling was enjoying it so much. The cares and frustrations of public life might have belonged to another age during those summer months. It was possible to forget that insufferable Palmerston and their disagreements with Russell over the German question, and the infuriating fact that Bertie was becoming slower and stupider than ever, though Gibbs watched and corrected as tirelessly as they could wish. Gibbs was really excellent; Stockmar was delighted with him and they had grown quite friendly. Every evening she sat by Albert's side while he read aloud to her the report on Bertie's behaviour, and every time it was unsatisfactory. The child gave way to bursts of temper, or suddenly started to cry during his lessons and always when he was corrected; he was secretive and, much as Gibbs grieved to mention it, not always truthful. As Stockmar said, he had a passion for romancing, and a mind which was only interested in trivial or highly coloured things.

She squeezed Albert's hand as she listened, growing inwardly angrier and angrier with her son, because he *would* not turn out as his father wanted, and it meant that Albert grew fonder than ever of his eldest daughter. Of course she was fond of her dear Pussy too, but how much more suitable if Albert's favourite had been a boy . . . Their private disappointment was bad enough, but rumours of the system imposed on the heir to the throne had become public, and the Press had been impertinent enough to print long articles deploring the fact that Bertie had no friends of his own age and was kept so hard at work. The sunshine of Albert's popularity had actually dimmed within months of the Exhibition because it was being said he was treating his son harshly. She had almost torn up the newspapers when she first read their comments; the innuendoes against Albert, the malice and downright rudeness were creeping back again, impelled by the jealousy and dislike which she thought had turned into love at last. Now she knew that his enemies had been only temporarily silenced but not dismayed; they were making a weapon out of her beastly little son and daring to use it against Albert. On the rare occasions when she visited Bertie, he invariably went to bed in tears; and the regime which was worrying the responsible members of the Press and Parliament grew more rigid and more merciless as his mother's dislike slowly turned to hatred.

The face that watched Victoria in the looking-glass when she dressed for dinner on those summer evenings had changed and hardened. Her lids were heavier, and her cheeks had filled out; there were lines of pride etched round the mouth and an expression of incredible determination in her eyes. Command had touched her face and marked it; the petulance and selfwill of her headstrong youth had vanished. At thirty-two she was mature beyond her years with the maturity of an iron will allied to personal power. That was the face that her Court and her Ministers knew; that was the expression her children saw, occasionally lightened by a distant smile when she was pleased with them; but when she looked or spoke to Albert, it fell from her like a mask. Love wiped clean the lines and smoothed the regal pride away; it lit her eyes with an extraordinary tenderness and her lips softened like a girl's. Albert was the shrine at which her heart and body worshipped; Albert had given her the peace and simplicity in which one side of her rejoiced, Albert had taken away the heavy robes and glittering crown, and in his arms and by his side she felt protected and a woman.

And Albert's hard work and selfless disinterest had increased the power of her nature's other side, the side that lived in a public glare as Queen of the most powerful nation in the world. He was planning to make it stronger still by increasing the strength of her army and expanding her fleet. He had given her everything: love, motherhood − she was quite philosophical about having children so often now − companionship and the dream of domestic simplicity; and he had done nothing in public life but try and add lustre to her crown. The intensity of her love for him removed her further than ever from the danger of affection for others, including her own children. She had no time and little feelings for anyone but Albert, though she liked those few people he favoured, merely because he favoured them. He was sufficient for her every need. And she had not realized then and never would, that she had failed to fill his life in the same way.

10

'Your Majesty. Your Royal Highness.'

Lord John Russell bowed to them in turn; in spite of her anxiety Victoria noticed the curt salutation to Albert, so different from the deep bow her Prime Minister had made to her. The discourtesy always irritated her. Her voice was steely.

'The Prince and I have been quite distracted with worry, Lord John. Could you not have come sooner?'

Russell shook his head.

'I left my desk the moment I could, Ma'am. Despatches have been pouring in every hour. It's a most deplorable business, most deplorable! Paris is in a ferment, but from what we can learn the *coup de'état* has been completely successful.'

On December 2nd, France had suddenly ceased to be a Republic. The man who had been elected President after the fall of poor Louis Philippe from his throne had seized absolute control of the country. Louis Napoleon, nephew of the great Bonaparte, had dissolved the elected Chamber of Deputies, arresting most of them and large numbers of influential men in the army and civil life, and after a massacre in which twelve hundred Parisians were shot down in the streets, emerged as the virtual dictator of France.

'It's unbelievable,' Albert said. 'To break his word and turn guns on his own people!'

'His name is Bonaparte, Sir,' Russell answered grimly. 'From the moment he was elected President he obviously intended to do exactly what he's done! He is Emperor in all but name.'

'Then I hope he remembers what happened to that other Emperor,' Victoria snapped. 'If he imagines that England will allow France to embark on another attempt to conquer the world under that loathsome dynasty, he's much mistaken! What we had to do once we can do again.'

'I doubt if he'll do anything rash just yet, Ma'am,' Russell said. 'He'll probably be only too anxious to allay those fears and gain English recognition.'

'Is it certain that France will accept him?' Victoria asked. 'Surely the country as a whole will rise against such a wicked and immoral action. I've never liked the French, but I can't believe they would approve of such a creature.'

'He became President on the strength of the name Napoleon, Ma'am,' Russell answered. 'That name alone swept him into office and I fear it will put him on the throne. The French are tired of dissension and muddle in their Government. They have forgotten the disasters the first Napoleon brought them and only remember the glory. I predict we will see another Emperor of the French, and every Frenchman with a Bee in his buttonhole. The question is – what attitude should the Government take?'

The Queen looked at Albert. They had discussed that point for the whole morning. If the reported rising was successful, if this horrible little upstart descendant of England's greatest enemy gained control of France, should he be acknowledged or should England protest? As Albert had pointed out, a protest was useless unless backed by action, and action could only mean armed intervention which was unthinkable. Time enough to embark on a war when France showed any sign of infringing on English interest. No, they could not protest, and congratulation was out of the question, of course.

'We must not commit ourselves in any way,' Victoria declared. 'England's attitude must be neutral, till we see the reaction of other countries, and what policy this person is going to pursue. Bonaparte! Just to think of it, dearest,' she turned to Albert. 'Little more than thirty years since we defeated one, and now we hear that name again!'

'He's unlikely to have his uncle's military genius,' Albert said. 'Thank God that doesn't run in families. We must be neutral, Lord John, and wait to see what happens.'

'That's my own view,' the Prime Minister nodded. 'No one has a greater detestation for the man and his actions than I have, Ma'am, and I'm only too thankful that you share it. I shall instruct the Foreign Office that nothing is to be said one way or the other, until the position is clarified.'

In the Palace and at Downing Street, the Queen and the Prime Minister worked and conferred all day and maintained an attitude of stony silence on the subject of the events in France. England had nothing to say.

In the Foreign Office Palmerston smoothed his whiskers and whistled cheerfully. What splendid news! France had been weak and undisciplined too long. Now a strong man had cleared out those boobies in the Chamber, some of whom actually favoured a return to the Bourbons again — some people *never* learned — and France had a leader at last. That would give the Prussians something to think about; that would remind some of these puny European princelings that any red-blooded man of action could pull the thrones from under them! And Russia, home of everything Palmerston hated most, Russia certainly wouldn't welcome a strong revitalized France to tip the scales of power in Europe. He glanced once more at Russell's letter informing him of English official neutrality, and then dropped it into a drawer. Still whistling, he sent a note of congratulation in a despatch to the French Ambassador in London.

'I have sent for you,' John Russell said, 'because you have such a habit of disregarding letters that you might have ignored one from me.'

Palmerston shrugged.

'Oh, come now! Not another complaint from the Queen!

What have I done, my dear fellow? You look as sour as a lemon.'

'You sent an official note to the French Ambassador, approving the *coup d'état* in Paris, didn't you?'

Russell glared at him; he was so angry that his hand trembled. He had just had a brief and shattering interview with the Queen at Windsor. He had never seen her so infuriated, and for once he whole-heartedly agreed with what she had said and what she demanded should be done.

'Why, yes I did,' Palmerston admitted ingenuously. 'But good God, Russell, don't you think it's a matter for congratulation? I know all the old busybodies are saying he's a second Napoleon and that we'll be at war in a few months, but it's a lot of rubbish! I've met the man, and he's no conqueror of the world; he's a strong man with plenty of sense, and we ought to be delighted. We need a sound French Government, and by Heaven, now there'll be one.'

'Your views don't interest me,' Russell said icily. 'Neither your views on Louis Napoleon nor your views on anything else connected with our Foreign Policy. You have disobeyed my authority once too often, Henry. I must ask you to resign.'

For a moment the ruddy colour faded from Palmerston's cheeks; his blue eyes glinted. When he looked at Russell his expression was amiable and slightly mocking as usual.

'Isn't this a little hard on an old friend?' he asked gently.

'You wheedled your way round Prince Albert, but you won't win the same trick with me.' Russell pushed back his chair and stood facing him. 'I repeat, Henry; I want your resignation. Granville will take the Foreign Office from you.'

'You're very adamant, I see,' Palmerston remarked. 'Very adamant. Ah, well, my dear Russell, if I'm dismissed, I'm dismissed. And all on account of a friendly little note to the French Ambassador. How I shall miss the dear old Foreign Office — and the pleasure of giving His Royal Highness a tweak on the nose now and again. I can't see Granville doing it, can you? I can't see him saying anything but "Yes, yes" to everything, but then that's what you want, I suppose.'

He looked at Russell for a minute, and the same unsmiling glint appeared. 'I accept my dismissal. I shall put myself at Granville's disposal until he comes in. I shall miss working with you, John I fear you may even miss working with me, in the end.'

Albert had wasted no time in investigating the state of the country's defences. No one yet knew what to expect from the new ruler of France and England must be able to confront him with strength. He discovered that the army was so badly organized as to be almost useless. The weapons were few and out-of-date, there was no proper system of training men, and the practice of buying command of regiments had deprived the army of any continuity of leadership. The navy had fallen into terrible neglect; the ships were antiquated and often unseaworthy, hopelessly ill-equipped to fight a modern naval war.

The country was alarmed by the disclosures, and urged on by a tempest of letters from the Queen and long memoranda from the Prince, Lord John Russell proposed the Militia Bill as a first step towards establishing a fighting core for the army. The Bill was debated in the House, and here Lord Palmerston revenged himself by splitting the Whig vote on the issue. With superb oratory he attacked the proposal, drawing the waverers on both sides of the House to his side, while Russell sat as Peel had done so many years before, watching the premiership being torn out of his hands by the skill and ruthlessness of his old colleague. The Bill was defeated and the Government fell. It was just two months since he had dismissed Palmerston.

A Tory Administration, headed by the highly individual Earl of Derby, took on the Government of the country. It was a feeble composition, with the exception of Derby, who had both courage and ability, but an unfortunate knack of making enemies; its one claim of distinction was the appointment of the talented Mr Disraeli as Chancellor of the Exchequer. The Queen, who had a typical dislike of Jews, was pleasantly surprised by the Chancellor's skill and tact in her few dealings with him, and impressed by the fact that unlike so many of her statesmen, Mr Disraeli expressed the deepest admiration of her beloved Albert. There was an interval of peace during Derby's term of office, but it was only an interval and painfully short. Before the end of the year the Government resigned; Mr Disraeli's budget had been defeated by an adherent of Sir Robert Peel, a brilliant, if rather ponderous man, who had been Secretary for War in Sir Robert's last unhappy Ministry. William Gladstone demolished Mr Disraeli's budget as Mr Disraeli had once demolished Sir Robert Peel; a Coalition between Whigs and Tories brought Mr Gladstone to the Exchequer, which the Queen did not like at all. She found Gladstone hectoring and humourless, and was glad she had little to do with him.

But worst of all, like some indestructible old demon, Palmerston was ensconced in the Home Office. The new Prime Minister, Lord Aberdeen, had avoided a direct crisis with the Queen by denying him the Foreign Ministry, but he was back in the Cabinet and back in public life as irrepressible as ever when she and Albert had supposed his political career was closing. They wrote bitter letters to Uncle Leopold and showed their displeasure so openly that some of those who liked Palmerston least began resenting the partisan attitude of the Crown. It was bad enough that the Queen should spend so much time at Osborne, and worse that she fled to Scotland for months every summer; everyone was inconvenienced by this passion for seclusion. Ministers had to make long journeys and wait for the return of documents, and it was all the fault of the Prince. The Queen used to live in London, the grumblers remembered; she never wanted to go further than Windsor until she married. But Prince Albert hated the capital, Prince Albert didn't think Windsor was private enough or even Osborne, so great was his passion for the quiet life. It was a great pity, his critics said, that he didn't indulge his fad of playing the simple country gentleman to the point where he stopped interfering in public affairs!

Certainly the Exhibition had been a huge success; it had brought trade worth millions to the country and showed a profit of one hundred and sixty thousand pounds when it closed in the autumn, but all that was soon taken for granted; success was always less spectacular than failure, and in their hearts so many had wanted it to fail, just to prove their prejudice against him. He was a meddler and a foreigner, and nothing annoyed public opinion more than the idea of a power behind the throne; the fact that it was eminently respectable only caused further irritation. It was also said that the Prince was bitterly opposed to France, though the new ruler, Louis Napoleon, earnestly desired England's friendship.

The Duke of Wellington died in that same year, and the Queen who had once disliked him so bitterly, now joined with Albert in genuine sorrow at his loss. He, too, had come to like and understand the Prince, and he stood for so many stable things in a world which seemed to be in a state of constant change. Wellington died, and the whole magnificent panoply of death reached a climax in the funeral England gave him. Soldier and statesman, a national hero after Waterloo and then so politically hated that his carriage was stoned by the mob, no man within living memory had born the vagaries of fortune as stoically as he did. It seemed only yesterday to Victoria that the great man had come into the Council Chamber at Kensington Palace to hear the eighteen-year-old Queen deliver her first address, and knelt to kiss her hand. How foolish she had been in those days, how obstinate and how blind, guided by the shallow opinions of people like Lord M. and Lehzen — it was nearly six months since she'd written to Lehzen and there were a dozen letters lying somewhere still unanswered — how Albert had changed her, and how she thanked God for him. As the carriages passed in a long procession through the city to St Paul's Cathedral, following the hearse decked out in plumes and velvet mourning draperies, the Queen's handkerchief touched her eyes. Albert had taught her to appreciate the Duke, and the Duke had appreciated Albert. That alone was proof of his greatness, and for that she wept openly before her people.

The Victor of Waterloo rested at last in his splendid tomb, and almost the last trace of Regency England was buried with him. That age of elegance and squalor, so paradoxical in its extremes of tyranny and freedom, with its moral laxity and its exacting codes of honour, passed out of human memory with the death of one of the greatest men who had lived in it and shaped its history. The England which mourned Wellington was rich and growing richer, the power was passing from the aristocrat to the manufacturer, the politicians who lauded his memory in both Houses spoke a new language and thought new thoughts, and the plain little Queen with her studious husband and her growing family, epitomized the change which had transformed the whole country. Virtue was the fashion, the sturdy, steely virtue which seeped through from Osborne and Balmoral, and the art of the new England was as stolid as the furniture. Grace and inutility were not compatible; wax flowers and potted plants made their appearance in the homes of England, chairs and sofas developed bulbous legs and broke out in a rash of bobble fringe, and in the Royal Palaces Prince Albert had the Gainsboroughs moved so that the Winterhalter portraits could be better hung. And within two months of that stately funeral, Louis Napoleon proclaimed himself Emperor of the French, with the approval of the English Government.

It was certain now that England had nothing to fear from France. The new Emperor Napoleon III, well aware of old associations, had made his desire for friendship so clear that even Albert accepted it, and in due course Victoria could write to the upstart as 'Mon Frère', admitting him into the jealously guarded circle of sovereigns. There was nothing to fear from France, and, thanks to Albert's efforts, Her Majesty's army and navy were being properly equipped.

But as the new year advanced it became more and more obvious that the martial preparations had not been in vain; for Russia was obviously manoeuvring to attack Turkey, and England, roused by preparations and months of war talk, was boiling with aggressive spirit, and quite ready to substitute the Russians for the French. The name of Russia filled Victoria with alarm; she had entertained the Emperor Nicholas at Windsor soon after her marriage and thought the Russian Autocrat a most forbidding creature. Russia was *dreadful*, she said to Albert, and Albert heartily agreed with her. And how dare the Emperor Nicholas try to expand his dominions any further! The Queen who had just returned from visiting her children in the nursery studied the map with the keenness of a general, tracing the areas under her authority with one finger, and pointing out to Albert that it was unthinkable that Russia should over-run the Sultan's principalities.

'If he makes any attempt, we must go to war!'

In spite of himself, Albert was surprised. He was always surprised when she dropped the role of wife and mother and returned to her old tone of autocracy. How ready she was to speak of war! Women were not supposed to make decisions of such magnitude, or to contemplate them with calmness, far less enthusiasm. He had helped to reorganize the armed forces, but then he had thought France meant to begin aggression. He bent over the map and studied it with her. The size of Russia appalled him too; it sprawled like a great sinister octopus, and the mentality nurtured on the miniature Duchy of Coburg, on pretty little castles and close frontiers, recoiled from the immensity of Russia. It was a land dark with ignorance, multi-racial and held in the grip of the fiercest oppression in the civilized world. Much as Stockmar admired and advocated independent power for the monarchy, neither he nor his pupil could countenance the ruthless absolutism of the Emperor Nicholas. He envisaged the spread of that power, creeping out over Turkey, turning to Europe through Poland, where a revolt had been mercilessly crushed, advancing like some evil tide against Germany itself . . .

'If it does come to war,' Victoria said, 'We shall have France on our side, dearest.'

France was already involved in the quarrel, ostensibly over the rights of some Christian shrines in Jerusalem, where both Orthodox and Latin rites were making claims. There was a touch of human pique about the attitude of Louis Napoleon; of all the European monarchs, only Nicholas had refused to recognize his Imperial title.

'It's a terrible prospect,' Albert said. 'But if it should come, then we shall face it together.'

'Of course we shall,' she turned to him immediately. 'Dearest love, I feel you'll worry more than I shall. Promise me you won't; it pains me so much when you don't sleep well and look so tired.'

He often slept very badly, lying awake in the early hours while she slept deeply and woke full of vigour. As he lay beside her, his thoughts wandered, back to Coburg and his childhood, back to his studies at Bonn University and his youth with Ernst. There was so much to think about, and the day was too short and always filled with problems. There were letters to be written and endless memoranda, nothing must be overlooked or left to chance, his son's education to supervise . . . If only he showed more promise! If only he could find one spark of sympathy with the boy or see a gleam of serious purpose in his nature. There were so many worries and so many duties, he never seemed to have a moment for reflection or solitude. And he loved solitude; all his life he had gone for long walks alone, or played the piano or the organ for his own amusement. But Victoria claimed all his leisure; she wanted to go with him and walk too, and when he played he often found her standing in the doorway listening. He knew she didn't understand his longing to be alone at times, or know that the part of his holiday in Scotland he loved most was when he went deer stalking with a ghillie and she could not come with him. He knew it was disloyal and unkind not to want her with him all the time, when she grudged every moment he spent away from her. Only at night, when she was asleep — when there was nobody to come to his door and interrupt him or bring him a message from Stockmar, or a scribbled note full of endearments from Victoria — only then could he live in peace with his own thoughts and imagine that he was free. No, he didn't sleep well, but he could never tell her why. There were still so many things that he could never tell her, because he knew that if he did she wouldn't understand.

'It does worry me so dreadfully when I see you looking tired, my love,' Victoria repeated. 'I don't know why it is, but I never feel tired.'

He smiled at her, and slowly began rolling up the map.

'My hold on life isn't as strong as yours,' he said.

'Emily my love, come and kiss your old husband! I've had a tiring day.'

Lady Palmerston laughed and bent over him; she kissed him fondly on the forehead. They had been lovers for twenty years and married for fifteen, but the bond of affection and understanding was stronger than ever between them.

'You're always sentimental when you've been making mischief, Henry. Tell me all about it.'

Palmerston smiled at her; she really was a damned handsome woman, he thought, watching her sit opposite to him; handsome and clever, everything an ambitious man could want in a wife. Emily was tall, with the natural elegance of all the Lambs; the spreading crinoline and tight-waisted dresses, which were then fashionable, suited her perfectly. He was pleased to see that there was so little grey in her hair, and the new style, brushed smoothly back from the forehead and caught up in curls at the back, enhanced her fine features.

'Why should you suppose that I've been up to mischief?'

245

'Because I know you so well, dear heart,' Emily retorted.

'And so you should, after all these years. And I know *you*, when you look like that, and I see I'm not to escape. I've made up my mind about something, my dear. I think the Home Office is a dull Ministry, and I'm going to resign.'

'Resign? Good Lord, Henry, you're not serious?'

'Never more serious in my life,' he answered happily. 'Dull for me and damned dull for you. We're about to go to war, and I can think of more amusing positions to be in during the next year or two. As I see it, Emily, the nation wants a war; we're armed to the eyebrows, we've a fleet that's crying out to be used, and the people are longing for a fight. We'll be at war in a month, whether Aberdeen wants it or not. And I don't consider he's the right fellow to lead the country in such circumstances.'

Emily Palmerston leant back in her chair and said sweetly: 'And who is the right fellow, in your opinion?'

'Myself, of course. Who else?'

'I know I'm being stupid, Henry, but how do you propose to become Prime Minister by resigning from the Government?'

'By making myself an issue, my love. Aberdeen is for peace, I am for war. The whole country knows that; I shall take care to hammer the difference home. Believe it or not, the Court and I are in agreement for once; Her Majesty is bristling with martial fervour, one hardly dares breathe the word Russia in her presence, and a split in the Government, properly timed of course, will relieve Aberdeen of the party leadership.'

'If you're hoping to make an issue out of his peace policy, you may fail,' his wife pointed out. All her life had been spent in the milieu of politics; she was as skilful in the science of intrigue as any professional politician.

'Aberdeen's not that big a fool — if the Queen and the country want war, then he'll adapt his policy.'

'I've no doubt he will,' Palmerston explained. Dear Emily — sharp though she was, he always enjoyed proving that he was sharper.

'But Johnny Russell will provide me with my excuse. He's determined to push through with another Bill for Reform, and I'm determined to oppose it. I shall resign, my love, and I shall be swept back to office. And not to the Home Office! You will see.'

'I probably will,' Emily said lazily. 'Heaven knows, I'm used to upheavals. You really are a rogue, Henry, I'm quite ashamed of you!'

Palmerston grinned at her, and after a moment she smiled.

'If I hadn't been a rogue, you wouldn't have married me,' he said. 'And you know very well, you like upheavals. And you'll like being the wife of the Prime Minister, won't you now?'

'Yes,' she admitted, 'I shall certainly like that. I shall be very disappointed if you fail.'

'Have I ever failed,' he asked her gently, 'to give you anything I've promised?'

The door of Albert's study opened very quietly; for a moment Victoria hesitated on the threshold. She saw him standing with his back towards her, gazing out of the window over Windsor Great Park. The sun was going down in a blaze of crimson, a Christmas sun, their children called it, dyed a deep blood red, and the room was full of that strange December light. She noticed that no candles were alight, and the curtains had not been drawn. He, who was so methodical and considerate, had not allowed the servants to disturb him. He was standing alone in the red dusk, and she knew, without seeing his face, that his heart was broken.

'Albert.' She closed the door very gently, and now that she had come to him she had stopped trembling and her eyes were dry.

'Albert, darling.'

Slowly he turned towards her, and she knew when he answered that he had been weeping as he stood by the window.

'Victoria . . . is that you?'

'I have looked everywhere for you; then I thought you might be here, working.'

They were face to face and she reached out for his hand and held it between both her own, against her breast.

'My darling love,' she said at last, 'I don't know what to say to you.'

'There is nothing you can say,' he said wearily. 'I had hoped to keep it from you, but I suppose it wasn't possible.'

'I saw the newspapers, and Lord Clarendon came to me with the report of what had happened in London. They had to tell me, my love, and all I prayed for was that I might have been able to soften the blow for you in some way.'

'There is no way to soften truth.'

Albert moved back to the window and sat down in the cushioned seat; she drew her skirts aside and sat with him, the red sun lighting them both.

'Your people have been waiting in their thousands all day long to see me brought up the Thames and imprisoned in the Tower for treason. There is no way, my poor Victoria, that you can soften that. They hated me from the day I came to England and they hate me still. Nothing I have done has made any difference.'

'It was just hysteria,' she said. 'Clarendon said the newspapers have been working everyone into a frenzy. They didn't mean it, my darling love − don't you know they expected to see me arrested too? They were waiting there, in a holiday mood, looking for their Queen and their Prince to pass under the Traitor's Gate. It's horrible − it's unforgivable!' For a moment her passionate anger and bitterness transcended the calm she was trying to preserve for his sake. 'But you mustn't take it seriously. Clarendon said they're mad with war fever; they would have made anyone the scapegoat!'

'But they didn't,' he reminded her gently. 'Palmerston is a national hero − Palmerston resigns over the Reform Bill, and the whole of England jumps to the conclusion that I forced him out of office because he wants war with Russia and I do not. They didn't make *anyone* the scapegoat — they didn't even know the facts, but they invented them and then blamed *me*. I believe that nothing would please your people more than if they heard I'd been executed in the Tower!'

'Oh, Albert, Albert, don't!' She broke down then, choking with tears, and covered her face with her hands. Everything he said was true, and she knew it. He was hated. Clarendon had paled while he described the scenes of popular enthusiasm and the bloodthirsty attitude of that mob thronging Tower Bridge, hanging over the parapets and shouting at the sight of any craft coming up the river in the hope that the man they hated was aboard. They would have rejoiced to see him die, to revive the barbarism of the past when kings and queens and princes shed their blood inside that awful fortress. And it was no use pretending to him, no use telling him that the papers and agitators were responsible, there was no refuge in excuses for either of them now. The people had shown their feelings for Albert, and nothing could erase the memory of that demonstration. She had forced every detail out of Clarendon, though she was trembling from head to foot, and the murderous temper of her Hanoverian ancestors had boiled up in her until Clarendon stammered and looked away at the expression on her face.

'Melbourne was right!' she burst out suddenly. 'He said they were animals and they are! Wild beasts, ungrateful, vile, unworthy of anything but tyranny. That's what they understand, my darling — tyrants to rule over them, not saints! I shall never forgive this.'

'Don't cry,' he begged her. 'Please, dearest, nothing can be changed by grief. I have accepted it, and I'm calm now.'

'Grief? Oh, Albert, I'm only grieving for *you*, for all your efforts and your hopes — you've worked so hard and done so much and this is your reward! I shall never be able to forget or forgive as long as I live. When they turned on you they showed themselves to me as they really are! God help anyone who comes to me and talks about bettering the working classes! They took their little children with them, the brutes, hoping to see us!'

'Hoping to see me,' Albert corrected. 'They love you and they're loyal to you. I am the one. I'm the foreigner. It was foolish of me to think it could have been otherwise. I have never been accepted by *any* class — what's the use of blaming the ignorant masses? They're only following the example of educated people.'

It was strange, he thought, how the roles had been reversed. She had come to comfort him, and now he was trying to ease the pain of his own heart-break, trying to quell her temper and her bitterness because of what had been done to him. It had always been so, and always would be as long as he lived. Duty expects no reward. He had heard that somewhere, but the source escaped him. He had built his life upon the performance of his duty, but he had been human enough to want to be appreciated. And he knew finally that whatever he did he never would be; and now it didn't matter any more. All that mattered was Victoria's feelings; she mustn't hate her own people and revile them like this, she was the Queen and she must be above taking sides, even with her own husband. That was important, but at that moment a strange lethargy possessed him; he could see how important it all was but he couldn't find the energy or the words to do anything about it. Not just yet. Later, when the pain and unutterable disappointment had been accepted, perhaps submerged a little, then he could really soothe Victoria and remind her that she was the Queen and show her where her duty lay.

'I am so tired,' he said suddenly, 'so very tired. I'd like to have dinner alone with you and go to bed.'

'They've broken your heart,' Victoria said slowly. 'Oh, Albert, don't look like that — try not to suffer so. I love you so terribly, I should simply *die* if you were to lose hope and be unhappy. Albert, think of me, think how much you mean to me! I couldn't go on without your support. Bear up, my own angel love, please, please bear up!'

'I'm only tired,' he said again. 'And I don't want to talk about it any more. It's over and done. Palmerston will rejoin the Government, I shall be exonerated, and the whole thing will be forgotten.'

'Not by me! Never by me, as long as I live.'

She raised one hand and put it against his cheek, stroking it as a mother might have done to comfort her child, and all the depth and force of her love for him was expressed in the gesture. She herself could bear unpopularity. She was above them all and she knew it; the opinion of the mob could never hurt her. All her life she had been able to meet criticism with contempt, but she fully recognized that Albert, her beloved, sensitive Albert, with his dreams of human nobility, was pitifully vulnerable to the baseness and ingratitude of the world in which he lived.

'I love you so,' she whispered. 'From the moment I saw you at Windsor, when I was so headstrong and didn't want to marry and give way to anyone, I loved you with all my heart, Albert. And I love you more with every day – every minute. I know how lonely you've been here in England, and how few friends you've found; I know how hard you've worked, not for yourself, but for me and for the country. *You* thought of the Exhibition, you organized it when everyone was trying to stop you, you made it the most splendid thing that's happened since I became Queen. *I* know what I owe you and what England owes you. If I'm a good Queen, my darling, it's because you've made me one. You've taught me everything. Nothing can alter that.'

He smiled at her, and taking her hand from his face, he kissed it. He remembered suddenly how he had once dreaded her affection, how possessive, even suffocating he had felt her love to be. But that evening when he had plumbed the depth of loneliness and tasted the bitterest gall of personal failure, he was glad of it. He had hidden from her in his study because his feelings were so painful that he didn't want to share them, above all, he hadn't wanted her sympathy, her angry denunciations and excuses. But now he was glad she had come to him. On the day he had married her, knowing that he was not in love and never would be, he had thought of her as the only friend he had in this alien country, and that early instinct had been right. The English would never accept him or like him. In less than two years they had forgotten the Exhibition, the trade and the wealth which had accrued through his idea and efforts, and believed him a traitor in the pay of the Russians. Whatever he did would always be wrong. But in *her* eyes, he was always right. He knew how strong she was, with a power of character and will that he could never possess; he knew that without the backing of her authority, his interference would have been swept aside again and again. She was the only one he had, yet he had never loved her; even what he felt at that moment was only the gratitude of a very tired man.

'You would have been a good Queen whoever you had married,' he said quietly. 'Just as you are a good wife. Oh, Victoria, how I wish we were back at Rosenau, on holiday again – just you and I.'

Gently she put her arms around him.

'We will have our own Rosenau when Balmoral is finished,' she whispered. 'And we shall live there in peace together, my love. And when all this is forgotten, you will be happy again, I promise you. I will make you happy, Albert. I know we have long years of happiness to come.'

They sat on in the window seat with their arms round each other, while the last red streaks faded to pink in the sky and merged into twilight.

In January, Lord Derby, the former Prime Minister, received an invitation to attend on the Queen at Windsor.

He had pleasant memories of the term served under Her Majesty, who seemed to like him and had been far less difficult than he had been led to expect. It was damned awkward about those rumours of the Prince being arrested and crowds gathering round the Tower, and he had heard from Aberdeen and others that the Queen was considerably annoyed. It would be quite awkward meeting the Prince, after such a demonstration of his unpopularity. To his surprise, Victoria was alone in the White Drawing-room. She looked very small in the enormous room, and rather dowdily dressed as usual, in a gown of blue velour with an ugly bead trimming.

'Ma'am.'

She gave him her hand to kiss.

'I know you are busy, my Lord, and I am overburdened with work, so we will dispense with formalities. I have sent for you because I know you are one of the finest speakers in public life. Therefore I have chosen you to speak on behalf of His Royal Highness Prince Albert.'

'Your pardon, Ma'am, I don't quite understand . . .'

'You will,' she interrupted. 'I am going to explain to you. No explanation is necessary, I am *sure* of the need for a prompt and public rebuttal of the unspeakable lies which have been circulated against the Prince in the last few weeks. You have heard, my Lord, of the infamous suggestion that he is disloyal to the country's interest and a friend of Russia?'

'Ma'am, such talk has been going round, but I assure you that I wouldn't dream of listening . . .'

'I am quite sure you wouldn't,' Victoria said. 'Nor would any responsible person. Nonetheless these things have been said, and the disgraceful exhibition given by the people round the Tower was one of the results. Now, my Lord, I have made my wishes clear to the Government, and they naturally agree that the Prince's good name must be vindicated and his position established once and for all.'

'Yes, Ma'am.' Looking down into the flushed determined face, Derby noticed that Her Majesty's rather receding little jaw was set like a vice. He had no doubt whatsoever that she had made her wishes *very* clear . . .

'You are a marvellous orator, my Lord,' she continued, 'and I would like you to put your gift at the disposal of the

Prince. Walpole will speak for him in the Commons, and I would like you to do so in the Lords.'

He bowed. 'It would be an honour, Ma'am. I can speak for His Royal Highness's loyalty and integrity from my own experience. But what am I to say regarding his official position?'

'You are to say,' Victoria answered, 'that as husband of the Queen he has the right and duty to advise her in all matters of State. I wish this to be emphasized beyond doubt. He has the *right*, do you understand?'

'I do,' Derby said. 'And I shall not leave the question in doubt, I promise you.'

'I'm sure you won't. I'm sure that now that Lord Palmerston has returned on a tide of hysterical acclamation, it's time the Press and the public recognized how badly they have behaved and what an apology is owed to my husband. I should also like to ask you whether it's true that Lord Palmerston gave the impression the Prince had contributed towards his resignation? I heard a rumour to that effect.'

He was not deceived by the guarded tone; her eyes gave her away. They were glittering with an expression that might have made the irrepressible Palmerston himself shake in his shoes if he could have seen it. Where had she heard that, Derby wondered. It was quite true of course, the whole outburst had been engineered by that unscrupulous old devil, posing as a patriotic martyr. He hadn't been able to resist a dig at the Prince at the same time.

'No, Ma'am, I have never heard anything, and I'm sure Lord Palmerston would be terribly distressed if he thought you believed such a thing.' Of course one needn't like Palmerston's methods, but one had to admire his skill. They had sat opposite each other in the House for years. He was not going to sacrifice him to His Royal Highness of Saxe-Coburg.

'I don't think Lord Palmerston can possibly be blamed,' he added.

Victoria turned away.

'I'm glad to hear it,' she said. 'I know I can rely upon you, Lord Derby, to make a speech worthy of your subject.'

On March 28th, 1854, England and France declared war upon the Czar of all the Russians. Excited crowds gathered in the streets, cheering and dancing with delight, and Victoria appeared on the balcony at Buckingham palace to watch the Scots Fusiliers march past on their way to the coast and embarkation for the Crimea.

She was nervy and excitable, and full of a bounding energy that scorned sleep or tranquillity, even insisting on following her troops to the ports, and standing on the deck of the *Victoria and Albert* to see her navy set out for the Black Sea.

Stockmar had returned from a holiday in Germany, and he paused in his joint persecution with Gibbs of the Prince of Wales to be thoroughly irritated by the Queen. He was annoyed by her sentimental tears when the bands played, and her hard-headed assessments of the political and military situation. He was devoted to Victoria, but it irked him to see how eagerly she shouldered the terrible burden of governing a country at war, and how she seemed quite independent of Albert's support. It was not seemly, the Baron grumbled, bitterly jealous that a woman should receive the plaudits of the army, while his protégé stood in the background. It was all very well for the Queen to represent popular frenzy, and draw cheers and hysterical crowds wherever she went, but the real organization of the war was quite beyond her scope. He saw a chance of Albert fading out of the public eye, and urged him in the strongest terms to concern himself with supplies and armaments and strategy, and to bombard the hapless Government and Her Majesty's Generals at the War Office with his views on all these matters.

The Generals, most of whom had last seen active service under Wellington, received the meticulous enquiries and suggestions with a good deal of irritation, and paid as little attention to them as they dared. Damned foreigner, meddling as usual — what did a comic opera German Prince know about the mighty science of war and what the devil had all these questions about supplies and lines of communication and transport got to do with winning battles? If only the old Duke had been alive he would have known how to put him in his place . . . But Wellington was dead, and the system of aristocratic preference in the choice of command soon showed itself pitifully inept without his genius.

Disturbing reports reached England of casualties through overcrowding and disease at the chaotic base camp at Scutari. Public enthusiasm for the war was damped by tales of nightmare voyages where men died in hundreds of heat and cholera, and the magnificent cavalry horses perished by scores. There were stories of officers too inexperienced and inefficient to lead their men on a simple reconnaissance against the Russian enemy without losing three-quarters of their force, of a lack of arms and equipment, of desertions and futile bickerings between commanders, and particularly of the lack of medical care for the wounded. The glorious war to protect Turkey from the rapacity of the Czar assumed an ignoble aspect of muddle and impending defeat. There was a general impression among all classes that the best was not being done for England or her soldiers. There were angry debates in the Lords and Parliament, where Lord Palmerston's speeches proved him as patriotic and forceful as the rest of his colleagues seemed inert. His popularity grew every day; in the disappointment and uncertainty of those months in 1854, his confidence and clear speaking raised him far above the Prime Minister Aberdeen in the people's estimation. 'Pam' was the only man among them, 'Pam' wouldn't waste time mouthing platitudes while English troops died of cholera and fell victim to the enemy through the stupidity of their commanders.

It was at this moment, when doubt and frustration had almost reached explosion point, that Aberdeen's Government fell.

'Well, Emily, have I kept my promise, or haven't I?'

Emily Palmerston shook her head and smiled at her husband. It was a mocking smile, but it was full of triumph and admiration.

'You've kept it,' she admitted. 'You're an impossible, terrible old rogue, my Lord, but I love you, and I shall adore being the Prime Minister's wife. Good heavens, I can still hardly believe it!'

'Never thought you'd see the day when the Queen sent for me to head the Government, did you? ' he asked. 'Ha, I don't suppose she did either. Lord, my love, she looked as sour as a lemon.'

'Well, you can't really blame her. After that dreadful scandal when you resigned and the demonstrations against the Prince . . . My dear, I should expect her to loathe you!'

'She does, she does,' Palmerston chuckled. 'But I've a feeling she'll get over it when she sees what good service I give. She's a militant Madam, I can tell you, and as soon as I began reviling the Russians she was agreeing with me as if we'd never had a cross word in our lives. And I positively fawned on the Prince.'

'He's not pro-Russian, is he?' Emily asked.

'Good God, no, of course he's not! I know people said so, and I may have let a word drop here and there just to gain a little sympathy, but there's no truth in it. He hates the Russians like the devil hates holy water, as they say in Ireland. I almost felt sorry about all that business when I heard him. Needless to say they were both as stiff as boards with me to begin with, but I do believe they thawed a little. Just a little, at the end.'

She put her arm through his and leant against him.

'You'll have to be tactful with them, Henry, or you may not last. It's one thing to be Foreign Secretary and let Russell take the knocks, but it's quite another when you're Prime Minister.'

'I know that, Emily. I'm not a fool, my dear. This is my opportunity; it's what I've been wanting and waiting for the best part of my life. Don't think I shall throw it away. We've got a war to win, and we'll have to work like the devil to make good our mistakes. That's the most important link between me and the Palace. They want victory and so do I. And I feel sure that he'll work with me whatever he feels, out of duty. And where he leads, the Queen will follow. She's a sensible woman, too, my dear. She knows the country is behind me; I think she probably realizes Aberdeen and the rest were a pack of muddling idiots, and that whatever I do I won't muddle and stray off course. I left office once, and, by God, the throne she was sitting on rocked under her! I daresay she hasn't forgotten that –'

'Or forgiven,' his wife retorted.

'Or forgiven,' he agreed. 'But then she's not the forgiving kind. I don't expect her to forgive me; or like me. But she'll work with me, and that's all I ask.' He yawned and stretched.

'I could put down a good dinner and some port, Emily. And then we'll go to bed. I've had a heavy day.'

Emily Palmerston blinked innocently at him.

'So have I, Henry dear. I've been so busy making plans to move into Downing Street, I'm tired out!'

In the months that followed, Victoria sometimes paused in the middle of her work to wonder whether she were dreaming, and if it were really possible that that detestable old man she had fought with so bitterly a year or two before, was the tireless, brilliant Prime Minister who seemed to be the easiest person in the world to deal with.

She didn't like Palmerston; she never would like him, but in spite of her feminine prejudice, she had to admit that his conduct was now faultless. He was still rather startling to look at with his dyed red whiskers and his brightly coloured clothes, but his manner to her was impeccable, and most important of all, he sought Albert's advice at every opportunity.

It was incredible, but the raffish, headstrong characteristics which had caused her so much annoyance in peace, were ideally suited to conditions of war; she could not help responding to his courage, his contempt for their enemy, and his confidence that England would win a sweeping victory. The fighting raged in the Crimea; the forces of England and France, decimated more by disease than by battle, struggled to capture the Russian fortress at Sebastopol, and an Englishwoman, Miss Nightingale – such a pretty name – had taken a band of nurses out to Scutari to succour the wounded. It was a wonderful thing to have done; Victoria, whose opinion of her sex's intelligence and ability was as low as any man's, decided that Miss Nightingale was an exception to the rule, and sent her a little brooch to the Crimea with a note of commendation. It pleased her very much to imagine the excitement and gratitude of that busy woman when she received a personal present from the Queen.

She visited the wounded on their return, and shed tears of emotion over her brave soldiers, her own children almost, who sat up in their beds to cheer her as she passed. They looked so splendid and so sad in their clean bandages, and her imagination pictured the worst battlefields and base camps of that frightful war as looking much the same as the hospitals prepared for her inspection. One did not think about lice and dirt and dreadful pain; one did not imagine men screaming for relief from their wounds. One only saw them brave and washed and on their best behaviour, and one felt very proud to think that they were her men and had fought for *her*. She had quite forgotten, and Albert did not remind her, that these were the sons and husbands and brothers of the common mob who hated her husband and, in her view, were not much better than beasts.

And early in the spring of 1855, the Emperor Napoleon III and his Empress Eugenie, paid a State visit to England.

Victoria was as excited as a girl at the prospect of seeing them; the very name of Napoleon had a sinister sound, and this was the great Bonaparte's nephew . . . There were so many different opinions of him: some people said he was the most charming man imaginable, while others said he was

259

little and ugly and sly. Her darling Albert had gone to Boulogne and met him the year before, and had given a reserved but favourable view of him. It was also said that Eugénie was one of the most beautiful women in the world, and without a trace of jealousy Victoria longed to see her too. She had several new dresses made, splendid Ball gowns of satin, trimmed with priceless lace, some plainer day dresses for informal occasions, and decided that since her present wardrobe suited her so well, the additions should be made in the same style. Albert did not like innovations in dress, and he always said that simplicity became her best. The magnificent state jewels which she so seldom used were polished and taken out, for while it would have been foolish to go to fashionable extremes in clothes, the wealth and power of the Crown were judged by a Queen's jewels.

The Emperor and Empress arrived at Windsor, and they stayed in the Golden state apartments. Victoria's first impression of Napoleon was of a small man with an ungainly figure and an ugly, melancholy face. But as soon as he spoke to her she felt the extraordinary magnetism of his charm; he had a delightful speaking voice, and very fine eyes, and though she was close to forty and idyllically happy with Albert, a buried instinct stirred and responded to an appeal she could not understand. She liked him immediately and, most surprisingly, she liked the Empress too. It was not in her nature to be jealous; when she saw the dazzling beauty of the French Empress, she admired wholeheartedly. She had never had beauty or even prettiness herself, but it did not occur to her to compare herself unfavourably with the gorgeous red-haired Eugénie, with her superb carriage and rare violet-blue eyes. She was the most exquisite creature Victoria had ever seen, and she was also absolutely charming.

After a magnificent state banquet, the whole company gathered in the Waterloo Chamber for a Ball. Palmerston, colourful as a peacock with his handsome elegant wife beside him, watched the Queen of England open the Ball with the

Emperor of the French. They were well matched; he was short and her tiny stature seemed less incongruous. But she was badly dressed in an old-fashioned crinoline of gold, smothered in Brussels lace, her head and neck and arms blazing with diamonds so big that she seemed to be on fire when she moved. She was a stout, plain little woman, with a rather red face, but he watched her steadily for some moments, and then glanced at the Empress Eugénie, who was dancing with Albert. They were both tall, both exceptionally good looking really, though the Prince looked tired and his hair was receding. The French Empress wore a glorious white dress which displayed her famous shoulders; she had the figure of a goddess, and a 'paling' tiara thick with diamonds and emeralds sparkled on her burnished hair. She was undoubtedly one of the greatest beauties he had ever seen − he reminded Emily in a whisper that Napoleon's original intentions towards her had been dishonourable as they were to most women; but her virtue, and her extraordinary loveliness had driven him to marriage. She was everything Victoria was not; tall, striking, superbly dressed, and she moved on Albert's arm like a swan on water.

But no man would ever bow instinctively to her, as they would to the dumpy little Queen of England. Victoria was inherently Royal, Palmerston thought suddenly, almost as if in that brilliant setting he were seeing her for the first time; beauty and elegance had nothing to do with the kind of majesty Victoria possessed. Albert did not have it either; but it was in the voice and the personality of the nephew of Napoleon Bonaparte. That was why he and Victoria dominated the whole room, as if the other pair, the lovely woman and the handsome man, did not exist for the spectators.

The visit was a great success; everywhere the Emperor and Empress went crowds cheered them enthusiastically; there were dinner parties and Balls and a review of troops in Windsor Great Park, and when they left for France, Victoria felt such a sense of anti-climax that she burst into tears on Albert's shoulder. She really liked Louis Napoleon, and she had so enjoyed having the Empress to stay; it was all very well, but she had never had a woman companion who was an equal; and it had been so amusing to talk about the children and ask questions about Paris, and look at some of Eugenie's dresses, made by a new designer called M. Worth. She was really sorry they had gone.

But in August they returned the visit. Victoria prepared happily to see her dear sovereign brother and sister again, and her eldest son was informed that his crushing routine of lessons, lectures and short walks with Mr Gibbs would be interrupted while he accompanied his parents to Paris.

Bertie expressed his delight so loudly that he had to be reprimanded, and in a pained interview his father explained that the French Court would naturally be interested in the character of the future King of England, and closely observe his behaviour. A display of frivolity would be disastrous, he said sternly, and added sharply that Bertie was not to hang his head when he was spoken to like that – it looked so sly! He was coming to Paris, and it was his mother's hope that he would acquit himself properly for once. They would both like, Prince Albert said severely, to feel that he could be trusted to behave as the Prince of Wales should.

He was annoyed and bewildered to hear from Gibbs that the boy had come back to his schoolroom and burst into tears.

They landed in France in August, in brilliant sunshine, and Victoria was so overwhelmed by the magnificence of St Cloud that she forgot to reprove Bertie for being sick on the boat. When she saw her apartments she exclaimed with pleasure. They were exact duplicates of her own rooms at Windsor. The furniture, hangings, the colour scheme – everything had been copied so that she might never have left England. How thoughtful of the Emperor! How charming and kind of them both! Laughing, she said she only needed to see her dog and the illusion would be complete. Her remark was repeated to the Emperor and the very next morning her spaniel, barking joyfully, bounded into her bedroom.

Victoria's enthusiasm was infectious; the cold and calculating heart of Napoleon III had already warmed towards her in spite of himself, and Eugénie, whose beauty had subjected her to so much feminine spite, was completely won by the generous admiration of the English Queen.

In their own apartments at St Cloud, Napoleon and his Consort discussed their guests. The Empress sat by her dressing-table, swathed in a bedgown and robe of palest pink satin trimmed with swansdown; though they had been married for only two years, the Emperor had begun to share his affections with other women, women who could not compare with his wife for beauty or charm, but who gave him the essential warmth that Eugénie lacked. A lot of nonsense was talked about women with red hair, Napoleon thought idly, watching her scenting her throat, but it was typical of men to worship goddesses and then be disappointed by the very qualities which had first attracted them.

But in spite of his mistresses, he was still in love with her. Eugénie sighed.

'What a long day it's been! I thought they were supposed to go to bed early, but Victoria was as fresh this evening as if she had just woken up!'

'She's enjoying herself,' the Emperor said. 'She was very gay as a young woman; it's the Prince who likes early hours. He looked exhausted.'

'I don't think he's very strong; he's so pale, Napoleon, and I've thought everything was a terrible effort for him at times. I watched him when we visited the tomb at Les Invalides and I could have sworn there was a moment when he nearly fell asleep!'

The Emperor smiled. 'I was also watching, my dear, and he did!'

There had been a state drive through the streets of Paris,

where an enormous crowd had given the Queen of England an hysterical reception, and the newspapers had hailed the visit as the symbol of the alliance which now existed between the two hereditary enemies, England and France. The soldiers of both countries were fighting on the same side in the Crimea, and it was clear at last that they were winning. The Queen of England's charm and dignity were described in flattering terms; with Gallic courtesy her old-fashioned costumes and lack of good looks were generally ignored. There was nothing but praise and enthusiasm, and when the Royal party made what was almost a pilgrimage to the tomb of the great Napoleon at Les Invalides, Nature blessed the occasion with a dramatic thunderstorm as if the soul of the mighty Bonaparte had called up cannon in the Heavens. It had been a strange sight for Louis Napoleon to watch Victoria kneeling at the grave of her country's greatest enemy, with tears of emotion in her eyes, and to see her motion her eldest son to kneel and pay homage with her. The boy had seemed quite dazed by the whole scene.

'Did he really sleep? How funny,' the Empress said. 'But after all, the Prince is a German; he can't be expected to appreciate what such a visit meant to French and English people. I hope nobody else noticed him dozing.'

'I doubt it,' Napoleon shrugged. 'He is not really important, everyone was looking at Victoria and the boy. Tell me something, Eugénie – you don't care for Prince Albert much, do you?'

'Not much,' she admitted. 'He's exceedingly polite of course and he's been charming to me, in his way. But he's cold, you know. And oh so stiff! His conversation bores me to distraction. Don't tell me *you* find him amusing?'

'Compared to the Queen – no. He's better informed, he knows too much about everything in fact; it leaves one with nothing to contribute oneself, which is irritating. But I pay him careful attention because it pleases her. I told her I was content to listen to him for hours and improve my mind, and she was simply delighted. She's an extraordinary woman; all she wants is for him to be praised and liked; when the crowds cheered him she blushed like a girl!'

'I like her,' the Empress said warmly. 'She's so genuine; I had expected a formidable creature full of her own importance, but she's really good-hearted, I think. France has a staunch friend in her.'

'That's what I wanted,' Napoleon answered. 'It's odd, because she looks such a little bourgeoise at first sight — until you speak to her. I think she could be formidable too, if she chose. She likes you, my dear, she's always telling me how beautiful you are, and she likes me, and she likes France . . . It's been a great success.'

'There's only one thing,' Eugénie said. 'I do feel rather sorry for that poor little Prince Bertie. They both give me the impression that they dislike him. Do you know, the child came into my room this morning and said he wished he could stay here with us instead of going back to England tomorrow! And when I pointed out how his Mama and Papa would miss him, what do you think he said? "Oh, no, they wouldn't notice it at all. There are six more of us at home!" Wasn't that sad?'

'Few sovereigns like their heirs,' he said. 'And she is no exception. Neither of them love the child; whenever they've talked about him they've practically apologized, as if we must think him dreadful too. When I said what a fine little fellow he was, they were quite annoyed!'

'Poor boy,' Eugenie said again. She yawned and closed her eyes. 'It's been such a tiring day. I'm quite exhausted.' The Emperor stood up and for a moment their eyes met in the mirror.

'I quite understand, my dear,' he said. 'I'll leave you then. Sleep well.'

Balmoral Castle was finished at last. When the Royal party returned from France they travelled on up to the Highlands for their private holiday, and moved into the completed manifestation of Albert's architectural dream. Hand-in-hand Victoria and Albert gazed at the enormous grey stone structure, at the turrets and ramparts, at the medieval grandeur of design which conjured up Scotland's romantic past. It was perfect, the Queen agreed, so much nicer than the rough and crumbling walls of an *old* castle, and their Court could only stare at the monstrosity and murmur compliments. Ludicrous as the exterior seemed, Albert's carefully planned decorations reduced even the Queen's dearest friends to giggling despair. The furniture was covered in Dress Stuart poplin, the curtains were an affront in Royal Stuart tartan and the carpets were Stuart tartan too. It was so awful that it was quite beyond description; the colours glared and clashed in a nightmare of ugly contrast, everything in it was brand new and so tasteless that the cluttered rooms of Osborne seemed like the Tuileries by comparison. Landseers and antlers and stuffed heads lowered from the walls; in the vast entrance hall a life-sized figure of the Prince in Highland dress made the ladies almost jump out of their skins. Mahogany abounded. Massive chairs and tables, covered with nicknacks, miniatures, wax flowers under glass, silhouettes and fussy photographs of the Queen and the Prince, their animals, their children . . . and porcelain views of every mountain scene in Scotland. It was incredibly middle-class, sham and uncomfortable; the aristocracy of England stood in dumb groups and exchanged glances while the Queen walked through the rooms in raptures of delight, and the Prince's ghillie John Brown bustled round them, pointing out this feature and that, and pushing past his betters. It was beyond comment, it was so ridiculous that it pained those who genuinely admired the Queen and had tried to excuse the Prince on her account. Palmerston travelled there to see them and hear details of their Paris trip; he roared with laughter and told everyone on his return to London that he had suffered a bilious attack from the colour scheme.

Word crept through the London drawing-rooms. There were titters of contemptuous amusement, and the general opinion was well, what could one expect? The Prince was simply not a gentleman . . . He chose the Queen's wardrobe, which had been a disgrace, for the State visit of Napoleon; he packed up the artistic treasures in the Palaces and made every room an eyesore with his own taste, and now he had perpetuated his vulgarity in that ghastly Gothic nightmare in the Highlands. Caricatures of Albert, balding and stooped, arrayed in kilts, appeared in the gutter press, and his old enemy *The Times* printed a scathing article. In his new home Albert heard the jibes and said nothing, there was nothing he could say, and no way Victoria could protect him from the constant hurts inflicted by a hostile people. He merely worked harder than ever, even curtailing the deerstalking he loved, in order to sit at his desk, endlessly writing memoranda to the Government and the War Office and the heads of State abroad. His closest companion was his daughter Vicky, the eldest of their eight children. She was a quiet, worshipping girl of sixteen, who listened to her father talking about all those subjects like science and history and metaphysics, which his devoted wife could never really understand, however hard she pretended to be interested. But the daughter had inherited her father's brain; like him it was methodical, painstaking, and deeply serious. In her company he found the sympathy that was so lacking with his other children, especially his son Bertie. Vicky was content to study; she showed no weakness for the lighter things of life and her judgment was not spoilt by any sense of the ridiculous. Over the years they had grown closer and closer with a strong tie of mutual interest and affection, and Victoria's jealousy of their relationship suddenly found a means of destroying it that autumn. Prince Frederick of Prussia came to stay at the new Castle; Victoria noticed with pleasure that he spent as much time as he dared with his young cousin, and when Albert tried to intrude upon them, she firmly restrained him. Frederick William was very nice, very suitable. If anything came of the cousins' devotion, it would be an *excellent* thing. The fair-haired Princess and the tall young Prussian went riding together, and one evening he approached the Queen and Albert and solemnly asked for Vicky's hand.

'She's too young,' Albert said. He was frowning, half-turned away from Victoria.

'She's sixteen,' she retorted, 'and she's very advanced for her age. Darling Albert, I know you think of her as a child, but I assure you, Vicky's quite marriageable. And Frederick is such a nice young man. I know he'll make her very happy.'

She was careful not to sound irritated. It was only natural that Albert, who was so kind, should fuss over his daughter, but then men didn't understand these things. *She* had been Queen of England with the most terrible responsibilities at eighteen, and no one had thought anything of it.'

Personally, I shall give their marriage my blessing,' she continued. 'But only if you agree, my love.'

'I've no objection to Frederick,' Albert said. 'You know that, my dear.' His thoughts flew back across the years to his own feelings when he had married, his homesickness, his intense loneliness in a foreign land. He couldn't bear to think of Vicky suffering as he had. 'But I do think she's too young.'

'Then they can wait a year,' Victoria suggested quickly. Nobody could say seventeen was too young . . . Besides, it would be a useful alliance to have the future Queen of Prussia with English birth and sympathies. Albert really must not be sentimental over it. It made her feel quite cross to see him pale and frowning over that silly girl. She was not a silly girl really, she corrected herself, she was a very *good* girl, and had never given them a moment's trouble. But it was not right to single her out from all the others as Albert did; it would only spoil her . . .

'I should like her to marry Frederick,' she said. 'Dearest, don't stand in their way; I know they're devoted already.'

'In their way?' He turned round in surprise. He had never thought of it like that. He had thought of nothing but how miserable he had been all those years ago, and imagined that the daughter he loved so much was going to be precipitated into the same circumstances when she was still so young. 'You know I'd never do anything like that. I only want Vicky's happiness.'

'Then give your permission,' Victoria urged. 'Marriage is the only thing that makes a woman happy. Darling love, *I* ought to know that!'

'Prussia is not like England,' he continued; 'I want to be satisfied that the King and Queen will be kind to her, that she won't be lonely.'

'Of course she won't be lonely — she'll be too busy being Crown Princess, and bearing children. Come, Albert, think of it, we could be grandparents before we were forty!'

He sat down, suddenly weary of arguing, weary of combating the will he knew was operating behind the facade of wifely argument. Victoria wanted the marriage, and Victoria was probably right. She only had Vicky's interests at heart, and unlike him who would miss the child so badly, she had no selfish motive for opposing the marriage.

'I only want Vicky's happiness,' he said at last. 'I know we said we would never have favourites, my dear, but I love her the best of all our children. I can't believe she's grown up and ready to marry and go and live miles away from us. I shall miss her terribly.'

Victoria suppressed a pang of most unmotherly annoyance. How that child had twisted him round her finger! Really, his eyes were full of tears just because he talked of losing her, as all parents must lose their children when it was time for them to marry. And if Vicky was going to cause friction between them, the sooner she married Frederick the better for everyone. Why couldn't Bertie have been his father's favourite — why had he to be so alien, so unsympathetic, so that Albert was driven to making a favourite out of a daughter, when he already had a wife to love and share things with?

There were moments like these when she regretted her self-imposed isolation with Albert, when a confidante, someone like poor old Lehzen, would have been God-sent. She could not tell Albert that she thought his opinion of Vicky was too high, or that she had wormed her way into his affection in a way that was not quite loyal to her mother. Albert would be hurt and horrified; he had such a noble mind that she couldn't voice such suspicions to him. And it was so *hard* to have secrets from him, to feel that there were things she could not say.

'I shall miss Vicky too, darling love. But I think this marriage is best for her, and I also think that as future Queen of Prussia she could do immense good for that country and for our own. Let them wait a year, Albert. Please, dearest, give Frederick that answer.'

She came and slipped her arm through his and smiled pleadingly into his face. It was strange, he thought, as he looked down at her, smiling automatically in return, how gentle she appeared, how wifely in the true sense of submission which he believed was the woman's proper relationship to her husband. Perhaps he had imagined that she was forcing him to agree to Vicky's marriage; she always gave way to him, deferred to his opinions, why should he be unable to avoid the suspicion that her formidable will had woken on this issue, and that somehow he was agreeing to part with his daughter against his better judgment.

'They will be so happy,' Victoria said. 'I think we should send for poor Frederick this evening and not keep him in suspense. *I* will go and see Vicky right away.'

Had he actually consented? It seemed he had; she was kissing him on the cheek and slipping out of the room to tell her daughter that her parents approved her marriage to the Prussian Prince. Albert sat down in the leather chair and stared into the fire which had been lit in the middle of the wide stone fireplace. Even though it was early September, he felt cold, and needed fires. He would be parting from Vicky in a year. Sometimes he felt as if his life were spent in saying good-bye to those he loved and living with people he could so easily have done without. Death had taken Anson and Peel from him, the only two men he had come to love and understand in the whole of England, and then Wellington, who had given him such a feeling of support. He saw Ernst at long intervals, embittered by scandal and change, and Stockmar's visits to Germany were more frequent and protracted as he grew older. He would lose Stockmar, too, one day. And now Vicky, the only one among his children who had come close to his heart, was going to marry and live in Prussia. He would have to help the child, he thought desperately; he must give her the advice learnt by his own bitter experience, save her from making his mistakes and suffering as he had done. He must teach her everything about the country she must adopt as her own, prepare her to make the most of her position and be a help to her young husband. He was so tired and so dispirited, and a mountain of paperwork grew on his desk if he left it for a few hours, but he had to help Vicky. It would mean denying himself more exercise, and spending part of his short evening leisure with her, which would certainly annoy Victoria, but it would have to be done. He leant back in the chair and closed his eyes. If she loved Frederick and Frederick loved her, she would be happy. Victoria seemed so sure of it; mothers usually knew these things. Dear God, how he prayed she would be happy.

'It is your father's wish,' Victoria said firmly. 'Naturally I hesitate to lose you, my dear child, but we are quite sure that Frederick will make you an excellent husband.'

'Yes, Mama.'

The Princess Royal was not looking at her mother. She was very pale, and if she raised her eyes Mama would see the tears in them and that would never do. She was several inches taller than Victoria, but she never felt anything but a small child in her presence, and she stood like a child, with her head down and her trembling hands clasped in front of her. She was to marry Frederick. She had gone riding with

271

him, and walking over the Scottish moors, and played amateur theatricals with him in the summer evenings with her parents in the audience, and he seemed to be very nice. She didn't *know* him very well, and she had never thought of him as anything but a pleasant cousin who came on an occasional visit. But her mother said she was going to marry him.

'I am sure that you are very fond of him already,' Victoria continued. 'Aren't you?'

'Yes, Mama.'

'Look at me when I am speaking to you, Vicky dear, it's not polite to stand like that. It reminds me of Bertie, and it's not becoming.'

'I'm sorry, Mama. I – I'm a little confused, you see, I hadn't thought of Frederick . . .'

'As a husband,' Victoria finished it for her. 'But you will. And I do *hope* that you are not going to worry your father by letting him see silly tears. Come now, you should be very happy. Besides, you have a whole year to prepare for the wedding.'

'A year? Oh, Mama, I thought you meant I should have to marry him quite soon. Then I shan't leave Papa – and you – for a year?'

'We thought you were too young to marry before your seventeenth birthday,' her mother explained. 'I think you should dry your eyes, Vicky; I know Frederick will be overcome with happiness and I can't have you looking pink and puffy, it's not pretty at all. You must always remember, dear child, that tears do not improve you. And Princesses don't cry. I know your father will tell you how best to conduct yourself when you go to Prussia – there's plenty of time for that, but *I* want to impress one thing on you myself. Prussia is a very fine country, but you must always remember that you are an *English* Princess, and that in marrying you, Frederick has made a very great alliance. Wherever you go and whatever you do, you will represent England and me, and though I know you will love Prussia, you must never forget that.'

'I promise I won't, Mama. Mama – is that why he wants to marry me? Just because I am your daughter and a good match?'

Victoria looked into the wet blue eyes, so large and pretty and just like Albert's, and said more kindly, 'He's fully aware of the honour done to him and to his country when he marries you, Vicky, but I'm sure he's genuinely very fond of you. I thought so long before he approached us. Your father and I would never give you to someone who wouldn't make you happy. Now I expect to see you smiling and looking happy at dinner this evening. You're a very good child, and your father and I are very pleased with you. Bend down, so that I can kiss you.'

She touched Vicky's forehead and, according to their custom, the Princess curtsied and kissed her hand; a moment later Victoria had gone. She was gratified to notice that her daughter showed no sign of having cried or been stupid in any way when they gathered for a family dinner that evening. She smiled and blushed when Frederick spoke to her; they were seated next to each other and he was laughing and full of good spirits, obviously very happy. Vicky was a dear child, and now that she knew she was leaving them for good, Victoria felt fonder of her than she had for a very long time.

11

The Crimean War was over. When the news of the fall of Sebastapol reached Balmoral, bonfires blazed across the purple Scottish hills: pipers played and the Queen and the Prince danced reels in the great Castle Hall, and turned a tactfully blind eye to the number of toasts drunk in whisky by the ghillies. England and France were victorious, and the London crowds sang in the streets and gathered to cheer outside the gates of empty Buckingham Palace, and Palmerston celebrated with a dinner party where the port bottles emptied as fast as if the good-living days of the Regency had suddenly returned. Russia's ambitions had been curbed; the pagan tyranny of Turkey had been maintained by the might of the two great Christian countries England and France, and for the moment the maimed, the dead, the widowed and orphaned were cheerfully accepted as part of the price of that inglorious and eventually inconclusive war.

Miss Nightingale received the unprecedented honour of an invitation to Balmoral, where she was congratulated by the Queen, and had a long discussion with Prince Albert on the lamentable conditions prevailing in the army during the campaign. Describing the miseries of her soldiers to the Queen had been rather difficult, even for a woman as courageous as the little Angel of the Crimea. She had an uncomfortable feeling, rather like that experienced by Peel in dealing with the Irish famine, that suffering did not excite Her Majesty's imagination, and that pity was not an emotion which came as naturally to her as to the Prince. Her

274

Majesty's enthusiasm cooled for the subject. Dirt and pain and inefficiency were apt to tarnish the gloss of victory. She disliked having her illusions spoiled. Miss Nightingale reserved her complaints and her suggestions for the sympathetic ears of Albert.

Later that year Lord Palmerston travelled to Windsor to receive the Garter from the Queen; he told Emily afterwards that she had managed to smile at him quite warmly, and that his old enemy the Prince had been generous in praise of his administration during the war. They had worked well together, he and Albert, and some of Albert's suggestions had been quite sound. He had a new respect for the man, more so since close contact with Her Majesty had convinced him the Prince must have exercised the most marvellous tact over the year. He was undoubtedly a bore, but a tragic bore, because nobody liked him when he was at least trying to do his best.

Emily smiled mockingly at him.

'Dear Henry, I never thought I'd hear *you* praising the Prince, of all people. Everyone's been expecting an explosion between you ever since you took office.'

'Ha ha, and they've been disappointed, eh? Well, I told you, my love, that I wanted to win the war, and he wanted to win the war; that's firm ground for even the most incompatible characters to work on. He's hardly what I'd choose for an after dinner companion, but he's a lot sounder than I thought. And in a funny way, Em, he's a patriot. Not because he loves this country, but because he thinks it's his duty. And, by God, I really believe that's what keeps him going. Damn it all, he has no amusements; he doesn't like his food – now *she* does. I've never seen a woman eat so much. He'd just as soon drink water as a good wine, and he'd rather spend hours stooped over a desk than go out in God's good air and get some healthy exercise. He's a prig and a bore, and I feel in my bones that now we've won the war, I shall quarrel with him and the Queen just as frequently as before. But he was a friend to England, and I'll never say otherwise.'

'You have a generous heart,' his wife said gently, 'and I love you for it.'

He winked at her. 'Only where you are concerned, my love. What I've said makes no difference to what I'm going to do. I intend backing Italian independence; the Queen and he are dead against it; I don't agree that Germany should be united under Prussia, and they do, and I'm not sure I approve of our Princess Royal marrying a Prussian Prince. So I fear there may be squalls ahead!'

'Fear?' Emily Palmerston shook her head. 'You mean you *hope*!'

Europe was at peace, but the voice of the Italian patriot, Cavour, disturbed everyone's complacency by demanding a united Italy under the House of Savoy, and in spite of the furious remonstrances which poured into Downing Street from Windsor, Palmerston gave the project his blessing. There was peace in Europe, even if it was uneasy; and then suddenly Italy and Europe were forgotten; and England, already settling down to greater prosperity in peace, was rudely shocked by a revolt in India. A horrified nation heard of the sudden massacre of English officers and their families, of bands of Indian renegades, still wearing the Queen's uniform, burning and torturing and killing. The rebels had struck without any warning or sign of discontent. But whatever the reason, it was lost in the chaos which swept over the country. Murder, rapine, and looting were highlighted by terrible atrocities, and the English soldiers, reinforced by Indian levies from the Punjab, punished the mutineers with equal brutality. The Queen learnt of a particular method of reprisal with pained resignation. It was all too horrible; she could not imagine men being tied over the muzzle of cannon and blown to pieces without shuddering, but when she reminded herself that these same men, or their relatives, had slaughtered English women and children, and at Cawnpore the entire white population had been murdered and their poor bodies thrown down a well . . .

Albert took the whole thing so seriously; he really grieved over the bloodshed and the cruelty, necessary though it undoubtedly was, and he wore himself out urging the Government to send more troops from England and bring order to the distracted people as soon as possible. He expressed the view, which she did not quite share, that the mutineers were ignorant heathens, and that it was wrong to stoop to their methods. He agreed that they had to be punished, but surely there was no need to execute on quite such a wide scale, or to permit English troops to avenge their fellows with a ferocity the equal of the Sepoys at their worst?

It was all most distressing, and it proved again that Albert was right when he said the Government never prepared for an emergency until it was upon them. The Crimean forces had been disbanded much too quickly. As usual, Palmerston had been too busy encouraging lawlessness in Italy to provide for trouble within his Queen's dominions. The relationship between the Crown and the Prime Minister deteriorated sharply; a mischievous quirk had decided Palmerston to place his old colleague John Russell in the Foreign Office, and it was his turn to suffer the endless memoranda, the rebukes and protests which had been Palmerston's lot in former days. He was as stern in his Liberal ideas as ever, but he lacked Palmerston's jaunty disregard of snubs; the Queen had always been able to upset him, and his life was a misery at the Foreign Office.

It was a turbulent year, a year when France decided to increase her power by espousing the cause of Italian freedom, and a French army under Napoleon III marched into Italy to secure independence from Austria, and then made peace with the Austrians before a decisive victory had been won. It was said that the nephew of the great Bonaparte had been haunted by the scene at the battlefield of Solferino; he bore the name but lacked the genius and the heartlessness of that other Emperor who had led his armies on to the field. In their secluded homes at Osborne and Balmoral, Victoria and Albert worked at their despatch boxes, read every page of the newspapers, marking such articles as they considered important — how extraordinary it was to think that when Melbourne had been with her, she had barely skimmed through the mountain of official papers, and never even read a newspaper unless there was something in it relating to herself — and wrote letters to Ministers, Ambassadors and Heads of State. They seemed to do nothing but work, and work had become almost a disease with Albert. He looked so tired and so old that there were times when she felt quite frightened, and putting aside her papers, knelt beside him and begged him to go for a walk or even lie down for an hour and rest. *She* was not tired; even though she was pregnant again, she could adopt his killing routine and still feel fresh by the evening. She had a wonderful constitution, which seemed to bloom under the pressure, while Albert wilted visibly. And he seemed so sad. He had never recovered his spirits from the day Vicky sailed for Germany after her wedding.

It had been a beautiful wedding. At one juncture Victoria had been considerably annoyed by the suggestion that her daughter should go to Prussia to be married. A very angry note had reminded Prince Frederick's parents that it was not every day a member of their family married the eldest daughter of the Queen of England. They would be married in England, or the inference was that they wouldn't be married at all.

But it had been a beautiful wedding. Vicky had looked so pretty and behaved with such dignity that Victoria forgot she had ever been irritated with her or wished her out of the way, and cried copiously at the parting. The grief of father and daughter had been less obvious; they talked and tried to smile in the few minutes before the ship sailed from Gravesend. It was snowing and, in spite of her furs, the new Princess of Prussia shivered as she stood on the quay, looking up at her father. They looked uncannily alike at that moment, the pallid, drawn face of a prematurely aged man with empty eyes, and the young girl in her teens, biting her

278

lips to keep back the tears. She was setting out for her new life and her new country, and in those few silent moments of farewell a premonition touched her of the long years of unhappiness which lay ahead.

'Dearest Papa—'

For a minute he held her in his arms, more closely and tenderly than he had ever been able to do since she was a tiny child. He could not show emotion easily; by nature he was shy, and years of living with an extrovert like Victoria had only dammed up the few outlets he had. He loved his daughter Vicky, not coldly and with his intellect, as one might have supposed to see them together, but with a deep and tender warmth. Only now, as he was about to lose her for ever, could he unbend and embrace her.

'My dear child, God bless you and keep you safe.'

The next moment she had run up the gangplank and disappeared below. Her tears were still wet on Albert's cheek. Though he waited in the icy wind until her ship sailed out of sight, Vicky did not come back on deck to wave to him. She was sitting in her splendid cabin with her embarrassed husband beside her, crying as if her heart would break.

'The Baron Stockmar, to see Your Majesty.'

Victoria was sitting alone in her study at Windsor; when she saw the slight, bent figure of the Baron come through the door, she got up and came across the room to meet him. Her footman had closed the double doors; they were quite alone when she gave him both her hands and he bent down to kiss them.

'Dear Baron, come and sit with me.'

The invitation was a singular honour and Stockmar knew it. As a young bride she had been inclined to treat him with informality because he was so close to Albert; but the latter years had changed her habits. They had hardened, like her face, into a fixed mould of pride. When the Queen sent for them, even her intimates stood, sometimes for an hour or more.

How stout she had grown, he thought, as he thanked her and lowered his frail body into a chair close beside her. Her arms were very plump; the portrait bracelet of Albert she wore seemed to have sunk into her flesh. Her cheeks were quite full, too full really, for they accentuated the hard, considering eyes and the beaked nose. She was a plain and formidable woman now; there was no trace of the impetuous, high-spirited girl who had caused her advisers so much anxiety in the past.

'I don't have to tell you how distressed I am, Baron, or how I hoped we could persuade you to remain with us another year.'

He was old and rapidly failing, and he had at last decided to go back to Germany. He knew he was close to death, and the longing to spend what time remained to him in his own country was stronger even than the pleas of Albert and the Queen. His usefulness was much diminished; his memory was weakening, he was always tired and frequently ill. He had devoted his life to making Albert into the selfless perfectionist he had become, and now there was no more for him to do.

'I ask your forgiveness, Ma'am,' he said. 'I would have granted what you asked, if it was possible.'

'I am not asking for myself,' Victoria said. 'I am asking for Albert. You know how much he loves you and relies upon you. I dread the effect on him when he loses you.'

Stockmar gazed at the carpet. She was not interested in his health or his wish to die with his neglected family. She had no feelings for him as an individual at all. She would sacrifice him or anyone else to Albert or to herself without a qualm. In that moment of revelation he admitted that he had never really liked her. She was not likeable, much less lovable. Poor Albert. How wretched he must have been all these years. At last he looked up at her and smiled. He could resist her will; it was difficult, but he was so old and weary now, and there was only one thing he wanted to do.

'Albert has you, Ma'am. He will learn to do without me.

Much as I would like to please you and stay on, I am an old man, and my powers are failing. The time has come for me to go home. I can be of no more service to the Prince.'

'You can't be moved, I see,' Victoria said. 'I'm very grieved, Baron; my poor darling will be so lonely – Heaven knows he misses Vicky badly enough.'

It was strange how the parting from his daughter had affected him. His spirits were never very high, but they had sunk to a more muted level from the day of Vicky's marriage, and they had never recovered. He spent many hours writing to her every evening; sometimes Victoria felt it was almost as much of a nuisance as if she had never gone away at all . . . Now Stockmar was going home for good, and she was really alarmed. She had never been jealous of Stockmar: he was too good a friend to them both, too much a part of their early lives. He was staunch and his advice had guided them through many crises. But above all, Albert would miss his companionship. He had no intimate friends left after Peel and Anson died, and now Stockmar was leaving him, too. And before he need; just because he wanted to be selfish and live at home in Coburg until he died. Really, there was no such thing as gratitude or even a sense of responsibility in the very people one respected most.

'If I may suggest it,' Stockmar said, 'I think a trip to Coburg would do Albert a lot of good. He needs a rest, Ma'am, and as long as he's able to get at the papers and see Ministers he'll never relax. Try and persuade him, even if you cannot be spared yourself.'

'I will,' she answered. 'He looks so tired, and lately he's been sleeping very badly. He worries so much, Baron; he works harder than the whole Cabinet together. And now Vicky's in Prussia he's taking the burdens of that country on to his shoulders as well. How I wish,' she burst out suddenly, 'how I wish God had sent him a good eldest son!'

'It would have made all the difference,' the Baron agreed.

The Prince of Wales was nearly seventeen, and as far as

Stockmar could see his character had successfully resisted all attempts to fashion it in his father's image. He was a true offspring of the disreputable House of Hanover; light-minded, pleasure-loving and superficial. There was nothing in the boy which connected him with Albert; neither physical beauty nor moral stature. He was a lazy ne'er-do-well, and the fact that the combined efforts of his parents, his tutor and the Baron had failed to break his spirit, pointed to hidden strength of character which deeply worried Stockmar. Supposing Victoria were to die — it wasn't very likely when one gazed at the ruddy face and keen eyes, radiating health — but supposing she pre-deceased his beloved Albert and that wretched boy came to the throne . . . What would his father's position be then? It was a recurrent nightmare to Stockmar, and he suddenly sat forward and said with some of his former vigour: 'Ma'am, there's something I must say to you. I don't know whether you've thought of such a thing, and God forbid there should be any need, but if Prince Albert is still alive when Bertie becomes King, what will the Prince's status be in the country?'

'Victoria stared at him.

'Status? Why, his status is only second to mine!'

'As long as you live,' Stockmar pointed out. 'But if Albert were left alone . . . Supposing some bad adviser were to put it into Bertie's head to disrespect his father, Albert has no official position here at all. He's not an English Prince, Ma'am — any of his children could displace him in precedence. I'm not suggesting that Bertie would be wicked enough to take advantage of such a situation, if it ever arose, but he's a weak character, and if he fell under an undesirable influence, God knows what he might be persuaded to do. Forgive me for mentioning this, but I know Albert would never speak about it himself.'

'It's unthinkable.' Victoria was quite pale. 'Baron, how perfectly *awful* — and you're quite right — my dearest has no official title; the matter was dropped before we were married when my uncles made a fuss over their precedence. Oh, if the day ever came when that wretched boy was in a position to humiliate my darling I should rise from my grave! Thank God you mentioned it. Something must be done to prevent anything like that. Parliament shall grant him a title.'

Stockmar avoided the Queen's eyes.

'Parliament has often been less than fair to the Prince,' he said quietly. 'I'm afraid they may see some sinister design to limit Bertie's eventual power, and refuse your request.'

'Less than fair?' Victoria said bitterly. 'Parliament and *England* have been less than fair to Albert. I can see them refusing. It's extraordinary how my son has managed to gain sympathizers, just by dint of being a failure. Yes, Parliament might reject it. But I shall put it to them; it would please my darling if they agreed; it might even wipe out some of the slights he's suffered from them in the past.'

'And if they refuse?' the Baron said.

'I am prepared for that.'

She looked at him, and he saw that there was something close to hatred in her eyes.

'My son will be a man soon. Nothing I can do can prevent him succeeding me, though God is my witness that I'd disinherit him tomorrow if it was in my power. He'll be seventeen in a few weeks, and before long he must have a separate establishment. Think of it, Baron. I've got to give his independence to a boy that can't be trusted not to disgrace himself idling or choosing bad companions if he's left alone for any length of time.'

'I am afraid,' Stockmar said, 'that it is bad blood, Ma'am; and there's nothing you can do about that. Even Gibbs hinted as much to me one day. You can punish him, he said, and lecture him, and talk reasonably to him, pointing out this or that, but he only stands there looking at the floor, and the next time he does exactly the same thing again. Forgive me, but I dread to think of England passing to him after you.'

283

'So do I,' Victoria said. 'But we have plans for him, Baron. I can't stop him going to ruin when I'm dead, but I can oversee him while I'm alive, and whether he's grown up or not, that's what I intend to do. He may be too old for Gibbs now, but I think we should choose three Equerries for him, and a Governor directly responsible to me. I have a man in mind, an excellent man – his name is Bruce. He's a retired army officer, and a splendid disciplinarian. If my son can't be trusted to conduct himself as he should, then I don't see why there should be any pretence about it. He must be trained for his future responsibilities; that is our duty as his parents. Albert wants him to go to Oxford and study. Personally I think it's a waste of time, but he has set his heart on it. He said the other day that no one could live in that beautiful atmosphere, surrounded by learning, without eventually improving their minds. He judges everyone by his own standards, that's what's so tragic. Just because *he's* sensitive and noble and clever, he thinks Bertie can be, too.'

'I suppose a miracle might happen,' Stockmar murmured dubiously.

'I don't believe in miracles,' Victoria said. 'Nothing will change my son. If he could resist his father's example, there's no real virtue in him. And he knows what *I* think of him. I've made it plain enough, Heaven knows. And I intend to make it plainer still.'

Sometimes, the Baron thought, she had shown her dislike of Bertie a little too openly. A great many people had seen the boy stammering under that gimlet eye, and remarked in whispers that, even if he was rather slow, the Queen's attitude was distressingly harsh. People like Lady Lyttelton and his former tutor, Birch, had actually told others that the Prince was intelligent and lovable, and only in need of affection to bring out his best qualities. The stories had spread and, as Victoria had just remarked, the Prince's failure to please his parents had won him a great deal of sympathy in the country.

'All you can do is maintain a strict discipline,' Stockmar said. 'And pray for a change of heart. An early marriage might be advisable. And you know, Ma'am, that though I shall be in Coburg, my thoughts will always be with you and Prince Albert — if there is anything I can do to serve you, any advice — anything — you have only to ask.'

'I know that, my dear friend,' the Queen said. 'I shall feel very alone without you, but you needn't fear for Albert. I shall take care of him. Promise me that you will write to us often; I know how much your letters will mean to him.'

He bent over her hand.

'I promise, Ma'am. May God bless you and the Prince. I shall never cease to think of you both.'

'His Royal Highness and Prince Consort of the United Kingdom of Great Britain and Ireland! I hinted as broadly as I dared that Parliament wouldn't sanction the title, so she bestowed it on him herself!' Palmerston grinned at Lord John Russell, and threw him a folded newspaper. 'Have a look at *The Times* — she won't be pleased with that comment.'

'It's a high-handed thing to have done,' Russell said. He did not open the paper. 'I can imagine the Press reaction. And I've no doubt that I shall suffer indirectly because of it. Every time anything goes wrong, the Queen sends a sharp note to me about something else. I don't want to see the article, Henry. I expect I shall hear about it.'

'I'm sorry she's difficult.' Palmerston laughed outright. 'But now you know what I had to put up with, when you dismissed me so summarily a few years ago! Well, well, we had better support this — it's done now, and I suppose some kind of recognition was due to him.'

'I have already heard that it's aimed at the Prince of Wales,' Russell remarked.

'I shouldn't be surprised. She detests the boy; everyone knows that. But it won't make any difference in the end.

He'll be King, and whatever she makes Albert can't alter that.'

'I don't approve of the way he's treated,' Russell said.

'My dear fellow, nobody approves. But what can one do? Suggest to the Queen that she's strangling the boy, keeping him on such a tight rein? I'd like to meet the man who has the courage — I'm damned if I have! No, he'll just have to wait till she dies, that's all.'

On November 11th, His Royal Highness the Prince of Wales came down to breakfast in his new establishment at Royal Lodge, Windsor. He no longer lived with his parents. Albert had considered him old enough to have a home of his own, and a household.

It had sounded very well when he first heard of it. He had stood awkwardly in front of his mother and father and tried to thank them, until Victoria interrupted to assure him that the new arrangement did not mean that he could neglect his education or his duties, or presume to manage his own affairs. He had listened in silence while his father explained the plan in that tone of tired resignation which he knew so well. He would live at Royal Lodge, and arrangements for his household would be communicated to him on his seventeenth birthday.

He was seventeen that November morning, and as he came down to breakfast, some of the servants managed to whisper their good wishes. Bertie thanked them under his breath, so that Gibbs would not hear and get them into trouble, and then took his place after saying Grace. He had inherited his mother's short figure, and like her he was inclined to fat; his chin receded sharply, and rather spoilt the effect of bright blue eyes and a good clear complexion. The Prince was not handsome — he had privately decided to grow a beard and cover that chin as soon as he was allowed, but he had a warm smile which compensated for his features. Unfortunately it was seldom seen. There was a hearty breakfast set in front of him; wholesome porridge and cream — Lord, how it reminded him of Balmoral and the interminable meals where the pipers played, even in the mornings — dishes of fried and scrambled eggs and cutlets and fish. He was hungry as usual, though his tutor said that he placed too much emphasis on food. He had always wondered why it was proper for his mother to have a large appetite and one of the Seven Deadly Sins for him.

There was a thick envelope beside his plate with the Royal Seal stamped on the back of it. It must be his birthday present from his parents. Inside was a letter so many pages thick that it was more like a document, covered in his father's beautiful neat handwriting. The food grew cold on the table while the Prince read. He was seventeen. He was gazetted as an Honourary Colonel and the Queen had been pleased to make him a Knight of the Garter. Gibbs, who had rendered him such faithful service, was to leave. For a moment the Prince glanced up at the tutor sitting opposite him, waiting to begin his breakfast. He had never liked Gibbs, but over the years he had grown used to him. Now Gibbs was going and Colonel Bruce was to become his Governor. Bruce. He knew him. He was a dour, cold martinet of a man; his name alone drove all the colour out of Bertie's cheeks. His Equerries — those three dull, carping men — were to take their orders from this Governor, who would receive direct instructions from the Prince Consort and the Queen. 'You will never leave the house without reporting yourself, and Colonel Bruce will settle who is to accompany you, and will give general directions for the disposition of the day . . . Life is composed of duties. You will have to be taught what to do and what not to do . . .'

Under the eyes of Gibbs, the gentlemen-in-waiting, and the astonished servants, the Prince of Wales threw down the letter, covered his face with his hands and burst into tears.

In Berlin, Vicky's first child was born. Albert and Victoria had visited her earlier in the year, and though she was homesick and nervous of approaching motherhood, Vicky had been alarmed by the change in her father. Mama was just the same; she had given birth to her ninth child, a daughter, and she looked healthier and stronger than ever; but Albert was pale, stooped and perpetually tired. He had been so kind and gentle to her, calming her fears about life in her new country, explaining how to please her in-laws and spread English influence without causing offence, and when they left her she had sunk into depression. The birth was a nightmare, but she had given her husband a son. It was not till long after that they discovered the little Wilhelm's shoulder had been dislocated in the delivery; the boy would have a permanently crippled left arm. Her brother Bertie had paid her a visit, too. He had seemed very downcast, and evidently loathed his Governor, Colonel Bruce. She obeyed her father's written instruction, and when they were alone together, read aloud to Bertie out of improving books. When he left, she could not help feeling that he had not enjoyed his visit. He had gone to Edinburgh to study applied sciences, and she knew by his letters that he was restless and bored. Then he was going to Oxford, but not to a college, as he had hoped. His father had chosen a house, Frewin Hall, for him to live in, under the supervision of Colonel Bruce, of course. When it was suggested that the Prince would benefit more from university life by mixing with the undergraduates, his father had retorted sharply that Oxford was a place of *study* . . .

Exiled in Prussia, Vicky spun nostalgic dreams of home, of happy hours spent at Osborne and Balmoral, with all their homely comforts, so different from the horrible bleak Prussian Palaces, and remembered the walks and rides through the wild highlands, where the scenery was so beautiful it brought one close to God. She looked on the flat, cold Prussian countryside, as her father had once looked at England, and like him she yearned for the country of her birth. Papa's advice was so good, so encouraging, but she had to admit she had few friends among the Prussian

Courtiers, and that for some reason her English tastes antagonized her husband's relatives. She had always thought of Germany in relation to her dear Papa; she had imagined that his studious mind and love of culture were common things. Instead, she found herself an oddity; over-educated for a Prussian Princess, suspected because she attempted to widen her knowledge of things which in his country were regarded as exclusively male.

Frederick loved her, and she could not deny that he was a good husband, a doting husband by Prussian standards, but the general atmosphere was hostile. She was an alien, as her father had been when he came to England.

Albert's careful training in the months before her marriage was a handicap instead of a help. She thought along the lines he had laid down; she voiced the opinions he had taught her were the right ones; she read his letters and wrote copious ones in reply; and all her efforts only made her seem more Anglicized in the eyes of her adopted people. The conflict was too much for a character which was narrow by nature. Vicky was failing, but it was beyond her or her father to see why. She adopted airs of aggressive Prussianism, which did not convince the Court or the Royal Family that they were genuine, and made the mistake of exhibiting them in letters to her mother. Victoria's rebukes were swift and crushing. She considered the Prussians pompous, and said tartly that she disliked her daughter assimilating the trait, however loyal she felt she should be to her new country. It was infuriating and humiliating, but Vicky trembled, exactly as if she were living at home, instead of being married and independent, many hundreds of miles away. It was so confusing to hate Prussia in one's heart and to miss England so much that a familiar song could bring tears to her eyes, and yet to resent the feeling that she was still subject to her mother, that the kingdom of Prussia was no protection against the authority of the Queen of England. It made it seem all the more incongruous that Bertie, who was so stupid and had no sense of responsibility, should one day inherit that power. Bertie had gone to Rome in accordance with Albert's hopes that travel might improve his sluggard intellect. He had actually met the Pope, which most people considered extremely dangerous, but the presence of Colonel Bruce had prevented any attempt at contamination. It was some comfort to know, as she waited for the birth of a second child, that if Bertie was a constant source of anxiety and disappointment to his father, Albert's letters to her were full of affection and praise.

'There's no doubt, Ma'am, the tour has been a wonderful success.'

The Queen stared coldly at Lady Lyttelton. It needed courage to tell Her Majesty that anything her eldest son did was successful, but Lady Lyttelton was notoriously brave. The other ladies waited nervously. The Prince of Wales had gone to Canada and to America on a tour. And the reports of his reception had delighted the country as much as they annoyed his mother. Huge crowds had cheered him; he was mobbed wherever he went; his speeches and manners were praised to an extent that Victoria thought quite out of proportion. He was only a stupid boy, and nothing Albert, with all his wisdom and nobility, had said or done had gained such recognition. She was furiously jealous for his sake.

'So it appears, if one can trust the hysterical outburst in the newspapers. Personally I find them unreliable. I shall be happier when the Prince returns and I hear from Colonel Bruce exactly what happened. Perhaps you imagine that to attract a crowd of curious vulgarians is a wonderful success, Lady Lyttelton?'

'Indeed not, Ma'am. But I believe His Royal Highness has inspired the Canadians with great loyalty to you. He is very young, after all—'

'If you suppose,' Victoria's voice was freezing, 'that I depend upon my son's efforts to maintain my subjects' loyalty, you are sadly mistaken. As for his youth, the Prince

290

has the very wisest advisers to make up for what he lacks. And always will lack, I fear, whatever his age. It would oblige me, Lady Lyttelton, if you reserved your opinions in the future; if you cannot, then be so good as to refrain from expressing them to me.'

I beg your pardon, Ma'am.' Lady Lyttelton had blushed; she had known and served the Queen for many years, and nothing but genuine love for the Prince of Wales had given her the courage to mention the tour at all. Everyone knew that the Queen would rather it had been a failure, that she read the reports of his popularity with mounting anger, and told everyone that it was due to the vigilance of the Prince Consort that her son had managed to behave himself at all. Really, she thought angrily, Victoria was a monstrous mother. It was no use criticizing Albert because he had no understanding anyway, but a mother . . . She curtsied and sat down, out of the Queen's view.

'Lady Augusta, would you kindly play for us? I am quite distracted with all this talk of tours and nonsense.'

Victoria sat staring ahead of her while the piano was opened. Absorbed in her thoughts, she did not hear a note of music, though Lady Augusta Bruce, choosing everything she could think of that Her Majesty usually liked, played for nearly an hour.

That wretched boy. How grossly unfair that he should have done so well, that the speeches others wrote for him should be applauded and written about in the papers, while her own darling worked himself to death for the common good and never received a word of unqualified praise. Just to think how much Albert had done! — the re-organization of the army and navy — how long would the Crimean War and the Indian Mutiny have dragged on without his efforts? The Great Exhibition. She often thought of that day when they went to the Crystal Palace and opened it, and she had believed in her heart that at last he would be recognized and appreciated. And what had happened then? — would she ever forget that evening at Windsor, when he stood by the window looking out on to the red sky, with his beloved head drooping on his chest, knowing that a crowd of thousands had been picnicking round the Tower, hoping to see him brought there as a prisoner. That was the worst moment in her whole life; she sometimes woke in the middle of the night, having dreamed it all over again, and trembled with anger at the memory. He worked on and did his duty without sparing himself, but the hope of her people's love had died in him that day. How he had suffered, and *still* suffered. Articles in the newspapers attacked him. *Punch* satirized him – how she loathed that horrible, *vulgar* magazine – all the advice he gave was accepted and made use of, even by Palmerston when it suited him, but nobody gave Albert credit. If Albert could be recognized, praised, *loved*, as he deserved, she would gladly give ten years of her life. With that burden of disappointment, her darling had to listen to the raptures about Bertie in Canada opening a bridge over the St Lawrence, Bertie attending a Ball in New York . . . Bertie being fêted, honoured, praised. His charm of manner – who had ever remarked on her darling's charm? Bertie's frank and pleasant looks – to think of the chiselled beauty of his father, and to read rubbish like that! Bertie, who was stupid and a liar, who had to be made Knight of the Garter, who had to be Prince of Wales and one day King of England . . . It was too unfair. And if Lyttelton *dared* to mention his name again, she would relieve her of her post.

Those sitting in the Queen's sitting-room saw the deep line between her brows and the gleam in her eyes under the heavy lids. Nobody moved or even coughed until Augusta Bruce finished her recital.

'Stockmar said he thought an early marriage was the only solution, my dearest.'

Victoria gazed into Albert's face, pleading with him not to be anxious. Poor darling, he looked so worried. There were deep lines across his forehead and at each corner of his mouth. He had lost so much of his beautiful brown hair that he was really rather bald. She squeezed his hand and gave the back of it a little kiss.

'And I know Stockmar's right; marriage will settle him down, give him a sense of responsibility. After all' — she disguised her annoyance with the whole subject of Bertie and tried to make a joke of it — 'remember how headstrong and pleasure-loving I was, until you married me? Nobody knows better than we do how the right husband or wife can change one.'

Albert sighed. It was kind of her to try and make light of their anxiety, but he knew her far too well to be deceived. Their son had returned from his trip abroad with an exaggerated idea of his own importance. He was objecting violently to Bruce's supervision. The Colonel wrote to the Prince Consort that his son now lost his temper, and actually shouted when he was corrected. He had once tried to travel up to London without permission. The escapade was discovered, and a Royal carriage was waiting at the station to convey the culprit straight to Buckingham Palace, but everyone felt that a major scandal had only just been averted. Bertie was addicted to every vice from which his father had tried to protect him. He wanted to play cards, he drank, and he had paid unseemly attention to a pretty lady-in-waiting when his sister Vicky came on a visit from Germany.

'I've been so disappointed with him so often, that I have no hope left,' Albert said. 'My greatest fear is that he will involve himself in some immorality if he's not married soon.'

'Albert!' Victoria exclaimed in horror. She was genuinely shocked. It was so unlike Albert to speak about such horrible things, and in connection with their son . . . 'Albert dearest, you don't think he would ever do anything *wrong*?' She became suddenly pale. 'Albert, you're not keeping anything from me?'

'Nothing, my dear, I promise you. But it is a danger and we must face it. He should be married. He's heir to the throne and he's twenty, nearly twenty-one.'

They had confided their anxieties to their daughter Vicky, and Vicky had inspected every eligible German Princess. The selection was poor; the candidates were either too young or else so plain that on meeting them Bertie had refused to consider them. And he would not be forced into an uncongenial marriage.

They appeared to have reached an impasse. Albert wished his son to marry a German, but none of the German Princesses would do. Now a letter from Vicky had mentioned a young Danish Princess as a possibility. She was reputed to be both pretty and charming, and the Crown Princess intended meeting her to see for herself, if her parents agreed.

'You never know,' Victoria said, 'this child Alexandra may be suitable after all.'

'An alliance with Denmark will upset Prussia,' Albert said gloomily. 'But I suppose Vicky had better see her. There doesn't seem to be anyone else.'

'My darling, if she is as nice as Vicky's heard, we can make it clear that the marriage doesn't tie us to Denmark in any way. Marriage to the Prince of Wales will be a sufficient honour in itself. Now I shall write to Vicky myself and tell her to see this girl and let us know her opinion. And I *beg* of you, don't worry about Bertie until we hear.'

As a guest of the Duchess of Meckleinburg-Strelitz, Vicky saw Alexandra of Denmark for the first time. Alexandra was seventeen years old, and the first thing which came into Vicky's mind when she saw her was that 'pretty' did not describe her at all. She was not only tall and graceful she had the most beautiful face Bertie's sister had ever seen. Red hair, wide blue eyes, which seemed almost violet in some lights, a perfect complexion, lovely teeth . . . It was hardly possible. And there was not a trace of arrogance, not a suggestion in her voice or expression that Alexandra herself

294

knew how beautiful she was.

The young Princess was nervous. Her parents, who were desperately poor, had run into debt providing her with suitable clothes, and the whole happy, close-knit family had sat up the night before her journey hopefully discussing the outcome. So much would depend on the Crown Princess; Alex *must* make a good impression on her. As Alexandra curtsied to the daughter of the Queen of England her exquisite skin turned pink with momentary embarrassment, but after a few moments her natural sweetness and gaiety became apparent. She sat side by side with Vicky, gazing up at her with those astonishing eyes, full of gentle admiration, and within half an hour Vicky had decided that this was the only possible wife for Bertie.

No one could resist the child: certainly not Bertie, who had managed to be polite to some of those dreadfully stodgy German girls, however cross he had been about them afterwards. Alex was perfect. Most important, she would be a perfect daughter-in-law, too. Vicky was quite sure that Papa, and especially Mama, who was very dictatorial at times, would find her easy to manage.

She stayed at Strelitz for two days, and then wrote to her parents that the search for Bertie's bride was over.

In February of 1861 an old lady sat in an armchair by the fire, watching the logs burn, and dozing. An embroidered handbag lay in her lap, the needle threaded through an unfinished stitch. The house at Frogmore was full of the Duchess of Kent's handiwork; fire-screens and cushion covers, beautifully embroidered, some of them in beading, which was becoming very fashionable. The volcanic, bustling Duchess, who had once made herself such a nuisance to King William IV, had turned to gentler pursuits in her old age. Her ambition had died years ago; like her spirits it had not survived the struggle with Victoria. No one mentioned those early days; it was so long since she had been at enmity with her daughter that the snubs and disappointments were as blurred as the details of a bad dream. For years she had been safe within the family circle, the beloved mother and grandmother, respected and secure.

Life was so tranquil for her now. It moved at a slow pace which was very pleasant compared to the storms of her youth and middle-age. Sitting in her chair at Frogmore, surrounded by comfort and reflection, the old Duchess sewed and dozed and played whist with her ladies, and looked forward to visits from Victoria and Albert. She loved Albert. Albert had rescued her from that awful limbo of neglect and disfavour and brought her and Victoria together. Albert was the link between them. She owed everything, her position and her peace of mind to him.

One of the logs in the grate crackled, and the old Duchess woke up. She felt the pain again; it was more persistent than usual, and she realized that she had been dreaming of her dead husband. How strange that the Duke of Kent should come into her mind after so many years. Her memories of him were suddenly clear, as if they had only just parted. She could almost see him, with his red face and ungainly way of standing, going round the room winding up that interminable collection of clocks. She smiled, thinking how the routine of setting and winding used to irritate her, and the noise of their chimes kept her awake. But she had got so used to them that after a time that she didn't notice. He had been a good husband in his way, and though he lived and died in debt, they had come very close together in the end. She remembered his last words mumbled as he lay dying forty years ago: 'Do not forget me.'

She closed her eyes again, trying to escape the nagging pain in her breast, and then rang a little bell which stood beside her chair. Though the fire was blazing and the curtain drawn, shutting out the grey February evening, she felt cold. It was early, too. The little household had not dined, but the Duchess did not feel like eating.

When her ladies came she asked to be helped up to bed. The last thing she did before she fell asleep was to take out the Duke's old tortoiseshell watch, and carefully wind it up.

When the Queen and the Prince arrived from London the Duchess had passed into a coma. They stood in the shadows round her bed, and Victoria slipped to her knees and caught the slack hand in hers. The years fled in that moment.

'Mama! Oh, Mama!'

She was dying; her own dear mother with whom she had been so happy for such a long time. She was lying there in that awful stiff attitude of unconsciousness, breathing so noisily and the hand she kissed and stroked was damp and lifeless.

The tears began pouring down her cheeks. The Duchess's ladies withdrew further into the background. There was something rather frightening about the Queen's grief. It seemed unreal that she should kneel there and cry tears and call her mother just like any ordinary woman. One by one the ladies slipped away, leaving Albert alone with her.

His eyes were dry. Weeping would never have expressed his feelings at the sight of the old Duchess lying there. His grief was almost tinged with envy. He had been fond of her, and his efforts to make her life easier had been repaid with deep gratitude and affection. He knew that she had looked on him as if he were a son. Thank God he had been able to reconcile her with Victoria. Thank God that as Victoria knelt there, she could feel easy in her conscience. Gently he put his arm around her and drew her away.

'You must rest,' he whispered. 'There is nothing anyone can do. We will be called if she wakes.'

But the old Duchess never woke again. Through the night the Queen came down to the bedroom, carrying a lamp, and waited for some sign of returning consciousness. At half past nine the following morning, Victoria heard the harsh breathing suddenly stop. As it did so, her father's old watch chimed.

'Oh, when I think how unkind I was to her!'

Albert gazed at Victoria's distracted face, her eyes swollen with incessant crying, and wondered whether he had better send for the doctor again. Sir James Clark had already seen the Queen, and said that only time would ease the extravagances of her grief. Albert thought he should have prescribed, but then he had never liked the man or had much faith in him. He had a rough manner, which the Prince found disconcerting. There was an old story about him and one of Victoria's ladies, Flora Hastings . . . Or was she a member of the Duchess of Kent's household? He could not quite remember the details, but he was sure that Sir James had not emerged from the affair with credit. However, Victoria had the greatest faith in him. And he did say that she would recover from the shock of her mother's death in her own time. The effect on her had alarmed everyone at Court, and caused some anxiety in the Government. The Queen had suddenly collapsed after the funeral. She could not eat or sleep or attend to business. She spent all her time going through the Duchess's belongings, reading her old diaries and weeping and lamenting until Albert seriously feared a breakdown. He had never suspected that Victoria's nervous system was so delicately balanced that it could be almost unhinged by the Duchess's death. He never suspected, nor indeed did Victoria herself, that the agonies of regret, and the floods of hysterical tears, were an expression of a much deeper feeling than sorrow for the loss of her mother. She had never really loved her mother, until late in life, and her affection then had been fostered by Albert, and encouraged by her mother's love of Albert. She cried and worked herself into a frenzy because she had experienced the omnipotence of death. And death meant only one thing to Victoria, however she covered her terror with talk of the Duchess of Kent. Death had taken her mother. Death could take Albert. Death *would* take Albert, unless by God's mercy she died first. And though it would not be for many, many years, the inevitability of that separation nearly unhinged her mind.

'When I think how I once turned against her, I can't bear

it, Albert. It was all the fault of that wicked Lehzen. She was so good to me − I've found things in her diaries when I was a little child − such sweet things . . . Oh, Albert, I'd give anything in the world to have her back and make everything up to her.'

'You've nothing to regret,' he insisted. 'You were a perfect daughter to her: you made her wonderfully happy.'

'But only towards the end,' Victoria cried. 'I should have been good to her *all* the time. Oh, Albert, Albert, isn't it terrible to think that when that happens one can never call the person back. I never realized it before. I can't believe I shall never see her again.'

'You must accept it,' he said gently. 'You must calm yourself and remember, dearest, that your mother was a very good woman, and now she's safe with God. And it would only grieve her to see you making yourself so unhappy and neglecting your duties. And you will see her again. We will all be re-united one day.'

'If only I could be sure of that.' Victoria wiped her eyes with a very wet handkerchief.

'But you *must* be sure of it.' Albert was quite shocked. 'My dear, we will all meet again in the next life. You know that, don't you?'

'Yes, of course I do. It's just that one has doubts sometimes. When I think how Mama looked afterwards, I couldn't believe that there was any life *anywhere*.'

'That was very wrong,' he said.

How strange to think that religion had run such shallow roots with her, after all their years of Sunday attendance and daily prayers. He had never suspected that she had not really shared his steadfast convictions, that a good life was rewarded in Heaven, or that loving families were gathered in eternal union in what he described to himself as their Heavenly Home. It was a beautiful, touching belief, and he was horrified to think that Victoria doubted it. That explained her unreasonable grief for the Duchess; what a hard and comfortless thought to harbour in her heart.

'You must have stronger faith, dearest,' he said earnestly. 'You must never, never allow yourself to doubt what you know to be true. And when the time comes for one of us to die, it will help the other to bear it so much better if we realize it is only a little separation.'

Victoria suddenly threw her arms round his neck. She clung so tightly it was quite uncomfortable. 'I won't think about that. Albert, you are not to mention that happening to us, or I shall break down completely. I can't bear the thought of it. Please, darling, don't talk about it any more. I'll try and control myself and not fret over Mama so much. And I know I shall see her again and we'll be just as happy as we were before. But don't mention one of us dying.'

12

November 22nd was bitterly cold; the rain drenched down from a sky so dark that it might have been evening instead of early afternoon. Alone in her sitting-room at Windsor, with a good fire burning, and a pile of papers on the table beside her which needed careful reading, Victoria paused to look out of the window and wish that Albert had not gone to Sandhurst on such a wretched day. She had tried to dissuade him; he looked particularly tired and she knew he had been suffering from acute insomnia.

But the Military College was his brain child; one of his solutions to the problem of keeping an unmilitary nation like England from losing interest in the army when the country was not at war. The College would train officers, and there would always be a corps of efficient leadership if an emergency arose. And though it was wet and freezing cold, he insisted on inspecting the new buildings as arranged.

If only he would rest more and relinquish the killing burden of work which he imposed upon himself. He seemed anxious to take more and more responsibility from her, when she was strong and quite well able to sit up late and work without feeling ill effects. It was as if he were driven by some force that would not let him rest. If they went to Balmoral and he agreed to go shooting for one afternoon, he often came back in less than two hours and returned to his desk.

He seldom walked in the gardens at Osborne where he had once spent so many happy hours of leisure; his time was passed in his study, the green-shaded light he used for writing casting a sickly glow over his face. He was thin, too, she said to herself, and put her papers down with a sigh. She was so worried about him that she couldn't work. He had no appetite. And he refused to see a doctor, insisting that there was nothing wrong with him.

Not that there was, of course. He was just overworked. With an effort Victoria settled down to read, making pencilled notes in the margins, and the habit of concentration Albert had taught her drove her anxiety about him out of her mind.

But it returned the moment she saw him that evening. He stood listlessly, while his valet helped him out of a soaking great-coat, and then bent down to warm his hands before the fire. The College buildings were very impressive, he said, in answer to her questions. He was pleased by them and by the warmth of his reception from the Generals and War Office officials who had been there. The whole thing had turned out very well; he was very pleased. When she touched his hands she found them icy cold and trembling. She was amazed when he lingered in the drawing-room after dinner, instead of going to his study to work before bedtime. He looked terribly drawn, and there were lines between his brows as if he were in pain. He confessed before they went to sleep that he had severe pains in his legs and arms, and that after walking through the freezing rooms at Sandhurst he had not been able to get warm again.

When Victoria woke she found that he had already gone. She could not even see the time, the room was still so dark. She lay there, waiting for him to come back to bed, and an extraordinary sensation of fear began to attack her as she lay there in the quiet room. There was no superstition in her nature, except what existed artificially, because the Highland legends were so charming it was a pity not to believe in them, but she had never been troubled by portents in her life and was inclined to be impatient with others who claimed to be. It was not a portent that came to her now; only a vague and horrible sense of fear that was connected with that sudden wakening before dawn and the discovery of Albert's empty bed.

She threw back the covers and struggled into her dressing-gown and slippers; she lit the candles beside her bed and was able to find the long string which tied her robe modestly at the neck and the wrists.

She could also see the clock at last. No wonder the room was dark. It was only half past five.

There was no one on duty in the corridors; no one saw the Queen gliding down them like a pale ghost in the gloom, and disappear into the Prince's study. There was a light under the door, and she knew her suspicions were confirmed. She turned the handle so gently that he did not hear anything, and for a moment she stood watching him, bent over his desk under the green-shaded light in the attitude she had come to know so well over the years. He was writing, and the despatch box he had not opened last night was on the floor by the desk, half empty.

'Albert! Albert darling, what are you doing at this hour?' He glanced up when she spoke and blinked as if he did not recognize her. Dear Lord, it must be that horrible green lamp which gave his skin that ghastly colour . . .

'I was awake, my dear,' he explained gently. 'So I thought I would do better to work than lie there wasting time, not sleeping. I do hope I didn't wake you.'

'How long have you been here?' She came and knelt beside him and caught hold of his arm. There was no fire and the room was icy.

'Albert, you will catch the most dreadful cold, sitting here without even a fire. Why didn't you ring and have one lit?'

'It was too early to ask anyone to do it,' he answered. 'Besides, you can't have anything warmer than this dressing-gown. I will say I was glad of it.' It was one of her many presents to him, made of red velvet with fur-lined collar and sleeves. It was warm; thank God he had thought to put it on.

'Albert, I was so alarmed when I saw you had got up. I lay there waiting for you to come back and I felt so lonely and frightened. What is the matter with you? I don't believe you can be well, whatever you say.'

'I'm perfectly well,' he patted her shoulder and managed a smile. 'I am merely tired, and made more so by not being able to sleep when I do get to bed. I'm sorry I frightened you, my dearest. Now I want you to go back to bed; it's far too cold for you in here, and I still have a few more papers to go through.'

'I am not going till you come with me. I insist, Albert. I shan't leave the room without you. You can finish your writing later, but now you are coming back to bed and I am going to send for a hot drink for you.'

It was so rare for her to disobey him that he gave way without arguing. Besides, he suddenly wanted something warm inside him. He was not hungry; far from it, his stomach closed at the thought of meat and fish and a half a dozen hearty dishes which would be served at breakfast. But he would like some hot soup or a cup of chocolate. And he was too tired to resist her. His body was aching so badly that he was afraid he must have written some rather poor memoranda; they would have to be done again later on.

He stood up, grimacing, and immediately Victoria's anxious eye saw the expression.

'What's the matter, my love? Why did you look like that?'

'I have such pains in my legs and arms,' he confessed. 'And in my back. I can't find a comfortable position. I think it must be rheumatism. I shall be glad to go to bed for another hour, and have something hot to drink. It seems very early to disturb the kitchens.'

'Nonsense, that's what servants are for. And you shall rest in bed for the morning, not for *one* hour!'

They went back to their rooms together, and soon the Prince was propped up with an extra coverlet over him, a large fire roaring up the chimney, and a tray of soup and biscuits, which Victoria insisted on feeding him herself.

He drank the soup and managed to eat the biscuits to please her. She was a strange little creature, he thought. She had such a strong face, and such a direct glance. He had seen people quail when she looked at them; what would they think if they could see her then, gazing at him with an expression of love that transformed her whole appearance. She was very kind to him, and very loving. She had a wonderful character, full of strength and purpose, immune from the self doubt and despair that corroded his spirit, forever denying him peace of mind.

'Dearest child,' he said gently. 'Let me lean my head on your shoulder. There, that is very comfortable.'

They sat like that until she knew by his regular breathing that he had fallen asleep.

'It was no use, Alice, I could not stop him! I begged him not to go, but he became so upset that in the end I didn't like to worry him by arguing.'

Princess Alice was a fair, tall girl, with her mother's patrician features. She was both gentle and obedient, and Victoria occasionally confided in her. But so occasionally that she was still embarrassed by the intimacy. She was even more embarrassed by the subject. Her father, sick and tired out and still suffering from rheumatic pains, had insisted on travelling to Cambridge to see Bertie. Bertie had been behaving badly again; Alice knew he was in disfavour for the simple reason that the Queen told everyone she spoke to how her eldest son was upsetting her and his father. It appeared he had made friends with two rather undesirable young peers, both of whom hunted and spent enormous sums of money; he was also smoking, which horrified his mother. It was a disgusting and vicious habit, second only to drunkenness. He was not studying well, and Colonel Bruce was finding him more difficult to manage.

The news had roused Albert from the lethargy into which he had fallen since visiting Sandhurst. He had been quite unlike himself since she found him working in his study; he was silent for hours and inactive, which was extraordinary, for he could never bear to waste time. And terribly depressed, in spite of the efforts she made to cheer him, even bringing the baby Beatrice into his room because she knew he liked the child and was amused by her. She had spent the whole morning, as she had just told Alice, begging him not to journey down to Cambridge when the weather was still wet and cold – to leave Bertie's correction to her.

Princess Alice could imagine the force and sting of the rebuke which would have fallen on Bertie, had Mama prevailed. Mama looked so angry that she really didn't know what to say.

'I will never forgive Bertie for this,' Victoria went on, without noticing her daughter's silence. 'Just when your darling father is not well and in need of rest, he has to be worried like this!'

'Couldn't Papa have written to him?' Alice suggested timidly.

'Letters have no effect whatever,' Victoria retorted. 'I understand he just reads them and puts them aside. Your father said this morning that he had to talk to him; nothing less would do. Oh, why did God have to burden us like this? Why couldn't Alfred have been the eldest?'

'I'm so sorry, Mama,' her daughter murmured. It was awful of Bertie, because her father was patient and kind, not like Mama, of whom they were all afraid. He always seemed so depressed, and that grim Colonel Bruce shadowed him everywhere he went. She could remember one afternoon at Osborne when Bertie was about nineteen, and he had burst into her room where she was quietly reading and shouted, 'Damn Bruce, damn him, damn him!' at the top of his voice. He had looked so furious that at that moment she had been startled by the resemblance to their mother, and she ran to the door, and glanced up and down the corridor in case anyone had heard. When she turned back to remonstrate with Bertie, he was sitting in a chair with his head hanging down; he had seemed so miserable after that burst of impotent temper that she had not had the heart to say anything cross.

'I do hope Papa will be all right,' she said to Victoria. 'If only he would go to bed, Mama, and rest. When will he come back from Cambridge?'

'Tomorrow.' Victoria had said all she wished to say on the subject of Bertie; she had no intention of discussing what Albert should or should not do with a mere daughter, and she nodded towards the door. 'You may go, my dear child. I shall see you at dinner this evening.'

In the long corridor outside the Queen's apartment, Lady Lyttelton and Lady Augusta Bruce stood and talked in whispers, watching the ante-room door.

'Why won't she call in another doctor?' Lady Lyttelton said. 'I think that old Clark is a perfect idiot; he knows nothing about medicine.'

'I can't bear to think of him lying there, just wasting away.' Augusta Bruce blinked away tears. She was devoted to the Prince Consort; she could never enter that sick room without crying and the Queen had snapped at her unkindly, saying that red eyes would only upset the Prince.

'Why has she got such faith in Sir James, then? Surely she would want the best doctors in the world, for *him*?'

Lady Lyttelton shrugged.

'My dear Augusta, Her Majesty believes in Clark because he tells her only what she wants to hear. I've no doubt that's what he's doing now. "He's making good progress, Ma'am, good progress! There's no cause for alarm!" I've never heard him say anything else, even when his patient was dying.'

'It's too dreadful. Surely she'll call another opinion soon.'

'She won't face it,' Lady Lyttelton said. 'She just won't admit that he's really ill. Heaven knows she loves him, it's not that; she reads to him by the hour and waits on him hand and foot. But she won't have it that there's any danger to him. And anyone but that wretched man would come out and tell her the truth.'

'I heard,' Lady Augusta said, glancing round, 'that Lord

Palmerston was trying to interfere. There is a Doctor Watson who is supposed to be very clever. I heard that Lord Palmerston is pressing the Queen to consult him. I do pray she does! I saw the Prince this morning and he looks dreadfully ill; I wouldn't have known him, he's changed so much in the last three days.'

'Everyone can see it; everyone but the Queen. I tell you Augusta, his life is in her hands, and she's letting it slip away!'

At that moment the door behind them opened and Sir James Clark came out. He stopped when he saw the two ladies, and Augusta Bruce went up to him.

'Sir James, how is the Prince? We are all so anxious . . .' He grunted and glared from her to Lady Lyttelton.

'The Prince is doing very well,' he snapped. 'Very well indeed. Rest and a light diet are all he needs, as I've just told Her Majesty. I'm more worried about *her*; she's wearing herself out with anxiety. I'd be obliged if you ladies stopped trying to alarm her!'

Then he turned his back on them and stamped down the corridor. He was an old man and tired, and the business of reassuring the Queen a dozen times a day was trying his nerves. The Prince was ill, but as he didn't know what was the cause of his illness, he saw no reason to suppose it was serious. When in doubt he always prescribed a rest for the stomach. In his opinion it was a great pity that good old-fashioned bleeding had gone out of fashion. He was particularly irritated because the Queen had told him she was under pressure to consult another doctor. The Prime Minister had upset her dreadfully by suggesting that the Prince was not getting the best attention and that this new fellow Watson should be called in. If he was, Sir James growled to himself, he'd get precious little help from him! And he told Her Majesty quite plainly that he wouldn't be responsible for the patient if he was subjected to a lot of experimental dosing by someone he'd no professional regard for at all.

'My love, would you like me to read you another chapter?'

Victoria put her finger in the pages of *Peveril of the Peak* which she had been reading aloud.

Albert turned his head on the pillow.

'No thank you, my dear. That was very nice, but you must be tired. You've been reading for nearly two hours.'

'I'm not a bit tired! Are you sure you wouldn't like to hear some more?'

'Quite sure. Perhaps before I go to sleep tonight.'

She read well; it was an accomplishment he had taught her, and in the beginning of his illness he had enjoyed Walter Scott's book. But in the last two days he had been content to lie there, soothed by the sound of her voice, without trying to follow the story, letting his thoughts wander uncontrolled. He had little command of them now. He could see the bare tree tops from his window, moving in what must be a cold February wind, but often they seemed as green as the majestic pines which flanked Rosenau like sentries, and then he was back in Coburg, calling to Ernst, and they were children again. He could see the pebbles at the bottom of the swift little stream, while he made a rod out of a stick and some string and then settled down on the bank to fish. He heard Ernst shout with excitement and show him a small wriggling catch. Ernst had always been more skilful; he did not throw his fish back into the water . . .

He felt the strong mountain air on his face as he walked through the woods, and his back was no longer bent with working at a desk and his step was firm. He was young and happy, surrounded by the people he loved, and marriage to his cousin Victoria was something he and Ernst and his father talked of for the future.

He was not surprised to find that sometimes he was in his room at the university at Bonn, absorbed in study, and then Stockmar was with him, not grey and feeble as he had been when they last saw each other, but full of hope and plans for him. There were moments when he knew he was at Balmoral; he could smell the heather and feel the gun against his shoulder as he sighted a stag.

'You are smiling, my darling — are you feeling better? You *look* much better!'

He was back at Windsor, and Victoria was bending over him. He remembered that she had been reading something to him.

'Yes, I feel better.' He squeezed her hand, thinking irrelevantly how easy it was to conquer time and space. He could leave Windsor and the cold weather whenever he wanted to; he could go home, and unlike the visit made last year, Coburg would not be empty and disappointing. Ernst, old and dissipated, the bright flowers and clear stream, even the romantic little Rosenau itself, less real and important than they had ever been before. Now when he returned to his childhood, nothing had changed; when he re-lived an incident it was always a happy one and it was always true while the tragedies and disappointments of life were magically fading so that he could hardly remember any of them.

It was so strange to look up and see Victoria sitting beside him when he had been so far away from her a moment before; but he was glad that she was there. She was a good wife, and a sense of impending departure made him appreciate her with a tenderness he had never known. It pained him to see her looking anxious, and to realize in moments of clarity that she would not admit that he was ill, when he knew that he would never leave his bed, and all her plans for a long holiday were only dreams. He would be so sorry to leave her for her own sake; he hated to think of her grieving and lonely, and once or twice tried to recommend the children to her in the hope that she would find comfort in them. But she had seemed almost impatient when he suggested that Alice or Alfred or even the little Beatrice could pass the time more pleasantly for her than her long vigils by his bedside. She wanted no one but him; she clung to him as if she were about to die and all the strength and hope of life were in his failing body.

'I hate to worry you, my love,' she whispered, 'but it's been suggested that you see another doctor . . . If you don't

310

want to he will be sent away, you have only to tell me. But he's here, at Windsor.'

'Who is he?'

He had no objection; he knew that whoever the man was there was nothing he could do.

'His name is Watson. Lord Palmerston recommended him.' She would not let him see how the interference had angered her; she had cried for an hour after reading Palmerston's letter with its cruel implications that her love was seriously ill. It would be a tragedy, the letter said, if the country were to lose one of its most valuable servants for want of giving him the best attention. It was clearly the duty of everyone connected with him to preserve so precious a life.

When Palmerston wrote that he knew that fear would prevail on Victoria and gain Watson admittance. He only hoped that it was not too late.

'That was kind of Lord Palmerston.'

How he disliked and distrusted that old man, and now he was trying to save his life.

'I'll see Doctor Watson, my dear. And thank Lord Palmerston for me. Tell him I fear I can't yet write to him myself.'

'Sir James says you will be well in a few days,' Victoria encouraged. 'I have such trust in him, my darling; I know you need a holiday and then you'll be yourself again. And we'll go to Balmoral in the spring, and you shan't do any work at all until you've got your strength back. Do you remember that wonderful summer we spent there, after the Castle was finished? Everything looked so beautiful — do you remember how we used to take the trap out with Brown driving, and picnic in the heather, just you and I? I have all my sketches, my darling, and this year I'll make a folio. Why, we can stay there right through the summer! I know how you love it, and you're always so well there.'

'It will be nice,' he said gently. He reached up suddenly and touched her face with his thin hand.

'Meine kleine Frau,' he said, 'gutes Weibchen. Go and get some rest. And let this Doctor Watson come this afternoon.'

'I am very sorry, Your Royal Highness. I would give anything in the world to tell you better news, but your father is gravely ill.'

'What is it?' Princess Alice whispered. 'Nobody has even diagnosed . . .'

'Watson looked away.

'I find that difficult to understand. The Prince is suffering from typhoid fever. May I suggest that you sit down,' he said quickly. The young Princess had become so pale that he was afraid she might faint.

'Typhoid? Oh, Doctor! How can he be . . .? We never suspected more than a cold or just fatigue.'

'The Prince has been in a high fever for some days, I believe,' Watson went on. 'The illness has already passed its crisis.'

'Then he'll get better?'

He was a blunt man, and he was so outraged at the neglect and ignorance which had thrown away a human life that he answered without hesitating.

'No, he won't. As I said, Your Royal Highness, I am very sorry. The Prince cannot live more than two or three days at the most. As Her Majesty will not see me, I can only advise that someone should tell her the position. I have done all I can. There is nothing anyone can do now but ease his sufferings and wait for the end.'

'It will kill my mother,' she said slowly. 'It will kill her. You realize that I will have to tell her, Doctor? I begged her to see you even before I knew this . . . What am I going to say to her? She won't listen, I know she won't.'

'For her own sake, I hope she does,' Watson answered. He was not very interested in the Queen. Any woman who could be obstinate enough to entrust her husband to that fool Clark and to see him burning with fever and wasting

312

away before her eyes and still cling to what she believed, had no claim on his sympathy.

'If she refuses to accept your word or mine, then I fear she'll believe the evidence of her own eyes before too long. Again, I am deeply sorry. The Prince is irreplaceable. Even if I never practised again, my career in medicine would have been worth while if I could have saved his life.'

'I forbid you to speak like that!' Victoria pressed her hand against her heart. It was beating with such speed and violence that she felt unable to breathe. 'I forbid you, Alice, to repeat a lot of irresponsible opinions given by a man who knows nothing about the case at all!'

'Mama . . .' Alice's voice trembled. 'Mama, he's not irresponsible! He's a very clever doctor and I believe him. He says Papa has typhoid fever and that he *can't* get well now!'

'He is a liar,' Victoria's eyes blazed at her; they were alight with fear. She stood like a cornered lioness, rousing her temper to combat that feeling of unbearable terror.

'How can you stand there and talk about your father in that way? How can you dare to say he isn't getting better? You must be the most heartless and unnatural daughter in the world. I used to think,' the Queen continued, 'that you had some sense, Alice. Now I find you a gossiping ninny. And I refuse to be upset by you. As for Doctor Watson, I wouldn't see him yesterday and I certainly won't see him today. I disbelieve his diagnosis, and no gentleman would have sent you to me with such a message.'

'Mama, I beg of you –' the Princess was crying as she spoke, 'I beg of you to listen. I'm only so afraid of the shock to you when Papa leaves us. And don't say I'm heartless because I speak of it; you *know* how much I love Papa . . .'

'Love?' Her mother's voice was harsh with tears. 'What is your love of him compared to mine? I love him as he deserves. Don't try and intrude yourself! Go out of the room at once!'

There was nothing to do but obey; Victoria waited, her back turned to her daughter until she heard the door close. For a moment she stood without moving, without knowing that her cheeks were wet. 'He says Papa has typhoid fever and he can't get well now.'

She put her hands to her ears, as if to shut out the sentence which was going round and round in her mind. Typhoid. He had been feverish at one stage, complaining of headaches and alternate heat and shivering fits . . . and pains in his limbs. She could remember that beloved voice, so patient even in his distress, asking if Clark could give him a powder or some relief.

At last she moved, one hand groping for a chair, and when she sank down into it she looked suddenly lost and old. 'He can't get well.'

She seemed to see the pale wasted face gazing up at her with all the abstracted expression she had never seen until the last few days; it was a kindly look, but distant, and remembering it in that moment of revelation alone in her room, Victoria suddenly knew what it meant.

Albert did not think he would recover. Every time he pressed her hand or whispered loving words to her in German it was his way of saying farewell, and in her confidence she had refused to see it. He was lying there, her darling, the light of her existence, preparing quietly for death, and strangers like Alice and this Doctor Watson had seen it while she had not. Had Clark known? He must have done; kindness had prevented him from telling her.

She took out her handkerchief and wiped her streaming eyes; she had never cried soundlessly like this before. For a second her mother's image flitted before her imagination, laid out on her death-bed with her hands folded peacefully across her breast and the familiar features drawn and changed until it was the face of a stranger. . . . When the picture threatened to turn into Albert, the room became suddenly dark. Some vestige of will, superhuman in its strength even at that moment, banished the illusion, and the

314

imminent fainting attack passed with it.

'Albert.' —Albert, lying there, suffering and patient, facing that dreadful thought of death, so weak and wasted, while she had strength and life enough for two and could not give it to him.

Where was her power, her majesty, she cried in agony, that it could not stay this parting? He couldn't leave her! He couldn't die. God would not inflict it on her.

She slipped out of her chair and knelt, beseeching an authority greater than her own, not to take Albert from her; it was the first moment of true humility she had felt for more than twenty years.

When she got up she was calmer. God would hear that prayer. God knew what Albert meant to her; He knew that she had led a good life. Only the transgressors were punished. God would not be so cruel to her. Whatever anyone said, she would still hope.

The clock on the mantelpiece struck two. He would have had his lunch and she had promised to go and read to him. She went to the looking-glass and straightened her dress and wiped her eyes again. He must not notice that she had been crying. When he was well and they were at Balmoral as she planned, she would tell him of the moment when she had knelt in her study and prayed God to save his life.

Peveril of the Peak lay on the table by his bed with the marker in it, but Victoria did not continue the story that day. The sky outside was grey but the room was full of light. Candles and lamps had been lit and Albert was propped up high on his pillows. As she reached him she saw that he was combing his hair as if he were making himself ready for a journey. When he looked up at her, his face was blotched and bluish; there was no recognition in his eyes and she did not speak. She noticed Lady Lyttelton in one corner, and the two nurses who had attended on him day and night, and several other faces. Alice was there too, crying silently. Victoria beckoned to her.

'Send word to Cambridge,' she said slowly. 'Your brother

315

must come immediately if he is to see his father.'

They set a chair for her and she sat down beside the bed and took Albert's hand in hers.

It was nearly daylight when she at last agreed to go to her room and rest. All through that endless day she had sat by his bed, stroking his cold hands; when he showed that he recognized her she whispered to him in German, so low that no one ever knew what she said. Time was suspended until the twenty years they had been married seemed no longer than those few hours. Even the arrival of their children hardly disturbed them. They came, their sons and daughters, headed by Bertie who cried and hung his head, and touched their father's hand and spoke a few words to him. And then they withdrew, leaving their parents alone, apart from them all as they had always been. There was a moment when Albert raised himself and asked for Vicky, and then fell back. She was in Prussia; he would never see her again. He had loved Vicky but it was God's will that he should die without her. He would leave England as he had lived in it, alone except for Victoria.

Lying there he could feel the force of her love willing him to live; it flowed through him from her touch, it was in her voice and her eyes, and it was fighting his battle with death for him. For her sake alone he wished he had the strength or the wish to struggle with her. But he had no will to live. For the first and only time in their married life there was a full understanding between them; now she could sense what he was thinking and feeling and share the thought and the emotion as if it were her own. The telepathy of love came to her as he lay dying. Holding the limp hand, inwardly agonizing for his life, Victoria realized the full extent of his sense of failure and disappointment. His struggles and achievements had been the mainspring of his existence. He had wanted to do well, to be appreciated and even loved by the people who had rejected him to the end. He had done his best and spent himself in that endeavour, and he lay there in the last hours of his life and welcomed death because he knew that he had failed. And she knew it too, and felt it with the new insight which was almost a transmutation of self, instead of the old angry partisan feelings which had merely skimmed the surface of what was hurting him. The inner soul of her husband with its rigid faults and shining virtues had always escaped her until then; she had seen him through a romantic haze, listening without understanding, but prepared to accept anything because he said it and because she loved him and thought him so wonderful. Now she saw the man himself in all his pathos, weary and defeated, and her love enveloped him, not possessively or greedily but with a pure passion of tenderness that quite transcended her own grief and terror of approaching loneliness.

'My love,' she whispered, 'how I wish I had made you happier. There was so much I could have done.'

He shook his head a little; the movement seemed to exhaust him.

'You gave me all the happiness I've known in the last twenty years. I have never been really worthy of you . . .'

He closed his eyes and for a moment his breathing faltered. He had never loved her. He would have died a happier man if he had ever felt the love she had given him so generously. Even now it would not come; tenderness and gratitude and pity mixed with guilt, but never that soaring of the spirit which he knew was part of love. He had never known that for her or for any other woman. At least, in that his honour was untouched. Never in thought or feeling had he given to another what he had denied to his wife.

'I wish you would go and lie down,' he murmured to her. 'I feel so much better, dearest, I could sleep . . .'

'I like to sit with you. I won't talk, my darling, or move to disturb you. You close your dear eyes and rest.'

Gently she drew the covers over his chest and tucked them round his shoulders; her fingers trembled as they smoothed his forehead and felt the damp, cold texture of the skin.

Without answering or opening his eyes he smiled at her and after a few moments his breathing grew quieter and more steady.

Two hours later Lady Lyttelton crept to the Queen's side.

'Ma'am, he's sleeping peacefully,' she whispered. 'I beg of you to rest a little while you can. I'll rouse you the moment he wakes.'

Victoria looked at her. Her eyes were red and pouched with strain.

'I think his colour is better. look!'

Lady Lyttelton bent over the bed; by the light of the candles she distinctly saw a slight flush in the Prince's cheeks. It was perfectly true that he seemed better. That ghastly drawn look had disappeared.

'Ma'am, I do believe he's improving . . .' Her voice quavered, close to tears. 'God's answering our prayers — he's lost that awful pallor and he's sleeping deeply. Oh, Ma'am, I pray it will be all right!'

'You could never pray more fervently than I have done,' Victoria said slowly. 'But now I am so tired I have no prayers left. If I lie down in my clothes, Lyttelton, you promise to call me the moment he wakes?'

'The very moment,' Lady Lyttelton promised. 'Take my arm and let me help you out of that chair.'

She was so stiff that she could hardly have moved without help; she leant on the taller woman's arm and walked slowly through the communicating door to her own room. It was Lady Lyttelton, who had disagreed with her so bitterly in the past, who now almost lifted her on to the bed and, in spite of her tired protests, unfastened the collar and cuffs of her dress and slipped off her shoes. When she covered the Queen with a quilt she was already fast asleep.

It was strange that she should see Melbourne, because after all he was dead and she had not thought of him for years. But telling her how wise he thought her choice of husband. He was there he was, as elegant and handsome as ever, and

318

he was such an excellent young man, and certain to be kind to her. She heard her own voice, very clear and imperious as it was in her youth, interrupting to say that Albert was far more than all these things. He was the most perfect man on earth and soon everyone would see his perfection as she did. And Lord M. could go now, because she had Albert and she didn't need him any more. The figure in her dream seemed to bow down and shrink, and as it disappeared the back view suddenly wore a bombazine skirt and looked like Lehzen . . .

And there was Albert; surely taller than usual, but so divinely handsome that his face literally shone. He was smiling that beautiful thoughtful smile which had enchanted her the first time she saw it at Windsor. Her hand was on his arm and they were walking together through a green and brightly coloured place which she knew was the formal garden at Rosenau. She felt so happy; she could hear her own laughter and she felt as if she were dancing rather than walking. There were times when she actually floated beside Albert. She could move so fast and so easily that she let go of his arm and glided ahead, calling gaily to him. Then, as dreams do, everything changed; the sunny Rosenau garden disappeared; she was no longer floating like a cloud but standing alone in the middle of a vast room with stone walls and narrow windows like the old Keep at Windsor, and Albert was not with her. She was alone and in prison and Albert had gone.

She began to shriek his name in terror and the word would not come out properly; she cried for Albert and her voice sounded like 'Mama . . . Mama . . .'

It was that voice which finally woke her. She sat up in a violent fright and saw Alice standing by the bed.

'Mama, Mama for Heaven's sake! Wake up and come — I think Papa is dying!'

She sprang from the bed and ran in her stockinged feet into the next room. The canopied bed and the still figure lying in the middle of it were bathed in a pool of candlelight.

Victoria dropped to her knees by the bed. There was no sound in the room but the harsh failing breath which was the herald of death.

'Albert – Albert, my love – '

Her voice rose in a wail, when it died away there was complete silence. Some seconds passed before Victoria realized that Albert's breathing had stopped. Slowly, trembling with horror and disbelief, she rose from her knees, staring at the sunken features, pale as old wax, at the limp hand lying slack, palm upwards on the cover and back to the closed eyes. Closed for ever.

Through the room and the ante-room and out into the corridor of Windsor Castle there came the echo of one wild and piercing cry.

She was sitting at her desk as she had at the same early hour every morning for the past twenty years. Candles burned on either side of her. The green-shaded light on the other desk opposite had not been lit. The light and the pens and papers and books and the desk itself would never be used again. A black widow's cap hid her hair; the dark veiling hung down over the back of her mourning dress. Her engagement ring and a bracelet miniature of Albert were the only jewels she wore. From time to time she reached forward to dip her pen into the ink and turn a page of her Journal; the tiny rasp of the nib and the rustling papers were the only sounds. The room and the whole Castle were shuttered and silent. Outside, on the Keep, the Royal Standard flew at half-mast.

The Queen turned another page, dipped her pen into the golden inkwell, and began to write. The pen moved slowly, the firm powerful script suddenly wavered like the writing of an old woman—

'At a quarter to eleven last night my beloved Albert died. My heart is quite broken.'